ROYA SANDS

AND THE

BRIDGE BETWEEN WORLDS

SARYON MICHAEL WHITE

ROYA SANDS

AND THE

BRIDGE BETWEEN WORLDS

Sacred Stories
PUBLISHING

Books may be purchased through booksellers or by contacting Sacred Stories Publishing.

This is a work of fiction. Names, characters, places, and incidents either are the product of the author's imagination or are used fictitiously, and any resemblance to actual persons, living or dead, businesses, companies, events, or locales is entirely coincidental.

Roya Sands and the Bridge Between Worlds

Saryon Michael White

Tradepaper ISBN: 978-1-945026-44-7

Electronic ISBN: 978-1-945026-45-4

Library of Congress Control Number: 2018943757

Editor: Angela Valentine | www.eloquent-editor.com
Cover Design & Interior Layout: Danielle K. Taylor | daniellekristian.com

Published by Sacred Stories Publishing
https://sacredstoriespublishing.com
Printed in the United States of America 10 9 8 7 6 5 4 3 2 1

For Dixie,
My beloved partner,
Who journeys with me to faraway lands
and inspires me with her courageous love.
Her commitment to truth and her passion
for making a difference helped launch this series—
part of our shared purpose to create
a better world and a brighter future
for all the Earth's children.

PROLOGUE

They were instructed to travel inconspicuously, leaving a false trail of information regarding their whereabouts and the purpose of their travel; and though their meeting place was not a secret, they trusted their meeting was secure. It was doubtful that anyone outside this group would be able to comprehend the grand scale of deception that had guarded the plan over the decades, but still, every precaution had been taken to prevent the media from catching on to what was being orchestrated.

It was a hot summer day in June, and several of the co-conspirators were standing on the porch of the main house, smoking cigars and discussing creative ways to hide money from the IRS. Gradually, more cars were arriving, and men in both casual and business attire were being welcomed inside.

A quarter mile down the long entry road, two security guards were confirming the guests at a checkpoint. No official IDs were used, but cameras were focused on all the incoming cars, so the hosts could watch them on a display of security monitors. Only the last vehicle sparked any concern, because it was not as inconspicuous as the others. The participant had arrived in a limousine.

"Devilishly hot today," proclaimed the elderly man in the back of the limo who had rolled down the tinted window to speak with the security guard.

"Is anybody else traveling with you?" inquired the guard, ignoring the man's comment as he visually inspected the inside of the car through the open window.

"No," retorted the man, curtly. "Can we hurry this up?"

"I'll have to check something, first," the guard replied stiffly, as the elderly man scoffed at him for making him wait. The guard, a thick-necked, muscular young man, awaited a response from one of the hosts through his earpiece. He was well aware that the attendees of the meeting were forbidden to bring drivers, so he did not dare let the limo enter the property without official clearance. After a few tense moments, the guard waved the driver through. The elderly gentleman in the back seat had assumed that his billionaire status carried enough weight to allow him to bend the rules. But the hosts were already making different travel arrangements for his departure from the meeting, so the driver could be sent away.

If they could have met in one of the presidential bunkers deep underground to finalize their plan, that would have been preferable to the hosts, but not everyone attending this meeting warranted that level of treatment. Still, for security reasons, they wanted to handle any remaining paperwork in person without emailing, faxing, or mailing anything. This was one of the most sensitive financial arrangements that had taken place in a decade— sensitive because of how many government insiders were involved in setting up and participating in the opportunity.

When the elderly man from the limo entered the large living room, he saw several dozen men standing around. Many of them were holding glasses of luxury alcohol. A few were still signing paperwork with a lawyer to create the offshore shell companies necessary to shelter their money from taxes.

"Well, is someone going to pour me a glass of whiskey?" snapped the old man, with an air of impatience. Without hesitation, two men pulled up a chair for him and brought him exactly the brand of whiskey they knew he wanted. There was a fair amount of old money in the room and a couple of investors with family connections to the group that could hardly believe their fortune to play at this level of the game.

"How many shares did you buy?" asked one of the younger men to the man next to him, wondering if he should invest more.

"Fifty thousand," said the man quietly, "but if I were you, I wouldn't keep asking those kinds of questions in this crowd. Do you know how many people in here have above top-secret clearance?"

"No," said the younger man with chagrin. "I mean, it's obvious that some would."

"Look, you're part of the family, but some of these guys work on the most highly classified special access programs in the world. So, unless you know to whom you are speaking, I suggest you just listen and learn. These people take secrecy *very* seriously," the man warned.

"I know. If I talk, I'm dead," he conceded. He did not dare let anyone think he could not be trusted with such secrecy.

The younger man was grateful for the advice and immediately decided to increase his investment by three thousand shares. Even then, he knew that his investment was probably the smallest in the room, but he was beginning to think he would be foolish not to trust what this many powerful players were orchestrating for their own benefit. He felt lucky to have had a family connection that was respected by the group. This was probably the only time he would get to meet the people that made it possible.

Looking around, he could see that most of the men were crowding around a tall, well-dressed elderly man that was beginning to speak to everyone. He was obviously regarded as a celebrity among the group.

"The public will never know how we did this," began the retired politician. "I was actually in office when we wrote the spending bill that funded the first prototype," he boasted. "That's the best part about this. We spent billions of dollars in taxpayer money on the research and development phase, so the company didn't have to. It's taken decades to get the technology to the right level with the military applications. But now, we're ready to sell the patents to the company and just profit from the next phase."

"Yeah, if you've ever wished you could go back in time and buy shares of Microsoft, this would be the next best thing," bragged another man.

"Actually, we're working on that, too," chuckled one of the generals, and several of the men raised their glasses in celebration.

"So, when's this new technology going to hit the market?" asked one of the investors.

"It'll happen in stages. But it's not just a matter of having this ready for mass consumption. First, we have to get more people used to the idea of Augmented Reality," explained a man who seemed knowledgeable.

"So, we've been investing heavily in games and apps that overlay a digital reality onto the physical environment. We're also doing more with Virtual Reality. If we can get the younger generations hooked on this level of interactive gaming and software, they'll eat the new tech up like candy when it comes out. Eventually, everyone will be so lost in the digital world that they won't even care how much we increase the military budget."

"Here, here!" interrupted one of the military contractors.

"And you'll be pleased to know we're further along than you might expect," the politician conceded.

"Yeah, we're not just acquiring the patents," added another man. "We're also bringing people over from the military side of the project to set up the new tech division. We just need each of you to do your part to bring the other companies and systems into alignment with the new platform as this unfolds. That way, everyone will be forced to integrate with the new system just to stay in the game. If we can keep the media on script with the narrative we've written for them, it'll go *very* smoothly."

"Just wait—in a few years, the whole world will be talking about this thing, and you will *all* be billionaires," declared the politician.

"Yeah, you'll be able to buy real estate on other planets," joked another man, and everyone burst into laughter.

In their own minds, they all believed that they were making history and that they were each playing a role in creating a new world. They considered themselves to be the architects and key players of the new global plan, but they were unaware that their collaboration was part of yet another hidden agenda.

This was to be their only physical meeting. From this day forward, they were to quietly play their roles without any discussion and pretend that the meeting had never taken place.

"A toast," said one of the hosts as they all raised their glasses. "To the last investment you will ever need to make."

1

A SURPRISING FIND

For a long time, Roya Sands had waited for something big to happen, something that would define her sense of self. She often wondered why her parents had chosen to live in the little town of Adams, New York—a place far too small for her big imagination. "It's a quiet place to raise a family," her parents would often say, but that was never a satisfying answer for her. Roya always wanted to understand the deeper reasons behind why things were the way they were. She wanted a mystery to explore, something that would require her personal expertise, but she could find nothing unusual or mysterious about Adams. She had explored every inch of the town countless times, and the only mystery she had ever found was herself.

What Roya didn't realize was that it was not necessary to search outside of her small town for mystery or adventure. If anything, she was fortunate that the town had sheltered her all these years from a storm of historical forces at work in the larger world. It was the last place anyone would think to look for the secrets of the future, and that was a very good thing indeed. After all, there were many shadowy organizations that wanted to control the course of history and exploiting knowledge of the future was on the top of their 'to do' lists. What they never would have guessed was that a sixteen-year-old girl from Adams would be worthy of such knowledge. And for that reason, Roya's role in the unfolding plan remained safely hidden—even to her.

All across the world, however, secret and sinister forces were seeking to gain control over the most sacred forms of wealth and knowledge; to gain control over water and our perception of history, for example, both of which are more fragile and vulnerable than most people realize. If it could be owned, the greedy would seek to own it. But thankfully, the most powerful secrets and the greatest treasures were still well-hidden from those driven by greed. No amount of money could buy access to such discoveries, and only the most humble and pure-hearted people would be entrusted with such responsibility. It was precisely for these reasons that the greedy quest for these hidden resources had become more forceful; for in them, lie the keys to the future history of the world.

Roya was not completely unaware that there were great secrets and dangerous struggles for power in the world. More than most teens, she possessed an ability to look beyond her personal experience to notice how everything was connected. Even so, she often felt alone. Roya had an inner sense of mission and purpose that she could not explain; a quiet determination, known only to her, to achieve something fantastic, though she did not yet know what this would be.

Roya liked to pretend that there was a larger, less visible world all around her—one with fewer limitations—though she often noticed a stark contrast between the world of her imagination and physical reality. In her imagination, for instance, objects could float and hover, and she could move things around by the power of her thoughts. Time could speed up, slow down, or stop altogether.

Usually, such daydreams happened in school when she imagined freezing time and escaping on long adventures across a world of frozen people. She would imagine tapping certain people she liked, unfreezing them so they could go on the adventures with her. She could imagine fantastic scenes to entertain her mind, but there was little crossover between the two realms, and she longed for some new kind of experience that could bridge them together.

If great authors could bring worlds of fiction to life, she thought, surely her imagination could find its expression in reality. Some of the people she looked up to most were full of colorful stories of grand adventures, but little was going on in her remote corner of the globe. So, the neighbors down the street had a new litter of puppies, and a traveling theater group was putting on a play and inviting students to audition. But that was about all her tiny community had to offer. To her, these simple events were mere distractions from a sense of waiting for something more exciting to happen.

In the meantime, she often liked to watch videos of teen activists, and she felt inspired by what others her age were doing in the world to make a difference. The world's problems concerned her deeply, but she felt far removed from the front lines of any cause. Still, she kept feeling like she was bursting at the seams, desperate to create some kind of change. Sometimes, this desire could grow so intense, it was as if a sense of power surged inside her, yet she did not know what it was or what to do about it. She only knew that she felt different than most of her peers—so different, in fact, that she often felt invisible.

Because of her inner strength, however, she was confident in her intelligence and held a generally positive view of her appearance. Without deliberately trying, she had managed to stay physically fit simply through activities that she liked, and she was often complimented on how strong and healthy she looked. Kayaking and paddle boarding were among her favorite outdoor activities. And in the winter, she often went with her dad to his favorite indoor climbing gym in Syracuse, just for a change of scenery.

Roya stood about five feet four inches tall, and had long, dark brown hair that fell just below her shoulders. It was mostly straight with some natural waves that would twist into curls when not brushed. Her skin was somewhere between the fair complexion of her father and the olive complexion of her mother. She often had a natural blush to her cheeks and did not wear much makeup.

Her most remarkable features were her eyes, which had a look of intelligence to them that was striking enough to provoke a subtle reaction when first seen. A true friend would notice a genuine kindness and a passionate curiosity in them, but anyone with something to hide would feel penetrated by her alert gaze. Moreover, her eyes held a certain brightness, partly because they were so clear and seemed to reflect her mental alertness; but there was something more. Later on, some who knew her in her youth would say they had noticed light in her eyes. To Roya, her eyes were simply blue.

Following her mother's expectations, she dressed modestly compared to many other girls her age. Sometimes this felt restrictive and made it hard to fit in; but she had far bigger issues on her mind.

Roya had a heightened sense of social awareness, and her emotional capacity to feel things deeply was more highly developed than most of her peers. Because she was sensitive to the feelings of others, Roya detested any sort of meanness or foul play. She was unwilling to pretend that any one group was better than the others just so she could be accepted by them. Above all else, Roya valued fairness, so she had a hard time relating to the way her classmates would often put each other down.

Occasionally, some of her peers would open up to her. They would find themselves feeling drawn to her, momentarily reflecting her openness and sharing their deepest thoughts and feelings with her. Perhaps it was because she was a good listener. But this kind of connection was usually short-lived. She was fooled many times, thinking that the person who was opening up desired a friendship, but the closeness rarely lasted very long. They easily fell back to being superficial, which ultimately overruled Roya's more heart-centered approach to building friendship.

While this did not deter Roya from being social, by her sophomore year, she was beginning to feel like everyone had found their group of friends but her. If it had not been for a couple of new girls who had moved to town that spring, finishing that year of high school would have been a great deal more challenging.

The very first time she had seen Ami in class, there was an undeniable spark of recognition, as if they had known each other for years. It felt like she was meant to be Roya's friend from day one. Ami was unusually thoughtful in a way that piqued Roya's genuine interest. She always paid attention to the things that Roya liked, and she was calm and easy-going. Right away, Roya noticed a kind of synchronicity between her life and Ami's that made their connection effortless. After only a short time, Roya was beginning to feel like she had a true best friend.

Ami's younger sister, Mandy, was also very friendly, and though Roya did not have any classes with her, the three of them had started meeting up after school. Unfortunately, Ami and Mandy were gone for the first two weeks of summer break, and Roya was all alone—or so she thought.

That Sunday morning started out like any other, with a trip to nearby Watertown where she could visit the library while her mother did the shopping. Roya had already finished reading all her books and longed for something more exciting to do for the summer. At this age, it felt like she had exhausted the entertainment value of the Flower Memorial Library, and she found herself going straight to the new arrivals. Nothing new. She felt momentarily disappointed but stayed positive as she wandered into the aisles to see if anything interesting leaped out at her. As much as she loved to read, the library was also her sanctuary: a quiet place to escape the busyness of her house, which never seemed to be silent.

As she relaxed into the expansive feeling of the library, out of the corner of her left eye, a glimmer of light caught her attention. She turned her head curiously, looking down to find the source of the light that had come from the bottom shelf. There, on the end of a row, was a thin, mid-sized, hardback book with shimmering golden letters that read: *The Circle and the Stars*. Roya thought she knew this library like the back of her hand,

and yet, she could not recall ever having seen this book before. In fact, it was so out of the ordinary that she brightened up with the anticipation of finding something new.

She knelt down and removed the violet-colored book from the shelf, immediately noticing that it felt much lighter than expected for its size. It had no dust jacket, and the surface of the cover felt particularly smooth. Flipping open to a random page, Roya half expected to see something related to astronomy, but curiously, she found a section with recipes instead. At first glance, the recipes did not appear to be very interesting. The recipe she turned to for *Zucchini Bread*, for example, was nothing unusual, and yet she felt entranced by the strange stylistic font used for the golden letters. The pages were thick, and the writing was only on the front of each page. With her fingers, she traced the gold frame that surrounded the writing, and then began to touch the letters, which felt slightly raised.

The book felt warm in her hands, like it was greeting her with a hug, and she began to notice a faint sweet smell. Gradually, the smell drew her deeper into a mild trance-like state, and even though she could not remember having smelled freshly baked zucchini bread before, she was certain that she could smell it now. The fresh aroma continued to fill her senses until something strange happened. The golden letters of the recipe title, Zucchini Bread, began to shimmer, as if reflecting light from somewhere. Suddenly, the letters 'r-e-a-d' illuminated, standing out from the word 'Bread', as if the book was asking her to pay attention to what the letters were doing. Then, all the letters in Zucchini Bread lit up one by one, rising up from the page and rearranging themselves into a special sequence:

read chuZ B i c in

It was an anagram! The glowing, hovering letters formed a message as if projected onto a screen. Once her intuition engaged, her mind decoded what her heart knew the message to be:

Read, choose, be—I see in.

The words described her potential, inviting her to choose a new experience of being. "I see in," she said to herself softly. *I see inwardly*, her mind mused, playing with the phrase. Then she began to repeat it like a mantra. "I see inwardly," she whispered, pausing only to notice the effect. "I see inwardly." The trance was growing deeper. It reminded her of what it felt like when she was deep in a daydream or when she woke up in the morning and part of her dream was briefly superimposed onto the room around her.

Each time she spoke the words, she felt like the voice of the book was saying it with her, until the book began to somehow come alive. The letters seemed to give off a light of their own, and scenes were appearing in her mind. *This is a recipe for victory*, she read at the bottom of the page, and a scene filled her mind of people cheering. For just a moment, her sense of being in the library began to fade as she was seeing a vision inwardly with greater and greater clarity—until she snapped herself out of it. She wanted to make sure she had control of her mind and could break the trance if she needed to, before she explored further.

Roya was so excited by what was happening that she quickly turned the page, eager to see what else was there. *This recipe will make you more visible*, it said at the bottom of the next page. Now that was an interesting thought. All last year, she had wanted to make one of the guys in class notice her, but nothing she did ever prompted a glance. What exactly did it mean, *more visible?* Her mind filled with ideas about how she might like to change the way she looked, but how could a recipe be related to visibility? There was no doubt in her mind that the book possessed some sort of magical quality, but what was it? And how did it get there? She had the sneaking suspicion that someone had left it there just for her, but who?

Roya closed the book and took a deep breath, feeling the dreamlike awareness subside as she looked around to see if anyone had noticed her. The library was relatively empty, and she remained inside the aisle out of anyone's visual range. As strange as it sounded, she could not help feeling that the book had chosen to share itself with her in a personal way, and a part of her wanted to keep the whole thing secret. But just walking out with the book did not seem right to her. Perhaps one of the librarians could tell her something about it.

She quickly hurried upstairs to the checkout counter. The first librarian was a short man with a balding head and thick glasses. He looked up briefly before directing her over to the lady at the next checkout counter as he continued busily punching numbers into his computer.

Roya stepped up to the counter and cautiously slid the book over to the woman whose nametag read 'Claire.' She looked like she was in her thirties and had short black hair cut in a bob just below the ears, with short bangs. Her skin was unusually pale, and yet, she appeared strikingly vibrant and alive. Perhaps it was because her brownish-green eyes were so big and bright. They complemented the beautiful blue stone that Claire wore around her neck. Something about her seemed uncannily familiar, though Roya was certain they had never met before.

Claire's eyes flashed a look of approval that Roya had discovered the book. She looked at Roya with kind familiarity, as if she already knew her. As Claire held the book up to scan it, she glanced over at Roya and smiled in a warm and friendly way. In the silence between them, it felt like their souls were greeting each other with a profound sense of recognition. Roya smiled back, though she was letting her bangs hide her eyes just a little as she sometimes did when she felt shy. Claire appeared to study the round features of her face and her long, wavy, brown hair. When she handed back the book, she was very deliberately making eye contact.

"Will that be all?" she asked in a soft voice that made Roya think she was hoping for more interaction.

"Yes, thank you," Roya said politely, wanting to ask Claire if she knew anything about the book, but feeling a little intimidated by her piercing eyes. For once, she was experiencing how her own penetrating gaze must feel to others. As soon as Claire handed her the book, Roya's body began to turn toward the exit, but her head stopped. For a split second, she thought she saw a flash of color coming from a tuft of hair sticking out from underneath what she now suspected was a wig. Claire must have noticed her glance, because she casually lifted a hand to tuck in her hair. Roya darted out of the library imagining what Claire's real hair must look like.

That was more than just color, she thought. *A hint of blue, but it shimmered. Almost like the letters from the book. That's strange.*

Roya's mother was already waiting in the car at the curb. Roya hopped in, still with a look of astonishment on her face, but her mother did not even notice.

"What did you find?" her mother asked as her eyes landed on the book.

"Oh," she said, startled out of her daze. "Just a little something to pass the time."

Roya wished she had brought her backpack or checked out some other books to conceal her discovery. Quietly, she slid the book down between the seat and the door of the car, out of sight. She was not prepared to discuss the book, especially since it contained recipes. Roya was keenly aware that her mother had been plotting for some time to get her more involved in the kitchen, since she had been so unsuccessful with her older sister, Sarah. Not long after Sarah had turned sixteen, almost two years before, she had immediately taken a job at the local pizza parlor, and now, she often ate at the restaurant with her friends from work. This left their mother feeling disappointed that her oldest daughter had managed to avoid the family traditions.

Roya's mother, Soraya, had neatly curled, shoulder-length, dark brown hair that complemented her olive skin. She was of medium build and believed in setting a good example for her daughters by dressing modestly and professionally. She came from a fairly traditional Persian family, and like her own mother, Soraya was the master chef of the household. Unfortunately, Roya was starting to feel that the expectation to be like her mother had fallen on her, whereas before, the focus had been more on her sister.

Soraya had incorrectly assumed that the girls would be as interested in learning the family recipes as she had been at the age of sixteen. But by the time Sarah was in her mid-teens, she was too absorbed with her friends and her phone to care. And though Roya was less active on social media and more into books, she also struggled with her mother's need to define her. Caught between pleasing her mother and claiming space to define herself, she felt split about how to include her mother in the young woman she was becoming.

To Roya, the lack of family traditions on her father's side felt more freeing. Her father, Raymond, had never pressured her to be anything other than what she wanted to be. He accepted her as she was: intelligent, curious, and open-hearted.

"You're a free spirit, Roya," he liked to say. "Don't let anyone tell you what to believe. You can find the truth for yourself."

On the ride back home, it occurred to Roya that if she were to try any of the recipes, she might have to experiment while no one was home, because her family would want to try everything that she made. Roya's dad was outside mowing the front yard when they arrived, and she could hear music blaring from her sister's room upstairs. This was going to be another one of those days when there was no peace and quiet until everyone started going to bed. In theory, a quiet little town like Adams was supposed to be a haven from the busyness of the world, but Roya's mother created a world of busyness all on her own.

"Sweetie, tell your father that I'm going to run another errand," her mother said as Roya opened the car door, "and there's laundry that needs to be folded," she shouted over the sound of the lawn mower.

Roya held her breath as soon as she smelled the freshly cut grass and dust, waving at her dad as she approached the front door of their two-story house.

Like all of the really interesting books she had found before, she would wait until she could enjoy it without any interruptions—at night, when her sister had stopped talking on the phone, the TV downstairs was off, and all her chores were done. No matter what surprises were in store, it would be worth it to wait for the house to go to sleep.

It was almost midnight before Roya was finally settled in her room, and the only sound was a gentle summer breeze blowing through the trees outside. She pulled the book out from where she had stashed it underneath some magazines on her writing desk and sat on her bed cross-legged with her back to the wall. Suddenly, a gust of wind picked up, rustling loudly, as if to make some kind of statement. Even though she was already comfortable, she thought about getting up to close the window, but then the wind died down. In the distance, she thought she heard the sound of an owl hooting.

Roya often loved listening to the night sounds through her open window while falling asleep, but tonight, she was wide awake and captivated. She began to examine the cover. Strangely, she could find no author listed, but in the middle of the front cover was a golden symbol made of three interlocking circles. It almost seemed as if the symbol itself was the signature of the author. The rest of the cover had a rich violet hue which complemented the gold. She opened the book and flipped to a random page near the back, noticing a section that contained artwork in black and white. Landing on a full-page image of what looked like an angel, she was struck by how familiar its face looked. Its wings were spread open before a backdrop of stars, and its expression looked as if it was patiently waiting for something.

The angel's eyes drew her in, and she began to feel the presence of an immense being. Her eyes widened, and her breath quickened with her heartbeat. It felt like a gentle wind was blowing over her heart. The power of the feeling was both frightening and exciting at the same time. She wanted to surrender to the sensation, to be swept away by it, but a sense of caution kicked in, and she clapped the book shut.

What just happened? she thought. This was much more than a magic book. It felt as though something powerful was trying to reach her... something that knew her personally.

Instinctively taking several deep breaths, Roya felt inspired to attempt what she thought of as a brief meditation, to relax and clear her mind until she felt centered. Whatever these pictures were in the back of the book, she was not ready for them yet, so she decided to start at the beginning. This felt like the right thing to do. For months, she had been searching for something, but she did not know exactly what she was meant to find. Now she had finally found something—or had *it* found her?

She took another deep breath and opened the front cover of the book, noticing that it had no publication page or table of contents. On the inside of the cover, written in the same stylized gold lettering as the rest of the book, were the words: Flower Memorial Library, Watertown, New York. There was no introduction, only a title page that read: *The Circle and the Stars*; and then on the next page: *Chapter One: There's No Such Thing As Magic.*

Now that's a strange way for a magical book to begin, she thought, and yet that was the title of the first chapter. Suddenly, she became aware of how much her mind had been running wild with fantasies about tapping into mysterious forces that could magically transform her life. For a moment, she wondered again if her experience in the library had been real or not, but the feeling of the angel's gaze still present in her mind's eye beckoned her to keep exploring. The opening words of the book seemed to impact her with a force of their own, as if the author knew what she had been thinking about all day and wanted to begin with a reality check.

She had to admit that having grown up with the Harry Potter books and dozens of others about characters with magical abilities, she had always imagined that some of it might be true, or at least possible. The authoritative feel to the words challenged her deepest hope of discovering her own magical potential; and yet, given the extraordinary nature of the book, she was not discouraged, but intrigued. When she was finished pondering, she began to read:

Throughout history, human beings have often mistaken advanced abilities or advanced technology for magic. Take this book, for instance. To a human being in the early 21st century, it might appear to be a magical book, because it does things that ordinary books cannot yet do, but that does not make it magic. Let me assure you that this book is quite ordinary in the world from which it came. It is also one of a kind.

As you will discover, this is a book of recipes, but recipes can take many forms. What is a recipe, but a plan to create something desired by all the ingredients. Finding the right ingredients is like finding pieces of the desired future in the past. The ingredients may not know at first that they are part of a desired outcome, but they will feel a certain joy about combining that will make each step in the recipe more obvious. Before you know it, the desired future has become a new present for all involved, and that is the gift of transformation. As you learn to trust in the flow of synchronicity, you will discover the joy of transformation.

That's it? Roya thought, perplexed. The large stylized words of chapter one were all there on a single page. She read the page again to see if she could glean any more information from it, but the hidden meanings eluded her. What did it mean, *in the world from which it came?* She had barely spent five minutes exploring her new treasure, and already she was overwhelmed with feelings and questions. She turned the page and started reading the next chapter:

Chapter Two
The Secret Life of Ingredients

Everything contains memory. In fact, this book is made with special materials known to be good carriers of human memory. When you read, you will remember the author's knowledge as if it is your own. That is how learning works in the libraries of the future. Memory stored in books can be shared through what we call the *tilt medium.* Knowledge is simply tilted into the position of the reader through a shared medium of memory. The tilt of each book is designed with a specific audience in mind.

Most people in the early 21st century have yet to understand that matter is alive. Whenever a meal or edible treat is made well, matter remembers. The way it tastes to the people who enjoy it imprints the electrons, giving them subtle characteristics that pass into the memory fabric of the universe.

Roya saw vivid images in her mind of people passing a tasty dish around a table, *oohing* and *aahing* at the smell, their mouths watering. It felt like they were passing around a feeling of gratitude that bubbled up from inside them and heightened their senses.

As people enjoy the flavors, their joy of each unique food experience adds to the complexity of matter. When these impressions are rich enough and concentrated enough, they can become a reality unto themselves. Beings are created in this way. The field of matter is alive with beings that co-create with the world of form.

Such beings arise from joy, combined with the memory of sensation, and are endowed with the desire to share taste experiences with others. These beings can go on to create with the field of matter, informing people of new potential sensations. All the best cooks in the world have discovered how to tap into the subtle guidance of these beings, whether they realize it or not. These beings are called Flavors, and their essence is the joy of being in form. Flavors are part of the evolution of matter itself. Creating a treat is more than just measuring ingredients and following instructions; it is a matter of listening to the Flavors and feeling how they want to combine. They will want to impress those who will taste them, and when you learn to honor their intelligence, they will, in turn, inspire you. When you allow room for Flavors to play, every opportunity you give them will be reciprocated.

Roya played with the words in her mind: *recipe...reciprocation.* There seemed to be something magical about the connection between the words, though she was beginning to understand the word 'magic' in different terms, now.

On the very next page was the first recipe: *Apple Crisp.* At the bottom of the recipe, it said: *This is a recipe for freedom.* It was as if the book had known exactly what she longed for the most, but what kind of freedom did it refer to? She was not even old enough to get her driver's license, yet. But at this point, it didn't matter. She had already decided to trust in the book's design. Even though previously, she had not been drawn to cooking, the book inspired her, and she was excited to give it a try. Tomorrow, she would make her first apple crisp.

2

THE TASTE OF FREEDOM

The next morning, as the house began to stir, Roya focused intently on holding the dream state just a little longer. Something told her this dream was important. She found herself searching for something urgently as she walked briskly through a library—not the public library she knew, but one much, much larger. Her footsteps were light, as if her feet barely touched the ground. The vast temple-like space contained stone architecture that felt alive, and the books she passed by seemed to pulsate with living knowledge. After turning several corners, she found herself stopping about six feet in front of a wooden bookshelf that was much taller than she was. There, near the top, was a big yellow book. She instinctively felt that this book had something in it that she needed.

Without even thinking about it, she reached toward the book, and her will to access the information flowed through her like a force, causing the book to float right off the shelf toward her outstretched hand. Part of her felt astounded at this ability, and part of her felt like this was completely normal. As she relaxed her arm, the book floated down and opened in front of her. Almost instantly, a holographic image appeared that projected up from the pages of the floating book. The light formed into a moving image of a solar system that quickly grew to be many times larger until it completely enveloped the space she was in. It was a living scale model of another place in the Milky Way!

Her mind became entranced with the information until the very presence of the library simply faded into the background. Planets and asteroids zipped past her at incredible speed, like she was watching the history of the whole system on fast-forward. *"This is where the secret was first discovered,"* she heard from the voice of the book, and before she could receive the next piece of information, the sound of her sister turning on the blow dryer in the bathroom down the hall shattered the delicate vibration of the dream.

Roya awoke feeling annoyed, because this always seemed to happen at the most exciting moments of her morning dreams. If it was not her sister in the bathroom, it was the TV downstairs or the dog barking next door. She had learned some time ago to stop feeling angry at the interruptions and to appreciate that there was often a hidden timing to such things. Perhaps the source of the dream knew she would remember it better if she had the dream right before being woken up suddenly; if she had awakened more slowly, it might have just faded away from her conscious memory. And yet, she could not help feeling attached to seeing what would have happened next.

Both Sarah and her father were gone before Roya came downstairs for breakfast, and her mother was talking to a friend on the phone. As she walked into the kitchen to fix herself a bowl of cereal, she noticed that the fruit bowl was full of fresh, green apples—a family favorite. Her mother must have bought them the day before. She counted them and found more than enough for the apple crisp. Had the book somehow known what ingredients her mother would stock in the kitchen, or had her mother's intuition told her what to buy? As Roya began looking for the rest of the ingredients, she tried to imagine what Flavor-beings might look like, and how involved they were with this little project. Had they invisibly suggested to her mother which apples to select, knowing precisely how they would be used, or had their work begun with the apple trees?

Roya's imagination began to run wild with visions of supermarkets filled with invisible beings that were trying to teach people how to combine foods in new and exciting ways. With every cabinet she opened, she imagined that these invisible beings had left her a surprise, having already known that she would find the book and look for the ingredients.

It was a fairly simple recipe with typical ingredients: tart apples, rolled oats, flour, brown and white sugar, cinnamon, nutmeg, salt, butter, and lemon juice. After all this time, she felt like she was only now discovering the kitchen. Just as she located the last ingredient, her mother walked around the corner.

"What are you looking for?" she asked.

"Oh, nothing," Roya replied, hesitating slightly about what else to say. "I just wanted a little cinnamon, and I couldn't find it."

Roya knew that her mother would find out about the apple crisp, but she decided in a split second not to explain any further, because she wanted it to be a surprise.

"It should be right there with the other spices. Have you brushed your hair yet this morning?"

Typical, Roya thought. Her mother never seemed to understand that she liked the natural waviness of her hair, an effect diminished by too much brushing. Even so, Roya's response to her mother's comment was almost automatic. She bounded up the stairs and grabbed her brush, waiting until she was in visual range of her mother to start brushing. Her only intent was to keep her mother out of her hair, so to speak.

Roya had fewer boundaries with her mother than her rebellious older sister who had forcefully started to break away at this very age, and though she envied Sarah's freedom, she was determined not to follow in her sister's footsteps. Still, something inside her was screaming for change. Her aim was usually to please her mother, but this was far less satisfying when her mother only pointed out flaws. *Why can't she just say good morning instead of picking on my hair?* Roya thought.

"Going anywhere?" Roya asked, wondering how long she would have to wait until she could begin her project.

"Well, I have lots more to do to get ready for your grandparents' arrival," she said, looking up from the list she was making. "They're coming for a visit this weekend."

"Oh, I didn't know." *Extra chores*, she thought gloomily as she glanced over at the list: new towels, new shower curtain for the girls' bathroom, cleaning supplies...

Every time her grandparents came to visit, it was like preparing for the grand opening of a five-star hotel. She could already hear Sarah's excuses for not helping her clean the upstairs bathroom and was preparing herself for the tensions of the coming week.

"Do you mind if I stay here?" Roya asked, sensing what her mother was about to ask next.

"Sure, but can you work on your room while I'm gone?"

"Deal," Roya said, concealing that straightening up her room was not her top priority for the day.

"OK, I'll be back in a few hours."

Roya ate her cereal, patiently waiting while her mother checked her hair and make-up one last time in the downstairs bathroom, but as soon as she was gone, Roya flew back up the stairs and grabbed the book. In no time at all, she had the ingredients assembled on the kitchen counter next to the open book. She was ready to begin.

The recipe was easy to follow, but it was the personality of the book that made cooking feel familiar, even though she was a complete novice. With every line she read, the words gave her more awareness of the Flavors. Each ingredient was like a friend that had come to join the celebration. She never thought that cooking could be such an emotional experience, but with every apple she peeled, she felt like she was peeling back another layer of herself.

Somehow, the idea of Flavors as actual beings appealed to the most creative and sensitive part of her, the part that felt invisible to her family. The more she acknowledged the inspirational gifts of the invisible world, the more she felt acknowledged as a creative spirit. The rapport she felt with the personality of the book was transferring right into her relationship with the ingredients, but there was something more.

The experience seemed to be erasing some of her self-doubt. The very idea of baking the apple crisp was challenging her to rise above the inferiority she felt next to her mother's accomplishments. Her mother had won scholarships, graduated with honors, spoke three languages, and was an amazing cook. But suddenly, it no longer mattered. Gone was the idea of trying to be seen or measuring up. She was doing this for herself. She was no longer just following a recipe. She was surrendering to a field that was guiding her along a path that felt full of possibility, as if the promise of some inspiring future was calling her.

The whole project was finished, including clean up, before her mother arrived back home. The book was stashed beneath her bed, and the fresh apple crisp sat on the kitchen counter. The aroma had lessened enough that Roya could not detect it anymore from the couch where she was reading, but her mother noticed it as soon as she walked through the door.

"Roya, have you been baking? Something smells good," she said, surprised, while walking into the dining room to the left of the stairs.

From there, she could see the rectangular, glass, baking dish on the kitchen counter, next to the nearly empty fruit bowl. Roya had just entered the kitchen from the living room, as her mother unloaded several bags of supplies on the counter. Waiting for her mother to inspect the surprise, she signaled with her smile that it was hers to discover.

"It's just a little experiment," Roya said, nonchalantly, as her mother began to lift the foil and smell the aroma more deeply. "I hope you don't mind that I used up most of the apples."

"Mind? My youngest daughter, baking by herself? Why would I mind?" she said, with a twinge of pride in her voice.

"Go ahead, try it," said Roya cheerfully.

She already had dessert plates with forks and a spatula sitting on the counter, waiting in readiness. Her mother cut out a large corner piece for herself and then one for Roya. Both of them took the first bite in unison. "Mmmmm," her mother said, as she began to savor the first bite. Roya was enjoying the tartness of the apples, but she was more interested in her mother's reaction, anticipating that part of the mystery of the book might be unfolding before her very eyes.

"I didn't know you had any interest in baking. This is really well-made!"

"Thanks," Roya said, still chewing. "I just got inspired."

Roya watched her mother take a second and then a third bite, noticing how focused she was on the flavors. While her mother was expressing deeper and deeper satisfaction, Roya felt more and more pleased with herself and the effect of the apple crisp. Her mother didn't seem to notice that Roya had stopped eating as she continued, tasting pieces of apple by themselves, and then tasting the crust.

"Roya, this is really amazing! I hope you're going to learn how to make more than just this," she said, giving Roya a familiar glance of expectation.

Roya could not help thinking, *what have I gotten myself into,* but her curiosity about the ultimate outcome of the recipe was greater than her worry that she would be expected to become more involved in the kitchen. Roya was thanking the Flavors inwardly, wondering if they could feel her smile. Then she began to feel a sense of pride swirling within her mother as she opened her mouth to receive the last bite. Her mood had changed and become warmer to the point that she was glowing, and then something extraordinary happened.

Her mother took a deep breath, feeling the food settling into her stomach, and as she exhaled slowly, Roya sensed a warm ball of energy emerge from the center of her mother's chest, carrying part of her glow. She could not necessarily see it with her eyes, but the feeling was so clear, it was just like seeing it. There, floating in the space between them, was a ball of living energy.

"I bet my friends at the café would love this recipe." With that said, the ball of energy seemed to brighten, and then Roya felt it zip away.

The book was right, she thought. Her mother had wished for others to experience what she'd just experienced, and her wish was powerful enough to become a being unto itself. Her experience had added a new spin of inspiration to the Flavors that was informing the field of matter. Roya imagined that she could see the Flavors traveling within the ball of energy into the little breakfast café that her mother loved, joining with the dance of creative energy in their famous local bakery.

"Don't tell Sarah or Dad that I made it until they try it. I wanna see their faces first." Roya implored her mother.

"They will love it, I'm sure. I'm so proud of you," she said, drawing Roya into a warm embrace. "If you need any more supplies, let me know. Now, if you don't mind, I need to work on a little cleaning project before everyone gets home."

Quite unexpectedly, her mother had not drafted her into her projects right away, which felt like a rewarding reciprocation for her effort. The whole experience of making the recipe had been well worth it, but it was a surprise bonus to have the rest of the afternoon to herself. Freed from expectations, Roya decided to take a bike ride over to the Adams Free Library to see if she could learn more about the book on the library's computers.

She was hoping to solve the mystery of the book's origin right away, so she started by looking up the title, but she could find no listing for it anywhere in Jefferson County. She tried the internet as well, but still found nothing. After staring at a long list of related titles online, she suddenly remembered the words of the book reminding her, *It is also one of a kind.*

Roya had the eerie feeling that the book had known she would search for information about it on this very day and had already answered the question in the first chapter. Realizing her research was at a dead end, she retreated to a quiet corner and began to explore the book again. Flipping open to a random page, she read the first quote her eyes landed upon:

> A word lit with the invisible light of future knowledge will tilt into alignment with hidden dimensions of meaning once you reach the correct time reference.

Tilt, she thought. Somehow, the word felt different, as if she was just discovering its meaning for the first time. The word itself seemed to be showing her how certain words have the potential to *tilt* into alignment with new knowledge that was always part of the hidden future meaning of the word. Gradually, she began to find her focus on the inner dimensions of the book as she continued reading:

The keys to the future are hidden in the past. As you align with the path to freedom, the light of a more promising future will interact with your awareness, showing you signs and synchronicities to guide you on your way. Certain things may appear brighter or stand out in your awareness, as if beckoning you in a new direction. The light of the future can even illuminate a hidden encoded meaning to certain words and phrases. The words of instruction are hidden in plain sight.

Just like the ingredients in a recipe for change, the words and letters of a hidden message will vibrate with joy as they are combined in the right way. When your mind is playful and imaginative, you will receive the intended interpretation of the encoded messages, like a story that unfolds spontaneously.

A daydreaming mind can unravel the mysteries of time, and an open heart can unlock the secrets of nature. As Albert Einstein once said: "Look deep into nature, and then you will understand everything better."

The words of instruction are hidden in plain sight, Roya thought. Something about this phrase seemed familiar. *In plain sight,* she pondered further. She could not help but think of the Watertown Memorial Library where she had found the book, which had many quotes written on the walls. And then it hit her!

To know wisdom and instruction, to perceive the words of understanding. She recalled this quote inscribed in a circle around the inside of the library's famous stained glass dome.

Pulling out her notebook, she wrote the phrase down in all capital letters and suddenly noticed that her awareness of the word 'understanding' had just shifted.

TO KNOW WISDOM AND INSTRUCTION,
TO PERCEIVE THE WORDS OF UNDERSTANDING

In her imagination, she saw the words 'STAND UNDER' pop out, and then she was drawn to the 'DOM' in the word 'WISDOM'. *Stand under dome,* she pieced together.

Next, she wrote the new phrase underneath the original quote, using the 'E' from 'THE' to complete the word 'DOME', crossing out the letters she had already used. Just as the book had described, the new phrase seemed to vibrate with excitement as she was decoding the hidden message. As she continued to scan for more clues, the word 'RECEIVE' popped out of 'PERCEIVE'. Very quickly, the remaining words and letters rearranged themselves to form a new sentence:

TO KNOW PATH INSTRUCTIONS,
STAND UNDER DOME
OF WINDING WORDS TO RECEIVE

The new sentence was a perfect anagram of the previous one, *but how could that be?* Her next thought was about getting back to the Flower Memorial Library to stand under the dome, but then she had a clever idea.

She remembered that the Flower Memorial Library had a virtual tour on their website that allowed you to be positioned directly under the dome, with the ability to look in every direction—including straight up. Roya quickly found an available computer and started the virtual tour.

Just inside the main entrance was a foyer where the signs of the Zodiac were emblazoned upon the floor, encircling a marble bust of Roswell P. Flower, to whom the library was dedicated. Directly above the statue was the domed ceiling, capped with a stained glass window. By moving the cursor around, she could see everything, including the inscription of words winding around the inside of the dome. The dome contained eight figures created by Frederick Stymetz Lamb that represented muses for History, Fable, Epic Poetry, Religion, Science, Lyric, Drama, and Romance, each flanked by two famous names. The entire rotunda overlooking the signs of the Zodiac was Roya's favorite feature of the library. After turning her focus to the muses, something caught her attention.

The name 'Newton' was inscribed to the right of the muse for science, complemented by 'Darwin' to the left. *Sir Isaac Newton*, she thought. Then, the Flavors of the apple crisp began to connect her with the apple trees and the legend of how Newton discovered gravity. *Apples falling from trees...fruits of knowledge,* her mind mused...*the wisdom of the trees.*

As she continued staring at the muse, Roya began to have a humorous thought: that the tree Sir Isaac Newton had been standing near had, in fact, been dropping apples deliberately to get his attention. It was more than a thought, but a feeling that became extraordinarily vivid. Had the trees always known? Had they finally been able to impart one of their secrets to someone who had the capacity to listen?

Roya then found her gaze drifting down to an image of two trees with an inscription written between them. *This must be significant,* she thought, but unfortunately the image was not clear enough to make out all the words. She had seen these words a thousand times but could not recall exactly what they said. On the opposing wall, was a similar inscription between two trees, and she was intrigued by the possibility of finding another message.

Suddenly, she noticed the time and realized it was getting late. She did not want to miss the moment when Sarah and her dad tried the apple crisp. Just as she was about to exit the library, a flyer on the wall caught her attention:

Teen Baking Contest
1st prize $500

The contest was scheduled for Wednesday evening in the cafeteria of the high school. As she read the rest of the flyer, a message from the book floated into her mind: *This is a recipe for victory.* It was the very next recipe after the apple crisp. Was this just another coincidence? Or did the book know that she was going to see this flyer?

Roya arrived home just in time to see her dad pulling up in the driveway. She could hear Sarah's music and was already disappointed that she might have missed her reaction, but she soon discovered that her mother had hidden the apple crisp so that it could be presented as a surprise dessert after dinner.

That evening, over dinner, she told her family about the baking contest, and her mother was surprised and delighted that Roya wanted to participate. Of course, Sarah's first reaction was to shoot her sister a disbelieving look.

"What?" Roya demanded, glaring back at Sarah.

"Since when do you bake?" Sarah implored, somewhat bothered at how pleased her mother seemed with Roya.

"Well," Roya said mischievously, "if you must know."

There could not be a better moment. She got up, walked to the oven, and produced the apple crisp, placing it on the table right in front of Sarah. Roya had a look of satisfaction on her face, knowing her big sister would have never guessed what was coming. She smirked a little and raised her eyebrows as she watched her sister examining the dessert in disbelief.

"I didn't even know she made it until I came home from running errands," said her mother, as if to answer the question Sarah was about to ask. All her father could think of was the fact that they had already eaten a couple of pieces without him.

"Well, let's give it a try," he said, enthusiastically. His mouth was already watering as her mother went to the kitchen to get the spatula and some dessert plates. Sarah had to admit that it *did* look appealing. Her father did not waste any time digging into his piece.

"Yum! This is really good, Roya," he said, sharing a smile with his wife. "Was this your idea?" he asked Roya.

"Yeah. It was just an experiment though," Roya said, realizing the implications of what was unfolding. She was still trying to downplay it so her parents would not start expecting more of her, though she wondered if it was already too late for that. As if her sister could sense what she was thinking, Roya felt certain that Sarah's look of satisfaction was *not* about the taste of the dessert. At first, Sarah seemed annoyed at the praise Roya was getting, but then she gloated at the idea that Roya had just become a target.

"Wow, Roya, you're a really good cook," emphasized Sarah, with a note of sarcasm that only Roya could detect. This was Sarah's way of sabotaging Roya by redirecting her parents' expectations away from herself and onto her sister. Roya knew exactly what her sister was doing and gave her a look of disapproval.

Sarah could be very clever at activating a sense of rivalry between them, just to entertain herself, but Roya's secret relationship with the mysterious book was helping her shift her focus onto something more positive. By the time they were finished with dessert, Roya had decided not to worry about getting drafted into cooking projects. Something told her that everything connected with the recipes was an opportunity, and there was only one way to find out.

3

A WINNING COMBINATION

The next day, Roya copied the recipe for zucchini bread onto a separate sheet of paper and stashed the book underneath her bed. Even though the thought of winning the prize money was attractive, a part of her was simply enjoying how present her mother was being with her. It had been such a long time since she had acknowledged Roya the way she had the day before. Something was starting to shift in their relationship, and her mother's excitement about the contest felt like another opportunity.

Roya insisted that she would use the zucchini bread recipe she had copied from the book, even though her mother kept suggesting other possibilities. She was not sure about altering the recipe, either, but her mother was full of ideas about how to improve it.

"Mom, I just want to keep this simple," stated Roya. "I don't have a lot of time to experiment." Roya, still wanting to keep the book a secret, did not want to divulge her reasons for sticking with the recipe. *If I change the recipe, it might change the outcome of events,* she thought, but then realized that she did not know enough about what the book was intending. Something about her mother's enthusiasm reminded her of what the book said about a contagious joy shared by ingredients.

"I know what the recipe says, but trust me, there is an even better way to do this," her mother explained. "I know just what you need to make this really special."

Assuming that the book had known this would happen, she decided to be open to her mother's creative input. It was as if the book was hinting that the recipe had left room for this exact experience. Her mother could not have been happier, because now she had an opportunity to impart some of her cooking secrets to her daughter. The thought occurred to Roya that her mother might unknowingly already be in touch with Flavors, even though she had never read about their hidden dimensions. As they headed off to shop for ingredients, Roya began to have the impression that the Flavors were talking to her again, but this time through her mother.

First, they came to a natural foods store where her mother explained that ordinary white sugar was not the best choice for bringing out flavors. She suggested substituting organic raw cane sugar instead, with a touch of molasses. From there, they went to a gourmet shop with all kinds of specialty items. Her mother explained that too often, people just use table salt when many different kinds of salt with different flavors and mineral properties are available.

"The right kind of salt can bring out the flavors, depending on the ingredients," she said.

For the next ten minutes, they tasted samples of gourmet salt and tried to describe the differences in their flavors. The man at the cheese counter was happy to come over and give a little presentation as they tasted, and he even brought some bread and butter over to enhance the experience.

When Roya finally decided on the one she wanted, they both grinned at each other, because they had intuitively picked the same one. It might have seemed trivial, but they were both secretly relishing the feeling of being on the same page. By the time they got home with the ingredients, their conversation had opened up into a wider range of topics, and they both seemed aware that something was shifting between them in a very positive way.

We're talking like two adults, Roya thought. It was the beginning of a deeper healing between them.

One thing Roya noticed was that the stress of preparing for the weekend visit had all but disappeared. Her mother's busyness so often conveyed that there was no time for play, but as Roya began working on the first loaf of zucchini bread, the sense of being in the present moment with her mother seemed unaffected by the burdens of the future. Her mother suggested that Roya test the recipe several times, if necessary, before baking some for the contest the next day. That way, if all the loaves turned out great, there would just be more to share.

When Sarah arrived home from her afternoon shift at the pizza parlor, she felt like she had walked into someone else's house.

"Is this for the contest?" Sarah asked, not sure what to think.

Seeing her sister wearing an apron and chatting with her mother like they were old friends was an unusual sight to behold. Sarah did not have the same feeling about wearing aprons, with her own work apron rolled up and tucked under her arm. She still had on her work hat with her long, brown hair tied up in a ponytail, and she reeked of pizza.

"Yeah, we just finished the first loaf. You wanna try some?" Roya asked, offering her a small piece on a napkin.

Momentarily, Sarah was annoyed at being held up from disappearing into her room and getting on the phone, but it was hard to resist Roya's invitation.

Both Roya and their mother watched Sarah closely, holding a silent expectancy that their good vibes would be transferred into Sarah through the zucchini bread. It might have been wishful thinking, but Roya was certain that the bread had been imbued with some of their joy while baking. Gradually, it was dawning on her how much love her mother had always put into their food as they were growing up and how the simple act of baking was bringing out her own ability to sense the subtleties of living energy.

"Not bad," she said in a non-emotional voice, still chewing. "Thanks." Sarah hesitated as if she wanted to express more, but she stopped herself and headed up to her room. Her words felt like a little victory to Roya, even though Sarah resisted being more acknowledging.

"Don't worry, Roya, we'll get a better opinion from your father when he gets home from work. Personally, I think it tastes like a winner. Don't you?"

"Yeah, I love it!" Roya said. "Now I'll try making one with nuts."

Her mother's belief that she might actually be onto a winner lent an upbeat feeling to the project that carried both of them through the rest of the afternoon. By the time Roya's dad walked in the door, she had baked several loaves. Her father immediately smelled the aroma coming from the kitchen as he closed the door behind him and loosened his tie. He always wore slacks, a white, button-up shirt, and a tie to work at the herb shop.

"Raymond, you have to try this, and let us know which one you like best."

"Wow, you two have been busy," he said as he kissed his wife hello.

Soraya always thought he looked so handsome in dress clothes with his broad shoulders, powerful hands, and neatly cut, butterscotch brown hair. He had barely sat down at the dining room table before they were both hovering over him with several pieces of zucchini bread.

"There's one plain, one with nuts, and one with nuts and dates," explained Roya.

Raymond approached tasting new foods with the same gratitude and openness that he approached just about everything else. He considered anything made by his wife a blessing, and to think of his wife and daughter baking together made him smile even before he put the first piece in his mouth. Slowly taking in the subtle flavors of each piece, he weighed the contrast between each of them in his mind.

"Wow, they're all good. I think I like the one with nuts the best. I love the flavor of dates, but they kind of overpower the other ingredients, especially…what's that taste? It's not the nutmeg…not the cinnamon. I'm pretty sure you added a dash of molasses, but even that's not quite it."

Roya and her mother both looked at each other and smiled.

"That's the secret ingredient," Roya said conspiratorially. Her mother was famous for keeping everyone guessing when it came to flavors, but this time, Roya was in on it.

"So, shall I go with the nuts?" Roya asked her mother.

"Yes. I think you have your finalist."

They all tasted good enough that Roya wasn't sure it mattered too much, but it felt right that they all agreed on the same one. The next day, she baked four more loaves with nuts and set them aside for the evening event.

Later, Roya took some time to organize her room so that it looked ready for the weekend, and then she helped dust and wipe down the windows with her mother. She could not help noticing that everything seemed to flow with a feeling of effortlessness.

That evening, there were nearly 200 people in attendance at the baking contest. She knew some of the guys and girls from school, and others were unfamiliar. There were 38 entries laid out on the tables that lined the perimeter of the school's cafeteria. As local events go, it was a huge success. The ten dollar admission fee was more than worth it for those who had come to taste. A portion of each entry was set-aside for the judges, and the rest was made available to the attendees.

Roya was surprised to learn that some of the guys from her class were quite good at baking. Everywhere they looked, people were busy tasting and trading recipes. After setting up their display between a pyramid stack of fudge brownies and a tray of lemon bars, Roya and her mother began to make their way around the perimeter of the room to check out the competition. There were cakes, pies, muffins, scones, breads, and just about every dessert imaginable. Most of the displays had small samples cut up and ready for tasting.

After almost an hour of tasting only the most attractive treats and chatting with the other guests, Roya's mother spotted one of her friends from the café.

"Oh look, there's Kathy," she said, putting her hand on Roya's back and guiding her to the woman standing a short distance away. "I think her daughter is just about your age."

Roya expected that her mother would know a number of people at the event and had already decided to politely go along with the show and tell, but she was not expecting that her mother would get into her old habit of trying to pick out friends for her. Kathy had insisted that her daughter Marcy stand behind her display of pineapple upside down cake while wearing an embroidered apron to help promote their family's bakery.

"Hi Marcy," Roya said politely.

Marcy responded only by raising her eyebrows. Apparently, she had not forgotten the time that her mother had compared her to Roya after finding out from Mrs. Sands that Roya was making better grades.

"Hey, Roya!" came a cheerful voice from behind. Roya whipped around to see two smiling faces that instantly made her light up with excitement.

"Ami! Mandy! I'm so glad you're here. How was your trip?"

"Great," said Ami, pulling her into a hug. "We just got back. What have you been up to?"

"Just baking a little. I made zucchini bread for the contest."

As Roya began to talk, she thought of telling them about the book. It was the most exciting thing she could think of to share, but something told her to wait for a better time.

"I wanna try some," requested Mandy.

"Hey, Mom. I'm gonna go show Ami and Mandy my zucchini bread. I'll find you in a bit."

Her mother was so engaged in conversation that she hardly noticed the two girls and went right on chatting. Roya found herself smiling at the universe again for having provided an escape from an uncomfortable situation.

"So, tell me about your trip," Roya invited, as they made their way through the crowded room.

"We went all over Ontario," shared Ami. "I think my dad must have photographed just about every waterfall there is. Sorry we were out of touch for so long, but we kind of agreed to go phone-free while we were out in nature."

"That's cool," Roya said, as she walked them over to the table to try some of her bread. "I wish I could travel like that. My dad says we can't afford it."

Even as she said the words, it bothered her, and she wished it wasn't true. She was such an explorer in her imagination; she believed she was meant to experience more of the world. Her family had a nice house, and all their basic needs were met, but there never seemed to be a budget for vacations. It had been several years since the family had gone on a road trip, so she explored the world mostly through books and documentaries. Roya had the sense that there were complications with the bills, but her parents did not openly discuss anything about it with her and Sarah.

"Mmmm, this is *full* of yumminess," Mandy said, using her silly voice. "It's light and fluffy, sweet and spicy, like zucchini pancakes with cinnamon."

Mandy chomped with her mouth open and had a wild look in her eyes that made Roya think she was imagining herself as a quirky cartoon character. Mandy sometimes liked to pretend that she was being buzzed or electrified by whatever she was touching, often exaggerating her reaction to things as a way of putting on a show. She was definitely the more animated of the two sisters. She loved being dramatic in front of her peers, though Roya could easily imagine her doing the same things when she was alone, just to entertain herself. She had a thousand silly faces, and though Ami sometimes acted mildly annoyed, her unconditional tolerance of Mandy's antics showed maturity that went beyond being a little more than a year older.

"I didn't know you baked," Ami said, contemplating the taste of the bite she'd just swallowed. "Wait a minute, didn't you say you were resisting your mom's idea of traditional gender roles?"

Ami was always good at discerning the hidden layers of things, and her memory was excellent.

"It's a long story," Roya said, which, in their friend-lingo, meant, *I'll tell you when we're alone.* Again, she thought about the book, wondering how she would explain her experiences, but she knew that Ami was good at coaxing the details out of her, especially if it was something important. Ami's sincere interest in her life always felt refreshing, and her way of being present with Roya conveyed a loyalty to their friendship that engendered trust.

Of course, she would have to share the book with Mandy as well, but over the past semester, she had come to accept Ami and Mandy as a package. After all, because they had moved around a lot, their closest friendship was with each other. It was not that she didn't trust Mandy with her deepest secrets, but Mandy's contribution to the group dynamic had to do more with generating playfulness in the present moment, whereas Ami liked to delve into the history behind Roya's feelings, which Roya appreciated. Mandy's realm was of the imagination, and Ami's realm was the landscape of memories.

"I missed you both," Roya said, and they all smiled.

For Roya, their arrival marked the true beginning of her summer break. She stood silent for a moment and took in the details of their faces. Ami had a slender build, just an inch and a half taller than Roya. She was wearing overalls with a sea-foam green tank top underneath. Her dark brown hair was cut in an edgy style that was short in the back with side swept bangs that were long enough to fall over her eyes. The slightly boyish features of her face complemented the androgynous nature of her personality. Her only accessory was a tiny silver nose pin on her left nostril.

Mandy had a somewhat curvier physique than her older sister and was the same height as Roya. She was more into makeup and styling her hair and wore colorful bracelets and silver earrings in the shape of crescent moons. Her hair was a dark ash blonde, shoulder-length, and wavy with several lighter blonde streaks. She sported blue jeans and a pink lace camisole. Roya, a bit more muscular, always felt athletic standing next to the two girls.

"Ladies and Gentlemen, may I have your attention please," said a short, stout-looking woman in a grey, tailored dress suit. "We are ready to announce the winner of this year's competition."

The room gradually fell silent as the woman at the microphone stood waiting for everyone to quiet down. With clipboard in hand, she turned her head back and forth several times as she surveyed the people in the room. She had her hair up in a bun and wore horn-rimmed glasses which made her whole face look rather pointy. She kept pursing her lips and tightening the corners of her mouth, like she had a nervous twitch now that the whole room was looking at her. Roya's eyes briefly landed on her mother who had just spotted her from across the room.

"This year's competition is the largest we have ever had. With so many entries, it was extremely difficult to choose a winner. A few of our judges had to loosen their belts before we had even selected the finalists," she said, and a few people from the crowd chuckled. "But this year, the judges were most impressed by one entry in particular. Even though our judges are all known for having a sweet tooth, the incredible balance of subtle flavors and textures embodied in this one entry stood out above all others. It is my great pleasure to announce that our first place prize of $500 goes to…" she paused to look down at the clipboard, before pushing her glasses back up the bridge of her nose, "…Roya Sands and her zucchini bread!"

"Roya, you won!" Ami shouted.

Roya's eyes grew wide as the crowd erupted with cheers and applause. Turning to see her mother making her way across the room to meet her, she noticed Mandy doing a crazy victory dance while Ami watched and laughed. As she approached the podium, it occurred to her that she had never really won anything before. It was such a strange feeling to have money just manifest out of nowhere. It did not seem real at first, but then her mother embraced her and acknowledged Roya for insisting on the recipe of her choice.

"If it had been me, I probably would have made a pie. I never would have thought of zucchini bread," she said to Roya over the sound of the applause.

Again, Roya was struck by the feeling that she had done something right; that she was trusted to be her own person. The check for $500 that the woman handed her was merely a bonus, because the main victory was being a winner in her mother's eyes.

Having the whole room focused on her made Roya blush momentarily, but then she became lost in a feeling of wonder about the book. This was more than a victory. It felt like someone had given her a gift, both inwardly and outwardly. Ami and Mandy kept clapping long after the rest of the crowd had stopped. As the woman went on to announce a number of other smaller prizes, Roya pulled her mother over to see them and asked if they could give her friends a ride home later. She could hardly contain her excitement that the mystery of the book had just deepened. How had it known that this victory would take place?

For the next twenty minutes, she accepted congratulations, and Roya's mother chatted some more with Kathy. Roya only caught part of their conversation, when Kathy sampled one of the last pieces of zucchini bread, desperately trying to guess the secret ingredient. Meanwhile, Ami and Mandy were busy discussing what she might like to do with the prize money. Perhaps for once, her summer break would be more fun than she had imagined.

4

FLAVORS AND COLORS

When Roya awoke early the next morning, the victory from the previous night seemed like a dream. She yawned and stretched, and after a few minutes, she reached under her mattress and pulled out the book. Now that its guidance had proven trustworthy, she was convinced that its purpose related directly to her life. She imagined that the victory was part of a design to build her trust in the unfolding plan. Clearly, the book was revealing a path that felt promising.

The sun was just starting to peek over the roof of the house next door, illuminating the book as she held it out in front of her to catch the rays coming through the window. Roya liked seeing the sunlight reflecting off the golden letters as she admired the book. Though the blinds were down, she usually kept them raised just enough so that some morning light would land on a prism that hung in front of the window, casting little rainbows across the white walls of her room.

Flipping through the pages, she wanted to see if she could discern the outcomes to the other recipes. It occurred to her that if she knew the outcomes, she might like to choose what she wanted to experience next, but the descriptions of what each recipe did were too vague. Perhaps the author had known that she would try to figure things out and had kept the descriptions vague for exactly this reason.

So, trying to control the outcomes might limit them, but letting go and trusting will set them free. Yes! That's what happened when I let Mom add her ideas to the recipe, she thought, realizing that her experiences with the book had just crystallized a new insight: *The less we try to control the outcome of events, the more room we leave for unseen forces to help us fulfill the highest potential.*

Roya heard herself think the words as if she was reading them somewhere. Was this a line from the book? While holding the book in her hands, she experienced a heightened sense of clarity that caused her mind to align with coherent patterns of thought that contained wisdom. She was exploring how she could read the resonance of the book's knowledge with her inner senses. This method of learning felt both new and somehow familiar at the same time.

Every moment of her experience with the book seemed to confirm that its contents were created with a sort of omniscient awareness of her thoughts and needs. More puzzling was the fact that the whole book only contained five recipes, the last of which did not involve food; but Roya was beginning to wonder if the entire book itself was a recipe for something much more. She knew that synchronicity played a role in guiding her actions and that the book was aligning her with recipes for change that were woven into the very fabric of her reality.

As she considered how she might explain her experience of the book to Ami and Mandy, she found herself staring at the very next recipe after zucchini bread. Rainbows danced across the page, as if they were talking to the golden letters, until the idea, quite literally, dawned on her. If the book knew what she was going to ask in this very moment, then the answer was the recipe right in front of her, most appropriately titled: *Sunshine Cookies*.

Roya waited until everyone was gone for the day before she started nosing around the kitchen for ingredients, happy to have some quiet alone time. Plus, she liked the idea of having her secret book with her when she was making the cookies. Luckily, just enough cane sugar and nuts were left over from making zucchini bread. After a little searching, she found that everything else was there. She had never made cookies on her own before, though she had helped her mother make them dozens of times.

As Roya began to mix the first of the ingredients together, thoughts of Ami and Mandy floated through her mind. Ami Allison Carter and Amanda Marie Carter had moved to town with their dad in the middle of the spring semester. Their mother, Cindy, had passed away when they were younger, but their dad, Frank, was a dedicated father. As a nature photographer, Mr. Carter had a dream that he would one day take his daughters on adventures to photograph rare animals. Though he enjoyed his work photographing landscapes, he longed for something more interesting.

Roya had three classes with Ami and instantly felt that she was meant to be part of the welcoming committee. She took it upon herself to show Ami around, and Ami was really touched by the gesture. When Roya found out how much Ami had traveled, she was fascinated. Between Roya's interest in life outside her small town and Ami's interest in Roya's perspective on all the teachers and students, they had plenty to talk about.

Roya liked the fact that Mandy had freckles, because it made her less self-conscious about her own. Roya's freckles were sprinkled across her nose and the tops of her cheeks, under her eyes, whereas Mandy's were a little darker and filled her cheeks, nose, and forehead. Roya had always disliked her own before meeting Mandy, but Mandy wore hers with pride, like they were her little beauty marks.

Roya would never forget when Ami first introduced her to Mandy after school. Mandy went on about how she had more freckles than any girl in school, as if this was one of the perks of living in a small, relatively freckle-less town. "Freckles are flair," she said in a nonchalant way, which made Roya laugh out loud when she thought about Mandy later that day. The fact that Mandy's were more noticeable than her own helped shift her attitude so that she felt more attractive the way she was. In those three simple words, Mandy's carefree self-acceptance had given Roya a lasting gift that made her smile whenever she thought of it.

Roya wondered if this had anything to do with why the recipe said it would make her more visible. As she stirred in the final ingredients—oats, Rice Krispies, coconut, and chopped nuts—the Flavors began to speak to her again, and she intuitively knew that these cookies were for Mandy. Of course, they would be shared with Ami as well, but something made her feel like thanking Mandy for being there. She noticed that Mandy sometimes felt left out, especially because Ami and Roya were almost exactly the same age. They had quickly become high school buddies, but Mandy had not yet made any friends that were as close.

About an hour later, she was out the door with the mysterious book and a sealed plastic container full of freshly baked Sunshine Cookies in her backpack. It was a beautiful, warm, summer day, and the walk to Ami and Mandy's house was less than half a mile, which gave her time to think about the way her awareness seemed to be changing. A strange new feeling was welling up inside her—a feeling that she was on the verge of answering questions about reality that she didn't even know *could* be answered. She was beginning to notice how her life was being propelled by a mysterious sequence of events, and the thought of sharing this experience with her friends felt joyful.

Roya was wearing her favorite blue jeans that had a couple of little holes worn out just above the knee. There was an unfortunate small ink stain that had bled through the pocket from a leaky pen, but she didn't mind, because she was just happy to be wearing more casual clothes for the summer. As she rounded the corner to Ami and Mandy's house, she thought about how nice it was to hang out with her new friends without having to worry about school. Theirs was a one-story, three-bedroom house with a big back yard and a tree in the front that was good for climbing.

Roya knocked on the door, and then suddenly decided to dig into her backpack to have the cookies already in hand when it opened. She had just produced them when Mandy answered the door.

"Roya! Come on in."

"I made you something," said Roya, with a grin. Mandy looked surprised, her mouth in a round "O" as she looked down at the container of goodies.

"Well, they're for both of you, but I thought of you specifically when I was making them, because I wanted to say thanks."

"Thanks? For what?" Mandy asked, with a puzzled expression.

Roya was not sure how to best convey the sentiment, so she just came right out with the simple truth: "Thanks for being my friend!"

"Oh. Well, you're welcome. That's super cool that you should say that, actually."

"These are called Sunshine Cookies," Roya said, as she lifted off the lid to the plastic container.

"WOW, these smell great!" Mandy said, just as Ami came around the corner.

"What are those?" Ami asked, catching Mandy's excitement.

"Shun shine 'ookies," Mandy mumbled, having already stuffed a whole cookie in her mouth.

"I want one," requested Ami. Mandy tried to hand her one, but Ami stopped her.

"I wanna choose my own," she insisted, as she began to examine the container.

She looked around until she found exactly the one she wanted, and then she sniffed it a couple of times before taking the first bite. Mandy almost laughed out loud, imagining that her sister was a dog sniffing a dog biscuit, but she managed to restrain herself from spewing bits of cookie everywhere. Sometimes, she could not help the hilarious nature of the scenes that she imagined. While Ami was still contemplating the first bite, Mandy had randomly grabbed another and was happily munching away.

"Wow, these are great!" Mandy exclaimed as Ami nodded in agreement. "Where did you get the recipe?"

Déjà vu, Roya thought. When the rainbows were dancing across the recipe that morning, she had vividly imagined Mandy asking this very question.

"Let's go into one of your rooms, and I'll show you," Roya whispered, conspiratorially.

Roya and Mandy followed Ami back to her room, no doubt because it was less cluttered, and then proceeded to sit on the floor in a circle with the container of cookies in the center. Roya produced the book from her backpack and handed it to Ami with a mysterious grin as she immediately began weighing it with her hands.

"OK, is it just me, or does this book feel way lighter than it should?" she questioned, with a surprised look on her face. "That's really weird!"

"Yeah. That's what I thought, too. It's like you're holding the *shape* of a book but without all the weight."

"Where did you get this?!" Ami asked curiously as she passed it over to her sister.

"At the library, in Watertown. It's strange, though. I couldn't find any information about who wrote it."

Mandy's eyes got really big as she played with the book in her hands.

"Wow! I wonder how it got like this? Does it say anything about why it's so light?"

"Sort of. It's kinda cryptic, though. I think it's from the future."

"Whoaaaa, the future," said Mandy, with excitement. "Maybe time travelers work at the library."

"Funny you should mention that. This new librarian named Claire checked the book out for me. I've never seen her before, but I got the feeling she knew something about it. She wore a wig and had unusual looking hair underneath, almost like it shimmered with some color. Maybe *she's* a time traveler."

"Maybe everyone in the future has hair that glows," Mandy mused, staring off into space. She looked like she was dreaming with her eyes open as she vividly imagined a future society of people with hair that glowed every color of the rainbow. She then began to imagine them wearing wildly colorful outfits.

"*The Circle and the Stars*" read Ami, inspecting the title. "Why does it have a symbol with three circles on the front, but the title only mentions one?" she wondered aloud.

"Yeah, I wondered that myself," replied Roya.

"Does it say anything about it?" asked Ami.

"Not that I could find. There are certain things about the book that give you the feeling that there are hidden messages in everything. Here, I'll read some of it to you," offered Roya, wondering if they would be able to sense the inner dimensions of the book as she had. Ami listened intently, contemplating the messages, and Mandy looked like she was still lost in her imagination. Roya paused for a few seconds after the first chapter, but Ami looked like she was waiting for more, so she kept reading. As soon as she reached the end of chapter two, Mandy snapped out of her daydream. Something caught her attention and brought her back into the room.

"Let me see that," she said urgently. "What was that last part about Flavors?" Roya passed the book over to Mandy and watched as she became very focused, reading the passage about Flavors several times until she exclaimed, "Yes!" She rocked backward until she was lying flat on her back, hugging the book to her chest and giggling with a look of delight on her face. She looked a little like she was being tickled, and yet it was something more meaningful that had touched her.

"What is it?" Ami demanded. "What's so funny?"

"This book talks about Flavors the same way I relate to colors!" said Mandy excitedly as she sat up.

"This is what I've been trying to tell you for the longest time," she expressed to her sister. "When I work with fabric or design clothing in my sketchbook, it's like Colors talk to me. I can almost taste them, like they get sweeter when they're combined in the right way...the way they *want* to be combined. All this time, I've been searching for the words to describe this, and here they are!"

"But why is that so funny?" Roya asked curiously.

"Because they're laughing with me!" Mandy exclaimed with a big grin on her face. "The Colors, I mean. There must be Color beings that help me when I create stuff. Speaking of which, I have something for you."

Laying the book down in front of them, Mandy got up and turned around to go to her closet in the other room.

"You're going to love this," Ami predicted.

Ami was happy to finally see the culmination of Mandy's whole creative process. When Mandy returned, she was holding a beautiful, yellow, strappy summer dress.

"Mandy, that's beautiful! You made this? When did you have the time? You've only been back like a day."

Roya was flattered, even though she usually didn't wear dresses. Mandy and Ami's excitement about seeing her in it reminded her of how she felt about them when she had made the cookies.

"I started sketching it when we were still in school, but I didn't know it was going to be for you until this morning," she said, holding it up against Roya. "I nearly had it finished before we left for vacation, and I just did the last stitches after breakfast. We're about the same size, so it should fit."

"Go ahead, try it on," Ami encouraged.

Roya was speechless as she walked to the bathroom across the hall from Ami's room. She was really touched by the gift. While Roya was changing into the dress, Ami picked up the book again and started reading. The words somehow felt familiar, like they were narrating what she was witnessing in some way.

As Ami was pondering the deeper meaning of the words, Roya was standing in front of the bathroom mirror, checking out the way she looked in the dress and having mixed feelings about it. She wasn't used to showing off her legs, and the dress came up more than a few inches above her knees—something she expected her mother might scrutinize. Her shoulders, too, were exposed, as the straps were very thin. She was not accustomed to wearing anything quite like this. The neckline had a slight scoop, and it felt very adult-like. As she looked down again at her legs, she heard the words of the book: *This recipe will make you more visible.*

Once again, the book was right, but in a totally unexpected way. Roya looked in the mirror again, realizing the subtle parallel between 'Sunshine' Cookies and the bright, yellow summer dress.

And then it hit her: *Recipe...reciprocation!* Mandy's gift reflected the gratitude that Roya had imbued into the cookies as she was baking and thinking of Mandy. And Roya's gift was unknowingly reciprocating the love and creativity that Mandy had poured into making the dress. They had been reflecting each other remotely. It seems the book had prompted Roya to step into the flow of love energy between them.

"This is so strange," said Roya, coming out of the bathroom.

"What?" asked Mandy, taking in the sight of Roya.

"This dress was predicted in the book. I'm certain of it." Roya paused for a moment, but Ami and Mandy were both waiting for her to say more. "It said, *this recipe will make you more visible,* and now I am wearing this eye-catching little dress. And winning the contest was predicted, too. That was why I made the zucchini bread. It said, *recipe for victory,* and then I won the contest."

"Roya, that's amazing," said Ami. "And the dress looks great on you, by the way."

"Thanks," replied Roya, blushing at the thought of her new look.

"What do you think it all means?" Mandy asked both of them.

"Well," said Ami, "I was re-reading the first two chapters while you were in the bathroom, and I think it's talking about us."

"Yeah, I felt like it was talking straight to me," Mandy jumped in, almost cutting Ami off. "It gave me goosebumps."

"No, not *to* us, *about* us. This isn't just about cooking. The ingredients are people," stated Ami.

"Whoa," said Mandy, trying to think of something funny to say. Roya could tell that her imagination was running wild, but Mandy could not quite find the words to interject anything.

Ami had just stepped into the next level of the messages, bringing the awareness of the book to life even more. Again, Roya was noticing a reflectivity between them that felt deep and familiar. She was excited to hear her friends discovering the other levels of awareness that the book had started to open up for her.

"Listen to this," Ami continued. "*The ingredients may not know at first that they are part of a desired outcome, but they will feel a certain joy about combining that will make each step in the recipe more obvious.* It says that recipes can take many forms. What if this whole book is a recipe for something that involves all three of us?"

"But a recipe for what?" asked Mandy.

"An outcome desired by all the ingredients," Ami said, pointing at the quote in the book.

"But that could mean a lot of things," said Mandy.

"What do we all desire most?" prompted Ami.

"I just wish we could travel and get away from this town. I want an adventure," Roya expressed.

"Well, I wish I could skip a grade, so we could all be in the same class next year," said Mandy.

"I just want to make meaningful memories that will last a lifetime," Ami added thoughtfully.

"So, what do you think the book has to do with all of these things?" Roya asked.

"I'm not sure, but if all three of us are ingredients in some kind of recipe, we should be able to figure out what the next step is. The most obvious one that I can think of is to make the next recipe," said Ami.

"Let me see that," Mandy reached out her hand. Ami handed her the book, and she began to flip through the pages to look at the next recipe. "Oooh, a recipe for love. Aren't you glad I made you a nice new dress."

"I'm not sure it means that I'm going to meet someone," said Roya.

"Why not?" questioned Ami sincerely.

"Do you think it's like a love potion or something?" interrupted Mandy.

"Well, my mom always says that you can make a love potion out of anything if you put love into it," recalled Roya, suddenly realizing that there was a line in the book that, curiously, said something very similar. "But I don't know that it works like that. So far, these seem to be recipes for synchronicity. Besides, there aren't any guys around here that I really like."

"Is anyone else we know one of the ingredients?" Ami wondered.

"Well, things have really changed between me and my mom. When I decided to enter the contest, she had all these ideas about how to alter the recipe. At first, I resisted, but then I found my focus on the synergy between us. There's something I read in the book about it…something about not resisting the way things were meant to combine." Roya grabbed the book from Mandy and flipped open to the passage she remembered. "Here, check this out." They all sat down on the floor again, and Mandy helped herself to another cookie as Roya began reading the book out loud:

When Ingredients Resist Transformation

Transformation is inevitable when you are connected to the stars. The gift of any recipe is that it brings out the best in the ingredients so that together, they can become a new kind of resource to feed those who hunger for change. The value of the ingredients is always relative to what they bring to each other, but sometimes, the pieces of a recipe can resist transformation.

When some believe they are more important than others, they may try to control the outcome of the recipe they are a part of— tilting everything into agreement with their aim. The less you try to control, however, the more room you leave for unseen forces to interact with your reality, improving upon your wishes and dreams.

Negative tilt assumes competition and fears a loss of control; therefore, attacking, judging, or trying to control it will only reinforce its illusion. Negative tilt is found in the attachment to one's view and a resistance to change in the face of a transformational potential. Taken to the extreme, however, it reflects the will to dominate, or the refusal to share power in an environment of competition and distrust.

The best way to help clear it is to surrender to the challenge of integration and recognize everything as another form of love.

Negative tilt is not the opposite of positive tilt; it is based on the illusion that existence is unfair, warranting unfair advantages to those who can claim them. Negative tilt will often see itself as positive because of the advantage this stance appears to create in the world of egos—hence "my way is better." Therefore, positive tilt—or natural tilt—can only truly be defined by a balance that reveals the inherent value of every unique angle of perception. It is found in the absence of duality and the willingness to surrender to change. Simply opposing negative tilt does not equal being positive.

Roya paused for a moment to see if they had any comments.

"That's really deep," said Mandy. "So how does that relate to your mom?"

"Well, she used to always want me to see things her way. Sometimes, she can be really firm, because she expects that I'm going to disagree, so she tries to lay down the law ahead of time. She doesn't want to leave room for me to decide. So, her tilt is that she wants me to see her as the authority so that I won't argue."

"So, negative tilt isn't bad, it's just uncompromising, but if we treat it as bad, we create a reason for it to persist," Ami said, astutely.

"Wow, you really understand what this is saying," appreciated Mandy.

"Sort of," Ami responded. "It reminds me of some of the stuff we talked about in that peer mediation workshop that we did at school a couple of months ago, remember?"

"Yeah, except this is more advanced," said Roya. "There's a much bigger picture involved that I haven't been able to wrap my head around."

"Three heads are better than one," said Mandy, and they all smiled.

"So, what about your mom?" asked Ami. "Do you think she's a part of this?"

"It's hard to say. Feels like a yes, but I can't see myself sharing the book with her quite yet," Roya said. "Not until we explore it more. Here, let me read a little more. This next part is really interesting."

Any recipe can be a recipe for love if you put love into it. A recipe for love is a recipe for balance and harmony. Just as finding the right balance of Flavors can bring out their greatest synergy, the highest possible synergy in any combination of beings comes through balancing the field between them.

In every family of beings, a potential exists to bring out the best of what they have to offer each other by focusing on their higher nature as love. The potential for greater balance and harmony is always bringing people together to co-evolve, but fear, attachment, and resistance to change can turn relationships into power struggles. However, when you look for the recipe for love in every relationship, you can find your alignment with a dimension of love that is always working to guide everyone back into balance. In this case, a recipe for love is a formula for building reciprocity and aligning relationships with a more soulful level of exchange.

A key to balancing any relationship is to focus on the equality of all relationships. This strengthens your connection to the balancing power of love. The joy potential behind every recipe for love and co-evolution has the power to neutralize negative tilt until the shift into love has brought about an end to duality. When all sides see each other as equals, a synergistic radiance can be achieved. The transformation is complete when all beings recognize their value as an integrated whole.

Always remember, your intentions have creative power. When you come from conflict, you will create conflict. But when you come from love and neutrality, you will create harmony and balance with your field of intentions. To quote a master from your own century: "The consciousness you are in when you create is what you create." – Louix Dor Dempriey

"Who on Earth wrote this?" blurted Mandy. Roya had already pondered this at length, but the answer was still a mystery.

"I don't know," replied Roya, "but whoever it is, they're speaking about the whole 21st century in the past tense."

"I suppose the most important question is: do you believe that what it says is true?" posed Ami.

"So far, it's proving itself true," Roya observed.

"Hey, I just thought of something," said Mandy. "Look at the next recipe. The main ingredient is green beans. And guess what Dad just brought home?"

"That's right!" Ami realized. "A huge bag of green beans."

"That's perfect," Roya said, as she began reading the other ingredients. "Do you have feta, garlic, basil, sea salt, and olive oil?"

"Olive oil, maybe, but not the rest," replied Ami.

"Let's make it at my house, then. My mom has the rest of what we need. And she grows fresh basil in the garden," Roya said, once again realizing that her mother was entering the picture.

She could not help thinking about what her mother would say when she saw her wearing the dress. Her older sister had endured a great deal of scrutiny about her clothing choices at this age, and this style of dress was definitely something new and more revealing. For now, she would change back into her jeans and T-shirt, but she was already plotting how she could introduce the dress.

Half an hour later, they were in Roya's kitchen combining the ingredients in a large bowl. The recipe for love was called *Feta Greens*, and it was very simple. As soon as they had everything in the bowl, Ami suggested they pause to focus on energizing the salad with love.

"We should put as much love into it as we can," Ami emphasized, wanting to see the recipes in action.

"How do we do that?" asked Mandy.

"We do it with intention, like the book says," she explained. "I was thinking about this a lot on the walk over, and this line about putting love into a recipe totally reminds me of our mom. She told us that she read this book once called *The Celestine Prophecy*, and it inspired her to start energizing her food with love."

"That's right!" remembered Mandy.

"She used to do this all the time. It's like blessing the food with gratitude, but there's more to it."

The synchronicity was flowing again, as the idea of imbuing love into the food seemed to build upon her sense of what she had created when she was making the cookies for Mandy.

Ami was now holding her hands out as she began to formulate an intention, and then Roya and Mandy began to mimic her.

"Is it like a visualization?" asked Mandy.

"Sort of. You start by forming a positive feeling and then you focus on appreciating the food, but it's not just about the ingredients. You focus on appreciating the living energy that's *inside* the food."

"Like the Flavors beings," added Roya.

"Yes. It's like you see the food as a gift of love from nature, and then you love it back until you feel a flow of energy. It's supposed to help raise the vibration of the food before you eat it. You can visualize the energy you're sending, or you can just feel it."

"I'm visualizing pink," said Mandy playfully.

They all looked like they were warming their hands together near a fire, and something felt magical about the combination of their energies—though again, Roya found herself thinking of magic in different terms.

With imagination, intention and focus they were accessing their natural abilities to manifest through the power of love.

Roya could not help noticing that the presence of the Flavors seemed to respond to their intentions, as if their vibrations of love were dancing around inside the bowl. Then it occurred to Roya that this particular recipe was always meant to be a co-creation. With the salad as a focal point, she felt the presence of a balanced field of connection and synergy growing between them and filling the space around them.

For a moment, Ami thought she felt the presence of her mother, as if her spirit was joining in. It felt good to honor her memory with something that she had intended to pass on to her daughters, and she was surprised to feel how much energy was flowing through her hands.

As soon as they were finished blessing the food, Roya decided to add a dash of balsamic vinegar. It made her think about how her mother always liked to add a touch of herself to the recipes.

Roya was still mixing it up with her hands when Sarah bounded down the stairs wearing her work clothes. As soon as she rounded the corner into the kitchen, she greeted the girls with a look that suggested that they were in her territory. Sarah often did this when she wanted to claim the upstairs bathroom to herself, or the computer, or the TV, or the laundry room. She carried around a sense of entitlement about being the older sister, and so Roya mostly tried to stay out of her way.

Roya half expected Sarah to bark at her about being late for work, but then something shifted, and Sarah's attitude softened.

"Hi," she said to the girls. "I'm Roya's sister, Sarah."

"Hi," Ami said. Mandy smiled.

Roya was shocked. It was like a bullet had been fired at her, but it had stopped in midair and then dropped to the ground.

"These are my friends, Ami and Mandy," introduced Roya. "They're sisters."

"Nice to meet you. What's that you're making?" Sarah asked inquisitively, eyeing the salad.

"Green bean salad with feta. You wanna try some?" offered Roya.

Roya grabbed a fork and handed it to Sarah who promptly jabbed it into the bowl. All three girls gazed intently to see what would happen, as if expecting some kind of miraculous transformation right in front of their eyes. She was, after all, taking the very first bite.

"Mmm, can I take some with me to work?" asked Sarah, to Roya's surprise.

"Sure, let me get you something to put it in," Roya said, gladly. She quickly grabbed a plastic container from one of the lower cabinets and heaped a huge serving into it. When she turned around, Sarah was licking her lips, but her expression did not reveal anything about how good it tasted. She handed the container to Sarah with love, intending that the energy they had put into the food would transfer to her.

"Thanks. See ya later," Sarah said, taking the container from Roya before heading out the door. As soon as she left, the girls began to talk excitedly.

"What do you think will happen?" wondered Mandy. "Do you think it will have an effect on her?"

"I don't know. I wasn't expecting that she'd ask for some, so maybe it already has. I guess we'll have to wait and find out," said Roya.

"Do you think we should drop by the pizza place and check in on her?" asked Ami.

Roya remembered that Sarah didn't like it when any of them came to her work. The pizza place was her domain where she could pretend she didn't have a family. "No. Let's just wait and see," Roya recommended. "In the meantime, let's eat."

Hours passed by as they chatted up in Roya's room, and Mandy began to sketch out a few new clothing ideas as they were talking. Everyone agreed that the salad was the best they had ever tasted, and between the three of them, they finished every last bite. They all talked about the meaning of the recipe, and what they had witnessed with Sarah.

"I totally wasn't expecting Sarah to try it," said Roya, "but after she went to work, I thought of something. Did you notice how she stopped cold when she first came in the room? It's like her mood shifted when she saw us. I think our group energy neutralized her negative tilt."

"Yeah, I noticed something similar," remarked Ami. "When she asked for some, it made me think that maybe she was the final ingredient. It's like there was a hidden recipe for love and balance between the two of you, and it took the strength of our group energy to help bring it out. I just automatically felt to include her."

"I think it helps that you guys don't have any history with her. Sometimes when she enters a room, I feel like I'm bracing myself, but I felt more surrendered with you guys around. I'm just glad we're all friends. You two feel like sisters to me. It makes me think of how Sarah and I used to be when we were younger," Roya shared, wishing that some part of Sarah could hear her.

"Ahhh, we feel the same way," agreed Mandy, and Ami nodded with a smile.

That evening, when Sarah arrived home from work, she went straight up to Roya's room where Roya was folding her laundry.

"Hey, thanks again for the salad. It was really good."

Wow! She said thanks, Roya thought, stunned. Roya really didn't have any expectations, because she could not have predicted any of the synchronicities that happened when she made the other recipes. She was learning to just give unconditionally and let the rewards come as a surprise. *Recipe. Reciprocation.*

"No problem. What are sisters for?" expressed Roya, with a genuine smile.

"You know, I miss eating at home sometimes when I work in the evenings so much."

"I thought you preferred eating at the restaurant?" Roya looked surprised.

"Nah. I'm sick of pizza. I just asked for the evening shifts to avoid getting drafted into kitchen duty at home. At least there I get paid for what I do."

"Right," Roya nodded, not expecting their conversation would go much further. Sarah rarely engaged her in conversations anymore. Even when she was present with Roya, it was on her own terms. For a second, they were both silent, and Roya was prepared for her to excuse herself to her room, but then Sarah surprised her even further.

"I was thinking, since you're in cleaning mode, why don't we do the bathrooms together? Let me just change out of my work clothes."

Suddenly, Roya felt a sensation like butterflies in her stomach as Sarah turned to walk away. She stood there, trying to process the feeling. It was as if her sister had been away for a long time, and she had finally come home. The feeling of home was clear, like a warm glow that radiated from her solar plexus, almost bringing a tear to her eye. She could feel some part of herself returning, as if she was becoming more complete on the inside. It was a familiar feeling from childhood that she had forgotten: the feeling that Sarah was a part of her.

5

DRAWING CONCLUSIONS

Friday morning, when Roya's mother went into town to run errands, Roya seized the opportunity to go on a mission to the Flower Memorial Library. This time, the book was concealed in her backpack, along with the notebook she had used to decode the hidden message about the dome.

Everything is about to change, she thought, as they merged onto the highway to begin the fifteen-minute drive to Watertown. After travelling this way for so many years, she rarely took notice of the landscape, but today, a warm feeling of gratitude came over her as she looked at the trees and the rolling hills. Perhaps she would ask her mother to take the back way home, down Route 11, which she sometimes liked for a change of scenery.

On the way into town, Roya brought up the topic of her grandparents, since they were expected to arrive that evening. Roya's grandparents had left Iran for America when Soraya was very little. For Roya's grandfather, who was now an economics professor in New York City, leaving Iran had as much to do with the opportunity he saw for his family as for escaping the political turmoil of his country. Roya loved hearing about her family's history, because most of the stories took place in faraway lands. This always gave her another opportunity to daydream about the mysteries of the world.

By the time they reached the city, however, Roya was starting to feel an unexplained nervousness that brought her back into the present moment. Even though she was excited to look for more clues in the library, the prospect of seeing Claire again was stirring something inside her. Luckily, it would take well over an hour for her mother to complete all the shopping, which involved going to a couple of different stores. Since she was not in a rush, she paused to contemplate her approach before entering the library.

Several minutes after her mother had dropped her off, Roya was still pacing around outside, rehearsing what she would say if she saw Claire, until gradually, she found her confidence and began to walk toward the main entrance.

For years, the library had been her temple. Reaching the stairs, she greeted the two marble lions that guarded the entrance. She had named them Faith and Courage, and she looked at each of them as she walked by. She liked to imagine that they would have bowed to her as she entered, if they had been real. To her, they were the guardians of knowledge.

As she entered the foyer, she walked to the right to examine the message between the two trees near the entrance to the South Reading Room. The words, written in all capital letters, read:

TONGUES IN TREES   BOOKS IN THE
RUNNING BROOKS   SERMONS IN STONES
AND GOOD IN EVERYTHING

For a moment, she gazed at the letters, playing with the words in her mind, but nothing leaped out at her. She did, however, notice an odd parallel between this message and her thoughts about the apple tree whispering messages to Sir Isaac Newton. She was having that feeling again, that something was on the edge of her awareness, but she could not quite pinpoint it. She then pulled out her phone and snapped a picture of the quote before walking over to see the message between the two trees on the adjacent wall. Just at the entrance to the North Reading Room, the other quote read:

A LITTLE LEARNING IS
A DANGEROUS THING   DRINK DEEP OR
TASTE NOT THE PIERIAN SPRING

Again, Roya played with the words and letters in her mind, but nothing was obvious. She then texted the pictures to Ami and started to explain what she was up to. At some point, she realized that she was stalling and that the same nervousness about seeing Claire was still swirling around inside her. It occurred to her that she would only be having this feeling if Claire were in the building somewhere, and that this was an intuitive feeling. She knew she would have time to explore the quotes later.

She walked around the corner to the main circulation desk, but Claire was nowhere to be seen, so she decided to head downstairs to the main collection. Walking through the middle of the room, she looked up and down each aisle on either side as she went. Then, toward the back of the room, she saw Claire with a book cart, placing returned books back on the shelves. For a moment, she backed up out of sight, feeling a wave of nervous energy about meeting her. She had hoped to get a better look at Claire without being noticed, but that did not seem possible now.

All she could see was that Claire was wearing a white, button-up, collared shirt with sleeves that came down to the elbows. She appeared to be wearing dress pants, but it was hard to see with the cart in front of her.

Roya made a funny face to herself to break up her own tension, took a deep breath, and walked into the aisle until she was standing directly in front of Claire, who stood only slightly taller than her. Claire's eyes opened wide with recognition as she turned to face Roya, and Roya instantly felt welcomed.

"Hi, I'm Roya. Do you remember me from last Sunday? I checked out a little violet book with golden letters."

Roya was certain from the first glance that Claire *did* remember her, but she felt more comfortable opening the dialogue the way she had rehearsed it in her mind.

"Yes, it's a pleasure to meet you. I'm Claire," she said, offering Roya her hand.

Roya immediately noticed a gentleness to the way Claire held her hand without shaking it, really taking the opportunity to acknowledge her presence. She even felt a little zing of energy up the back of her spine that seemed like a kind of energetic *hello*.

"I was wondering, what do you know about that book?" Roya asked.

"I thought you might be back to ask me," she said as she continued to casually put books away. "I'm glad you came. I was given very specific instructions about you."

"Instructions?" Roya was surprised and immediately began to wonder what she was talking about. "What sort of instructions, and who gave them to you?"

"I'm not at liberty to say, but I *can* answer some of your questions." Roya was all ears. "The author of the book wanted you to have it. As you might have guessed, it was made just for you, to help you on your journey."

"What journey?" Roya inquired as her curiosity continued to grow.

Claire stopped putting books away, smiled warmly, and gazed at her silently for a few seconds, as if answering first with her eyes.

"The one you have always wanted to go on," she said in a soft voice.

These words were spoken directly from Claire's heart, and she appeared to have thought about her response carefully, as if she knew that Roya was going to remember these words for the rest of her life.

Roya became lost for a moment, feeling the impact of Claire's last sentence. It felt like she was still drinking in the words through Claire's big, bright eyes. It was not just a librarian speaking to her, but a vast soul presence that filled Roya's inner senses. Staring into her eyes, it was like the opportunity she had been waiting for had arrived…the beginning of a journey. This was it. It was like a switch had been flipped on, and she knew that Claire was to be a part of that journey. This was the moment when Roya began to accept that her life was being guided by something greater than herself.

"If that book was meant for me, then how did it end up here?" Roya asked.

"I brought it here—or rather, it brought me," Claire replied with an enigmatic smile. "The book must have known there was a volunteer position open, just like it knew you would be here. It said, *Flower Memorial Library, Watertown, New York* inside the front cover. I started a couple of weeks ago and slipped the book onto a shelf."

"But what if someone else had taken it? Someone it wasn't meant for," asked Roya.

"We didn't think that would be a problem. I'm not even sure most people can see it," she said a little quieter with another smile. "Besides, we suspected that the book would choose its reader, just like it chose me to come here."

"Umm, I hope you don't mind me asking, but who is *we*?" Roya was polite, but the answers could not come quickly enough.

"The community I came from," Claire answered, while considering how best to explain further. Roya sensed that there was something more that Claire was not ready to share quite yet.

"And, where are they? I mean, where are *you* from?"

"Well, we are not from the future," Claire said, obviously avoiding a more direct answer, "but the book certainly is. I'm sure you've noticed its lightness."

"Does that mean everything is lighter in the future?" *Now we are getting somewhere*, Roya thought, absolutely intrigued.

"Yes. In fact, this book was originally even lighter, but mass had to be added to it to entangle the book with our present time reference."

Something about this idea made sense, even though Roya had never thought in such terms before, and Claire said this so matter-of-factly that it just sounded real. She thought about getting out her notebook, not just to write down Claire's answers, but also to write down all of her new questions. There were so many of them, she hardly knew where to go next.

"So how did the book come to you?" asked Roya.

"It just appeared."

"It just appeared? Like out of nowhere?" Roya was astonished. Her imagination was stretched, but not challenged. "Is that sort of thing unusual for you?"

"This whole chain of events is *highly* unusual. Perhaps you could tell me about your experience with the book," invited Claire.

Roya then proceeded to tell the whole story, from finding the book, to winning the contest, to sharing the book with Ami and Mandy.

"So, there are *three* of you," Claire said suddenly with a look of surprise. She seemed to have deduced something from the story that gave her an epiphany.

"What do you mean?" asked Roya.

"I am not exactly sure what this means but let me ask you something. What do you think about the state of the world?"

Roya thought about it for a moment. It was a simple question, but she wanted to honor the depth of Claire's mind with some depth of her own. She could tell that Claire was patient enough to allow her time to think about it more deeply before answering. Something about Claire's presence helped Roya's thoughts become more focused. Even as she was looking away and considering her answer, she could feel Claire's eyes, as if they were radiating warmth, and she wondered if Claire could sense all of the memories and ideas that were rolling together into a single description in her mind. Finally, even though her sentences were not yet fully formed, she began to describe her perception.

"There's something very wrong with the way things are—with the world, I mean. I feel like we're inheriting a huge mess left behind by the older generations. And even though they know they're leaving this terrible burden for us, they aren't doing enough to try to change it. I think about it a lot—why it seems like so much power is in the wrong hands, and how so many people don't even care about the truth." She paused for a moment, grasping for something that was still on the edge of her awareness. "It's like…there's something hidden, but it's in plain sight. I feel like I'm seeing something everywhere I look: in people's faces, in the media, but it's… elusive."

"What's elusive?" probed Claire.

"Whatever it is that keeps interfering with all of us coming together. It's like most people are living in some kind of illusion, and they don't want to see past it, to see how we're all connected. We're being exploited, and yet, we're doing it to ourselves. People just seem so distracted by things that aren't important, even when they know our world is in danger. I know there's a better way, but it feels like time is running out for us to do something about it."

"You are very observant for your age. How old are you?"

"Sixteen. I'll be seventeen next February."

"So young. We expected you would be older. This is highly unusual, indeed."

"What does my age have to do with anything?" Roya questioned.

"A sixteen-year-old still has many restrictions—on the ability to travel, for instance. But other than that, you are young for what you are about to face. The whole world is going through a great change, and no one can escape it. It's affecting everything and everyone, but the final outcome of history has yet to be decided. There are many dangers, and every decision we make is important. That's why the appearance of the book gave us hope. It mentioned the possibility of a desired outcome for all involved, and as I see it, this is a matter of life and death." Claire paused so Roya could take this in.

"You still haven't told me where you are from." Roya reminded her.

"You wouldn't believe me if I told you."

"Try me," Roya said playfully, hoping to tempt some more information out of her.

"It's too soon." She paused. "It's not that I don't think you are capable of understanding, but I was given explicit instructions. I was told you would be able to find something that was hidden long ago, and that I could not reveal any more until you did."

"But how am I supposed to know what I am looking for, or where to look?"

"Here, come with me. Do you have something to write on?"

"Yes." Roya said, taking off her backpack where her notebook was stashed.

"Let's go up to the reading room so we can sit at a table."

It bothered Roya that some unknown person or group of people knew about her but wanted to remain anonymous. This might have seemed highly suspicious, but Claire's presence was so warm and reassuring that she decided to go along with the flow of things and not get too demanding for more information. More than anything, she trusted herself and was happy to have a private little adventure unfolding that gave her imagination more freedom to expand.

Just up the stairs and around the corner to the right was the North Reading Room, Roya's favorite sanctuary. It had a high ceiling and an old feel to it with all of the shelves of old books and antiques. Just below the antique clock that sat on the fireplace mantle was a large golden inscription with the words: Knowledge is Power. It was a statement that always reminded her that knowledge could be either creative or destructive.

Fortunately, the room was empty. Claire pulled out a chair for Roya at the table and sat down opposite her. Roya unzipped her backpack, retrieved her notebook and pencils, and looked across the table at Claire expectantly.

"What you need is a map that shows you the way to what's hidden."

"Where on Earth am I supposed to find that?" Roya said, humorously.

"You won't. You will have to create it yourself." Claire smiled.

"Create a map from nothing?"

"No, not from nothing. You can draw it from intuition." She made this seem like it was as easy and normal as taking a shower, but Roya was not as confident.

"How does that work?" she asked.

"Intuition is like a navigation system. It feeds you signals from a wider reality to help you enter the specific reality that your soul desires. Most people have just forgotten how to pay attention to these kinds of inner signals. And even those who *do* pay attention are often not in the habit of acting on the information."

"So, Mandy was really being intuitive when she made me the perfect dress."

"Yes. Her soul knew it was for you, but she acted on the intuitive signal, because she trusted a feeling that would take her into a desired reality. Intuition loves to bring you what your heart desires most. In her case, it was making you a gift that you would love. When you are willing to act spontaneously without needing to know why the guidance is right, your life can become more graceful and synchronistic."

"Spontaneity empowers intuition to guide you where you want to go, without the logical mind needing to be involved in every decision. The key is to let go of thinking linearly all the time. People so often think in straight lines, trying to get from point A to point B with no room for the creativity of the soul to dance with you on the path. When you are willing to follow the impulse of intuitive guidance, you will find surprises that you didn't expect as a reward for trusting in your inner senses."

"So where does the guidance come from?" Roya's mind was beginning to open even more.

"Part of it comes from you, that is, the version of you that is the happiest with how things worked out. The happiest version of your future self is always the guide for the part of you that is searching for direction," Claire explained.

"So that would mean that the future is communicating with the past," said Roya, remembering what the book had said about the light of the future.

"Exactly!"

"So how can this help me create a map?"

"Well, you already know you are meant to find something. Let's assume there is a version of your future where you have already found it. Then, ask that version of you to send you the map, complete with all the information you need to enter that reality."

"You can do that?"

"Naturally. The soul is much vaster than the incarnated personality. We are multidimensional beings. A part of the soul exists beyond the world of time and physicality as you know it, and so that greater part of you is capable of passing you information from the future in exactly this way. If you can believe that the book came from the future, this shouldn't be a stretch for you."

Claire was right. Roya's experience with the book had prepared her well to digest this kind of information, but that did not make her feel any more capable of the task at hand.

"I have a problem, though. I'm not good at drawing—not like my friend Mandy," said Roya. "She's really gifted."

"Perfect. You can borrow her abilities."

"What? How do I do that?" asked Roya. Clearly Claire's knowledge of reality was very different than her own, but nothing she said seemed impossible, just beyond what she was currently aware of.

"I'll help you. Just focus on the piece of paper in front of you, let go of all your thoughts, and pretend that you are Mandy. The part of her soul that is beyond time wants to help you, just like she would if she were physically here, so we will just call in her presence and invite her to participate," Claire encouraged.

"But, will Mandy know—I mean, the part of her that's in the body?"

"She might have some awareness of the connection, but the personality doesn't have to be fully aware for the greater self to be involved. Just trust that she wants to help you because she's your friend, and I will focus on the connection between you by seeing you both as one. Once the connection has been made, start to think about finding the hidden object. This is an object that *wants* to be found, so imagine that its energy is already arriving in your present, giving you signals that you can interpret as images. It is just a matter of remembering the future until the path becomes clear."

Roya stared at the page for several minutes while Claire focused on her. She imagined Mandy's energy all around her, until she began to vividly pretend that she was Mandy. She almost started to make one of Mandy's silly faces, but she didn't want to have to explain that to Claire. This was starting to feel fun, as if Mandy's soul could feel what she was doing and was entertained by it. For a moment, she started to get distracted by Claire's presence, whose penetrating gaze felt electrical, but Claire must have noticed, because she said, "Just keep focusing on Mandy as if you are two souls in one body. Feel the playful energy between your souls and ask her to help you draw."

Suddenly her senses began to heighten, and she felt a warm vibration running through her forearms and into her hands. Her perception of colors began to shift as well, and then images started to flow into her mind.

"Claire, are you doing this, or am I?" Roya asked.

"Between every two souls is a place of balance where you cannot tell where one soul ends and the other begins. My people call it *betweenergy*. It's part of a hidden universal structure that connects all souls together into a single matrix of being, but friends and soulmates tend to develop that connection into a resonance of shared personality. All I am doing is focusing on the betweenergy you share with Mandy and seeing you both as reflections of each other. Because of your need, all her abilities are tilting into alignment with you."

How did you learn to do this? Roya wondered. She thought about asking the question out loud, but then her hand felt the impulse to draw. She couldn't remember the last time she had attempted to draw anything. That was why it was so surprising to see the image of a bird coming to life before her. The image was present in her mind as she translated it right onto the page without thinking, and before she could finish, she felt the bird as if it was flying somewhere. Then, her hand drifted down and began to draw the outline of a single, large egg, resting in a nest below the bird. Next, her hand was guided over to another blank part of the page where she sketched a baseball cap. Somehow, she just knew to label it 'Red'.

Within minutes, she had drawn a set of swords that were clashing, a large flowing creek with rocks and trees nearby, and the mouth of a cave. The placement of each object appeared random. Discerning how they were connected did not seem important yet. As she practiced clearing her mind to create a blank slate, the images kept coming, and Mandy's presence continued to help her translate the images into drawing. There were moments when Roya became so excited about what was happening that she nearly broke her alignment with this unique convergence of creative energy, but with Claire's help, she quickly found the alignment again and continued drawing.

The next object was a large old oak tree, and then out in front of it, she was guided to draw the symbol of the three interlocking circles that were on the front of *The Circle and the Stars* book. Almost as soon as she finished drawing this symbol, she knew intuitively that this represented her, Ami, and Mandy, so she wrote 'US' beneath the symbol. Then she went back to the egg and was guided to draw rays of light coming out of it.

"Does any of this mean anything to you in terms of location?" asked Claire.

"No...not yet, but I feel there's still something missing." Roya relaxed her mind even more, trying to feel what wanted to happen next. She was guided to imagine standing in front of the creek, and then, she immediately thought of crossing it.

"A foot bridge. That's it!" Roya began to draw again until a simple image of a wooden bridge arched over the creek. There were no rails, only the pathway over the water. "I know where this is! It's part of a nature trail that I know. My parents took us there a few times when we were kids. But, what do I do once I get there?"

"It's clear to me that your friends have a role to play. What you must begin to do now is invest your focus on the outcome of a shared discovery. Holding this intention will energize each of you to discover what is yours to do."

Claire's words contained a contagious wisdom that spoke to a place inside Roya that was ready to listen and act on the guidance. She was excited to realize that this journey was more than a physical journey, but a journey to expand her understanding of reality. Up until now, she had felt unable to do anything about what was missing in her life. She had known for a long time that there was a greater truth worth seeking. But for the first time, she felt like she was gaining access to real tools she could use to create the breakthroughs she longed for, and she knew that intuition was one of them.

"So, how do I use this map?" Roya asked, wanting to know still more about it.

"When you see how this map works, you will understand something more about the design of the book. Just stay alert and watch for the signs. The key to navigating intuitive signals is not to be too attached to the form in which you first received them. The map is just there to help confirm your intuition, but ultimately, intuition will be your guide."

Claire smiled warmly at her, and Roya felt something energetic exchanging between them. Roya had a sense that Claire had been transferring some of her awareness into her, and for Roya's part, her feeling of gratitude was fueling the exchange.

"And now, I must get back to my duties," said Claire as she reached over and wrote her phone number on the edge of the map. "Feel free to call me. I am very confident that you will find what you are looking for."

"I can't thank you enough," expressed Roya. "I don't know what you did, but I feel like you've removed some kind of obstacle from my path."

"If you only knew, Roya, it feels like you have done the same for me. We'll talk more soon," Claire assured her as she stood up. "Good luck."

"Thanks again," said Roya, bidding her farewell as she headed for the door.

Roya decided to sit in the sun on the library's front steps while thinking over everything that just happened. With her notebook out, she scribbled a few notes, including the word 'betweenergy', and then she jotted down the two quotes from between the trees on the library walls. She could not help noticing that the intuitive map she had drawn contained some of the same components as the "tongues in trees" quote. *Trees, brooks and stones*, she thought. It was as if the message had been perfectly planned to help nudge her toward the right memory.

Allowing her mind to enter a daydreaming state, she began to play with the words and letters of the message until something leaped out at her.

A LITTLE LEARNING IS
A DANGEROUS THING   DRINK DEEP OR
TASTE NOT THE PIERIAN SPRING

The 'K' in 'DRINK' connected with the 'EEP' in 'DEEP' as if speaking to her mind the word 'KEEP'. Looking at that same line, all of the letters for 'ARRANGING' leaped out, followed by the word 'LIT', which seemed to light up from within the word 'LITTLE'. Her mind intuitively completed the first hidden message as she crossed out the remaining letters that she needed…and there it was.

KEEP ARRANGING LIT UP LETTERS

Out of all the possible word combinations, incredibly, this first message was speaking of exactly what she was experiencing and encouraging her at the same time. When she first saw the word 'KEEP' she could not have imagined where the process was leading. The next words came more slowly, and were also unexpected, but within a few minutes of feeling the letters lighting up in her mind, she spelled out two new statements:

ONENESS TRAINING
ONE EARTH

This felt right, but incomplete at the same time, and there were many letters left over that she did not know how to use. Then she recalled the previous decoded message: *To receive path instructions, stand under dome of winding words to receive.* From the middle of the room beneath the dome, both messages on both walls were equidistant, and so they might be equally connected to the same process of instruction.

TONGUES IN TREES   BOOKS IN THE
RUNNING BROOKS   SERMONS IN STONES
AND GOOD IN EVERYTHING

She began to play with the arrangement of the words and letters again, this time seeing a perfect use for the remaining letters of the first quote. Gradually, a new series of messages came together with a surprising energetic theme. The process did not feel forced at all, and she felt an exciting presence behind the messages, like the source of the guidance was beaming at the opportunity to communicate with her. After using every last letter, a perfect sequence of messages and ideas had come together, combining the decoded statements from both quotes. The encoded instructions read:

KEEP ARRANGING LIT UP LETTERS
ONENESS TRAINING
DRINK STRONG ONENESS VIBRATIONS IN LUNGS
TAKE DOOR UNITING DIMENSIONS
GO ON THE TONED BRIDGE
SHAPE HISTORY
ONE EARTH

Roya was stunned. Something about these words made her heart beat faster. The potentials they seemed to describe were breathtaking, even though she did not fully understand them. She had never faced such high expectations, and consequently, a terrible feeling of doubt was growing that she might not be able to fulfill such grand potentials. Finding the hidden object now felt even more intimidating, but she was committed. This was not just a mystery to solve. It was a calling, and somehow, she had to make this happen.

It occurred to her that this encoded message might have to do with the book, and in that very moment she felt the energy of the book vibrating in her backpack. The book begged to be read, and so she set her notebook aside and reached inside her pack for it. Flipping it open, she began to read the text of the final recipe for change:

> The light of the future is a calling that aligns you with the dimension of love. But when that calling comes, it takes courage, patience, and a commitment to face your fears in order to overcome the resistance to your potential. Doubt is not a sign that your greatest potential is merely an unrealistic dream. Dare to dream the impossible. When you feel doubt in the face of your calling, it's actually a sign of how great your potential really is. It is an invitation to let go of your limiting assumptions, as well as the way the world has taught you to underestimate your value.
>
> Embracing more of your potential involves continually learning to value yourself more than you did before. Step by step, you are entering a new kind of human experience, one in which you are being led intuitively by your potential. The calling of your potential will align you with opportunities to build confidence in your capacity to lead. They will be small at first but will always challenge you to rise to the occasion.
>
> Believe in yourself. Believe in your ability to make a difference. Take the initiative. The invisible world will help you. Before you can balance the world from within yourself, you must first start with a smaller circle of influence. In time, your influence will grow, and so will your trust in your ability to lead.

Roya put down the book and closed her eyes for a moment, feeling the sun on her face and a gentle summer breeze. The strange mix of both doubt and the calling of her potential were beginning to come into balance as she considered that her value was greater than she had ever imagined. If the light of the future was showing up to guide her, then her intuition could read the signals and align with the highest potential outcome of events—an outcome that would feel joyful for all involved.

In that very moment, she could have sworn she heard the voice of the book repeat: *Take the initiative.* The fact that this passage was presented as another recipe told her that this was an opportunity. This was not just about letting go of resistance and surrendering to change. This was about being willing to try something completely new and trusting in the power of her influence.

A sense of strength was arising within her, inviting her to take ownership of her full potential. Suddenly, she had an inspiration that began to make her feel visible in a whole new way. She became willing to consider something that surprised even her—a little test of leadership that made her smile, and somehow felt empowering. Tonight, she would flip the script and offer to prepare dinner for the whole family.

6

RECIPE FOR TRANSFIGURATION

That evening, just before Roya's grandparents arrived, Sarah pulled Roya aside to suggest an idea.

"Wear your new dress for dinner," she said. "Grandma will love it."

Both sisters were well aware of how much influence their grandmother's opinion had over their mother, and it seemed like it was worth trying.

Roya's grandparents were in their seventies and were very healthy. When they arrived, they were both dressed casually and were in a good mood. This was the beginning of their summer vacation away from the city. They planned to visit friends in several states as they journeyed west, stopping at some of the national parks. Their route went through Syracuse, and since Adams was less than an hour north, it was the perfect opportunity to stop in for a visit.

Roya's grandmother always made a boisterous entrance and was ecstatic to see everyone, while Roya's grandfather was more reserved. Roya still was not sure what her mother would think when she saw her in the dress, but it felt good to take Sarah's suggestion, like it was a little plot between sisters that she hadn't experienced with Sarah in a long time.

When Roya came down the stairs wearing the yellow dress, her mother was not yet present. Both of Roya's grandparents, along with her dad and Sarah, were still standing in the front hallway talking. As soon as Roya's grandmother saw her, she exploded with joy.

"My, how you have grown up into a beautiful young woman. Look at you! It's been less than a year since I've last seen you, and yet, you look so different."

As Roya reached the bottom of the stairs, her grandmother drew her into a warm embrace. Roya's mother had just rounded the corner when her grandmother had taken a step back, still holding Roya's shoulders and admiring her new look.

"You must have grown two inches since I last saw you, and what a beautiful dress!"

And that was it. Roya could not have timed it more perfectly. Before her mother could even remark, her grandmother's words had established the precedent. The dress had been accepted, and Roya's mother's opinion was instantaneously shaped by what she witnessed—sisterly plot fulfilled.

As they all went into the dining room, Roya realized the perfection of the whole plan so far. When she first found the book, she had no idea that her grandparents would come to visit; but in one short week, the book had prepared her to cook for her whole family. The very idea of taking the lead with dinner had shifted the balance of the family dynamic, and even Sarah briefly made an appearance in the kitchen to help with the preparation.

Roya's mother was so impressed by her daughter's recent accomplishments that it influenced a more positive mindset for appreciating Roya's mature new look. It was a dream come true. She and Sarah felt like sisters again, and Roya felt like her own person in the family. Everyone noticed a sort of glow about her, and for once, Sarah did not even behave competitively.

A little later that evening, as they smelled the aroma of homemade soup in their bowls, Roya swore she had seen this exact image in her mind when she had first read the opening chapters of the book. She was certain that the book had somehow already contained this moment of future-memory, imbued into the energy of the golden letters. The memory had tilted into her awareness from the knowledge of the writer, just as the book had explained, but how?

Is it my future self? she wondered. She had a feeling that this could be true but could not explain it. All she knew was that following the instructions had brought the family dynamic into a surprising feeling of balance and synergy, which gave Roya a renewed sense of personal power.

The last chapter she had read was called *Recipe for Transfiguration*, and that is exactly what had happened. Her appearance had changed. Her attitude had changed. Her sense of empowerment had finally found its expression within the family as they were all treating her as an equal. She had become a woman in her mother's eyes, and her grandparents were marveling at the transformation. Surely, the whole book was a recipe for freedom—and love, and victory, and visibility. They were all true at once. But where was it all leading? It felt like a preparation for something, but all she could think of was going on Claire's mysterious mission with Ami and Mandy.

It was hard not to call them right away with the exciting news after returning home from the library, but she had become busy with the dinner arrangements almost immediately. Ami's phone call later that evening could not have been more perfectly timed, as her grandparents were ready to turn in early, and Roya's dad offered to help clean the kitchen. For the moment, it seemed as if she had some free time, so she jumped at the chance to unload her new secret.

"Ami, I've been wanting to talk to you all afternoon! You'll never guess what happened," said Roya, excitedly.

"So, you noticed that it's gone," guessed Ami.

"What's gone? I was going to tell you what happened with Claire."

"Roya, I have the book!"

"What do you mean? It's up in my room," stated Roya.

"No, it's not. I have it right here," Ami insisted.

Roya raced up to her room to look under her bed where she had last stashed the book, and Ami was right. It wasn't there.

"So, wait a minute. How did you end up with it? I just had it earlier when I got home from the library," remembered Roya.

"Roya, it's the weirdest thing. It just appeared here. I was thinking about how much I wanted to read more of it, and then, when I went back to my room, it was just lying there in the middle of the floor. It's like the book *wanted* me to read it, and then I flipped it open and started reading, and it's totally describing what's happening again!"

"OK, this is really strange. I feel weird, like I'm in a dream or something. If it weren't for you, I would think I was crazy, but it's like there are so many bizarre things happening, I can't even keep track of them all."

"I know! It feels like everything is happening faster," said Ami. "I think when we energized the salad, something activated, and I'm feeling this flow of energy."

"Yeah, I'm feeling it, too. You know, I was looking at that same chapter before I went downstairs to start cooking, because Claire said that when the book first came to her, it just appeared. What does it say about dreaming things into a different position?"

"Here, I'll read it," said Ami.

Stirring Potentials

Memory is more than a living record of the past. It begins as pure living light, an invisible and infinite potential to become the history you imagine through time. It is also found in the readiness of the universe to change in the presence of creativity. Like an invisible disc that is everywhere, memory is always recording the experience of the co-creators.

Likewise, gravity is more than a binding force. It is a vast, living web that functions as a universal platform for memories. And your center of gravity is more than a physical center. It is part of a living center for the intelligence of the body and connects you with the power of the soul to co-create with universal forces. Just as stirring can transform ingredients, your intentions can stir the position of objects and energy through the illusion of time and space.

Roya was holding her hand over her solar plexus as Ami was reading, noticing how the words seemed to affirm a renewed sense of power and self-worth that had arisen over dinner. She was feeling more confident somehow, like she was feeling support flowing into her sense of purpose, and she was willing to explore wherever this transformation would lead her. As Ami continued to read, they both felt the book tilting more knowledge into their awareness.

The universe is constantly reorganizing itself to reflect the dreaming of the co-creators, and when the power of dreaming is aligned with love, the flow of synchronicity and manifestation is quickened. A dreaming heart can even dis-remember the distance between itself and what it seeks. Disremming is part of the art of dreaming. It involves changing your memory of the present and dreaming resources into alignment with your purpose. Disremming is the art of collapsing distance.

"That's what must have happened with the book," realized Ami. "I must have changed my memory of where it was and disremmed it into my room. OK, this next part made me think about us."

You are part of a living universe that responds to your intentions. And your field of intention has the power to tilt people toward one another through their attraction to the resonance of a shared dream, thus collapsing the distance between them. The most powerful calling to direct energy and resources into alignment with your vision is a shared purpose. A shared purpose will always draw from the talents of everyone involved. After all, it was a shared purpose that brought you into being.

"Ami, that sounds like something Claire was telling me earlier today. She said that I should focus on making a shared discovery involving the three of us so that we can manifest what wants to be found."

"What kind of discovery? What are we supposed to find?" asked Ami.

"I don't know...but I have a map!"

Having successfully manifested the potential of balance and synergy within her family, Roya was feeling a powerful new energy inside that heightened her intuition. Ami, too, was sensing that something had shifted with the appearance of the book in her room. Unbeknownst to them, an invisible field of connection was beginning to tilt both of their families into a deeper alignment with each other.

The presence of the new energy was even beginning to synchronize their lives with people in faraway places, opening doors and illuminating possibilities that contained a powerful calling for all involved. And because of this, in a dark corner of Chicago, two brave souls, named Zack and Echo, were about to make an incredible discovery.

In the spirit of adventure and curiosity, they had entered an abandoned building in an old industrial part of the city, hoping to have a paranormal encounter. It was almost midnight when they began their survey of the dark and eerie shell of a factory. Most of the windows were boarded up, making it impossible to see without their lights. Just inside the expansive structure, they stopped to listen to their new surroundings.

"This place is huge. Hey, Zack. Check this out," whispered Echo, while snapping his fingers to create an echo.

"Kinda reminds me of when I gave you your nickname," said Zack, remembering how they first met in an abandoned warehouse.

Echo was fond of the nickname Zack had given him. He had always wanted a cool nickname, and after Zack used it at a party, everyone just adopted it as if that had always been his name.

"It's creepy how quiet this place is. Ya feel me?" prompted Echo.

"Yeah, it's like the building knows we're here."

Zack and Echo had explored abandoned buildings before, but not usually in the middle of the night. The two nineteen-year-olds wore jeans and T-shirts, along with LED headlamps strapped to their heads. Both of them carried backpacks with just about everything they could think of to bring on such an excursion.

"Hey, it looks like there's a lower level," pointed out Zack as he headed for a ramp that went downward.

Echo was right behind him, feeling glad that Zack was going first, for once. The silence created a sense of safety, like they were truly alone, and yet the darkness had an ominous feel to it.

"So, do ya think there are really any ghosts in here?" asked Echo.

"I don't know. That homeless guy we talked to was certain of it, but I wouldn't think you'd find ghosts in an old factory like this. I'd expect 'em in places like an old hotel, or a mansion, ya know? Didn't you say you thought there were ghosts at Edgewater?"

"Yeah, maybe," replied Echo. "I didn't see anything for certain. It was just a feeling."

"Well, it used to be a medical facility, so there were probably people that died there," speculated Zack as he walked down the dark hallway, poking his head in a number of doorways that led to empty rooms. "You might expect to see a ghost in a place like that. But this just doesn't seem like the place."

"People die in factories," stated Echo. "Freak accidents with machinery?"

"I suppose," said Zack as he walked back toward Echo who was still examining a room near the bottom of the ramp. "Hey, look at this," he noticed as he walked past Echo, pointing his light at an old door with a padlock that was somewhat hidden behind the ramp they had just walked down.

"Where do you think it goes?"

"Let's find out," said Zack, as he produced a bolt cutter from his backpack.

Once again, Echo was impressed that Zack wasn't hesitating. After a moment of working with the cutter, the metal gave way, and the lock came off. Zack swung the door back to reveal an exposed metal staircase that went down two flights into a large open room below.

"No way!" exclaimed Echo. "This must be the boiler room or something. Man, this place is old. Just look at this. I bet we could pull off a killer party down here."

"I don't know. It looks like there's only one way in or out," observed Zack as he descended the steps to the basement floor. "What if the cops came?"

"There's no other way out from down *here*," admitted Echo, "but on the main floor upstairs, there's more than one exit. We would just have to have enough lookouts."

As they reached the bottom, Echo walked over to a huge pile of cinder blocks in one of the corners of the room.

"Check this out. We could totally use these cinder blocks to build a DJ booth," suggested Echo as he began to pull some of the blocks off the pile. "Come on man, just humor me."

For a few minutes, both Zack and Echo pulled blocks from the bottom of the pile and began stacking them to create Echo's DJ booth, until suddenly, one of the blocks Zack removed caused the whole pile to shift.

"Whoa, look out," Zack warned as several of the blocks toppled from the pile, kicking up dust. Both of them stepped back for a couple of minutes as the dust began to settle, until something interesting caught their attention.

"Hey, look. There's a door," said Echo. "Help me clear these out."

Block by block, they removed almost all of them, neatly stacking them up against a wall, leaving the large metal door exposed. Zack produced the bolt cutters again and cut away another padlock. And with a little pull, he swung the door wide open.

"OK, this is getting really weird," expressed Echo.

There, before them, just beyond the metal door, was a wall made of the same kind of cinder blocks. Echo could not help his curiosity and began pushing on the wall, testing it for weaknesses.

"Hey, it just moved," Echo noticed. "It's loose. Help me push on it."

Both Zack and Echo placed their hands on the wall, leaning into it.

"On the count of three," said Zack. "One, two, three!"

With surprisingly little effort, several of the blocks slid inward until the whole wall began to collapse. Zack almost lost his balance, but Echo braced him just as several of the blocks fell dangerously close to his head.

"Whoa! That was close," said Echo as a cloud of dust billowed up from beyond the door.

"Thanks," Zack coughed. "I didn't think it was going to be that loose."

They both stepped back for another minute or two, letting the dust settle once again, until they both stared in disbelief with their lights fixated on the far-left corner of the hidden room.

"Dude. Is this crazy or what?" Zack was stunned.

"Yo, I'm trippin'," replied Echo. "You seeing what I'm seeing?"

"Yeah. It looks like…"

"It *looks* like someone wanted to keep this a secret," continued Echo.

"I don't think anyone's been down here for a really long time."

"Yeah, maybe decades."

"OK, don't tell anyone I said this," confided Zack, "but I kinda wish there were more of us. I mean, I don't ever worry if it's just you and me on the street, cause I know you've got my back, and you're just as strong as I am."

"Word," agreed Echo. "So, what if we told the others?"

"You mean like Mel and Dominic?"

"Yeah, and your brother," Echo added. "What do ya think?"

For a moment, they both continued to stare at what they knew was a powerful mystery, waiting to be explored, until Zack broke the silence.

"I think I just had a brilliant idea for my film."

7

THE INVISIBLE WORLD

The next day, it was nearly 10 a.m. before Roya's grandparents left to continue on their summer vacation. Ami and Mandy already had permission to go with Roya and her dad for the day. All Roya had to do was convince her dad to join them, so they could look for the hidden object, but she waited until Ami and Mandy arrived first, believing that the will of the group would be more compelling.

"Let me do the talking," Roya said quietly, just before they entered the office where her dad was reading an article online. "Hey, Dad. Whatcha doin'?"

"Oh, just catching up on some news. What are you ladies up to?"

"We were hoping you might be up for a little day trip."

"What did you have in mind?" he asked, with a slight note of reservation. Roya knew this tone but was not discouraged.

"Well, Ami and Mandy haven't seen that much of the area, and I wanted to take them hiking. It wouldn't be a short trip, though. You would have to come with us for the day."

"Oh," he said, hesitantly. "That depends on your mother."

Classic misdirection, Roya thought—the old defer-to-the-other-parent trick. He often pretended to be disempowered to her will when he did not want to commit to something himself. *Be patient. Don't fight his resistance*, she heard herself say inwardly, determined to neutralize any negative tilt by being more inclusive.

"Dad, do you remember that place you used to take us when we were little, where we lost my Frisbee?"

"Yeah, we haven't been there in ages." Raymond's interest was piqued, and he looked like he was recalling something. Roya sensed a little nostalgia coming up in him about when she and her sister were little. But then his practical side returned. "You *do* realize that trail is almost two hours from here. We really can't afford the gas."

Instantly, Roya knew that the author of the book had placed the power right into her hands. The recipes had already handled the situation, knowing that money would be an issue.

"No problem. I'll use some of the prize money to take care of the gas. I'll even buy us all dinner on the road. Mom can have the night off."

Smooth move, Ami admired. She was always fascinated to see how other teens bargained with their parents. Roya's dad was easily persuaded. Roya knew him well enough to know that he liked random adventures; he just tended to say no until he was sure it was something he wanted to do.

"Roya, you shouldn't use your money for something like this. Don't you want to save for a car?" her dad admonished.

"No. What I *want* is to have a nice summer with my friends," she declared. "Besides, I need more driving hours so I can get my license at the end of the summer."

Raymond paused for a moment, considering all of the factors involved. Finally, he admitted, "You know, it *would* be interesting to visit there again to check for anomalies."

Mandy was struck by the word 'anomalies,' and she had a weird look on her face. She looked poised for laughter at the absurdity of such an unfamiliar expression, but she didn't know enough about it, so she held back. Ami was more inquisitive.

"What sort of anomalies would you be checking for?" she asked.

"Electromagnetic, Earth energy, or anything mysterious. It's sort of a hobby of mine. Let me grab my compass, and I'll go talk to your mother about it."

The compass, Roya thought with a sudden rush of excitement. While her dad went upstairs to talk with Roya's mother, Roya dug the map out of her pocket, and they all huddled around to look at it. This was the first time she had shown it to them.

"You see here where I drew a compass? That's the first sign!" exclaimed Roya, pointing to where she had drawn a cross with north, south, east, and west around it. "I knew when I was drawing it that it had some meaning that I would figure out later on. You see, an intuitive map is not a map of directions as much as it's a map of signs and synchronicities. This compass is actually a symbol that represents my dad."

"Cool. We'll go check for anomalies with your dad and his compass," joked Mandy, pretending to have a serious voice. "Maybe we can figure out where the aliens have landed," she added, almost cracking herself up in the process.

Before Roya had time to explain the rest of the map, her dad was already returning with a backpack. "Your mother is going into town, and she said it's fine if we want to take off for the day. She's happy to have the night off. Are you three ready to go?"

"Yeah, we're all ready," said Roya. "Let me just grab my other shoes upstairs and say goodbye to Mom."

Victory, she thought. *In more ways than one.*

The drive down was peaceful, and traffic was light for a Saturday in the summer. Raymond was highly entertained listening to his daughter talk with her friends. The first half an hour, they talked about the trips Ami and Mandy had taken or were planning to take with their dad. Raymond kept wanting to interject things about his travels, most of which were from before Roya was born, but he figured it would be a little rude, since Roya did not have as many stories to share yet. Roya was just happy that they could show Ami and Mandy something that was from their family's history, even though the map was foremost on her mind. At some point, Mandy began to interrogate Raymond about Earth energy.

"So, what's the purpose of finding these anomalies?"

Raymond had been waiting for a question like this, so he could find his place in the conversation.

"That's an interesting question. The purpose of finding them isn't really clear to me, yet. I suppose I'm trying to answer questions that I have about the Earth," he said, though the questions he was thinking of were much deeper and more fully formed than he was ready to explain. "As I understand it, the Earth is like a gigantic, living biocomputer. It stores tremendous amounts of living information, and like a computer, it also *releases* information. It *might* even be programmable."

"If the Earth is a living biocomputer, then what would *we* be, the operating system?" supposed Mandy.

"Yes, but if we are the operating system, then who is the programmer?" Raymond prompted.

The truth about how he became interested in this subject was not something he enjoyed trying to explain to people, unless they had experienced something similar. He was becoming more adept at engaging people in hypotheticals instead of trying to prove that he had encountered things from beyond this world. Roya just listened with curiosity.

"So, if we're just the operating system of a giant computer, then we're not really in control of our destiny," Ami considered. "We could be hacked."

"True. That is, unless the operating system evolves into something else."

"But what would we evolve into?" asked Mandy.

"The programmer," replied Raymond.

"You guys are deep. I still don't get what this has to do with finding anomalies," said Mandy.

"Well, if the Earth is storing living information, it must also release it in certain ways. The electromagnetic field of the Earth has a pattern, with strong points and weak points of flow. Many of the great monuments of ancient history, like the Great Pyramids, for example, are built on the strongest points. So, it stands to reason that some ancient cultures knew something about this."

"But why would ancient cultures build monuments on these energy points?" Mandy wanted to know.

"That's part of what I hope to find out. If more living information is present in these power spots, it might be possible to tap into the knowledge of the Earth and learn something about the bigger picture."

"How would you do that?" asked Ami.

"By feeling it, or seeing it inwardly, like a vision or a knowing," answered Raymond.

I see inwardly, Roya remembered, as she contemplated the map. Ami, too, was deep in thought.

"So, how do you detect these energy points?" Mandy inquired.

"Many years ago, I discovered that I could feel this kind of Earth energy with my hands. I visited several places that are considered to be power spots, or sacred sites, and I found that my body was sensitive to the stronger Earth energy there. Sometimes, you can even observe electromagnetic anomalies in such places. I was on Mt. Tamalpais in California once, at a place where the Native Americans used to hold ceremonies, and my compass started to spin. It only happened in this one area. The compass needle could not find north. It makes me wonder how the Native Americans knew that this place was different."

"Maybe they could feel things with their hands, like you," Ami suggested, noticing her own hands and realizing that she also felt sensations of energy with them at times.

"Perhaps. Ever since then, I wanted to try to map out other locations like that in New York. It's been a while since I had the opportunity to scout, and I haven't really checked this area since I started doing this, even though we used to hike here occasionally when Roya was younger. I can't explain it, but I feel like I am becoming more sensitive to this kind of energy."

Roya knew there was more to the story than he was sharing with Ami and Mandy. She had heard his stories before about strange encounters with mysterious phenomena. He had a series of experiences before she was born that seemed to have changed him somehow. She could hardly imagine what he would have been like before, so she had no context for how much he had changed. What interested her most about the conversation was the way her dad's quest felt like it was beginning to parallel theirs. Until now, she had very little idea of what they were looking for, but listening to him talk about Earth energy made her feel, somehow, like the search was already narrowing.

A while later, they arrived at the trailhead, which was just as well-marked as it had been years ago. They saw several parked cars that belonged to other people using the trail. Roya began to wonder how she would direct the journey without explaining to her dad that they were looking for something, but she decided to just go with the flow, for now. The trail was many miles long and linked with a much larger trail system that ranged throughout parts of Herkimer County, though the place she was thinking of was not more than a mile away.

The three girls began the walk together, with Raymond following a short distance behind. He easily agreed to give them a little space to themselves, which worked well for secretly discussing the map. The first key was to find the footbridge over the creek. Roya figured this was not far away, but it had been so long since they had been there, her sense of distance was off. After walking more than half a mile, Roya was starting to wonder if she had picked the right trail, until she began to hear the sound of water flowing in the distance. The trail must have started to run parallel to the creek, off to their left, but they had to walk quite a ways further to intersect it.

There was the bridge! It was just as she remembered it, but no matter how much she reflected on her memories, she did not recall any kind of cave. So many of her memories from hiking when she was younger had run together, it was hard to guess where the path would lead her. As they stood before the footbridge, they noticed a clearing off to the right that opened into a grassy field, while the trail beyond the creek veered off to the left into the thick of the woods.

"Which way do we go, Roya?" asked Ami.

"On the map, I didn't sense which part was more important: following the main trail or following the creek into that field."

"What's that?" Mandy paused. "Do you hear that?"

They all listened intently for a moment to what sounded like sticks clapping together until Roya broke off the main trail and began walking into the clearing. Ami and Mandy followed just behind her on either side, still trying to listen over the sound of the twigs breaking under their feet. Just past the clearing, they could see to the far side of the field where a couple of young boys were using large sticks as imaginary swords, or perhaps lightsabers. As they walked closer to where the boys were playing, a man that they presumed was the father stepped out of the forest.

"Roya, look at what he's wearing!" exclaimed Ami.

"I know!"

The boys' father was wearing a Red Sox hat that they knew was the hat from the map. When Roya first drew the hat, she labeled it with the *word* 'Red' because she thought it referred to the color of the hat. But only the letters on the man's white hat were red. Now, she could see what her intuition had been trying to show her, that the *word* 'Red' would be written on the hat.

Raymond had just caught up to them in the field, when a large raven swooped very close by them, continuing to fly up toward the far end of the field. It even seemed to announce itself with a loud "caw, caw" before flapping its wings to create more lift. Roya turned slightly to the left to look across the rest of the field and watch the raven until it flew behind some trees.

"Let's go that way," she said, pointing in the direction of the raven's flight.

Raymond had his compass out and seemed content to meander along with his own thoughts as the girls marched forward. Their pace quickened with the excitement of the synchronicities, and yet they were also trying to get far enough ahead to talk some more without being heard.

"Do you remember any of this?" asked Ami.

"I'm pretty sure I remember us playing Frisbee in this field. You see those hills off to the right with all the rocks? That's where I think we lost the Frisbee. It flew right into a crevice, and my dad couldn't reach it."

"This is really cool. It's like a treasure hunt, but I don't see how we can find something if we don't know what we're looking for," doubted Mandy.

"We've come this far, haven't we?" Roya encouraged.

Roya was holding the map out in front of them as they walked. After following the creek for a while along the edge of the field, the girls continued on into the forest where the raven had disappeared. They were surrounded by trees and lush green vegetation and had to hop on the rocks in the creek to get past some of it. The flow of the water seemed to speak to them, guiding them to keep moving forward until they could see another smaller clearing up ahead. As they approached it, they spotted a large oak tree. This was the sign they were looking for.

The old oak stood majestically watching over the clearing, towering above the surrounding trees, and was filled with the light of the midday sun. Roya imagined that they might be able to see something from up in the tree, and then she became absorbed in a familiar feeling. This was the place on the map where Roya had drawn the three interlocking circles, right near the oak tree.

"Hey, Roya," her dad said from behind. "You remember this tree, don't you? You must have been up there for half an hour one day when we couldn't find you."

"Really? Can you refresh my memory?"

"We were having a picnic out here. You must have been about seven years old, and you were playing and exploring nearby. At some point, we noticed that we couldn't see you anywhere. Your mother and I were really worried when we called, and you didn't answer. When we finally found you, you said that you hadn't heard us. You just walked right up to us like nothing had happened, and when we asked you where you'd been, you just said you'd been up in this tree. I thought it was really strange at the time, because you *had* to have heard us calling for you, and yet you seemed oblivious. You just said you'd been watching the clouds."

"Weird. I hardly remember that, but maybe it's worth remembering. Do you mind if we hang out here for a bit and have a snack?" asked Roya.

"No problem. I'm going to scout around those rocks over there. Just yell if you need me. I won't be far," Raymond said.

Roya had yet to show Ami and Mandy her favorite climbing trees around the town of Adams, but this was better than all of them. It was rare, with all the logging over the years, to see an oak this old and magnificent. The lower branches were easy to climb onto, with lots of places to go from there. The tree was at least fifty feet tall, and the branches extended out almost twice as wide. Mandy was already climbing up into the tree before Roya had broken out the water and snacks from her backpack.

"Mandy, don't you want a snack?" asked Roya.

"Just toss me a trail bar," she called down from about twenty feet up in the tree. It took three tries to get the trail bar up to her, and then she happily kept on climbing while Roya and Ami stayed at the bottom, enjoying the shade of the tree.

"This is really beautiful," appreciated Ami.

"Yeah, it's even better than I remember," agreed Roya, as she dug out a bag of trail mix and a couple of apples. "I'm trying to remember what happened when I was up in the tree back when I was seven. I honestly don't remember hearing my parents calling for me, but something seems familiar, like I remember coming down from the tree, and everyone was surprised to see me."

Ami took a bite out of her apple, and it was juicier than she expected. She slurped the juice off before her mouth closed over the next bite.

"Maybe you were daydreaming," she mumbled at first, with a full mouth. "Sometimes, in class, I completely lose track of what's happening. I get so lost in my own thoughts that when I come back, it's like a chunk of time is missing from my memory of the class."

"I totally do that, too," Roya smiled, thinking about how alike they were. "Hey, I just thought of something." She reached for the book in her backpack. "If the book was made with knowledge from the future, maybe it knows about us being here and what we're looking for."

"Do you think it left us a clue?"

"Yeah. Sometimes, I get this vibe when I feel it wants to tell me something. It happened yesterday at the library just after I decoded the messages, and now, I'm getting a similar vibe. Can you feel it?"

"Let me see it," said Ami. "Do you mind if I read?"

"No, go right ahead," invited Roya as they both sat down with their backs against the tree.

Ami was trying something new; she held her right hand above each page, searching for the one that held the strongest vibe. She sensed the book clearly had a message for them, and after flipping around for a minute, she landed on a page that called to her. She began to read:

Sometimes, those who guard knowledge of the future must demonstrate transformation. Knowledge from the future can be dangerous, but it is permitted to those who are destined to guard its purpose. There are some who will seek to steal it or distort its meaning. They want to profit from such knowledge—to control the outcome of the recipe that they are a part of—but the only way to truly profit from knowledge of the future is to surrender to the way it guides your heart.

Knowledge, power, and resources will always tilt into alignment with those whose focus is sharing. But a mind tilted out of alignment with the heart will seek to possess all forms of wealth that it perceives as separate. Sharing wealth is the best way to stay in the flow of resources, because physical resources are ultimately controlled by the invisible world. Greed blinds you to this world and binds you to the gravity of human ignorance. The more you seek to share, the more the invisible world will give you to share. The treasuries of the Earth will open to those who are devoted to loving service.

Ami paused for a moment and then asked, "Did anything from that passage stand out? Sometimes, I feel like a single phase starts speaking to me, like there's so much more behind it."

"Knowledge from the future," replied Roya. "I feel like there's something there…"

Roya could feel Ami's focus of attention trying to help her retrieve the memory, but she needed silence to look inwardly. "Let's just be quiet for a few minutes while I'm trying to remember."

At first, Roya concentrated on what she could recall, which wasn't much. She remembered playing next to the tree and watching her sister wander off to climb on the boulders on the other side of the clearing. She tried to imagine climbing up into the tree as her seven-year-old self, but nothing was clear. Then, she felt guided to just relax and listen to the sound of the breeze blowing through the trees.

Tongues in trees, she thought. *Books in the running brooks, sermons in stones, and good in everything.* She wondered for a moment if the tree remembered her, and then she began to ask the tree to reveal its secrets. She listened intently to the pristine sounds of nature, straining her senses to perceive any subtle messages. Then, an unexpected sound broke through her awareness. It was Mandy crumpling the plastic wrapper of her trail bar and stuffing it into her jeans pocket. She had to laugh inwardly for a moment, because even without trying, Mandy's actions often had a comedic timing. As the sound drew her attention up to Mandy, her consciousness began to align with their betweenergy.

Interestingly, she could feel more energy flowing through this focus, like the clouds that surrounded the memory were lifting. She was beginning to imagine something impossible: that somehow, Ami and Mandy had been up in the tree with her back then. This could not really be, and yet, there was a tremendous amount of energy building around this idea until the memory of what had really happened suddenly became crystal clear. It was true that she had not been alone in the tree, but it was not Ami and Mandy as they are now. It was a voice that spoke to her *about* them, and the words of the voice had the power to connect her with the living presence of two girls that she knew were her companions.

Guided by a feeling of joy, seven-year-old Roya had climbed the tree to a high point where she could see large billowy storm clouds on the horizon. There she sat, straddling a large branch and leaning forward, folding her arms in front of her so she could lie on her belly across the branch with her chin resting on her arms. Here, she continued gazing at the clouds until something unusual caught her eye. At first, the sun was casting beautiful rays that looked spectacular, but then the dark storm clouds seemed to become more illuminated from within. Roya became entranced with the radiant glow, feeling connected to the light somehow, as if it was alive.

The light began to dance and shimmer around the edges of the clouds. Every time it twinkled and grew a little brighter, a strange feeling of anticipation was building within her. The feeling kept growing more intense until a part of the light seemed to reach right out and touch her. It was a deeply peaceful and yet strangely familiar feeling that lasted a long time, gently filling her with light until she heard *the Voice.*

How could I have forgotten, Roya thought as she was reliving the memory. The Voice said things to her that she swore she would never forget; things that she knew were important, and yet, almost immediately after that day, the memory began to fade. She never talked about it to anyone. Even when the memory was fresh, she did not believe anyone would understand. That was before she heard her dad talk about strange encounters. By then, the tree and the clouds were long forgotten. Now, the pieces of her life were beginning to fit together in some way that she could not have planned on her own. She was witnessing something of a Grand Design, and suddenly, it made sense why she had forgotten the Voice so quickly. The context of the messages that were spoken to her had not yet arrived. She had been in the right place, but not the right time, and yet the messages seeded an awareness that the Voice knew would one day return.

The world is facing a great crisis, and you can help us change the outcome, the Voice had said. Somehow, in the awareness of the light, she knew who 'us' was, and yet there were no words for it. It was an 'us' that spoke to her from beyond this world, and yet a part of 'us' had been extended into the world through her. The gentle vibration of the words drew her into a state of group consciousness with the source of the communication.

We are waiting for you in the future, when the world will be ready to receive the gifts that you carry. Do not be afraid of your destiny. Do not be afraid of those who will attempt to disrupt the change. We have provided everything you need to fulfill your purpose. You are not alone. In time, you will find the others and remember the plan.

As she remembered the words, it was like she was hearing them again for the first time. A window had opened inside her, and she was in two places at once. As soon as the Voice said *you will find the others,* she remembered how the energy of the two girls had appeared within the tree. One girl appeared bright with rainbow colors dancing around her form. Her soul was leaping from branch to branch, playfully flitting around with a fairy-like energy. The other girl appeared with a soft blue and violet hue around her. She was sitting quietly on a nearby branch, steadily focused on Roya, beaming her constant support.

She will go with you into the places that you dare not go alone. As she heard this line and remembered this part of the vision, Roya suddenly became more aware of Ami's physical presence sitting next to her with her back against the trunk of the tree. Then, she remembered how the other girl had come and dressed her in rainbows, touching her with light that blended in with her own.

What you give to her will always bring out the best in you. The Voice had a way of speaking the very experiential truths that she was discovering but did not yet have words for. The connection with the two girls felt undeniably a part of her. And there were others, too, but they were more distant, until, for a moment, the tree lit up with the energy of other children, laughing and playing together along every branch. And then, the Voice spoke again.

I have given you the seal of the guardians. They will recognize you and protect you on your journey. They will bring clarity to you and guide you on your way. Roya felt these words going right into a point in the middle of her forehead. The words penetrated her mind and reminded her that she was connected to powerful forces of good. But there was something else. A familiar image crept into her mind that felt connected with the Voice. She could almost see it with her eyes closed, like someone was holding a book up to her mind's eye. The instant she recognized the image, it became clear. It was the angel from the book! This is what the picture in the book was meant to remind her of: the Voice and the Tree.

Roya opened her eyes and looked up at the sky, wishing she could see the light and the clouds again, but the sky was perfectly clear. The angel felt like a powerful ally, and she wanted to remember more about how she knew this being, but the pace of the synchronicities kept her mind racing along a different pathway. The image of the angel in the book was not just there to remind her of the vision, but to connect her again with the words of the book, which began to open like a doorway inside her.

The treasuries of the Earth will open to those who are devoted to loving service.

"Ami," Roya whispered.

"What?"

"I know why we are here. I think there's something buried in this field."

"What do you think it is?"

"I don't know," replied Roya.

She was still connected to her vision as she stood up, and Ami joined her, wide-eyed with interest.

"Did you remember what happened to you in the tree?" asked Ami.

"Yes. It all just came back to me. I had a vision when I was in the tree, and both you and Mandy were there! This was all meant to happen!"

"Really?!" Ami exclaimed. "That's awesome! I was praying that you would remember. It felt important. Tell me more."

"Wait. Just a minute…first, I need to write something down," Roya said, bending down to dig for a pencil in her backpack. As soon as she found one, she pulled out the piece of notebook paper with the map on it and wrote 'Seal of the Guardians' at the bottom, knowing that would be enough to help her recall the rest.

By this time, Mandy had climbed down the tree and jumped the last six feet, landing with a thud in front of them.

"Wow, this tree is amazing! You can really let your mind go up there. I almost fell out. I got so caught up imagining that I could fly and leap from branch to branch. It's a little disorienting to think about when you're up that high."

Roya could not be certain, but she felt that Mandy had been sitting up in the tree on the same branch she had been on when she had the vision as a child.

"I was just telling Ami before you climbed down that I think what we are looking for is in this field. Remember when the book said that the treasuries of the Earth would open to those who are devoted to loving service?"

"Yeah, I remember that part," said Mandy. "So, you think there's buried treasure here?"

"I don't know if that's what 'treasuries' is referring to," Roya suggested, "but I have this odd feeling that there might be something buried here."

Just then, they heard a voice coming from the rocks, and Raymond emerged, jumping down from one of the boulders and then walking into the clearing.

"Hey, Roya," he said as he got closer. "The strangest thing has been going on with my compass. It kept pointing over here every few minutes. It's happened five times now. I think there's something buried in this field."

Roya and Ami got chills. These were the exact same words that Roya had used. It was as if she had been speaking the same thing that her dad had been thinking from over on the rocks. It was time to let him in on their secret mission.

"Dad, we have something to tell you."

"What is it?"

"We were guided here for a reason. *We* think there's something buried here, too. Look at this," she said, showing him the map.

"I was guided to draw this intuitive map yesterday, and I recognized the little footbridge over the creek. Everything else in the picture represents things that we encountered on the journey, and these three interlocking circles in front of the tree represent Ami and Mandy and me. Even the north, south, east, and west that I drew next to the circles represents you with your compass. There's something here we're supposed to find."

Raymond was blown away by the idea that his daughter had drawn an intuitive map of their journey. Roya, Ami, and Mandy all looked at each other, realizing together that they had just taken a big step letting her dad in on the secret, but it seemed like a natural one. Raymond studied the map for a moment, and then handed it back.

"I have an idea," he said.

Raymond set the compass on the ground, and they all knelt down to look at it. The needle was pointing north, but they sensed that he meant to wait for something to happen. After about a minute, the needle twitched and briefly pointed directly away from the tree. They were about five feet away from the base of the tree, so the needle had pointed straight back out into the field that Raymond had just crossed.

"Last time it did that, it pointed *toward* the tree, so I must have walked past whatever is causing this."

Raymond grabbed the compass, and they all stood up and turned toward the clearing. He handed the compass to Roya and walked forward with his hands outstretched and his palms facing down, trying to feel the anomaly.

Mandy put her hands out as well, trying to imagine what she might be able to feel, and then Ami followed suit. Roya just kept her eyes on the compass needle until suddenly it twitched again. This time, it was not able to find another direction and took a minute to settle down.

"Dad, the needle just went crazy. I think we're getting close."

"Yeah, I can feel it."

"What's it supposed to feel like?" asked Mandy.

"It feels like…a vibration or a flow of energy passing through you, almost tingly or like a buzzing sensation. It might feel different for different people," said Raymond. "Some people get chills up the back of their neck. I feel things through my hands. But you might feel things in other ways, like in your gut, or on the tip of your nose. Lots of different ways for people to get vibes."

Mandy crossed her eyes, looking at her nose, and then closed one eye while making a funny face. They were about twenty-five feet away from the tree, and Raymond was starting to circle around a particular patch of grass. Then, unexpectedly, he took off his backpack and unzipped it, pulling out what looked like some sort of wand.

"What is that?" asked Ami.

"It's a metal detector."

He switched it on and adjusted some of the settings before he began waving it over the ground. The small black box that the wand extended from hummed and beeped as Raymond swept it back and forth until he locked onto something. There was a steady tone and Raymond was confident that he had found something. He switched off his machine and started feeling the ground with his hands.

The girls gathered around, placing their hands on the Earth around the same spot. Mandy thought the scene looked like a hand collage that would be used for an Earth Day poster. Raymond was actually checking the density of the soil, and it felt fairly loose. Reaching over into his backpack again, he pulled out a trowel and started to dig, breaking off the first layer of grass and roots to reveal the soft dirt below. From there, the girls were able to help remove the loose dirt as Raymond kept digging with the trowel, alternating between the sides of the hole and the bottom. Gradually, the hole became deeper and wider, and after about ten minutes, Raymond stopped them to take a break.

"Can you feel that?" he asked.

"Yeah, I sure can," said Ami.

"I'm totally buzzing with energy," beamed Mandy.

"Yeah. Me, too," added Roya. "Let's keep digging," she urged as she dove back in to scoop the dirt from the bottom of the hole.

Gradually, each of them moved back into action to follow her pace. They must have been digging for another ten minutes before Raymond's trowel struck something hard. They all paused and looked at each other in amazement. Raymond scraped around the edges, beginning to dig around the object until they could see the outline of a rectangular box. After scooping out enough dirt, they were able to brush it off and see that it was about a foot and a half long and a foot wide. The four of them wedged their fingers under it, and then they all lifted together. The box felt like it was made of stone and was about eight inches deep. It was somewhat heavy, but any of the girls would have been able to pull it out by themselves.

"What do you think it is?" asked Roya.

"I don't know. I'm not even sure how to open it," Raymond was puzzled. He continued to brush it off, feeling around the edges for any markings or cracks.

"I don't feel any hinges or anything," he said, perplexed.

Roya and Mandy had begun to feel around the edges as well, while Ami examined it very closely. The stone was black and very smooth. The edges of the box were slightly rounded, and there were little bits of the stone that looked more reflective than others.

"Hey, look at this," Ami pointed out. "A line runs around the surface near the edge."

Ami traced her finger around, rubbing parts of the surface to make the line more visible until she came to one of the shorter sides.

"There's no line on this side. It runs around three of the sides, but not this one."

Assuming that the top might just slide off, Raymond first tried pushing on it, but something obstructed it from moving. Ami continued to feel along the edges with her finger, and then she discovered something. She looked like she was trying to grip something between her thumb and her middle finger until finally, she pulled out a piece of the corner of the box that had a metal rod connected to it. Almost as soon as the rod was free, Raymond pushed the surface toward the edge where the rod had been, and the cover slid right off. Everyone stared into the box with a look of wonder and surprise.

"It looks like a giant egg," said Mandy.

"Yeah. It's like what I drew on the map," Roya realized, marveling at the accuracy of her intuition.

"What could it possibly be?" asked Ami.

"I have no idea," said Raymond. "It's not what I expected—but then again, I don't know that I had any expectations."

"Waiting for dragon to hatch," Mandy said in a funny robotic voice.

The egg was lying on its side in the center of the box. One end of it was slightly longer and skinnier, and the wider end with the base had three gold metal rings around it, stacked one over the other so that the smallest ring at the bottom was perfectly level with the base of the egg. It appeared that the object was meant to stand upright on the bottom ring. The surface of the egg almost looked like plastic, though it did not feel that way to the touch. It was even smoother than the surface of the box that contained it and was a light beige color. The base of the box on the inside was obviously thick enough to contain an indentation that perfectly fit the shape of the egg. The way the rings fit into the indentation seemed to secure the egg from being rattled around if the box were to move.

Just as they were about to discuss it further, the whole group noticed the sound of the boys playing in the adjacent field. It seemed like they were getting closer. They strained their eyes to look for movement through the trees. Then they saw the man they had passed before, walking with his boys in their general direction.

"What should we do?" asked Roya. "We don't want anyone to see this, do we?"

Just as Raymond was about to answer, a burst of energy came from the egg.

"Whoa, did you feel that?" he asked.

"What was that?" exclaimed Ami and Mandy simultaneously.

"It came from the egg," said Roya. "That must be what was causing the compass to go wild."

"I think you're right. But wait a minute, I can still feel something," noticed Raymond.

They all became very still, and sure enough, there was indeed a gentle vibration of energy beginning to flow from the egg. They all felt it, and it was gradually getting stronger.

"That wasn't just a pulse like the one that triggered the compass. I think this thing just started up," said Raymond. "I have an idea. I saw a small cave when I was exploring in the hills over there. It could provide us some cover until we figure out what to do next."

"Yes," agreed Roya, remembering the map. "The egg wants us to go to the cave."

Roya seemed to be a step ahead in her awareness of what was happening, and everyone else felt aligned. Raymond lifted the box with the egg inside and began to lead the way to the cave. As they grabbed their packs and headed toward the boulders in the distance, Roya was beginning to realize that the energy of the egg had been communicating with her when she made the map, just like it had been sending pulses to trigger her dad's compass.

The terrain was filled with rocks and trees, and ahead was a large hill made of boulders. It was the first of several, and the land behind them became more rocky and elevated. They followed Raymond into the trees, walking along the base of the hills until they could see a large slab of rock that leaned against a pile of boulders. This formed the entrance to the cave. Roya had seen lots of small caves like this in upstate New York and always loved to explore them, but she did not remember this one from any of their previous visits. It was well-hidden, unless you walked out of the clearing in just the right direction.

Raymond led them down into the cave without hesitating, having been there only half an hour before. The ceiling of the cave was well above their heads, and the floor was relatively even. The three girls fanned out around the room, which was big enough for about ten people to stand comfortably. Roya felt the rock walls, and Ami stared into the darkest corner, waiting for her eyes to adjust. Mandy stood close to Raymond as he removed the egg from the box and placed it gently on the ground in the center of the cave.

"Hey, is everyone still feeling this energy?" asked Roya. "I think it's getting stronger."

"Yes," agreed Raymond. "It's like it keeps shifting gears. I just wanna chill in here for a moment and study this thing. Maybe we can figure out what it's doing."

Raymond stood back near the entrance to the cave, gazing at the egg in bewilderment. The shadows of the trees outside only allowed in a little light, just enough to see the perimeter of the cave without turning on a flashlight, once their eyes had adjusted. Just then, a wave of energy washed over them, and they all felt a shift in perception. Somehow, they all knew that they had just experienced the same thing without needing to speak about it.

"Umm…does everyone think this thing is safe?" Ami worried.

"It feels natural somehow," Raymond reassured her. "I think if it were unsafe, we would have a stronger fear reaction. I feel like this device is entraining us with its frequencies," and almost as soon as he said the word 'frequencies,' another wave kicked in, this time with a ping that seemed to create a lasting gentle ringing sound in the inner ear. Then another. This time, the ringing shifted from the ears into more of a vibrating tone that filled the air.

"This feels really weird," said Mandy, sounding a little frightened, but more in awe than anything else.

Both Ami and Mandy had moved around to the left of the entrance where Raymond stood, blocking some of the incoming light, and Roya stood to the right forming a semi-circle around one side of the egg.

"It's like some kind of energy generating gizmo," Mandy observed.

"Hey, that's funny. You just spelled egg," Ami noted.

"What do you mean?" said Mandy.

Roya heard it, too. "Energy. Generating. Gizmo. E. G. G.—it's an acronym for Egg," Roya pointed out.

"Oh, yeah, right!" Mandy realized.

"Look at that!" said Raymond.

An ambient light began to fill the room, but it was not shining from any particular source. Though they could feel its connection to the Egg, the light seemed to be appearing as if out of nowhere. It was everywhere in the cave, like a glowing mist that was passing right through them. Even the sense of being inside a cave was beginning to fade as their minds became connected to a vast form of space that was enveloping them.

Roya took a deep breath and felt some of the glowing mist flow right into her lungs, causing her to feel even more connected to the light. She looked at Ami and noticed that she, too, had started to breathe differently.

Then, the Egg began to illuminate, and a luminous substance appeared just past its surface, producing a kind of ethereal vapor. As they watched, the vapor straightened into a barely visible beam that expanded until it enveloped them. Suddenly, their sense of depth extended right past the rock wall behind the Egg, and they saw several glowing forms in the distance that began to approach them.

"Don't be afraid," advised Raymond, and with those words, Roya knew that her dad's previous experiences with strange encounters had made him the perfect person to have with them. His fearlessness about what was happening permeated the energy of the room, giving Ami and Mandy a feeling of calm surrender. Roya was already calm, having absorbed the messages from the tree. This was something she had been waiting for since childhood.

The nebulous forms gradually moved in closer until they began to exhibit a subtle human appearance, while still remaining luminous. Glowing, scintillating clouds of energy surrounded the image of two beings as they positioned themselves hovering just above the Egg. Other forms of light appeared farther behind them. The two unique vibrations of living energy filled the space until everyone felt a personal connection with them.

"*Greetings,*" they said as one. The word was both audible and vibratory at the same time, ringing through the vibrational field that embraced all of them. They heard it simultaneously with their ears and with their minds. There was a palpable feeling of excitement coming from the beings, whose light radiated the essence of smiles. They both felt masculine, though the tone of their voices was more emotionally rich than men often sound.

"Who are you?" Raymond asked, and one of the two beings moved slightly forward and began to speak.

"*You can hear us. Good. My name is Houston,*" said the one in front, "*and this is Lance.*" The being next to Houston seemed to light up for a second when his name was spoken.

"*We have waited a long time for this moment*" continued Houston, speaking for both of them. "*We are colleagues of yours. You will recognize our vibrations from before. We were with you when you first tried to make contact,*" they said to Raymond, "*but the grid would not support it. Doctor Determined we called you, and now your persistent search has paid off. What you did not know then is that you would need an appropriate team of individuals to support the frequency of such an exchange.*"

"I *do* recognize your vibrations. How do we know each other?" asked Raymond.

"*We know you by the affinity that we share for your work. You have all studied in the same schools with us before you came to Earth. We are following along with your journey in the physical, to assist you in your quest for greater healing. A doctor needs all the help he can get.*"

"I hardly qualify as a doctor," deflected Raymond.

"*Oh, but a doctor you are by greater standards than those that measure your worth on the Earthly plane. You are what many are beginning to call a medical intuitive, and you have a most important quality: you never give up on a patient's healing potential. Too often, when traditional doctors run out of ideas, they give up and deliver disheartening advice to their patients, without even attempting to use the instrument of the mind and body to perceive the subtle nature of the imbalance. The time is coming when people like you will have abundant resources of energy medicine to work with, but for now, you are honing your skills in an environment that feels safe for you."*

"The herb shop," recognized Raymond. "It feels safer to give people advice when they don't expect me to save their lives."

"Yes, but they do not expect this of you, because you do not allow them to see their healing potential as separate from them. By your very nature, you work with the subconscious mind of your patients to help them transform their doubts so that they can believe in the healing power of the soul. Are you beginning to see the standard by which we measure your capabilities as a doctor?"

"Yes. I think I understand," replied Raymond.

"Hi!" said Mandy enthusiastically raising her hand, wanting to jump in and participate. "What do you know about us?"

This time, Lance moved slightly forward and began to speak, and his unique vibration became clearer within the field.

"We speak of you as three sisters, and it is a great pleasure to see you working together. We expect great things from this group. You three have come together to unite your families for a special purpose. We have much to share with all of you. However, we cannot continue this conversation for much longer. We risk the danger of being discovered by the sentries that monitor this part of the energy spectrum. You must take this device to the Guardians of Knowledge. They will guide you to a safe place where we can make contact again. Only they can be trusted with the secret of this technology."

"But this technology is one of the greatest discoveries in human history: a device that can connect us in a visceral way with the invisible realms of Spirit! How will the world ever change if this discovery remains secret? Isn't there a way to share it with the world?" hoped Raymond.

"Do not be discouraged by the necessity of hiding this discovery. The very fact that we are experiencing this breakthrough is now rippling through the web of humanity's collective consciousness. When the first light bulb was switched on, the shift in consciousness experienced by those who were there to witness it was felt invisibly throughout the world. So, it is the same with your experience now. You have demonstrated a new possibility in this time period, and the Earth's energy grid will not forget. Many people throughout the world are working on making such breakthroughs, and their collective intentions are part of what is forming the field of this communication. You have taken a fresh new step into a larger reality, so acknowledge the importance of this accomplishment. You could not have done it without each other."

"How do we find the Guardians of Knowledge?" asked Raymond.

"Roya has already made contact," Houston interjected. *"We know that you*

all have many questions, but for your own safety, we must go now. Be well, and trust that the same forces that brought us together will unite us again."

"Thank you," said Raymond, and they all followed with goodbyes.

Just as the energy began to wane, Mandy impulsively reached out her left hand to touch the energy of the guides as it was hanging in the air and was surprised when Lance seemed to anticipate her move by extending his energy in the form of a hand to touch hers. It happened so fast; she was startled and appeared dazed by what felt like a zing of energy that had rippled through her arm and into her heart chakra.

Everyone looked at Mandy, surprised at her little experiment, but then their attention turned toward the guides as they began to float back away from them to join the many glowing orbs of light in the distance. The gentle hum that filled the air began to fade, and the light grew dimmer until it disappeared completely. The collapse of the field generated by the Egg was slightly disorienting, because it happened quicker than it did when it was switching on. Everyone looked around at each other in a state of wonder.

"What the heck just happened?" Mandy broke the silence. "Was that amazing or what?!"

"I want to do that again!" bursted Ami.

"Mandy, what did you feel when you touched his hand?" asked Raymond, wishing he had done the same thing.

"Wow! It was, like, cooling at first, and then, this tingle happened, and it went right into my chest. I feel *really* open!"

"It looked like your hand went right through his," said Ami.

"That's what you call ectoplasm," explained Raymond.

"I thought ectoplasm was slimy," questioned Mandy.

"Oh no, you're thinking of the movie, *Ghostbusters*. It's not that way at all. Ectoplasm is more like smoke or vapor that can concentrate itself into a form according to the intentions of the beings that are creating it. Roya, what did they mean when they said that you've already made contact?" asked Raymond.

"Claire! She's the one that helped me draw the map. The Voice said that the Guardians would bring clarity to me. It was talking about Claire!"

"What voice?" Raymond probed further.

"Well, it's kind of a long story…" Roya paused, and Ami nodded.

"OK, I'd really love to hear all about it, but before we do anything else, I think we should get moving. I don't know exactly what they meant by danger, but I know I'll feel better once we are on the road. Let's rearrange our backpacks so I can fit the box inside mine."

Raymond emptied his backpack, and Roya packed his stuff into hers as best she could. With a little work, Raymond was able to fit the entire box with the Egg inside his pack. It took some work to get the zipper closed, but they managed to secure it.

Next, they filled up the hole where they had found the box. After a little effort, they were all satisfied with how inconspicuous it looked. Raymond asked that they hold the conversation until they got to the truck so that they would all stay alert and aware of their surroundings. They passed by several small groups of people on the way back, but nobody showed any interest in them. Though they had no idea what kind of danger to be on guard for, it looked as though their path was clear.

On the ride home, Roya recounted the whole chain of events connected with the book, including her experience of remembering the vision in the tree. Raymond was fascinated by how Roya's life experiences were paralleling his own quest for truth. Though Roya's search had only begun very recently, it had culminated in the same discovery that his life had been guiding him toward for decades. He was overwhelmed with emotion about how meaningful it was to have shared this discovery with his daughter; however, it did not feel like the right time to express it.

Roya must have sensed this, because she acknowledged how meaningful it was to have had him there. For Raymond, it felt like he had become more visible to his daughter, because she now understood the kind of experiences that had set his spiritual path in motion so many years ago. For Roya, it felt like her dad could see her path in life and trusted how she was being guided. They both felt more aware of each other in a way that made them feel closer.

On the drive home, they stopped at a small diner for some food while they talked about all that was unfolding. They revealed the book to Roya's dad and had a lively discussion about its origins and nature. Raymond effortlessly received it with an open mind, but they had to consider the manner in which they would share everything with Roya's mother and sister.

Roya then realized that the book had already made it easy by playing a direct role in her winning the contest and cooking dinner for her family. This had created the perfect bridge for her mother to step into the more expanded reality that they were all now exploring. She could not help wondering if the cooking references had been planned deliberately to engage her mother in the path that was opening.

Because Raymond did not know Ami and Mandy's dad very well, there was some debate about whether he should be included before Roya talked to Claire. Roya thought that when the guides mentioned uniting their families, this meant that Frank was absolutely included, whereas Raymond thought that the message about only trusting the Guardians took precedence. Ultimately, they agreed that they would try to arrange for all of them to meet at the same time the next day.

That evening, before dropping off Ami and Mandy, Roya began to think again about the messages she had received about them. The sense of soul recognition between them was stronger than ever, and Roya received an inspiring thought about how to honor their friendship.

"Hey, I have something I want to share," Roya said, turning around from the front passenger seat to face Ami and Mandy in the back. Her attention was first directed at Mandy. "I want to use some of the prize money to buy fabric so that you can make some of the clothes that you've been sketching."

Mandy was beside herself. She was silent for a moment, letting the words sink in, and then Ami and Roya both felt Mandy's heart expanding like a balloon until she looked like she was about to cry. She was grinning from cheek to cheek.

"Wow, that's the best gift I could ever imagine receiving. I have so many ideas. I am going to make you both the most amazing outfits. You can help me pick out the materials. It'll be so much fun!"

"Wow, that's so nice of you, Roya," said Ami.

"Well, it's easily a gift to all of us, because I know Mandy will make us something perfect. You have to make some things for yourself, though, too," she said to Mandy.

"Of course," Mandy replied.

Roya knew from the messages in the tree that giving such a gift would help sustain the good vibes, which felt important for their journey. Between channeling Mandy's soul presence to draw the map and being dressed by rainbows in the vision, Roya was beginning to understand something about how it is possible to wear the vibrations of others synergistically.

Ever since she had won the contest, she had tried to imagine buying material things for herself with the prize money, but something deep inside told her that she would get more for the money by valuing the potential of co-creation. Even before she understood this clearly, she had already felt very blessed by what the gift of sponsoring the daytrip had returned to her. Among other things, she had given Ami her wish, to enter into Roya's memories and become a part of them.

That night, when Roya and her dad arrived home after dropping off Ami and Mandy, they found a note on the door from Roya's mom explaining that she would be visiting with friends in town until late. Sarah was working the closing shift at the restaurant, so they had the evening to themselves. It was ideal because then they would have time to explore the book together and talk with Claire about setting up a meeting for the next day.

Roya's conversation with Claire was very brief, and almost unsatisfying, given how excited Roya was about having made the discovery. She had known that this was her ticket to more answers, but Claire insisted that they wait until they could meet in person to talk. Claire's voice did not match her own level of excitement, but she seemed pleased, and that was enough. She sensed that Claire was just being reserved for some reason, and she did not want to read anything into it. Tomorrow could not come soon enough, but for now, she was happy to share the book with her dad.

They even found time to clean and polish the box that contained the Egg, examining it for any markings they had missed, though they found none. They suspected that the metal rod that secured the cover was made of silver, though they could not identify the type of stone that was used for the box.

Before going to sleep, Roya laid in bed looking again at the pictures in the book. Because the picture of the angel now had meaning, she wondered if any of the other pictures might activate something in her awareness. There were five pictures all together. Along with the angel, there was a picture of what looked like a group of narwhals, surfacing to breathe. These arctic whales were easily identifiable by their long unicorn-like tusks sticking out of the water. She also saw a picture of a long, beautiful crystal rising up out of the ground, and an image of the Earth from space, but the image that drew Roya's attention the most was that of an open doorway.

As Roya studied the picture, it began to feel familiar, like some part of her knew what lay beyond, but it was not a pleasant feeling. There was something ominous about it, and yet, she also felt a sense of adventure that reminded her of the joy of a shared discovery. Just then, a part of the message from the vision in the tree resonated into her mind as if it had been waiting for this moment to describe what she was feeling. *In time, you will find the others and remember the plan.*

There was something comforting about these words, as if they were reassuring her that no matter how great the challenges were that she would face, she would never be alone. This thought, more than anything, gave her a sense of peace as she closed the book and began to relax into a deep and restful sleep.

8

THE SECRET DOOR

Halfway down a dimly lit neighborhood street in the suburbs of Chicago, an old grey van rolled to a halt in front of a small house where two teen girls wearing hiking boots and navy blue coveralls stood waiting just outside a chain-link fence. As the side door to the van slid back, the girls grabbed their backpacks from behind them and approached the van.

"Love the gear," said a voice from the van as a tall, young black man with a shaved head emerged from the shadows to greet them. "I'm Dominic," he said, offering his hand to the shorter of the two girls who had long, straight, black hair and light brown skin.

"Thanks. Andrea Martin," she said in a Hispanic accent, shaking his hand and checking out his grey coveralls. "Melanie said you're quite a break dancer."

Dominic smiled and gestured for both of them to hop in the back.

"We've all got skills. That's what I love about this group. Speaking of which, this is Aaron Taylor, one of the best street artists in the scene."

The bright-eyed teenager with short, wavy, brown hair nodded, enjoying the compliment, though he never liked to brag about his work.

"All right, let's get this show on the road," Dominic said as he slid the door shut.

"Here," said Aaron, handing both girls a particle filter mask. "We use them sometimes when we paint, but they come in handy for urban exploration."

"Thanks," said Melanie as Aaron went back to digging through a bag of gear.

"This is Echo," said Dominic, pointing to the well-built young man with short Rasta braids in the passenger seat. "He's a rapper and a beatboxer."

"Uh, correction," Echo interjected, "I'm a poet and a hip hop lyricist."

"And a one-man sound machine," Dominic praised.

"Respect," replied Echo, holding his fist up.

"And this here is Zack who was kind enough to pick us all up in the Mystery Machine." Zack cracked up at Dominic's joke, and everyone else smiled. "We met in college this last year. He's Aaron's older brother and likes to document our exploits."

"Yeah, I heard you're making a film. Thanks for inviting me," said Andrea politely.

"No problem," said Zack, as he began to accelerate. "Mel said you were cool. So, how'd you two meet?"

"Dre and I both graduated from the same high school this year, but we didn't really start hanging out until the very end. We saw each other at a show," said Melanie. "And then I found out that she loves dancing as much as we do."

"Yeah, we've just started practicing our moves together," added Andrea.

"We call each other half sisters," Melanie said with a smirk.

"Why's that?" asked Aaron.

"Cause we're half white," they both said in unison, giggling afterwards at how they so often say the same thing at the same time.

Melanie put her arm around Andrea, and suddenly, it seemed natural that she was part of the crew. The fact that they were all wearing coveralls and boots made Andrea less shy about her appearance. She was definitely the shortest and least known in the group, whereas Melanie was tall and confident and knew her place already.

"Her dad's white and her mom's Native Mexican," Melanie explained, "and my mom's white and my dad's black."

"Man, I wish *my* DNA was more interesting," Aaron commented. "You've got this crazy afro hair that's all curly and bouncy," he said to Melanie. "And both of your faces are this cool multiracial fusion."

Melanie laughed a little to herself about how much work it takes to make her hair look that way, if he only knew.

"Somehow, just being white seems a little boring to me," said Aaron.

"Don't let this guy fool you," said Echo from the front seat. "Hip hop is in his DNA. That's part of why Zack's makin' this film."

"Easy for you to say," Aaron replied. "You've got all these roots: Asian, Afro Cuban..."

"Man, I'm only one quarter Asian."

"Still!"

"So, what's this film about?" asked Andrea.

"Well, it started out as a project for my photography class last semester." Zack rolled up his window, so Andrea could hear him better in the back.

"I was shooting some of Aaron's work. Then, it became about the scenery. And *then*, Mel and Dominic brought music one time and started practicing their breaks, and I knew I had to start filming. Echo is the one who got us into exploring."

The van sped away from the neighborhood and onto the freeway, and they were all feeling an exciting vibe. The remaining light of dusk was fading fast, and the stars were as visible as they could be in the grand production of city lights. Their sense of mission and purpose made everything feel clear, like they could all read each other, and everyone trusted each other's motives.

"I don't really have a plot worked out or anything, but ultimately, it's about real people doin' real things. We're kinda makin' it up as we go along, so just be yourself and interact. Don't be shy."

"So, how'd you find out about this place we're goin' to?" Melanie asked as Echo turned around to face her from the front seat.

"Zack and I were scoping out some places to film, and then we started talkin' to this homeless guy. He said he'd been in a lot of the abandoned buildings. We asked about ones with cool graffiti, but then, he started goin' on about some place that he thought was haunted. He said none of his buddies would go near it, so we decided to check it out."

"So, is it haunted?" Melanie asked.

"Not sure, yet," teased Zack, "but we found this weird door."

"What do you mean? What's weird about it?" asked Andrea.

"I don't want to tell you anymore. It'll spoil the effect. All I can say is: this is gonna *blow... your... mind.*"

"So where exactly is this place?" asked Aaron.

"You're all sworn to secrecy, right?" Zack affirmed as heads nodded behind him.

"Yeah, the secrecy's important until we figure out what this is," added Echo. "We're going to an old abandoned factory. That's all we can say for now."

For the next twenty minutes, Aaron briefed the girls on all of the precautions they take when engaging in urban exploration. Echo selected a playlist for the stereo with his phone, but he kept the volume low enough for ease of conversation. By the time they reached their destination, they were having a lively discussion about some of their ideas for the film. Zack was adamant that he did not intend to control where it went and wanted the film to be directed by the interests of the group as they went along. Only the building with the mysterious door was part of the plan. He wanted to capture their expressions when they discovered what was behind it. Just to keep it interesting, he and Echo had deliberately not explored it much further. This way, they were all entering new territory together—where anything could happen.

"We're gonna park down the street a ways and cut across an abandoned lot," Zack explained as he rounded a corner and pulled over into a darkened street filled with old red brick buildings.

"Hey, should we have special code names?" Andrea suggested, just for fun.

"You mean like Echo?" asked Dominic.

"Yeah."

"Na, we don't need code names," said Aaron.

"Easy for you to say, *Airo*," retorted Dominic.

"Nobody calls me Airo, though. That's just my tag name."

Aaron leaned over to the window and breathed on the glass until it fogged over, then he drew a circle with a vertical line down the middle. Then, in the left half of the circle, he drew a letter A, and in the right half, he drew a letter R.

"This is how I sign my work. The line down the middle is an 'I,' which makes AIR, and the circle is the 'O,' so the word 'Airo' is sort of a hidden code. Someone once asked me if I knew who A.R. was, because they'd seen one of my pieces and didn't get the code," he smiled. "I just go by Aaron, though."

"So, where'd ya get the name Echo?" asked Andrea.

"That's how we met him," answered Zack. "Aaron and I were looking for a new place for one of his murals, and we heard someone making all these crazy noises."

"Yeah, he was playing with the echo in this old building, and we followed the sound around until we found him," said Aaron. "Zack gave him the nickname, and now he uses it as his stage name."

"I am: Echo Sound Machine," he said, following his declaration with a few beats. "I just love playing with sound."

Everyone grabbed their backpacks and hopped out. Zack handed Echo his other mini video camera. "Here, I'll handle the filming until we get inside, but be ready to shoot anything interesting. You can lead the way."

Everyone seemed to know what to do without needing instructions. As soon as Echo began to cross the street, everyone fell into place behind him, silently keeping pace with the leader. Aaron walked next to Zack, followed by Melanie, Andrea, and Dominic. The street was only dimly lit by an occasional streetlight, and it was hard to tell which buildings were abandoned and which were still in use. After only a minute on foot, the group disappeared around a corner into a dark ally, cutting across a row of buildings until they emerged from the building complex near a set of railroad tracks.

The ground sloped upward, raising the tracks slightly. The tracks were noticeably more well-lit than the surrounding area, so they quickly slid down the gravel embankment on the other side into the shadows of an empty lot between two old abandoned buildings. The walls on either side were covered with bad graffiti.

"Hey Aaron, you should fix this place up," said Dominic in a hushed voice as they all paused to take a look.

"No way," Aaron said. "These tags are territorial. Besides, vandalism like this provides a nice contrast to the work of *real* artists. If the city is ever going to transform, we have to show the difference between the new culture and crap like this."

Aaron was speaking deliberately for the camera as Zack panned from him over to the wall. There was just enough light to see half of it. Echo had moved on ahead, scoping out the rest of the lot. There were a few piles of junk in odd places around the property, and just past the buildings, across another street, was a small field.

"Hey guys. Let's keep moving," reminded Echo, waving everyone over to the edge of the field. "That's the old factory over there."

They all walked to the edge of the field, noticing a complex of abandoned buildings, barely lit by the ambient light of the surrounding city. The street they had just crossed curved around one side of the field to the left and ended in a circle drive just past the front of the old factory. The only well-lit part of the road was in front of the factory, and they were well-hidden in the dark of the field. From there, it was a short walk through dust, weeds, and the occasional odd piece of litter to the main parking lot.

As they approached, they could see a number of other smaller buildings in the shadow of the three-story factory. One looked like an old warehouse and another looked more like a small office building. The whole complex was well-hidden from any major city streets in the area, and the circle drive was the only road in or out of the property.

"Hey guys," Zack whispered. "Let's pause here for a moment and gear up."

"Why are you whispering?" Echo asked. "There's no one around to hear us."

"Good point," Zack said at a more normal volume. "But let's just keep our voices low anyway so we can hear anything else around us. You never know what might be hiding."

He was feeling cautious, though he also wanted to create even more suspense for the film.

Aaron was already digging in his backpack and produced a couple of LED headlamps that he offered to Andrea and Dominic who only had regular flashlights.

"I like these better, because I can keep my hands free," he said as he was tucking his hair under the strap of his light.

Aaron's hair was slightly longer and wavier than his older brother Zack's, who kept his short and neatly trimmed. Melanie was already wearing her LED light around her neck like it was an accessory while Zack and Echo were busy adjusting theirs.

"Just keep your lights off until we get inside," cautioned Zack.

Echo had a little pin light that he was using just to light the way around the back of the building. It was just enough light to keep them from tripping over each other in the dark of the building's shadow.

They walked in silence along the back of the factory, noticing that most of the windows had been boarded up. A feeling of excitement kept everyone on edge as they approached a door that was already opened just a crack. Echo seemed to have no fear, though that was partly because he had already scoped it out. He nudged the door open with his foot as it made a slight creaking sound. It stayed open and did not swing back as he walked straight in. By the time the girls had entered, Zack, Echo, and Aaron had already switched on their lights to illuminate the high ceiling of the main factory room.

There were steel girders visible across the ceiling, and one corner of the roof above the girders was caved in, leaving a big, gaping hole. Looking around to get their bearings, they noticed that they were on a platform with a ramp walkway that went down and to the left. The floor of the main room looked like it was about half a story below ground. There were piles of junk in every corner, and you could see holes in the ground indicating where heavy machinery had been bolted to the floor. The main room connected with many other levels and platforms that had concrete pillars throughout.

Dominic pulled the door in behind them, leaving it open just a little, and the whole group walked down the ramp. Echo and Zack were now walking together in the lead. The sound of their footsteps was complemented by the flapping of wings as the pigeons roosting on the girders near the hole adjusted to the presence of the visitors.

"This is the main factory floor," Zack said as they navigated around several piles of debris. "The other half of the building has a number of offices and workrooms, but *we* are headed for the basement."

The cavernous room seemed peaceful somehow, and the presence of the group filled the space. The sense of being explorers took over, and everyone began to feel the wonder of the unknown. Just ahead, beneath a long platform that stood overlooking the factory floor, a wide ramp led down to a lower level.

"So, what's down there?" Dominic asked.

"This is where it gets interesting," Echo said as he began leading the way down.

"On this level, it looks like mostly storage space, but…"

They all walked down the ramp and onto the lower platform, noticing doors that opened into rooms on either side. Then, he said, "Look behind you."

They all turned around except Zack, who had already been walking backward to film their entrance into the lower level. To the side of where the ramp ended, a hallway extended around behind the ramp that led to a doorway.

"We had to break the lock," said Zack, as Echo opened the door to reveal a staircase leading down.

"How many levels does this thing have?" wondered Andrea.

"That's an interesting question," said Zack, indicating that he might know more than he was letting on. They continued down two long flights of stairs into the basement: a single large room with numerous concrete support pillars. It stretched the length of the factory floor above, and it looked like it used to be the boiler room, even though it was hard to tell what anything was. The ceiling was high and lots of pipes were connected to it. Heaps of scrap metal and other pieces of equipment were scattered in small piles around the room. Some of it was recognizable, like an old broken jackhammer that Aaron nearly tripped over as they began to fan out into the room. The whole area looked like an abandoned construction zone.

"Wow, this is really cool. What's so weird about this place?" Melanie asked.

"Check this out," Zack said. "You see those cinder blocks stacked against the wall? Echo and I found them in the corner. We thought we might try to build something, so we started pulling them off the pile. That's when we found this." Zack pointed his camera and zoomed in on a large metal door. "It was hidden behind all of the blocks."

"Whoa!" gushed Andrea, impressed by the find.

Echo approached the door while everyone else crowded around behind him. Without hesitation, he lifted the large metal latch and swung the door back toward him until it opened wide. The group gathered around the entrance to what looked like another storage room, except down at the end and to the left, they saw yet *another* opening. For a moment, they all huddled around the entrance, eyes wide with curiosity, and then Echo stepped in.

"There was a wall of cinder blocks stacked in here when we first found it, but we cleared those out, too," said Echo as he turned around and started filming. "There was a padlock on it, but we cut that off."

"Come on in. Check it out," he said, walking backward to the far end of the room as the rest of the group cautiously made their way in.

Zack followed behind them with the camera while Melanie and Andrea moved in behind Echo, who now stood in front of a metal sliding door that was embedded into the wall of the storage room. Echo's fearlessness seemed to set everyone at ease, allowing curiosity to reign free. He waited until everyone was inside, and Zack placed a cinder block in the way of the entrance as a doorstop, just to make sure they would not get trapped. Even so, they always carried a hammer, a bolt cutter, and a pry bar, just in case.

Once everyone was in position, Echo slid the door back to reveal a hidden hallway about ten feet wide that extended to the left and to the right. Echo walked through and leaned up against the wall, raising his camera to catch the look on everyone's faces. Andrea and Melanie both leaned forward together, peeking around the corner to the right while Aaron peeked around to the left.

"What do you see?" asked Dominic, who could not quite fit between Aaron and the girls.

"Whoa!" said Andrea, "This is some kind of secret passageway."

Echo kept his face turned so everyone's lights did not shine directly into his eyes.

"What the heck is this place?" asked Aaron.

"This is crazy! Here," Melanie said, stepping into the hallway to make room for Dominic. "You've gotta see this."

Looking down the right passage, they could see that it went on for about sixty feet before disappearing around a corner to the left. The left passage stretched as much as a hundred feet, but several other hallways shot off to the right.

"All of these hallways that extend off this one go well beyond the perimeter of the building above us," Echo explained. "Is this freaky, or what?"

"What was all of this used for, and how did it get here?" asked Melanie, dumbfounded.

"I have no idea, but it looks like it's been abandoned for decades," responded Zack.

Echo took the lead down the left passage and took the first hallway that led off to the right. From there, they could see doorframes without doors on either side of the hallway stretching off into the distance. Again, Echo walked right into the first one on the left without hesitation, and the group followed until all of them were inside a long rectangular room with concrete walls that appeared clean and featureless.

"So, what do you think?" beamed Echo.

"My mind is officially blown," said Aaron.

"Yeah, that's kinda what I said to Zack when we first found this place," agreed Echo.

Zack was hanging back, trying to capture everyone's reactions as they were walking around the room.

Suddenly, Dominic sprang forward onto his hands, walking on them until he could lean his feet up against the wall. Then he looked back, smiling at the cameras from upside down.

"Man, this place is wild!" he said as he pushed off the wall with his feet and then launched into a backflip. "We could bring some music down here and film a crazy break video all through here."

"Right! Now you're talkin'," said Zack. "So, Aaron. What do you think? Is this the kind of canvas you've been looking for, or what?"

"It's got potential," Aaron acknowledged.

"We could make this into anything," Zack went on. "You could even bring in some other artists."

"Yeah," added Echo. "We could transform this place and make a film about it but keep everyone guessing about the location."

"I'd be a little worried about ventilation," said Aaron, always concerned with logistical matters. "We need to explore this further."

"So, how big is this place?" asked Melanie, stepping back out into the hall.

"We didn't go much further than this," said Echo. "To be honest, we were so freaked out at first, we just wanted to get back out and see what we could learn about it from the outside."

Everyone followed Melanie out into the hallway, and they began to walk farther down, trying to focus on what lay at the end.

"Yeah, we looked up this factory and found out that it was built back in the seventies," said Zack. "I think it belonged to some company that made tools and construction supplies and stuff."

"So, why would they need all this hidden space?" Andrea asked.

"That's what we're hoping to find out," answered Zack.

They all walked down the hallway, pausing at each doorway to peer inside. Each room was empty with no markings. The whole site was a hollow concrete shell. Coming to the end of the long hallway, they found another hallway that went both directions. Echo led them to the left about twenty feet before they came to an opening that made everyone's jaw drop. This was exactly what Zack had been hoping for: a surprise.

Neither Zack nor Echo had gone this far before, precisely because they wanted to leave some unknowns to share with the rest of the group. But this was more than they expected. The complex of underground rooms was larger than they anticipated. In their imagination, they had thought that the main hallways, visible from where they had come in, were part of a large rectangular complex with several sets of rooms, but now they were staring at the entrance to a set of stairs going down to an even *lower* level.

"Did you guys know about this?" asked Dominic, in awe.

"No way. I thought there was just one hidden level," said Zack.

"What do we do?" Andrea hesitated, a little scared to go deeper.

"Let's check it out," persuaded Echo, proceeding a little more cautiously than before.

Down two short flights of stairs, they found themselves on a lower level with more hallways and empty rooms, but this time, the floor was smooth, not concrete like the level above. The walls were painted white, and they could see where the ceiling once contained fixtures for fluorescent lights.

"What is this place doing here?" asked Dominic. "Is anyone as creeped out by this as I am?"

"I feel ya, man. This place is spooky," admitted Aaron.

"Let's split up and see if we can get a sense of the layout," suggested Zack. "Echo. You take Mel and Aaron. I'll take Dre and Dominic."

"Are you sure that's a good idea?" asked Melanie, concerned. "You don't think anyone could be down here, do you?"

The idea gave everyone the chills.

"No," replied Zack. "I think it's just us, but let's just take a quick survey and meet back here in about five minutes."

The team split up, each trying to find the end of the first hallway that they had just entered from the stairs. Even though they assumed they were alone, everyone proceeded as quietly as possible. The sound of their movements was so noticeable in the dead silence that being heard was unavoidable; it heightened their adrenaline to think that someone might be listening.

Echo, Aaron, and Melanie walked past a number of corridors, checking each one out just a little before moving on. Eventually, the hall began to curve off to the right, but they ran into piles of debris that blocked the way through. The rooms along the way looked more developed than the ones on the level above. Some of them were painted, and some had vents. Aaron wondered if the ventilation system ran through some part of the old factory that they had not yet seen. That was about all they found before they decided to scurry back to meet up with the others.

Zack, Andrea, and Dominic had not returned to the starting point yet, but Echo heard them coming and signaled them with his light from way down the hall. When they converged on the other group's position, Zack had this wild look in his eyes.

"We found another staircase!" he exclaimed, trying not to speak too loudly.

"What?!" whispered Melanie. "How far down does this thing go?"

"Check... this... out," said Zack, dramatically.

Just around the corner from the end of the hallway was the entrance to another stairwell, but this time, it went down more than one flight. Melanie leaned forward, adjusting the position of her headlamp so that it was better aimed down into the deep. Between the metal rails that ran down each flight of stairs was a space where they could see many more flights below.

"You've gotta be kidding me," gasped Aaron. "How did this thing get built without anyone knowing?"

"I don't know," replied Zack. "It just keeps getting weirder. Did you guys find anything?"

"Looks like the rooms down there have vents, but the end of the hallway was blocked off with junk. This whole floor looks a little bigger than the level above, but we'd have to explore the rest of the corridors to be sure."

"Forget that," dismissed Echo. "Let's see how deep this thing goes."

"Is everyone in favor of taking the stairs?" asked Zack.

Everyone looked around, absorbing a priceless moment of wonder, mixed with fear and insatiable curiosity. They did not even need to nod their heads yes. It was in their eyes. They had stumbled onto something truly mysterious and fantastic: a real adventure.

Down the stairs they crept, deeper and deeper into the hidden building structure, pausing at each floor to notice if there were any differences. The lower they went, the more developed it became. By the fifth level down, they noticed a different kind of floor: checkered, white and black. It was starting to look more like they were in an abandoned school or hospital.

On one of the floors, they could see a room at the corner of two intersecting hallways that was open with counters, which looked like a reception area.

Seven floors down, they encountered the first doors on some of the rooms, though the locks and handles had been removed. It looked like the whole building complex had been cleared of any evidence that might reveal what it was used for, or perhaps the materials had just been efficiently recycled. Only a few desks and chairs remained in some of the rooms and an occasional pile of debris—nothing with any information on it.

Floor nine appeared to be the bottom floor, and they were just beginning to debate how they wanted to proceed when a sound began to grow in the distance.

"Do you hear that?" asked Aaron.

"Shhh," whispered Zack. "Just listen."

Everybody heard it by now: a low rumble; more of a vibration running through the building than a sound, at first. But then there was a high-pitched tone, like air rushing through something and almost whistling—and then it was gone.

"What was that?" whispered Aaron, alarmed.

"It sounded a little like the subway," suggested Andrea.

"Yeah, but that's impossible," replied Zack.

"Well, it's pretty impossible that this building is here, and yet it is," stated Andrea.

"Girl's got a point," agreed Dominic.

"I think we have to keep going and find the source of that sound," prodded Echo.

"This time, let's stick together," Zack suggested.

They all walked down the main hallway toward where they had heard the sound until they came to an intersection. There was something very different about this level. The hallways generally looked wider. They found restrooms next to each other, but there were no mirrors, and the plumbing didn't work. For a moment, they had fanned out to examine several rooms near the intersection, but just as they were coming back into formation, another sound took everyone by surprise. This time it was the recognizable sound of footsteps.

Everyone quickly ducked into one of the empty rooms and became very quiet. Zack and Aaron immediately switched off their lights and everyone else followed their lead except Melanie, who looked stunned by what was happening. Zack reached over to her headlamp and clicked it off for her. Now they were totally in the dark. Melanie and Andrea grabbed each other and held tight for a feeling of security, as their hearts were racing, and everyone became perfectly still.

Down the hallway and around the corner of the intersection, lights began to appear, moving up and down as someone was walking until it became apparent that more than one person was coming. The footsteps grew louder and the lights brighter until they heard the voices of two young men. Their words started to become clear just before they reached the intersection.

"Are you sure this is safe?" asked one of them.

"Yes, absolutely," replied the other. "I wouldn't be in here if I didn't think we would get away with it. The Superminds have better things to do than patrol the abandons. If they were as alert as they want us to think, we wouldn't have even succeeded in making the hole."

"But what if they're waiting to catch us in the act?"

"Don't even think about it. Keep your mind clear," commanded the confident one. "If you start worrying that they will see you, then you might create it. Don't even give them a signal to hone in on. Just keep thinking about work. Easier to hide our memories that way."

"I'm trying."

"Looks like there's a restroom just down here. Probably out of commission, but I need to go either way."

Zack immediately tried to back away from the doorway, pushing several of the others behind him farther back into the empty room. They all ducked down trying not to make a sound. Zack's heartbeat was pounding so loud, he began to wonder if it was audible. They all froze as the two young men passed right by the door and turned into the men's restroom.

Across the hall, they heard the unmistakable sound of pee streaming into the empty toilet bowl, splashing at the bottom as it began to collect. Dominic was biting his lip until the second stream began to splash, and then he whispered, "Man, I gotta pee."

"Why didn't you go when we were in there?" Echo whispered back.

"Quiet," Zack admonished, frustrated with the noise.

Dominic had not really noticed his bladder until they had crouched down and been forced to hold still, but the sound of peeing made him hyper aware of his own bodily need. To make matters worse, he was about to crack up laughing, which was his way of dealing with the anxiety of the situation, though his fear had slightly diminished from the realization that there were only two of them.

Everyone held their breath as they heard the two young men coming back out. "Which way do we go next?" said one of them. They paused to take a look around, and then they froze at the sound of an unknown noise.

Zack's stomach had let out a sudden grumble, but that was not what they heard. Realizing that neither of their bodies were cooperating, Dominic tensed up all of his muscles, trying to hold in the laughter, but this caused him to lose his balance. In a split second, Dominic put his arm out to steady himself, and then his arm connected with Echo who lost his balance completely, falling backward from where he was squatting until the pry bar in his backpack struck the floor through the material, creating a loud thud.

"What was that!?" said one of the young men.

"I don't know, let's check it out."

The two proceeded cautiously to the door of the open room, which was ten feet away. At first glance, their lights fell on empty space as they stood at the doorway, but as they slowly panned around to the left, they began to see boots, hands, and then several pairs of eyes blinking in the light.

"Ho!" said the confident one as they both backed away with a look of shock and surprise.

"Let's get out of here," said the other as he turned around and ran toward the intersection. The confident one was still backing away to his friend's position, keeping his light focused on the doorway where he could still make out some of the crouching figures.

"Wait!" called out Echo. "Don't be afraid."

He had gotten to his feet now and stepped in front of Zack.

"We're not armed," he continued, stepping out into the hallway with his hands up.

The young men appeared stunned, like deer in headlights. They had stopped and were standing at the intersection, prepared to make a break for it down the hallway back the way they came.

"There are six of us. We're just explorers," Echo explained as the others began to switch on their lights and emerge from the room.

"Stay here, guys," he said to the group. "I'm just gonna make contact, first."

Echo had run into this situation before while exploring abandoned buildings. He was using what he thought of as explorer etiquette: do not do anything to intimidate; introduce yourself; be friendly and kind. The two young men relaxed a little when they saw that he was approaching alone.

"I'm Echo," he said. "We didn't mean to frighten you. We just didn't know who you were, so we were hiding."

He was about ten feet away but stopped to give them enough space to feel safe.

"Who are you guys?"

Both young men looked about the same age as Echo and the others. They wore jeans and black, long-sleeved shirts with a couple of buttons under the neck. Both had hats with lights on them, and one of them was carrying a backpack. Their skin was pale, and their faces looked somewhat Asian.

"We didn't think anyone would be here," said the confident one. "What sector are you from?"

"We aren't from any sector. We came in through the factory."

"Factory?" they both said in unison, looking at each other perplexed.

"How did *you* get in here?" asked Echo, becoming perplexed himself.

Gradually, the rest of the group inched forward, listening to the conversation. Echo then waved them over, feeling that the newcomers were a little less intimidated.

"These are my friends," he introduced as they all walked up. "This is Melanie, Zack, Aaron, Dominic, and Andrea."

"Hi," said Dominic, and everyone else just waved.

Zack was holding the camera down at his side, but it was pointed up and rolling.

"Sorry for my hesitation," said the confident one, "but what factory are you talking about?"

"You mean there's another way into this place?" asked Dominic in disbelief.

"We came in through the only entrance we know," stated Echo, "about eleven or twelve floors up in an old abandoned factory."

"Whaaa" said the nervous one. "You mean you're from the surface!"

"Where else would we be from?" asked Andrea, dumbfounded by the unusual question.

"Yo, dude just asked me what sector we're from," emphasized Echo.

"It is a great honor to meet you. I'm Lex," said the confident one, "and this is my friend Ram. We are also explorers."

Their whole demeanor changed as they began taking in more of the details of the newcomers. They seemed oddly astonished at the group.

"You must tell us more about the surface," entreated Ram, excitedly. "We've only heard stories. Can you really get there from here?"

"You've got to be kidding, right?" bursted Andrea.

"Kidding?" said Ram, as if he did not know what the word meant.

"Wait a minute. You mean you two came from somewhere down *here?*" asked Aaron, incredulously.

"Yes," replied Lex. "We are not supposed to be here, though. It's forbidden, but we wanted to explore."

"Can you show us where you came from?" asked Echo.

"Sure. Follow us," said Lex.

The excitement was unimaginably high as they followed Lex and Ram down the hallway from where they had entered. Questions were exploding in everyone's minds, but Lex knew that it would be important to establish where they had come from before the real exploration could begin.

Lex led them down one final flight of stairs. The hallway at the bottom continued straight until running into a brick wall. The odd thing was that the bricks were completely different than the surrounding walls.

Just before reaching the brick wall, Lex went through a doorway on the right where they could see a sledge hammer laying on the floor next to a hole in the wall.

"They sealed the main entrance with layers of bricks and concrete," said Lex, "but the wall of the adjacent room was still thin enough to break through."

He seemed genuinely proud of his accomplishment.

"What's on the other side?" asked Echo.

"This is an old transport terminal. But this stop hasn't been used in decades," explained Ram. He reached through the hole and slid back a piece of black plexiglass that had been covering the hole from the other side. "Go ahead, you can look through."

Echo was already on his knees. The hole was near the floor and was just big enough for a person to easily crawl through. Echo did not waste any time and was thrilled to go first. Lex and Ram followed him, and then the rest of the group. They all walked forward to the edge of the platform, shining their lights down on the tracks and examining the perfectly round shape of the tunnel. There were no lights, but they could see a flat walkway running along the other side of the tube.

At this point, they were all enthralled with a mixture of excitement, disbelief, and rampant curiosity. The fact that they were standing some twelve stories below a supposed factory in a secret underground transport tunnel that had been operating for decades was a shocking consideration. Lex and Ram were just as stunned to be standing in front of actual surface dwellers. Quietly, they stood by observing everyone's reactions.

"These tracks aren't anything like the subway, and it's way too deep to connect with anything on the surface," speculated Aaron.

"Yeah, I'm trying to figure this out," said Zack, who had to remind himself to keep filming. The sheer scale of anything this big so deep underground was mind-boggling.

"Well, you two wanted to blow my mind," acknowledged Dominic.

"So where does this go?" inquired Echo, focusing on their tour guides. "You say you live down here?"

"We live and work in sector nine," said Lex. "It's only minutes away by transport, but we had to walk for almost half an hour to get here from one of the working terminals. We only knew about this place because we found an old archive of architectural schematics. One of them showed what used to be an active terminal here."

"Wait a minute. What's sector nine?" asked Zack.

"Sector nine," began Ram, just remembering that, as outsiders, they would have no idea what he was talking about. "It's just another part of the city."

"You mean there's a whole *city* down here?" asked Zack with a shocked look on his face.

"Wow!" exclaimed Ram. "You guys know as little about our world as we do about yours. This is just one of *many* cities, and most of them are connected by these transport tunnels. We aren't allowed to visit any of them, though. You have to have the right clearance to move between cities."

"How many people live in your city?" asked Andrea.

"We don't know," answered Lex, "but I tried to calculate how many people live in our sector once based upon the number of living quarters. I estimated over thirty thousand, and that's just sector nine."

"I wanna see it," implored Aaron with a sense of determination as he turned to Lex.

"See what?" asked Zack, with his camera trained on Aaron.

"The city. Can you take us there?" he asked Lex.

"Whoa, I don't think that would be a good idea," replied Ram, nervously.

"Yo, I'm not gettin' caught down here. I say we head back to the surface," urged Dominic.

"Yeah, I'm with Dominic," agreed Echo. "Haven't you got enough footage?" he asked Zack.

No one had expected to make such a wild discovery, and their emotions were swirling with both excitement and fear. Nearly everyone felt the same way: that if they could get back home safely, they could protect the secret knowledge they had discovered. This was too important to risk getting caught, because then they would not be able to share this discovery with others. And yet, they could not help a lingering curiosity about exploring further.

Lex was silent, taking in everyone's reaction to Aaron's idea.

"Would that even be possible?" asked Melanie. "Would it be safe?"

"It would definitely *not* be safe," affirmed Ram, intending to register his opinion with Lex. "It's dangerous enough for *us* to be out here."

"He's right," agreed Lex. "We could never get all of you there and back safely past the main terminal. It would be too risky, but we might be able to take one of you," he offered.

"What?!" questioned Ram, with a look of surprise. "Are you crazy?"

"What if we showed the professor what we found?" he asked Ram emphatically. "Maybe we could finally get him to talk. You know how we're always trying to get him to talk about the surface."

"Hang on," asked Aaron. "What've you been told about the surface?"

"They say that you are a dying race and that there's nothing but disease and pollution up there. They say that we are the ones that were smart enough to find a way to survive underground."

"And you just believed it?" asked Andrea.

"Not entirely," Lex defended. "Some of us know that there has to be more to the truth. It's obvious that they don't want us to make a connection with the surface, but it makes sense to me that we're still connected. You guys are the proof."

"You don't really know what you are getting into, though," said Ram to Aaron. "Most people down here are a lot different than you. Our thoughts are different, and if you don't think like we do…if your minds don't vibrate like ours do, it would stand out."

"You don't *seem* very different than us," observed Aaron.

"That's because we are choosing to be more reflective," explained Lex. "If you want to come with us," he said to Aaron, "we would have to put you into the Frequency."

Everyone looked around bewildered at what was happening. They had discovered a hidden underground civilization. The threat of getting caught was ever present, and now Aaron was talking about separating from the group to go right into the heart of an unknown danger. Zack dropped his camera down and looked at his brother, Aaron, questioning with his eyes if he really thought this was a good idea. They gazed silently for a moment until Aaron felt clear about what needed to happen. There would never be another opportunity like this, and he was certain of it. He was already committed to the plan.

With surrender and a calm state of mind, Aaron turned to Lex and said, "Tell us about the Frequency."

9

THE GUARDIANS OF KNOWLEDGE

Being fairly new in town, Frank Carter welcomed the opportunity to get to know some of the other parents better, though the circumstances surrounding Sunday's invitation were highly unusual. Still, he always liked to take the time to prepare himself and look his best for any occasion. Standing a little over six feet tall, he had a medium build and short hair that was a little dark, but mostly grey. And even though he liked the way his hair looked, he often wore a favorite black Indy hat, made of 100% wool, with a bonded leather band. He was in his mid-fifties and had strong facial features with an intense expression that gave him a look of authority, even though a light in his eyes conveyed compassion.

Today, he emerged from his home dressed in a pair of grey slacks, a short-sleeved, blue, button-down shirt, and the Indy hat. Whatever this was about, he had never seen his daughters so excited. They could not stop talking all morning about the discovery, but they wanted to save the details for the meeting: something about a book, an egg, and some kind of energy that allows you to see spirits. While he couldn't possibly say no to something that had Ami and Mandy so excited, it was Mandy's words that had haunted him all night since they had returned from hiking: "What if this thing could allow us to see Mom?"

It had been four years since his wife, Cindy, had passed away, and not a day went by that he didn't think about her. The family bond they all shared was deep enough that they could never feel totally separate from her. Frank always said that a part of her spirit lived on in each of them, and he could easily see that in his daughters. Though Ami's contemplative nature was more like her dad, her empathy and her cute boyish features were a lot like her mother. Mandy was just Mandy, a light unto herself. She was the creative spirit that her mother always wished she could be, and her laugh reminded him of Cindy.

Roya was waiting on the front porch when they rounded the corner of her street, and she walked out to greet them. Frank had only seen Roya a few times, but already had a good sense of her character. He had observed that she seemed to have a highly developed intellect and was emotionally mature for her age. He could easily understand why Ami and Mandy liked hanging out with her, because she had a way of balancing their differences.

Roya invited them in and poured them each a glass of lemonade. Frank shook hands with Raymond, who was standing near the entrance to the dining area, and then he greeted Sarah and Soraya, who were already seated at the dining room table. The Egg was standing in the middle of the table, and the black stone box was resting on the nearby kitchen counter.

Raymond invited everyone to take a seat.

"So, what exactly is this thing, and where did you find it?" asked Frank, intrigued.

"We found it buried in a field over in Herkimer County," explained Raymond. "Roya basically guided us to the field, and a little technology did the rest." He did not yet feel like revealing that he could sense energy with his hands. "As for what it is, that can only be explained by what we experienced. Almost as soon as we dug it up, it sort of switched on and was creating these vibrations of energy. We actually ended up moving it into a cave, because there were some people nearby, and we didn't want them to see it. That's when it got *really* interesting."

"Yeah, the girls said that it filled the cave with energy that made you see spirits," remarked Frank.

"In a manner of speaking, yes," said Raymond. "It seemed to generate some kind of field that connected us with the realms of Spirit. It was like a bridge opened up, and two beings of light appeared to cross over into our space and speak with us."

"That's incredible! And where were the two of you?" Frank asked Sarah and Soraya who were sitting across from him.

"We weren't with them when this happened," responded Soraya. "We haven't actually seen it do any of what they described." Frank noted a slight tone of lingering skepticism in her voice but wondered if she was just taking that stance until she knew what everyone else was thinking. She did not seem like the kind of personality that liked to be the first to present a new view.

"Yeah, when I came home from work last night, they were all sitting around the table talking about this thing," contributed Sarah, reflecting her mother's tone.

"So, what did these beings of light say?" asked Frank.

"I wrote it all down afterwards, as near as I can remember. In my excitement, I could have easily lost some of what they said. Luckily, Roya has a good memory. It was short, but very meaningful."

Raymond handed Frank two pages of writing that contained nearly a word-for-word transcript of the dialogue with the two beings. "I want you to read this first, because they mentioned uniting our families for a common purpose."

Frank studied the words very carefully as the rest of the group sat quietly, waiting to hear his response. Sarah had *The Circle and the Stars* book in her lap and was reading one of the chapters.

Soraya had already read much of it with Roya over breakfast while Sarah was sleeping in, and they had a lively discussion about the meaning of all the synchronicities. Were it not for the book, the story of the Egg would have seemed unbelievable to Soraya, but the anomaly of the book by itself was enough to convince her that this was something highly unusual that called for an open mind.

"This is really fascinating, to say the least. So how can you make it work?" asked Frank. "And who are these Guardians we're supposed to get in touch with?"

"Roya already invited a woman that we believe may be one of these Guardians," explained Raymond. "She should be here any minute. I'm afraid I don't know how to make it work, though. I wasn't too concerned about that after what the guides said, but I think it might be controlled from their end."

"Can I touch it?" asked Frank, unable to contain his growing curiosity.

"Sure. I don't know how fragile the insides are, so I wouldn't shake it or anything, but you can pick it up," said Raymond, feeling a little protective of the device.

Frank ran his fingers over the smooth, beige surface and then tapped on it lightly a few times. It sounded hollow, and each time he tapped, something continued to vibrate for a second on the inside. Next, he picked it up and held it for a moment, feeling its weight and looking at it from different angles.

Just then, they heard a knock at the door, and Roya leaped up to get it. She opened the door, and in stepped Claire. She was wearing a dark grey dress suit and a white, button-up shirt with a collar, and to Roya's disappointment, she still had the black wig. As usual, she looked very professional, like she was ready to go to work.

"Hello, my name is Claire."

"Nice to meet you. I'm Soraya, Roya's mother...and this is my other daughter, Sarah, and my husband Raymond."

"And this is Ami and Mandy, and their dad, Frank," added Roya.

"It's a pleasure to meet all of you," said Claire, taking her seat. "So, is this the object?"

"Yes," answered Raymond. "And we heard you had quite a role in helping us find it."

Claire took the only seat that was left at the head of the table and looked around the room, acknowledging everyone with her eyes. Roya observed her behavior closely as she went back to her seat, opposite Claire, knowing better than anyone that Claire had a way about her that seemed more conscious. Her movements always seemed graceful and deliberate.

"It's true. I told Roya that she was meant to find something, but I did not know exactly what it would be," said Claire.

"And how did you know Roya?" asked Soraya.

"I suppose I should start at the beginning; or, at least, *a* beginning. Sarah, do you mind?" asked Claire, gesturing for her to pass over *The Circle and the Stars* book, which she then held as she began talking.

"Several months ago, I was attending a meeting with a council that I'm connected with, when we were met with an extraordinary light, many times more intense than what you encountered through this device. Through the presence of this light came many pulses of energy that focused right into the space in front of us, and then this book appeared. We spent a long time examining it and were certain that it was an artifact from the future. We often work with light from the future, but we had never received a physical object before."

"What do you mean when you say that you work with light from the future?" asked Soraya, perplexed by Claire's casual way of speaking about such unusual things. Claire could tell immediately that Soraya was trying to make what she had just heard fit into her current paradigm, a process Claire knew would have to shift.

"This technology is not foreign to me," she said, glancing at the Egg. "It's just a different version of what I'm used to, but it's very ancient. Most of the time, when you work with beings of light like the ones you encountered, you are working with a more expanded awareness of time. Light from the future, as we are learning, is part of how reality is created on a very large scale. The future can create its own past leading up to it."

Claire handed the book to Frank, so he could examine it as she continued talking. Again, Roya noticed Claire's actions carried an elevated level of conscious intention behind them; from the way she told the story, to the way she was handling the book. Roya could almost see what looked like a blue ball of energy that Claire had formed around the book with her gaze, using the book to then pass over the ball of energy to its intended recipient.

Frank looked quite astonished when he felt the lightness of the book, and the blue energy seemed to be absorbed through his hands. He looked as though he was becoming aware of something that Claire intended for him to realize: that he *was* connected to all of this, and that he was no less important than anyone else at the table, even though he felt like he was the last to know.

"When we examined the book," Claire continued, "we found the inscription that mentioned the Flower Memorial Library in Watertown, and we decided that someone would have to take the book there. The only way to find out what this meant was to carry out the intentions of the author, and it was decided that I was meant to go. We expected that once the book was placed in the library, someone would be guided to it, but we also received instructions that this person would be able to find an artifact that symbolized humanity's potential for transformation. This was to be the sign that we could trust this person with our secrets. What we did not expect is that this book was designed to bring all of you together to make a shared discovery. Only now does it make sense to me that Roya's age necessitates that her family accompany her, and the same is true of her friends."

Claire knew that she had just opened up a difficult conversation, but she was prepared to lead it toward her intended outcome. It was a delicate path to walk. She knew that even possessing this technology was dangerous, and she was concerned that it had already been activated. If the energy signature had been noticed, it was only a matter of time before they were traced. Her challenge was to convince everyone to follow her, while still empowering them to make their own choice. She was calm and patient with their process, but alert for any intuitive danger signals that might prompt a more straightforward approach. Her task now was to keep everyone aligned within an intuitive corridor of safety that would complete her mission—a mission that she could not yet fully disclose.

"Accompany her where?" asked Raymond.

"The place where I must take this technology to keep it safe," replied Claire, "but before I get to that, are there any other questions?"

"Yes. How does this technology work? Where does it get its power?" Raymond continued to question.

"This device is what we call a Resonator. It contains a set of filaments and structures that act as conductors. They work with the harmonic frequencies of the human body and chakra system, like tuning forks that entrain you with a range of frequencies that the guides use to communicate. It amplifies the natural ability humans have to connect with the invisible world, but it also acts as the physical vocal cords for the higher beings of light that you are connecting with. Devices like this can be used to strengthen the connection between dimensions, making the connection more accessible from both sides."

"That's fascinating!" exclaimed Frank.

"But what about all of that light?" inquired Raymond. "Was the device generating energy or just receiving and dispersing it?"

"A Resonator like this is designed to be a bridge," Claire continued. "It's powered by you, the Earth, and energy from the realm of the guides. Your bodies have a natural but mostly dormant connection to the light of the higher dimensions. The guides are just using a very powerful focus of attention to bridge many different levels of light vibration together with the help of this Resonator. The most important part of the connection that makes the communication possible is your rapport with the guides and with each other. There is a spiritual bond that ranges through many vibrations of reality, making it easier for the guides to reach you."

"So, could we learn how to make such connections without the technology?" asked Roya, thinking about her connection with the angel.

"Absolutely," assured Claire. "A whole hidden world of people exist who are adept at communicating with Spirit." As Claire said this, she looked into Roya's eyes, and Roya was certain that Claire was sending her the image of where she was talking about.

"We were hoping you could clarify something that the guides said to us," invited Raymond. "They said that we were in danger of being discovered by the sentries that monitor this part of the energy spectrum. What did they mean by that?"

"I am glad you asked that, because it will help explain what we must do next. To put it simply, this device is a form of suppressed technology. There are powerful psychics and even nonphysical entities who work for this suppression agency and have the ability to sense the use of devices like this. If your guides had not broken contact, you might have attracted a lot of unwanted attention, and we can't rule out the possibility that you are already under observation."

Roya could tell that Claire did not want to frighten anyone, but she sensed there might be some kind of real, yet elusive, danger that Claire was concerned about.

"Who exactly is suppressing this technology and why?" asked Frank.

"That is a more difficult question to answer. It is not just *technology* that is being suppressed, but knowledge and awareness of a greater multidimensional reality that humanity is starting to remember. The knowledge of what this device is capable of—and of what the human body is capable of, for that matter—is dangerous to those who want to keep humanity in the dark. But ask yourself: would anyone be able to suppress knowledge of human potential if humanity itself were not afraid of that knowledge?"

"It sounds like you're suggesting that we are just as responsible as they are for creating the suppression," questioned Raymond. "But aren't they creating karma with all of this secrecy and control that will come back on them at some point? I always thought that we were just tolerating the ignorance and arrogance of the people who needed these karmic lessons."

"That's one way to see it. But from another perspective, the suppressors are only doing what humanity's denial of the truth demands. They are only playing the roles that humanity creates for them. Most people believe they are disempowered under the structures that run the world, but the world is only a mirror of their own thoughts. Part of the knowledge that is being suppressed is the fact that you can change the world with the power of thought." She paused for a moment to let that piece of truth sink in.

"Even with what the four of you witnessed yesterday, you've barely begun to explore how much humanity has hidden from itself. But what you must understand is that this denial of a wider reality gives an advantage to those who want to exploit humanity. The sooner humanity chooses to remember what it has forgotten, the safer it will become," Claire explained.

Until that moment, Soraya had not considered that she was in denial of a greater reality, but the idea that she might be contributing to a collective pattern that made humanity vulnerable to exploitation was unsettling. Claire knew that she was conveying a level of responsibility about one's creative power that was confronting to the part of the human ego that feared its connection to the greater reality. But she also saw the potential that the journey of the group could catalyze a shift in consciousness for everyone present.

Frank looked like he was deeply considering everything Claire was saying while he was staring at the Egg, and around the room, Roya noticed sparks of recognition in everyone's expression as Claire continued.

"You all sense it, I can tell…there's an elusive presence of control that's lurking behind many global organizations and events, exploiting and even reinforcing human ignorance. And you're hoping to find the doorway into a world where such control does not exist before it's too late."

This last statement excited Roya. She could feel her family beginning to experience Claire's ability to crystallize awareness of the unseen into something familiar. Claire was speaking consciously about a realization that had been on the edge of everyone's awareness to one degree or another for some time. On some level, Roya had felt that part of her purpose was to push the boundaries of her family's consciousness, but up until this point, she had not known how. All she knew is that it felt like Claire was helping.

"So, are you saying that if humanity stopped being afraid of this new awareness and embraced it, the control would come to an end?" questioned Frank.

"I'd like to think it could be that easy," replied Claire sincerely.

"Easy!" Soraya snapped. "I don't have that much faith in humanity. It's hard to imagine that so many people would just stop being afraid and choose some other reality that we can't even see."

Roya was fascinated by her mother's words, because she sensed that she was speaking subconsciously about herself.

"But that is where *you* come in," said Claire to Soraya. "If you wait around for humanity to get over its fears, you will miss the opportunity to correct the course of history. Humanity needs more than an awakening. It needs bold and courageous action that can cause the change that is needed."

"Like what? What kind of courageous action is needed?" Roya asked.

Claire smiled at her, feeling her willingness to go the distance. "That is what we are here to discover. It is what brought me to you."

"You said you would explain where you wanted to take us," Raymond reminded her.

"There's not much time," Claire warned. "But my hope is that what you have learned from the book and this ancient technology will be enough to convince you to trust me. The book was clearly designed to bring all of us together for a shared purpose. Now I believe that shared purpose holds the answer to a Great Dilemma," she paused for a few seconds, "which is why I have been given permission to show you what my people have been guarding." Roya and Ami looked at each other, and their eyes were wide with excitement.

"It's the only way you will be able to have another experience of this technology, but where we are going, you may not be able to come back from immediately. And in order to get there, you must be willing to let go of everything you think you know about human history and the nature of this planet. If you are too attached to your current worldview, your resistance to change will prevent you from completing the journey before we have even arrived at our destination. It's essential that we stick together as a group from here on out."

Sarah and her mother looked a little resistant to the idea of going somewhere they could not return from immediately.

"I have to work on Monday," said Sarah, slightly annoyed. "I'm fascinated, but this really doesn't sound like the real world that I live in."

"Yeah, some of us have jobs," said Soraya. "We can't afford to miss any of our work. There's no escaping the bills."

"That's not exactly true," said Raymond, taking his wife by surprise.

"What?" she replied. "Of course, it's true. We can't just leave unexpectedly."

"I don't *have* to be at the herb shop. My employees are trained well enough that they could handle it for more than a week, if necessary. And you only have two clients right now, so that accounting work can easily be rescheduled. As long as you have it done by the end of the month, you could take some time off."

"But we don't know how long this will take, or what the cost will be," said Soraya.

"I can promise all of you that you will not have any expenses. All of your travel, food, and accommodations will be taken care of, and we are not going very far," explained Claire, "we just need some flexibility with time."

Raymond then looked over at Frank, but he seemed deep in thought until more of the attention at the table shifted to him.

"This may sound strange," volunteered Frank, "because I walked into this meeting knowing less about this than any of you, but I'm willing to go. Whatever this is, I think it's worth our trouble. I believe that these girls have a right to know why they were chosen. I don't have any deadlines for several weeks, so I have some time. You can count me in," he said to Claire. "That is, if Ami and Mandy are truly interested," he said, knowing they would jump at the opportunity to have an adventure like this.

Ami, Mandy, and Roya all looked at each other, and their faces lit up with excitement. They already knew that half of the battle had been won without even having to speak up.

"Of course, we want to come," said Ami, and Mandy nodded.

"Roya, what do you think?" asked her dad.

"I'm in. I trust Claire," she said, looking over at her. "I know this might sound inconvenient to just leave unexpectedly, but we need to trust. Does this really feel like the wrong path?" Roya asked her mother and Sarah.

"I don't know, yet," Soraya hesitated. "I don't like not knowing what we are getting into."

"I know how you feel," Claire assured her. "Where I come from, very few people were willing to make the trip to come and bring the book to Watertown. If you understood more about what a leap of faith it was for *me* to come *here*, you would appreciate that sometimes a leap of faith is needed to experience a miracle."

"Couldn't I stay behind?" requested Sarah. "I can take care of the house by myself. I promise I'll be good. I'm the only one who can't just postpone going to work. I don't see how I could come with you guys."

"If you stayed, later on you would regret not having come," said Claire with absolute certainty. "Once you heard about what I showed the rest of the group, you would wish that you had been there. I also think we need time to assess whether or not there is any danger. I would prefer if all of you came with me for a time. I can promise that once you see where we are going, you will not be in such a hurry to get back."

"So, what am I supposed to do, just quit my job?" The moment the words came out of her mouth, Sarah could not help thinking that she actually liked the idea. Her main concern was that there weren't any other places hiring that she could go to when they got back. Glancing down the table, Roya was nodding her head yes in answer to the question, and Ami and Mandy were beaming her with the intention to let go and join the adventure. Still, she knew having that job was a sign of maturity in her parents' eyes, and she did not want to give it up without their approval, even though she would never admit this to them openly.

"Sarah, this feels important," encouraged her father, "and I would be happy for you to be a part of it." Sarah looked like she was pondering a solution.

"How far away is this place?" asked Soraya.

"We could be there in a couple of hours. We only have to drive over to Lake Ontario and take a boat."

Suddenly, the whole idea did not seem so farfetched. Perhaps Claire's community lived on one of the islands. Some of them were privately owned. This was starting to sound more like a surprise summer trip.

"I don't mean to be rude, but why would we be doing this again?" Sarah asked.

"It might seem like I am asking all of you to trust me a great deal, but the knowledge that I will entrust you with through this journey is far, far greater," said Claire.

"Can't you just tell us where you want to take us?" asked Soraya.

In her mind, Claire thought, *you wouldn't believe me if I told you.* But out loud, she said confidently, "If I told you, it would ruin the surprise."

"Do we need to pack anything?" asked Ami.

"You might like to bring a change of clothes, but please bring only what you can easily carry with you in a small backpack, if anything at all," said Claire.

"What about cameras?" asked Frank.

"No cameras or phones. But you might like to have a journal and something to write with."

Frank looked momentarily disappointed. Documenting the journey with film was foremost on his mind, and this felt like a major setback.

"I can promise you this: very few people such as yourselves have been entrusted with what I am going to show you, and there is no doubt in my mind that this will change your lives forever. It is a great honor for me to be a guide for this group. I am merely serving the destiny that I find in you and recognizing how this complements me."

"Sarah, I think you should call work, and tell them you have a family emergency," decided her dad. "Just tell them that you have to leave unexpectedly, and you don't know exactly when you'll be back."

Sarah looked at her mom, waiting to see how she would react, and finally she nodded in agreement. Gradually, Soraya had come to the conclusion that this technology could help unlock her understanding of her husband's mysterious past. Some things he believed in, like extraterrestrials, did not fit into her paradigm of life experience. The idea of having contact with ETs had always seemed a little scary to her for some reason but having a spiritual contact experience through this technology felt like a safer way to explore the unknown.

"So, is everyone in?" rallied Raymond. They all looked around nodding their heads. There appeared to be a consensus now about trusting the journey with Claire. "So, what happens now?"

"How quickly can all of you be ready?" Claire asked, relieved that she had succeeded at getting them all onboard.

"I think we can be ready in less than an hour," estimated Frank. "We just have to run home for a bit to grab a few things."

"Just meet us back here when you're ready," agreed Raymond. "We shouldn't need much longer than that ourselves."

Roya had already started to feel like a Guardian, realizing that they were all acting to protect the knowledge of this technology. While the rest of the group was busy getting ready and making arrangements, Roya found time to show Claire her room. She was anxious to absorb more of Claire's way of perceiving and wanted to learn more about how to bridge energy with people.

First, the experience of creating the map, and now, watching how she helped each person find their place within a group dynamic; Claire could see the potential of group unity wherever she focused, and there was something empowering about being able to facilitate people in that way. Claire assured Roya that all her questions would be answered through the journey, and that she would have to be patient. That was a small request, considering how quickly all of this was coming together.

In a little under an hour, they were all assembled again downstairs. Phone calls had been made, a few small backpacks had been packed, and everyone wore clothes that were comfortable for travel.

Claire rode with Roya's family while Roya followed with Ami, Mandy, and their dad in their blue minivan. The Egg was secured in the trunk of the car, and Roya carried the book with her in her school backpack along with a notebook, a change of clothes, and some bottles of water.

It only took about thirty minutes to reach Sackets Harbor. Claire showed them where they could park the vehicles, so they would not be disturbed if they were gone for more than a day. From there, it was only a short walk to the harbor where Claire's boat was docked. It was a large, white motorboat, big enough to hold about ten people up top with room for about six people to sit below in the forward cab. Claire had life jackets for all of them stowed on the boat, and in a short time, they had all boarded and were ready to go.

"Before we embark, I need to prepare you a bit more. Even though we are taking a boat, our final destination is actually underground." Claire was subtly planting seeds, gradually stepping them into an awareness of what was coming.

No one knew exactly what to expect from the journey, but everyone was content to have an adventure on Claire's boat. After all, she seemed to really know what she was doing.

It was late in the evening when they pushed off and began the trek out of the harbor and into the surrounding bay. The sun had set, and the full moon was rising. Only a few clouds dotted the sky. Claire waited until they were in open water, past all of the docked boats, before increasing the speed. The boat had a maximum speed of about 37 miles per hour in calm water, but they were going 30 to be safe.

Just out of the bay to the left, they passed a little privately-owned island called Horse Island where there was an old lighthouse, though they were too far away to see any details. Still farther to the left, they could barely see another tiny island, but everyone was more focused on seeing what was out in front of them, expecting a physical destination of some kind on the horizon.

About twenty minutes passed, and it seemed like all they were doing was getting farther away from land. Soraya was becoming anxious to ask some questions, but she did not want to yell over the sound of the motor. Finally, after they reached a point where they could barely see any lights from shore, Claire cut the motor. Soraya was relieved, and everyone turned around to face Claire.

"Wow, we're in the middle of nowhere," noticed Mandy. "Why did you stop here?"

"It's not so important *where* we are but where we are *not*. This is as far as we need to go to be well beyond anyone's visual range," said Claire.

"Why would we want to do that?" asked Soraya.

"To protect the secret location. You'll understand in a few minutes, but first we need the Resonator."

Raymond had stashed the stone box with the Egg in the front cab of the boat, along with everyone's backpacks. After going down to get it, Claire guided him to take the Egg out and place it at the center of the deck where everyone could see it. Roya could not take her eyes off Claire, though, who seemed to have more of a glow about her. The whites of her eyes glistened in the moonlight, and Roya was poised for what was coming next. Just when Claire was about to explain further, there was a sudden pulse of energy that came from the Egg, creating a brief, mild ringing tone.

"Wow, did you feel that?" asked Sarah.

"It's starting again," nodded Raymond with excitement.

"You mean, this is how it started last time?" asked Frank.

"Yeah, if it's happening again like before, we should start to feel an increase in energy," informed Raymond.

"This is the signal I was expecting," stated Claire. "The guides are using the Resonator to help synchronize all of you with the energy that will open the pathway. We all have to be at a higher vibration before we can continue on."

"Pathway to where?" asked Roya. Claire just smiled at her, asking through her eyes for Roya to keep trusting. Roya was very aware that her trust in Claire was part of what was holding her family in alignment with the journey.

"Mom, can you feel it?" marveled Roya.

"I don't know. I thought I felt…" and then another pulse resonated through the air, followed by a noticeably sustained vibration, just like before. "Yes, I can feel it!" Soraya looked at her smiling husband.

"Are we going to be able to see the guides out here?" asked Ami. "Last time, we were in a cave."

"It's not time for the guides, yet," said Claire. "They are just signaling to give you a confirmation that you can trust where we are going. They are aware that I told you that you would all get to have an experience with this technology once we reach our destination."

"So, where do we go from here?" asked Ami.

"A good question," responded Claire, standing to face the whole group. "I have no doubt that the means by which we will arrive at our final destination will be surprising," Claire prepared them, "so it is worth mentioning that if any of you feel at all…um, hesitant, just know that this will pass quickly." She said this playfully, as if to conceal the potential of something more shocking, to make it seem less scary.

"It is also important to understand that we are not just traveling to a different *physical* location, but also to what I would describe as a different *psychological* environment. The closer we get to our final destination, the more different you will feel, but in a good way. For that reason, I want to suggest that we all do a meditation to get in a calm and centered space before we continue," recommended Claire as she knelt on the deck and straightened her spine.

Roya immediately followed her lead, and sat up with her spine straight, and then Ami and Mandy followed. Soon they were all poised and ready.

"I would like to invite all of you, while I am focusing, to meditate on the water. Not just on the sound of the waves and the presence of water around us, but also on the *living* connection we all share with water through our bodies." Claire's tone of voice began to change. It felt like she was sharing her meditative brainwave state with the group through the sound of her voice. Her words became softer, and the cadence of her speech was more clearly focused.

"The human body is made of mostly water," she continued, "so imagine that *your* water is not separate from the water of the world, but that *through* the water in your body, you are *one* with the whole of Earth's water. Imagine that we are one through the living water and hold this focus while emptying your minds."

Everyone closed their eyes and listened to the gentle sound of the waves lapping against the sides of the boat. Sarah occasionally peeked to see if anyone else's eyes were open, but everyone seemed to be giving the meditation their best effort.

"Focus on our oneness through the living water, and take slow, deep, rhythmic breaths," guided Claire after a moment. "We are all one with the living water."

The gentle vibration of the Egg continued to resonate through them in some way that made it easier to meditate, and Claire's presence felt like it was reaching out to envelop them. There was a warm glow that began to touch everyone on the inside as the state of connection grew deeper.

Claire had entered into a trance state and was expanding her awareness into her surroundings. A mild breeze occasionally gusted, and then the air would balance for a moment before gusting again.

Roya had never contemplated water like this before, but they were in a perfect place for it. She began to think about all of the fish in the lake and in the rivers and in the oceans all over the planet. Then she thought of all the water in everyone's bodies until a vision with surprising clarity arose in her mind.

Roya was vividly imagining being inside the nucleus of a cell, and she could feel the water that surrounded it. Her eyelids had grown heavy, and yet, she was alert and aware of her breathing. A feeling of deep peace came over her and then balance. For a moment, she thought that this awareness was coming from Claire, but before she could explore that any further, something shifted in the air.

Until that moment, she had felt a strong breeze caressing her face with mild fluctuations in temperature, but somehow, as she connected with a more balanced state of consciousness, she felt the physical conditions balancing out around her. The wind began to die down, and the temperature felt perfect. Then, the sound of the wind and the waves became distant, and everything around them became quiet. The boat was perfectly still, and Roya began to fight the heaviness of her eyes to come out of the meditation.

When she opened her eyes, she became engaged with a feeling of deep unity with everyone and everything around her. Everyone else was looking around, speechless. Frank was still deep in meditation, and everyone began to observe Claire who was just beginning to open her eyes. None of them could ever remember feeling such tranquility.

Roya beamed expectantly for answers, and Claire gave her a soft smile as she began to look around at the rest of the group. "I am sure you are all wondering what is happening."

"The boat is perfectly still, and where did the wind go?" Raymond wondered. "Are you doing this?"

"Yes and no," responded Claire. "Right now, we are inside an invisible vehicle that is much larger than this boat. Just breathe in the feeling of calmness and feel your connection with everyone and everything around you. This is part of the preparation for the psychological environment we are about to enter. We are entering an environment of oneness."

Frank was just coming out of the meditation, and he began to look around as if he did not know where he was. He might have thought he was dreaming for a moment, but then he became more alert and amazed at what he was perceiving.

"Why is everything so still?" Frank noticed.

"We are in a field right now that has complete control over the elemental forces," elucidated Claire, as she continued to align herself with the hidden structure of the universe.

"I thought you said we were in a vehicle," corrected Soraya.

"The field and the vehicle are one and the same," Claire replied. "The vehicle is geometric in nature, and it contains a perfect balance of universal forces, like the eye of a storm, if you were to consider the turbulence of reality itself as a storm."

She paused for a moment, taking a slow, deep, conscious breath. "It's quite extraordinary to share this with all of you, even though this is normal for me. The only way for any of you to be in this field is for you to surrender to the unity consciousness that is present, and you've all integrated with it nicely. It says a lot about what kind of people you are."

"I guess I never thought of us being a whole like this, but I can really feel it," expressed Roya. Everyone noticed a feeling of inner balance, both mentally and emotionally, and the fact that the wind and the water around them was perfectly calm reflected their consciousness: as within, so without. It was like a little bubble of stillness had enveloped them, and everything felt perfect.

"Claire," continued Roya, "I was having a feeling like I was inside a cell. Then it changed right into this feeling of peace."

Claire tuned in and immediately seemed to access Roya's experience through the field. "The field of this vehicle is very much like water to the nucleus of a living cell, and we are like the nucleus."

Roya looked around and noticed that everyone was intentionally taking deeper breaths to feel their connection to the energy of oneness that was in the air, and then she distinctly felt Ami vibing with an expectancy to share. Roya noticed how Claire began to energize Ami with her focus of attention, deliberately acknowledging her presence within the field so that she lit up more. The field was making it easier to feel everyone's flow of attention!

"I was wondering about whether there are oceans with life like ours on other worlds," shared Ami, "and then I felt like the stars were saying: YES!"

"Very good," acknowledged Claire. "The field of this vehicle is *connected* to the stars. You will find that it's easier in the presence of this field to access information that comes from the Greater Reality."

"I thought of dolphins," Mandy just blurted out. "So, what is this invisible vehicle for if we already have a boat?"

Claire knew that Mandy's question was more important than exploring the dolphin connection, so she began to describe more about the vehicle.

"Up until now, you probably thought of a vehicle as something physical like a car, a plane, or a boat. But the vehicle we are in now is made of light and sacred geometry." As soon as Claire said *sacred geometry*, the symbol known as the Star of David flashed in Roya's mind.

"This vehicle is also part of my body, and part of the body of my people. It spins around us invisibly, but it can also change according to the preferences of its hosts."

Just then, the remaining light became dimmer, as if a tinted glass bubble had appeared around the boat, and they had the distinct feeling of a dome over their heads.

"That's better," said Claire. "This will help your eyes adjust more before we proceed."

Everyone was looking around with wonder. Mandy couldn't help herself, and she leaned over the side of the boat and splashed some water over to the wall of the bubble, watching it bounce right off.

"Wow! It's a force field," exclaimed Mandy in awe.

"Right now, we are invisible, but we shouldn't stay here for long. There are ways that your military can detect the energy field that this vehicle creates, and we don't want them to take notice, so we have to get moving," Claire advised.

Suddenly, the water outside of the bubble began to rise. It was only an inch at first, but visually noticeable to everyone in the group. By the time it was at two inches, a slight feeling of panic arose.

"What's happening?" Soraya asked urgently. "It looks like we're sinking!"

"Do not be alarmed. We are not sinking. I have done this before," said Claire reassuringly. The water was rising higher now. A foot and a half. Two feet. "We are perfectly contained and safe."

Roya noticed that the water outside the bubble had begun to swirl like a vortex. As the wall of water continued to rise, almost everyone instinctively stood up as if to counteract the feeling that they were sinking.

"Uh, I take it we are going down?" guessed Raymond. Claire's calm surrender was reassuring, but nothing could have prepared them for this.

"Yes. As I said before, the place we are going to is underground," reminded Claire.

"I wasn't expecting this!" Soraya was not protesting, but still looked concerned.

"Just relax, you can all sit down," said Claire who was still kneeling on the deck.

The wall of water outside the bubble was four feet high now and was beginning to close over the dome. The water inside the bubble just around the boat was perfectly still as it continued to descend with the boat.

"This will only take a few minutes. It's important that you all maintain the feeling of surrender. My people are sending forth a great welcome to all of you to help you feel at ease. Just feel the vibrations of the field and take a deep breath if you feel nervous."

As soon as she said it, they all felt the gentle waves of welcome, coming through the field. The water had nearly closed over the top of the dome, and they could still see the moon through the water. Roya felt a rush of adrenaline, and it was clear that everyone else was on edge. Sarah had grabbed onto her mother, and Frank had his left arm out protectively around both Mandy and Ami. Finally, the last part of the bubble was covered with a splash of water sloshing over the top.

There was something deeply peaceful about watching the moonlight fade, inch by inch, as the bubble continued to descend. They were all in a state of surrender, trusting and knowing somehow that they were perfectly safe.

"I want everyone to remember this feeling," emphasized Claire. "This is important, because this is what makes it possible to travel in these vehicles. You all just made a leap of faith together. Whenever you are called to make a leap of faith, others are always extending help to you invisibly to energize your path. Surrendering to your path is a process of letting go and trusting where the field of the future is guiding you. When your trust is complete, the path will open like a form of living gravity that pulls you along, making all of your movements lighter and more graceful. Just feel how light you are right now."

"You're right, I noticed it when I stood up," acknowledged Frank. "I actually feel lighter and more balanced." Everyone looked around and nodded. Mandy kept looking at her hands.

"Where is this light coming from?" asked Mandy. "I can't even see the moon anymore, but I can still see everyone."

The movement downward was slow enough at first that it was hardly noticeable, but the light that filled the bubble made everything look crystal clear. It did not seem to be coming from anywhere, but then Mandy looked up and noticed a soft glow around Claire.

"The light is coming from the field inside the vehicle, but you are also seeing auras," Claire elaborated.

Claire was right. They were all starting to see it. There was a soft glow around each of them that looked bluish-white at first, but the more they focused, the more they noticed subtle details in the energy pattern emanating from each person. Claire's was the most noticeable. She was getting brighter by the minute. Her aura was a bright blue with a pink glow around her throat chakra and a seafoam green dancing around the outer edges.

"Watch my field," Claire instructed, and everyone looked. "I am feeling the excitement of returning home, and if you look closely, you can see the intensity. Every emotion has a specific pattern that moves and vibrates and communicates the living expression of a being."

"Like the Flavors," Roya realized.

"Yes. Just observe, and you will see the feeling of connection that is building between my people and me. Try to learn from everything that you observe in people's energy fields, and your knowledge will increase very quickly."

The group began to feel an energy building in Claire's chest. At first, they noticed her blue and pink hues strengthening, but then they noticed dances of white, and they could all feel the presence of several other people in her field that were connecting with her. She was talking without talking as she shared her emotional vibrations with them through the field.

"This is the pathway we must travel. The vehicle obeys the will of the higher heart. Now watch what I do with this energy."

Claire then looked at Roya sitting near the back of the boat, directly across from her, and with a single breath, she released the greater portion of the white light that had been building. It transferred right into Roya and everyone watched her take in a deep breath. She was overcome by an incredible feeling of connection with Claire and her people. Roya could feel Claire's emotions, and her own aura became noticeably brighter.

"Now share the feeling of connection with Mandy," suggested Claire. As Roya looked at Mandy, she found that the energy was easy to extend, as if the energy *wanted* to be shared. Roya was not sure why Mandy was chosen first, but she took a deep breath, and as she exhaled, she willed the feeling of connection over to Mandy who instantly began to laugh as if the feeling tickled. Somehow, Mandy's laughter made her aura flicker, and the white light of connection amplified the power of her laugh. The white light brought out the rainbow colors in Mandy's aura, and her flickering permeated the space around them.

Roya felt every nuance of Mandy's laughter and started laughing with her, and it quickly spread until everyone was flickering.

"I've never had so much fun in my life!" admitted Soraya.

She was completely letting go of her normal sense of composure. By the time the laughter calmed down, they were all at a deeper level of connection. Roya could sense everyone's unspoken questions, and yet the field of connection was answering their questions before they could even speak them out loud. They were all remembering that they were a family of eternal souls, and that the body was merely a container for the soul's vibration.

"How could I have forgotten this?" Ami wondered out loud, and everyone around her knew precisely what she meant. It was as if she had spoken what everyone was feeling.

"You will notice in this state of being that your words may feel more guided and may reflect more unifying truths. It is the way of my people to speak words of connection instead of words of separation," Claire explained.

Everyone understood without needing to know more. Her words were backed by the living knowledge of the field.

"If this vehicle has a fuel, it is joy. If you can hold the expectancy of greater joy, we are ready to accelerate."

With that, the vibration of the bubble began to increase. There was a sense of movement, but they did not feel any inertia. They were traveling down, and it felt like the field was guiding them to let go of the world above. Water rushed past the bubble, but the inside was still. They felt no difference in pressure as they went deeper.

Roya tried to remember how deep Lake Ontario was, but she could not recall. They must have been moving along the bottom, because she could not imagine that they had gone straight down for very long.

Finally, the bubble entered a tunnel of some kind, and they felt several barriers open and close behind them as they moved through it. They continued to descend, angling downward, until the tunnel leveled out and became horizontal.

Roya had been turned around with Claire behind her, looking to see what they were moving toward, but when she looked back at her, she noticed that Claire had removed her wig. Her hair appeared black but with a noticeable shimmer of blue and turquoise. It reminded Roya of those Amazon butterflies that have an almost luminous blue pattern on their wings.

"I didn't want to have to explain to anyone how it got that way," Claire said to Roya as everyone looked around to notice. "You can't make your hair look this way artificially."

"Drats," said Mandy. "You just answered my next question."

"How *did* it get that way?" asked Roya.

"It's natural, but it's not the norm, as you will see. There are a few of us with very unique physical features like this, but that's a story for another time."

Before anything more could be said, there was a gentle swooshing sensation as the water around the dome of the bubble disappeared. They had emerged out of a large pool of water that filled a dimly lit domed room. There were small lights evenly spaced along the perimeter of the room where the water met the wall. The lights partly illuminated the water, which appeared more clear and pristine than the lake water from above.

They all stood up as the bubble moved the boat gently over toward solid ground where they noticed a man standing near the edge of the pool. As they approached, he raised the palm of his hand to greet them, opening his fingers slowly, and Roya watched as Claire did the same.

"It means, I acknowledge the Spirit that brought us together," explained Claire. "It's like touching the field that is between us and acknowledging the force of love and guidance that all share in as equals," as she did the same gesture to Roya. Mandy quickly mimicked it with a fake serious look on her face.

Claire's aura brightened when she saw the man, and Roya was fascinated to notice that a subtle arc of living energy had appeared between them. Mandy leaned over and whispered in Roya's ear, "Doesn't he look a little like Justin Timberlake?"

Roya laughed a little and gave Mandy a funny look. She could tell that having her friends with her on this adventure was going to be fun, but she wanted to quietly observe for a while and save the chatting for later when they could hopefully break away from their parents.

The bubble seemed to have disappeared without anyone noticing, and Claire placed the ladder over the side of the boat, gesturing for Soraya to go first. One by one, they each stepped down.

"This is Amaron," said Claire as she embraced him heart to heart. For a moment, they looked deeply into each other's eyes and smiled. Their connection was so deep that everyone felt touched by it, and it was apparent that they knew each other very well. After a long moment of silently gazing into each other's eyes, Claire stepped aside and Amaron greeted everyone again with a smile.

"It's an honor to meet all of you," said Amaron. "Welcome to Lys."

10

FORBIDDEN FOOTSTEPS

Aaron felt like he was somewhere between asleep and awake. He had never been hypnotized before, but he was certain that it would be similar to this experience of being in the Frequency. Were it not for his trust and his sense of adventure, it might have felt more like he had been ensnared by a spider's web. But under the circumstances, he felt protected somehow. The presence of Lex's mind was holding him in some kind of trance-like state that felt very mental and slightly uncomfortable at first, but Aaron was still impressed with Lex's ability to extend consciousness.

No more transports were scheduled for the night, according to Lex and Ram. They walked in front of Aaron, down the maintenance path of the transport tunnel, and he followed without thinking. In an odd sort of way, Aaron felt a sense of oneness with his new companions through the mind-link. His movements felt automatic, though he also felt their alertness for any sign of danger. Half an hour must have passed before they reached a stretch of tunnel that was lit at the end by a station. Though they did not expect anyone to be there at this hour, they exited the tunnel through a maintenance door on the left, just before they reached it.

The doorway led to a set of stairs going up, and then a long maintenance corridor that ran the length of the station. They stopped after a while at a door with a window that went out onto a metal platform overlooking the tracks below, part of an emergency exit route. From the window, Aaron could see four more maglev rail lines with platforms between them for people to stand and escalators going to the level above. Lex relaxed the trance-field a bit so that Aaron could take it all in and remember it before they moved on.

"If it weren't for all of these service paths and emergency escape routes, we would never have managed to explore as much as we have," said Lex.

"Being this deep underground, there are all kinds of reasons why you might want an alternative way out of an area."

"You mean like earthquakes and stuff?" asked Aaron, noticing that his words sounded more monotone in his trance state.

"Earthquakes, flooding, tunnel collapses, fires, contamination…" explained Ram. "They made it hard to go from city to city, *and* from sector to sector, but we've found lots of alternative routes like this one that come in handy if you want to avoid being seen."

"Come on, let's keep moving" said Lex.

Around a corner, they entered another maintenance corridor that had pipes running along the walls. Here they stopped to stash their lights and some other gear, so it would not be obvious what they had been up to. Lex wanted to make sure that if they were caught, they would not be seen coming from the transport tunnel itself. They had already planned their cover stories before they ever began the journey and wanted to avoid suspicion as much as possible. Before moving on, Lex insisted that Aaron remove the coveralls he was wearing over his jeans and plain grey T-shirt, so he would blend in.

After turning down several long hallways with pipes, they came to an exit door that led to a stairway connected to the central plaza above the transport hub. Having often used the subway, Aaron found it easier now to pretend that he was not out of place.

"We're less than ten minutes away from our living quarters," explained Lex, "so stay focused, and do not become distracted with any sights along the way."

Aaron felt his mind being gripped again, this time a little tighter. He wondered if he would be strong enough to break the trance if he wanted to, but it didn't make sense to do anything but surrender. It felt like Lex was pulling him along with his mind.

From here, they marched up a wide tunnel walkway that was slightly inclined until they reached a vast atrium with white walls. There were numerous tunnels branching off the main floor and several stories of walkways around the perimeter of the room. This was the first of three atriums they would pass through before taking an elevator down. Finally, after more turns than Aaron could count, they came to their living quarters in one of the residential areas. Among the few people they passed, no one seemed to take notice of them, though Aaron could feel how mental and emotionless they were through the Frequency.

Everyone relaxed as soon as the door shut behind them. Even though Lex had released his mind, Aaron felt a little disoriented. The living room was small and featureless with only a couch and a small table with a couple of chairs. A set of bunk beds were around the corner. There was a bathroom without a mirror, a shower without a tub, and a small closet that they both shared for clothing. The whole space was no bigger than a small studio apartment without a kitchen.

"I've got a headache from that trance thing," complained Aaron.

"Just relax on the couch," said Lex. "I'll go see if I can find the professor."

Lex was out the door before Aaron could say anything, but all he cared about was collapsing on the couch. Ram quickly produced a map and a pen and started making marks on it.

"If for any reason you have to leave on your own, this map will show you the way out." Ram had marked all the turns they took to get to the apartment and noted the location of the transport tunnel they had used to get to the city.

"Wow! Is this a map of the whole city?" The sheer size and complexity of the underground city snapped Aaron back into a more alert state of mind.

"No," answered Ram. "These are just some of the areas my group is allowed to roam freely in. The city is much larger, but many of the other areas are restricted. We don't even know how big it really is, but we think there must be hundreds of thousands of people living down here. We've been told it's becoming one of the largest underground cities in the world."

"I have so many questions. I don't even know where to begin," said Aaron.

"We do as well, but I should wait for Lex."

"Whatever you can tell me about the city, I'd love to hear about it," requested Aaron, who was still trying to orient his consciousness.

"This is sector nine, one of the newer parts, mostly residential, for the workers. It was completed ten years ago, and now, they're working on sectors ten and eleven, which are even deeper and larger. Our sector is mostly filled with students, trainers, managers, maintenance people, and construction workers. Sometimes, we get passes to go work in other sectors. Lex and I tested high enough to be trained in multiple fields. We get to see more that way."

"What's in the other sectors?"

"Sector one is resource management. That's the only one still connected to the surface. Supplies are received, stored, and sometimes distributed to the lower levels. Lots of offices and really vast storage spaces up there. We've only heard about it, and apparently, the people that live and work on those levels don't even know about most of the other levels below them. Sector two is medical. *They* don't know about us either. Beneath that is sector three, which has most of the greenhouses, water treatment, and a lot of other research facilities. Probably genetics. We're not entirely sure after that. This place is *full* of secrets."

"We think a lot of scientists and elite managers live on those levels, and we've heard stories about luxury living spaces and highly classified research. The sectors are not all stacked one over another, if you're wondering. Once you go down a ways, there is more overlap, but even within sectors, many compartments are restricted. Some common areas exist, but you have to have clearance to go beyond them, and you have to have clearance to go to other cities."

Aaron's head was spinning. He had read about secret underground military bases on the internet, but nothing of this scale. *This is a whole separate civilization*, Aaron realized.

"How many other cities are out there like this one?" he asked.

"They don't tell us. We've tried to ask some of the ones who travel between cities, but unless you have clearance, they won't talk to you. Professor Alton says there are lots of them, though."

"What about your parents? Do you have any family down here?" asked Aaron.

"We never knew our parents. They gave us their DNA, but we were raised with our group. Lots of us don't know our parents. It's rare to meet the ones that do, at least in our sector."

"So, you spend your whole lives down here? Is anybody down here from the surface?"

"Oh yes. Professor Alton was raised on the surface. But down at this level, we don't get a lot of exposure to new arrivals."

Just then, the door swung open, and in walked Lex with an older, very stern-looking man. He was mostly bald on top with closely shaved hair around the sides and back of his head. He wore a white button-up shirt and dark grey slacks. He looked muscular, but with a little extra weight, and he had a pale complexion. His nostrils flared as he was looking Aaron over, and his stare felt intimidating.

"This is professor Alton," introduced Lex. "Professor, this is Aaron."

"This is quite a dangerous business you two are engaged in: smuggling in someone from the surface. Very dangerous, indeed," he said with a commanding voice while pulling over a chair to sit in front of Aaron. But then he softened a bit. "Still, it is a pleasure to meet you."

"Thank you, sir," Aaron said respectfully. "Might I ask, what exactly are you a professor of?"

"I am a professor of mathematics, architecture, and engineering," he spoke proudly, sounding like a military officer. "I manage quite a number of students, including these two. So, tell me, how did you find your way down here?"

"We were exploring an abandoned factory on the surface, and we stumbled onto all these hidden levels below it. We met Lex and Ram about twelve floors below the surface," Aaron explained.

"We? You mean there are more of you," stated the Professor, glaring at Lex, letting him know he was aware that Lex had hidden that detail from him on the walk over. Professor Alton often expressed anger when his students withheld information, which worked well to keep everyone honest. But Lex was always testing the boundaries. Lex was discerning enough to know that much of his anger was just a show meant to intimidate. And he knew another side to the professor that reflected Lex and Ram's insatiable curiosity.

"Yes, there are six of us all together." Aaron disclosed.

"Fascinating!"

"What do you think this means?" asked Lex, believing that this was more than a chance meeting.

"What does it mean?" repeated the professor, pondering for a moment. "It means there's hope."

"Hope for what?" asked Aaron.

"Hope that there's still a possibility for integration," expressed the Professor. "That there's still a way to end the secrecy. So, wait a minute. Where were the two of you when this happened?"

"We went to one of the abandons connected to where they came in," explained Lex. "We hadn't gone very far inside before we met them. Ram nearly fainted when we saw them."

"I did not," snapped Ram. "*You* stood there like a pole, not knowing what to do."

They both looked at each other and laughed.

"You see how these two just laughed?" noted the professor. Aaron nodded.

"Very human, isn't it?" Alton smiled brightly at both of them. "They have a greater emotional range than most of the people who live and work down here. Lex tells me that they put you into the Frequency until they got you this far."

"Yeah. What *was* that? I felt really stuck in my mind and almost hypnotized. It was like being pulled into a non-emotional trance-state, or something."

"We just call it the Frequency. It's the mode of operation down here. I've been part of it since it was set up by the Superminds, but it doesn't feel as natural to me as it does to those who are raised with it. Lex and Ram here are an exception. I feel affected by it most of the time, but I've noticed that some of my students can drop out of it whenever they feel like it. They've helped me rediscover what I lost when I joined the colony," he smiled at them warmly.

"More and more of the young people have the ability to modulate their brainwaves with greater control," he continued. "They can mask themselves within the Frequency, but they don't like to stay there too long. They're looking for ways out so they can understand what's missing down here."

"Who are the Superminds?" asked Aaron.

"They are the controllers. They introduced the Frequency to manage the population through a kind of psychic hierarchy. It's a way of limiting emotions and controlling creativity so that people lose their ability to question reality and simply accept what they're told. By setting up colonies like this that are based on the Frequency, they're also intending to affect those of you who live on the surface."

"Because we are all connected..." Aaron mused out loud.

Professor Alton was pleased with Aaron's remark, because he was sharing information very deliberately to provoke such thoughts. He knew that some of the information might be shocking to Aaron, but he enjoyed feeding a truly curious mind.

"It's true, and the organization is using that knowledge against you. They want to change the resonance of human consciousness globally, to make the surface culture easier to control. Take the media, for example. They've been using propaganda for decades to manipulate your perception of reality, justifying whatever the organization wants or needs. They just trick you into creating with your thoughts what *they* want, as if their desired reality is inevitable. They have people embedded in your mainstream news media, your academic institutions, *and* your government. There are even teams of people posting on social media now to drive the global conversation. They work on everything—from shaping public opinion on mainstream topics, to messing with the minds of people who are into fringy new age stuff. They want the government to remain perpetually polarized, so your people never become unified. What you call liberal media and conservative media, in some forms, are part of a larger project to fragment your consciousness and keep you all in duality."

"You know, I've thought about that before," remarked Aaron assertively. "My dad talks about this, too...how it seems like over time, there's less objective reporting and a lot more people with viewpoints that seem intentionally polarizing. It's like the media is just becoming another form of entertainment."

"It goes beyond even that," interrupted the professor. "A lot of what you *think* is news is completely orchestrated. Most of your journalists think they're reporting on what's happening, but they're being led by master manipulators and are often reporting on events that are manufactured for them. This keeps you all busy with distractions, so you never notice what's *really* going on. Behind the scenes, there's a massive hidden operation transferring resources into these underground cities. And they're setting up more funding sources all the time to support the project."

"Can it be stopped? Is there a weakness in the plan?"

"I don't know," admitted the professor, though it was worth considering what he could offer to Aaron.

"You seem to have thought about this a lot, though," prodded Aaron.

"Well…if some of my students can modulate their frequency of consciousness, I suppose it proves that human beings have the ability to resist, maybe even to become immune to the Frequency. But for the whole surface culture to reject frequency control, they would have to identify with another source of vibration that's stronger and more unifying."

"Like love?" proposed Aaron optimistically. "I've always thought that love was the most powerful force in the world."

"If you could get enough people to love humanity as a whole," the professor responded, "it might be possible. If *our* people can form into a psychic collective—which is what we are developing down here—then the surface culture must have the same potential. You're fighting an uphill battle, though."

"So, this is all about what frequency of reality we're choosing?"

Aaron was way more perceptive than the professor had expected a surface dweller to be, and he could tell that Lex and Ram were very in tune with all that was being shared.

"I suppose so," he agreed, "but your people would have to know that they *have* a choice. From what I remember, most people on the surface are not discerning enough to understand how oppressed they really are. They've all been raised inside a maze of illusion with very little knowledge of the power of thought and intention. Most are not strong enough in their knowledge of reality to resist this kind of hidden oppression with their consciousness."

"But things have changed a lot since you were on the surface," informed Aaron. "I think more of us are discovering the influence our consciousness has on the whole world. And there are more of us than there are of you. Couldn't *our* frequency change *yours* if we became more focused?" Aaron challenged.

Lex and Ram were beaming.

"Yes, but there's still a lot you don't know about frequency control. The organization is doing a *very* good job at reinforcing the superiority of our Frequency by convincing you not to recognize the power of your own. They're programming you to accept a disempowered state, so you believe you no longer have a choice to resist something so powerful and well-organized. You're being taught to see yourselves as subjects of the emerging new hierarchy. And the more they are able to expand the project, the more our Frequency of reality affects everyone on the planet."

"But the surface culture is affecting us, too. We're all reflecting each other, right?" Lex interjected. Ram nodded his head in agreement.

"In theory," continued Professor Alton. "That may be why some of the young people down here can still access their emotions, because they are connected to the surface culture…to you. It's an invisible war at this point, though. I hear they're rolling out the Frequency in more of your cities now. Their goal is world wide."

He said it so matter-of-factly. The professor did not seem to have much of a connection to the emotional impact Aaron was feeling about the scale of the manipulation. Yet, he was being very straightforward so that Aaron could understand. His intention was not without compassion. Both of them felt that they did not have much time, and there was a sense of hope behind the encounter that suggested that the fate of this secret war had not yet been decided. The thought occurred to Professor Alton that somehow, Aaron might be able to shape the outcome of history by taking this information back to the surface and sharing it. Though he believed it was a long shot.

"How are they rolling it out?" inquired Aaron.

"It's a combination of things. The Frequency is part of the human resonance field, but you guys on the surface are in a different kind of conversion experience. The Frequency *we* know contains a resonance of psychic superiority. It's how we relate to each other within a hierarchy of psychic influences. But on the surface, they're using radio waves, electronics, propaganda, as well as psychic manipulation to influence your thoughts and emotions. You are very gradually being entrained with the minds of those being trained to manage you. They will wait until people have been in it for a while, and then they will turn it up gradually. That way, people become slowly acclimated, so they don't realize how much they are being affected by it over time; and the incoming generations are being raised with it, never knowing what it feels like to live without it."

"That's shocking!" Aaron exclaimed. His emotions were rattled, but he tried to stay focused on gathering more information. "How does it work?"

"They're trying to zap you out of your natural state of being so that the human nervous system becomes unplugged from the natural environment and is more susceptible to the influence of the managers. The more unplugged you are from the natural environment, the more bonded you will become with electronic technology, which is right in step with their plan of control."

"And how do these managers operate? I mean, where are they, and how do they influence us?"

"They walk among you, but most of the time, you don't notice who they are. Many of them stay well-hidden, extending their influence psychically to entrain your minds while working to confuse your knowledge of history and human potential. *Their* minds are considerably more powerful than the average person on the surface. They're better at manipulating mentally, and they understand things about the subconscious mind and how to use it against you. They're using the Gateway to entrain you and make you more suggestible."

"What's the Gateway?" asked Lex, leaning forward with interest.

This was the kind of information they had been hoping he would share. Until this moment, there was no reason for Professor Alton to risk sharing this kind of classified information with his students, but the teacher in him just wanted to remember what it was like to be free to tell the truth. There was something about Aaron's innocence that demanded it.

"It's one of the scariest things I have ever seen," he paused, realizing he had never before expressed how he actually felt about all that he had witnessed. "I was part of the original experiments on the surface decades ago when they were testing the Gateway on military subjects. The Gateway is a set of frequencies designed to prep you, to get you ready for the next level of frequency control. They want to keep you distracted and mesmerized with entertainment that limits your imagination and pacifies you while they are changing your resonance with the Gateway."

"Some of the frequencies they use are an assault on your senses designed to agitate you, while the Gateway is designed to reward you for thinking less and zoning out on distractions. They want to make you feel comfortable when you're in the Gateway and uncomfortable when you're out of it."

"The managers are trained to extend their field of consciousness *with* the Gateway to feel the difference between those who are accepting the program and those who are resisting it. They look for people who are influencers that could potentially lead humanity away from their plan of control—people who hold the frequency of love and light in a stronger way. The managers want to hack their influence so that it will carry some part of their indoctrination, even if only subconsciously."

Professor Alton realized that he was also speaking about himself, and how his own influence had been corrupted, though not entirely. He was beginning to recall his heart connection with the surface culture, remembering the pain of severing ties with people he cared about. He could not help seeing something of his own humanity in Aaron that had been overshadowed by the change in his resonance from being underground for so long.

"A lot of influencers in your society will be contacted telepathically to imprint them with programming. They are implanted with thoughtforms designed to either intimidate them from opening further or to indoctrinate them into giving power to the psychic hierarchy of the Frequency. They want people to think they're being psychically watched all the time, so they'll be afraid to use their abilities to investigate. Influencers with strong psychic aptitude, however, might actually get recruited into the organization if they're noticed."

"That's really clever," said Ram, appreciating with terrible awe how brilliant the controllers could be.

"That's what always worried me about it," said Professor Alton. "The average person on the surface is almost completely unaware of this invisible assault on their freedom and sovereignty. When I first experienced it, they said the Gateway was being developed as an enhanced interrogation technique, but I always knew they had bigger plans for it. It took living down here for years before I put more of the pieces together. Now, it's clear to me that with a wide enough implementation of the Gateway, they can do to a whole world what they did to the original test subjects."

"What exactly went on in those experiments?" asked Aaron.

"They were experimenting with how to make human beings vibrate in specific ways: to feel terrified, or to feel stimulated, even in pleasurable ways." For a moment, he looked like he was recalling something from the experiment. "They were able to record our experiences of terror, for example, and somehow play back the frequency of our emotions to other test subjects so they would feel the same way."

"They could also simulate what it feels like when the brain is rewarded by entertainment, which is how they can distract you from meaningful thought. The Gateway Program basically trains you to avoid the agitating frequencies by seeking out and going into that mesmerized state as a shelter. In this way, they are seeking to corral the population into a very specific docile zone of consciousness where you are easily convinced to hand over your power to minds that are more organized and capable than your own. I think the next step will involve some kind of personal technology, because the entire population is too big to manage the way they do it down here. They will need to trick people into choosing the next level of control, thinking that it's something exciting and beneficial to them."

"Wow! I can't believe it. It's…in-human." Aaron had to stop and breathe for a moment to take it all in. "So, is that how they did it down here, with the Gateway?"

"Down here, it's a bit different, though I suspect a lot has been kept secret from us as well. The Frequency is maintained through a series of agreements that have become ingrained in the subconscious minds of every one down here. It makes it easier for everyone's brainwaves to be synchronized into a pattern that serves the purposes of the Superminds. A lot of the people who were brought down here were chosen for their psychic aptitude, and people are even being bred for different purposes now, including for their psychic abilities."

"That makes a lot of sense. Pool them together to create some kind of psychic collective," concluded Aaron.

"Right," said the Professor. "Lex, here, is probably going to be trained as a manager. In every group that was raised with the Frequency, usually one or two emerge as leaders. The leaders have a stronger aptitude for projecting mental commands, and the rest of the group feels safe when they are entrained with a leader that they know."

"So, would you say that the Frequency is telepathic in nature?" suggested Aaron.

"Yes, but only in the crudest fashion. If you are taught not to think as an individual, but to focus only on the goals of your collective, you don't participate in meaningful exchanges between minds. Some are taught to command. Most are programmed to respond. The Frequency is both technological and psychic. They use technology to make everyone vibrate the same, and then telepathy to establish a psychic hierarchy. The most creative and intelligent minds are the ones that get trained to use their gifts to become skilled manipulators of consciousness within the system. There is no true freedom of thought, though. People like us have had to learn how to hide our thoughts from people who are loyal to the system."

"That seems like a real waste of psychic potential, if you ask me. If I were going to create a telepathic society, I would want it to be more meaningful and emotional."

"Exactly," said the professor. "An outsider such as yourself can easily see this, but most people down here are lost in a different kind of experience. All they care about is fulfilling the plan."

"What plan? What is this place for?" asked Aaron.

"The answer to that depends on your level of clearance. Take the people closest to the surface, for example. They are told that they're part of a contingency plan to protect the human race from dying out if a supervirus were to wipe out the surface population. It's a great excuse to entice surface people from the medical field to join the program, but once they are in, they're not allowed to return to the surface. They must sever all ties when they join the program."

"Yeah, Ram was saying that they don't even know about the lower levels," confirmed Aaron.

"That is correct. They function as a separate colony, believing they are part of a top secret surface government program. They are like a stockpile of medical expertise, taking care of elite personnel and helping to manage the process of receiving and storing all the incoming supplies. Many of them are being used to conduct research, the purpose of which they may not even fully understand. They pride themselves on being part of an elite group that is more prepared for the future than the rest of the surface culture. They know nothing about us down here, though, or how we are connected with other colonies through a transport system. The whole system of colonies and bases is highly compartmentalized in the way they function. *We* have been told for decades that these cities were created to preserve the best from the dying race that is on the surface, but I never liked that explanation. Would you say that *you* are part of a dying race?" The Professor posed his question deliberately for the benefit of his two students, knowing that the truth they had been raised with was distorted.

"No. Absolutely not! Just the opposite. We're thriving!" exclaimed Aaron. Lex and Ram looked stunned at these words.

"True, our society has a lot of problems," Aaron continued, "and we don't know how to solve them all yet, but I think, like a lot of people my age, we're optimistic about finding the solutions. I don't believe my people are willing to give up. Otherwise, there would be no future for anyone. Only for those who survive."

"Yes, well I know what our leaders would say. *We* are the survivors, and this city is our solution to the problems that are destroying the surface culture. *We* are the future," said the Professor. Lex and Ram were captivated.

"If you are the future," said Aaron, "then it's a future you have stolen from those of us living on the surface. Where would your cities be without everything we do for you? No offence, but your relationship to us on the surface is parasitic."

"Right. Did you ever think about that?" the Professor asked Lex and Ram.

"I thought everything was made by machines," assumed Lex.

"Yes, but who made the machines, and who runs them? Who collects the raw materials that are used? Where do all of the waste products go? And do you think all of the food we eat is grown in the greenhouses?" tested the Professor. They were speechless.

"The surface of the planet is covered with factories and workers and people who are unknowingly doing all kinds of things that support the plan and functioning of these cities. The boy is right. Our future may indeed be stolen from them, but what kind of future will it be if the surface of the planet is destroyed?"

"I thought that the destruction could not be prevented," said Ram, "that it was too far along to be stopped."

"But what if that were *not* the case?" suggested the Professor. "What if we are stifling *their* progress for the benefit of our own? And what if they actually hold the key to *our* potential."

The Professor looked at each of them, profoundly interested in the connections they were making. And then his eyes landed on Aaron again. "My boy, you are a link to a new future, but a fragile one at that. I have long suspected that many of my students are somehow connected to others on the surface, and now it looks like that connection has brought us all together. Unfortunately, I can't think of anything else to do but return you to where you came from. It's too dangerous for you to be here. You two better get him back to his friends. And I don't want either of you boys talking about this to the others."

"What am I supposed to do, now that I know about this place?" asked Aaron. "I still have so many questions."

"We've risked enough with our time here. The psychics that work for the Superminds could notice if we keep talking like this, and I don't want to deal with security. Until you're back on the surface, try to erase this conversation from your memory. Just pretend that none of this ever happened. I won't be able to protect you if you get caught. I hope something good comes from this, young man. Good luck on your journey."

Getting the professor to talk felt like a major conquest even though Lex and Ram still had a million more questions for him. Now that he had left, they became immediately focused on the dangerous task of returning Aaron to the surface.

"The professor is right," said Lex. "We should really go."

"I'm ready when you are."

"Then I'm going to put you back in the Frequency now. Just relax your mind, and follow my lead," instructed Lex.

Aaron stared into Lex's eyes, and a feeling of pressure entered his mind until his awareness narrowed. He could feel his emotions being restricted, and his whole presence felt pulled into a mental space as he began to zone out. It happened quicker this time, partly due to the presence of the Frequency in the underground city. His mind felt like jelly for a moment, but he relaxed and let his thoughts drift away as he surrendered to the influence of Lex's mind. This time, he felt Ram joining in, and they quickly became a cohesive unit.

Seconds later, they left the apartment and began the journey through the maze of tunnels. Aaron noticed even less of the details on the return trip, focusing only on Lex who was walking in front of him. Ram, who walked to the left of Aaron, was looking around more cautiously, trying not to make eye contact with the people they passed by in the dimly lit halls.

The transport plaza was completely empty, and they passed a large digital clock that said it was just after 2 a.m. They quickly made their way back through the maintenance corridors and began the half hour trek down the transport tunnel, back to where the others were waiting. They were silent most of the way, and Aaron became fascinated with observing the connection between their minds. Were their minds inside of his, or was his inside of theirs? He felt pulled along, like he was tethered to Lex, and Ram just flowed with the connection like he was a part of them both.

His head was buzzing, and he was glad to feel Lex relaxing control of their shared mental field as they got closer to their destination.

When they returned through the hole, they could hear the others talking at the top of the stairs. Everyone fell silent momentarily as they entered.

"Whoa!" said Melanie. "You guys scared me." Everyone stood up and walked down the stairs to greet them.

"We were seriously wondering if we had made a mistake by letting you go," said Zack. "I'm just glad we have you back."

"Yeah, I'm glad to be back," admitted Aaron, still a little zoned out. "How long were we gone?"

"About an hour and a half," Dominic informed him.

"We were able to see the professor," said Ram proudly.

"Yes, professor Alton had some interesting things to say, but our meeting was short. He didn't want us to be discovered," said Lex. "We really should be going now. Aaron can explain the details."

It was a shame not to explore each other's worlds further, but it would have to wait. The only goal now was for both parties to return safely with what information they had.

"He's right," said Aaron. "We should leave now, too."

"Just one question, though," asked Ram. "What do you and your friends do for fun?"

"Man, what don't we do?" joked Dominic. "Tonight, we went exploring, but usually we go out dancing or cruise around the city. There are lots of places to go. Sometimes we go camping. We just make it up as we go along."

"I do a lot of art," added Aaron, "and everyone has some kind of creative hobby."

Lex and Ram had never danced before or made art, and camping was not even in their vocabulary, but they understood one important thing about their new friends: they had freedom.

In Lex and Ram's world, everyone had a purpose that was defined by a highly organized social plan. There was little room for personal growth and exploration. More and more, the purpose of individuals was determined by aptitude tests, and even sometimes before birth as a product of their DNA. Each new class of subterranean humans was being programmed to affect the consciousness of their DNA, and thus, future generations of offspring. A new social order was being created, based in part on the organizational structure of the city itself, and the role of traditional families was quickly disappearing.

"Would you ever come with us to the surface?" asked Aaron.

"We would like that very much," expressed Lex. "But I'm quite certain that the memory of such an experience would change us too much, and we would be noticed. I'm afraid it could only work as a one-way journey, and our home is here. If there is a way though, I hope we will find it."

"Yes, let's just intend to meet again. This can't be the end," affirmed Ram.

"When *can* we meet up again?" asked Zack, thinking about the documentary.

"I'm not sure. We need time to process all of this. Whatever you do, don't try to come find us. We have to think very carefully about what to do next. We can't even think about making any more plans for meeting you. If we do, security could extract this information from our minds. It's enough just knowing that there is a way to the surface. I hate to say this, but I think this has to be goodbye."

As Lex said the word 'goodbye,' it struck everyone just how significant their meeting was, and how much of a barrier still existed between their two worlds. There was an invisible wall between them that wanted to be taken down, but for now, it had to remain in place for everyone's protection. They could all feel a new revelation about the nature of the world beyond, hanging in the air between them. There was silence for a moment as they all smiled at each other, appreciating everything that had happened. Each soul felt the gift of all the others and was grateful.

"It was a pleasure to meet you," said Dominic emphatically, reaching out to shake their hands.

"Yes," said Echo, "I do hope we meet again."

Lex and Ram took turns shaking everyone's hands, and then Andrea placed her hand in the space between them. "Put your hands on mine," she said, and they each placed their hands, one over the other, forming a stack in the middle. "We *will* meet again."

"Right," declared Melanie, recognizing how Andrea had changed hope to certainty with the power of her words. "We *will* meet again." It was a group affirmation, and each of them took turns saying it as they were holding their hands together until the circle of agreement was complete.

"Thanks, guys," appreciated Melanie, as they all released their hands. "Now it feels like we can go."

"We'll walk you to the stairs," offered Lex, wanting to at least see that much before they headed back. The whole group walked for about a minute before reaching the main stairwell. Lex and Ram only poked their heads in, taking one last look at their new friends who were beginning to walk up the first flight. Between the rails through the middle of the stairwell, they could see that many more floors were obviously above them. The mere sight of this stairwell sent shivers of wonder and fear up their spines. *This is as far as we go*, Lex said to Ram telepathically. And from there, they waved goodbye.

11

THE COUNCIL OF LYS

Raymond carried the Egg inside the black stone box as the whole group followed Amaron through a network of tunnels, leaving the boat pool far behind them. Roya was beginning to sense that they had arrived on the outskirts of a much more developed area. Every turn they took revealed more elaborate details on the carved stone walls.

"It's extremely rare for outsiders to be allowed into Lys," Amaron revealed. "You will all be treated as honored guests."

"Do all of you speak English down here?" asked Roya.

"No, but many of us do," he answered. "It has become like a second language, ever since we received a prophecy about its purpose. We believe it is a key that will help bring about the eventual integration of our cultures. We started speaking English when we realized that we could help raise the vibration of this language to reflect more universal frequencies of thought. By sharing in a common language, it is creating a resonance of shared mind between us. This allows us to help you evolve the practice of language, to purge it of duality and progress toward more unifying expressions of knowledge and awareness. The more people who use this language with an intention of oneness, the more the words can be imbued with unity consciousness, which will help bring our cultures into resonance with each other."

"Wow!" remarked Raymond, about to continue, but then he became lost in thought.

"What?" asked Soraya expectantly, wondering what her husband was thinking.

"I've never thought of language like that," replied Raymond. "How does using our language actually create that level of interconnectedness when your culture is so far removed from everyone's awareness on the surface?"

"By using your words and introducing some of our own through telepathy, we are creating a kind of quantum entanglement between minds through shared patterns of resonance. Even a single word can become a bridge that connects many minds together in a way that acts as a medium for living information to flow."

"Like betweenergy," said Roya.

"A perfect example," stated Claire. "We are using language to activate the betweenergy that we share with you on the level of our DNA."

"That's fascinating! So, what is your first language?" asked Frank.

"We are a telepathic race, but our telepathy also evolved into resonance with the Language of Light itself," explained Claire. "We communicate through pure emotional meaning, but the Language of Light allows us to share in the consciousness of living symbols that contain powerful universal insights."

Roya was remembering the flash of the Star of David from the boat. Somehow, it felt like more than a symbol, as if their journey into Lys had connected them with the living consciousness that the symbol reflected. She was beginning to see it spinning in her mind and vibrating with living information, as if the consciousness of the symbol was greeting her like an old friend.

As she walked along, the symbol began to reveal its hidden dimensions. Sometimes it appeared small, like a spinning ball of light inside her mind, and at other times it would expand to encompass all of them.

After a short walk, they entered a circular, domed room with several other tunnels leading off in different directions. A soft white light glowed from a spiral pattern that began at the center of the ceiling and expanded to fill the dome. The archways over the tunnels were also engraved with symbols that glowed, and the tunnels beyond had arched ceilings. Roya was overcome with wonder. Her mind filled with questions, first and foremost about the power source of the light.

"Where exactly are we?" asked Raymond, beating Roya to the next question.

"We are very close to the city of Sharindaya, one of the many cities of Lys. This pathway over here leads to the heart of the city," Claire explained, gesturing to the left. "Some of these other pathways lead to a more ancient tunnel system."

"There's a whole city down here?!" exclaimed Roya's mother in disbelief.

"Oh, yes," said Claire, as Amaron led them into the pathway on the left. "We will be there shortly, but first, we must go see the council. They are the ones that have made it possible for you to be here."

The pathway was lit by the most intricate pattern of glowing, curving lines, which covered the walls like artwork. Again, the source of light was a mystery, but the artistry was amazing. It resembled a complex maze. Occasionally, ripples moved through the pattern, making the light appear to be liquid. Ami and Roya both explored the pattern with their hands and noticed a very mild current of energy that felt exhilarating, as if the energy was happy to interact with them.

Mandy had fallen behind the group and was becoming lost in the pattern. As she traced her fingers over the lines, something interesting began to happen. Some of the light was absorbing into her skin. As she continued to gaze at it, she began to notice that when she breathed, she was drawing in the light with her breath. It felt pleasantly uplifting, as if the pattern was a beautiful living energy that was greeting her personally. She was beginning to feel connected to the light of the city.

"Hey, Mandy," called Roya, who was nearly at the end of the pathway. "You have to see this!"

Mandy trotted down the rest of the way to catch up just as they were all entering into the largest domed room they had ever seen. The ceiling must have been five stories tall at the highest point. A set of twelve glowing symbols encircled the upper part of the dome, most of which looked reminiscent of animal forms. The whole group stood quietly for a moment, taking it all in. To the far right was a wide, elongated archway, and there were several other exits with smaller archways like the one they had just passed through. They all began to hear the distant sound of a waterfall. Though barely discernible from their position, the gentle, meditative rhythm of the falls in the distance permeated the space, adding a sense of depth that was much greater than the room itself.

"Roya," said Claire quietly, "can you guess what these symbols are?"

Roya looked perplexed at the idea that she would know anything about something she had never seen before, but then she realized Claire expected her to be capable of making an educated guess. After studying them for a moment, she had an idea.

"Are they like the muses at the library?"

"Yes, very good," said Claire. "These symbols represent twelve forms of living knowledge common in the system of libraries our people hold sacred." Claire then pointed to an inscription on the floor that looked like a series of light symbols flowing into one another. "It says: *From these twelve forms, knowledge flows like water through the channels of the life code.*"

"When you say 'life code,' are you talking about DNA?" asked Raymond.

"Yes," said Claire. "Though we do not use a chemical name for it like you do."

"So, you believe there is a relationship between DNA and inner knowledge?" he continued as they walked along.

"Yes," Amaron responded this time. "That is one of the teachings we preserved from the ancient past. We relate to the human body very differently than your people do, but that is beginning to change in your culture. All of the great teachers from both of our cultures have taught us that knowledge comes from within, but down here, we have progressed much further in our ability to access such inner knowledge."

"So, what is this place?" questioned Roya.

"Do you remember the intuitive map that you drew to help guide your journey?" asked Claire.

"Yes."

"Well, this whole room is like an intuitive map that is responsive to the seeker. If you focus on the symbols, they will speak to you about the knowledge you are seeking. Sometimes, they even guide you where to go on the path of knowledge. That's why across the floor, you see symbols for each of our cities."

Roya now noticed several of the people across the room walking around while looking at the floor, sometimes appearing to follow a pathway. Then she realized that the pattern in the floor contained a labyrinth. As she walked forward, watching more of the pattern come into focus, she saw an intricate network of pathways weaving connections between the city symbols. At times, one of the city symbols would light up for someone, as if to invite them to journey there in their quest for knowledge.

"How many cities are there?" asked Roya.

"Lys is comprised of a hundred and thirty-two cities, all together," replied Amaron, "but not all of them are currently in use."

"A hundred and thirty-two!" Sarah exclaimed loudly. Everyone else was just as shocked.

"Just try to let go of all your questions, for now," requested Amaron, quietly. "We should be quieter when others are in the space. This room is meant for contemplation."

"Oh, sorry," Sarah whispered.

Amaron then led the group toward an archway to the far left, passing by several curious onlookers. Roya was struck by how easily she could now see people's auras. She wondered if this was because the people of Lys had more light in their bodies, or if she had somehow been psychically activated by the experiences of the previous week. Around each person was a kind of energetic egg containing a vibrating, scintillating field of colors. Each person's energy looked different, and sometimes, she could see a connection flowing between those who were together. Amaron and Claire's energies looked merged when they stood next to each other, as if they were both inside a larger egg, and their auras became more reflective. She could really see the way they complemented each other through their colors.

Thinking back, she realized that she had begun to glimpse this new living energy awareness when she connected with the Flavors, and then again when Claire helped her draw the map; but it had been more of a feeling at first and not as visual. When they had the experience with the Egg in the cave, her awareness expanded, opening her inner senses even further until it became a visual experience. Now, it was clear that being in the presence of others who had the awareness had boosted her own. She wondered if she would still have this level of heightened perception when they returned to the surface.

After they exited the map room, they entered a great hallway and passed by several entrances to other domed rooms with unique designs. It was hard not to stop and look. Each room had an inviting ambiance that wanted to be explored, but their guides had another destination in mind for them. The hallway came to an end in a circular room, the first they had seen without a domed ceiling. This one was lit almost normally, according to the standards of surface dwellers. A number of glowing white orbs set into the ceiling lit the room, and the floor was made of a smoothly polished stone that shimmered in the light.

As they entered, they noticed white walls and a large, circular, white table with enough chairs around it to accommodate almost twenty people.

It looked like they were in some kind of conference room. Amaron was the first to take a seat midway around the left side of the table, and Claire joined him, followed by Roya's parents, and then Sarah and Roya. Frank took a seat on the right side of the table, followed by Mandy and Ami.

Roya wondered why the council wasn't already there, since their group was expected, but as soon as they all sat down, something amazing happened. A short ringing tone buzzed through the air, and suddenly, a part of the wall just disappeared on the other side of the room, creating a doorway. Immediately, a group of three regal-looking people entered and took their seats next to one another. Then, just as quickly as before, a tone chimed again, and the wall rematerialized, appearing perfectly seamless and solid once more.

"Wow, it's magic!" said Sarah, awestruck.

"No," Roya whispered to Sarah. "It's just advanced technology."

"An excellent observation," recognized the man in the middle of the group of three. "Though, we do not normally refer to the elemental beings that form such structures merely as technology. That is, unless you were to say that matter itself is the technology of dreams." Roya began to ponder his words. *Matter: the technology of dreams.*

His voice was warm and friendly, and he seemed deliberately welcoming. Roya blushed, and she felt a flutter in her chest as he glanced at her momentarily, reading her response. His face was beautiful and warm, and she felt like her heart was naked. She was not used to men who were so present and acknowledging. *Can he feel what I'm feeling?* she wondered. She was relieved when he broke eye contact, and she took a deep breath as he looked around at the others.

The members of the council smiled at the group, looking around and making eye contact with each of them individually. The look in their eyes was powerful, yet kind. This had intimidated Roya when she first met Claire, so she wondered how the rest of the group was feeling about the presence of such powerful beings. She looked around, assessing the energy of her group, and felt that everyone was adjusting well. For a moment, the three seemed to hold everyone in silence, as if to help them focus inwardly on the feeling of connection they all shared before speaking. Their sense of command made everyone in Roya's group want to pay close attention to what was unfolding.

The two men and one woman wore green tunics with gold trimmings.

"My name is Shumayan," said the man in the center with short brown hair. "It is an honor to meet you. This is Shemazae," he said, looking to his right. She then raised her hand, slowly spreading out all five fingers to bare an open palm, just as Claire and Amaron had done when they first arrived. She had long dark hair that was pulled behind her ears and woven into a braid, and her eyes were just as big and bright as Claire's.

"And this is Twa'amatae," he continued, looking to his left as the man with long blonde hair made the same gesture. "We are part of the Council of Lys, a much larger circle of individuals. We thought it would be easier for you to acclimate to just a few of us, at first. We already know each of your names. We've been observing everything that has happened since Roya found the book."

"You could see us?" Ami blushed.

"Yes, we've kept a close eye on our emissary, and we are quite adept at seeing through each other's eyes," said Shumayan as he turned his gaze to Roya, sensing her next question.

"Claire. Is that your real name, or do you have one like theirs?" she asked.

"I took the name Claire when I came to the surface, to blend in with the culture, but Claire is short for Clairadinda."

"Are you the leader of this council?" Frank asked Shumayan.

"We do not have a leader, but I was invited to facilitate this meeting. I am sure you are all wondering who we are and how we came to be here," Shumayan answered.

"Where do we begin?" asked Frank. "This is a previously undocumented civilization as far as our people are concerned. Claire said we had to be willing to let go of everything we thought we knew about history. I think I speak for everyone when I say: we are ready to be enlightened."

"Very good, then," proceeded Shumayan. "We are excited to have this opportunity to tell you our story." He looked around at his companions, and they all smiled in agreement.

"Our people originally came from another star system to make a home on the Earth for a time. We came from a system of worlds that had surpassed the use of physical technology, though we did not experience as many obstacles to our spiritual growth as you have here. We lived in harmony with nature, but our knowledge was incomplete. There was something missing inside us that compelled us to search for another experience, a way to contribute to the galactic community that we knew existed beyond the womb of our homeworlds. When we began to explore outside our local system of stars, we found many inhabited worlds struggling to achieve the unity that had become so natural for us. We witnessed extended periods of warfare between factions of the same planetary culture and even war between worlds. A great tragedy occurred when one of these inhabited worlds was destroyed completely in warfare. It was then that we realized a new purpose. Can you imagine what that was?

Mandy raised her hand with excitement. "To bring peace to the galaxy," she said, smiling, because she believed she had it right.

"That is an *excellent* idea, Mandy, and one our ancestors debated over at length, but we found that peace could not simply be brought to a planet by outsiders. It had to be born from inside a planetary culture and claimed as a personal value by each participant."

Roya instantly noticed a conscious intent behind how Shumayan responded to Mandy's answer. Most of the teachers she had from public school would have just treated it as a wrong answer, but Shumayan met Mandy's energy from a place of equality that acknowledged her creative expression as being valuable to the field of the group. He was ensuring that she felt included in the flow of the conversation.

After a moment, Roya suggested, "To preserve knowledge?"

"Yes," Shumayan smiled brightly, and Roya's parents both smiled at each other as if Roya had just brought home a report card with straight A's. Sarah suddenly became more poised, ready to show that she could answer a question correctly, as well, if another came up.

"It's clear from the twelve symbols that your culture values knowledge," explained Roya, "and when you mentioned war, I couldn't help thinking about all of the great libraries that have been destroyed in human history. When we started learning about world history in school, that part always struck me as a great tragedy. I couldn't understand why anyone would want to destroy a library."

"You are very observant, Roya. To preserve knowledge is indeed part of our cultural mission. We decided that if we could preserve the knowledge of emerging planetary cultures, we could ensure that such knowledge would be protected until those cultures reached maturity. In order to do this, we had to work from behind the scenes. We have seen on other worlds how intervention from the outside destroyed emerging knowledge systems before they could bear their fruit. So we have developed a policy of noninterference with cultures that are not advanced enough to meet us as equals. For hundreds of thousands of years, our people have experimented with this role in the galaxy with some surprising results, but the most surprising of all may be about to unfold right here on Earth."

"Now, I have to ask," interjected Raymond, "have your people preserved parts of *our* history that have been lost?"

"Yes, we have," replied Shumayan.

Roya heard her dad swallow hard, and a palpable feeling of both shock and excitement came over the room. Something inside them was awakening and coming full circle, as if humanity itself was crossing a new threshold through them, much like when Neil Armstrong and Buzz Aldrin first walked on the moon. Ideas were flashing through all of their minds about what kinds of secrets from history the council possessed, and Roya's inner senses were alive with impressions coming from the group through the field of connection between them.

She could feel the council focusing gently on their minds, coaxing them all to relax into a presence of group consciousness. Sensing what was possible, Roya let go and felt her mind opening up like a container. She imagined her mind as a chalice being filled with the presence of the council. Just as she could sense their auras outwardly, she was beginning to sense their presence inwardly, like a band of living energy that was wrapping around her mind. It was like wearing an energetic headband, and when she looked around at them, several of them seemed to acknowledge with their eyes that she had achieved the next level of connection. A second later, her focus shifted, and she felt Claire inside her mind as well, and then Amaron. She could feel some of the others being apprehensive about entering such a level of connection but testing the waters in their own way.

"Our mission to preserve knowledge here began with a call that came to us from the Earth herself, inviting us to become a part of her," explained Shumayan. "This was an incredible honor, because we knew that Earth was a great storehouse of living knowledge. Preserving it would be the work of many ages. The way our culture measures time would be foreign to you, but we came here long before modern humanity came into being."

"When we first arrived, we did not look like we do now. We were luminous beings who could change form according to our thoughts. We came here as beings of light, traveling in vehicles made of light, but we soon began to densify ourselves to blend with the planetary environment. The human pattern was already familiar to us, being one of the most successful evolutionary patterns in the universe, so we began to develop a human-type form for our people here on Earth. The first version of us was semi-physical. We were shorter than we are now, our heads were more round, and we had less individuality to our appearance."

"For thousands of years, we worked with the plants and animals, taking in their knowledge as a pure vibrational essence. We lived on the surface then, and we like to think of this as the time when we became married to the Earth. During this time, we witnessed the activities of many other galactic cultures and the beginnings of *your* civilization. By then, our bodies were becoming denser and more physically developed, which is part of the reason why we felt drawn to you."

"From the very beginning, we noted qualities of individuality in your species that intrigued us. We saw more than just an evolving planetary culture that we could document. How can you document such a diverse culture from the outside?" he paused, leaving room for the thoughts of the group. "Because we shared the Earth in common, we chose to present ourselves as companions to this new human culture, to co-create with you." He said this now as if he was addressing the whole of human history inside each of them.

"For many ages, we shared your cities and worked side by side with your people, building a planetary culture that could connect the Earth with a vast community of intelligent space-faring races. The idea was to develop a civilization that could assimilate knowledge from across the galaxy: a galactic melting pot that could represent a potential for galaxy-wide cultural integration, and we were there to document this noble effort."

"Whatever happened to this culture? Why do we have no record of this?" asked Raymond.

"Despite our best efforts, we did not have the influence to prevent the corruption of this project. More than thirteen thousand years ago, our people chose to leave this corrupt society and make our home inside the Earth. By this time, we had wisely chosen to incorporate some of your DNA into ours, and thus, we carry a remnant of yourselves from this time, which is why we look so similar. It was the best way to preserve the knowledge and achievements of your ancient ancestors. Technically speaking, we are your cousins."

"It was not long after this that a great destruction occurred. Once again, warfare created a major setback. So major, in fact, that almost none of your people can remember what came before. You had to start over."

"Are you referring to Atlantis?" asked Raymond.

"Yes. However, the culture you know as Atlantis was much vaster than your people realize. Plato's story of Atlantis has led you to believe that it was contained on a single island that sank, but there were once Atlantean cities in many other parts of the world. Atlantis was a global, technologically advanced, sea-faring civilization."

"You have also called our ancient home in the Pacific Lemuria. But again, our civilization was more global, as well. Now that we carry the genetic memory of both civilizations, we see both Atlantis and Lemuria as equals in our DNA."

"As to your other question, Raymond, your scholars have found many records of Atlantis, but you do not yet know how to read them properly. However, all of the keys to unlocking humanity's ancient past are right there in your DNA. The challenge of piecing together your ancient history has never been one of finding evidence, but rather of remembering how to access the truth that is within you. We watch your debates over the origins of humanity with great humor because your people so often testify against the truth stored in their own bodies. It is a great wonder to us how so much of your wealth in knowledge remains invisible to you."

"For thousands of years after the destruction, we watched your culture experimenting with primitive social structures on the surface. We watched, and we waited, looking for signs that you would remember and begin to seek after the knowledge that you had lost: knowledge of the soul itself. Approximately six thousand years ago, we sent emissaries to the surface, because we saw the light in human consciousness beginning to increase again. We sent teachers to Egypt, India, and the Americas, to plant the seeds of the knowledge-sharing culture that you could become. This was when the great mystery schools of your modern civilization began—a time when you began to reconnect with the stars."

"Then we watched and waited again. We saw the light struggling to claim its place, and each time the light increased, darkness would arise to stamp it out. But a part of you continued striving for the light. We watched with great interest the advent of humanity's messengers and the great social changes that began to take place as you entered an age of discovery. Gradually, we began to sense the coming integration of our two cultures."

"Over the last several hundred years, we have seen signs of a great awakening, and many of our people began to dream about being born into the surface culture to take part in it. We believe this is part of a plan that is even greater than our original mission, a calling we have not felt since we first came to Earth."

"You're talking about reincarnation, right?" Soraya questioned.

"Yes, though there is far more to this process than the concepts taught in your Eastern religions. We did not expect that integration between our cultures would happen in this way, but this meeting is a sign that such activity has begun to break down the barriers."

"Are you suggesting that some of us may have reincarnated from your culture into ours?" Raymond considered.

"Yes. Feel the truth of this, and tell us, who among you forms the bridge that you crossed to come on this journey?"

"Roya," Raymond recognized, turning to look at her. "I suspect Ami and Mandy as well."

The two sisters both looked at Roya, trying to sense if she believed this could really be true of the three of them. The idea that they had somehow known each other before, though unspoken, was a feeling they all shared, but this was an exciting twist. The thought that they could actually discover something of their history together as souls was intriguing.

"It makes a lot of sense," agreed Frank. "Ami and Mandy have a way about them that's different, and until they introduced me to Roya, I thought it was just them."

"And what about Sarah?" asked Soraya, sensing that she might feel left out.

Sarah was suddenly embarrassed by the comment as she felt the council turn their attention toward her. For a moment, she *had* felt left out, but it was far more uncomfortable being put in the spotlight of the council members.

"Sarah, we sense that you have been Roya's sister before in several lifetimes," said Shemazae, "though not during her incarnations in Lys. Like many from the younger generations on the surface, your soul has followed a pattern similar to Roya, Ami, and Mandy's. Whenever there needs to be a bridge between cultures, to bring about integration, each of you, in your own way, will form part of a bridge to help break down the barriers."

Sarah was now looking at Roya, seeing them both through the eyes of the council, and Roya was opening up to a feeling of deep gratitude for Sarah. The council was describing something that Roya was beginning to remember about their relationship as souls.

"In this case," she went on, "because Roya would not meet Mandy and Ami until she was in her teens, she called for the assistance of a familiar soul to help her adjust to life on the surface and to help her make it through the first stage of her journey. We are deeply grateful to you, Sarah, for choosing to be Roya's older sister, because she would not have done this without you. You are also a system buster who breaks new ground and challenges people to let go of their old ways to discover the new. It's no wonder she chose you."

Instantly, as Shemazae said this, Sarah burst into tears. Many things at once spoke to her heart: the feeling of gratitude from Roya; the fact that her parents were listening to this wise council speak positively about her will to test the boundaries of freedom. Then, a memory flashed through her mind that was as clear as the day that it happened. She could feel herself being carried by her father at the age of two into a little gift shop at the hospital where Roya was born. Her father asked her to pick out a stuffed animal as a present for Roya. She was not even sure she could comprehend all of his words at that age, but she remembered understanding clearly that, on that day, she was getting a baby sister. Perhaps she only understood the emotional intentions of her father, but she remembered pointing to a little stuffed baby owl and knowing that was the one she wanted to give to her sister.

What touched her so deeply about the memory was not just the excitement about the arrival of her sister, but that she remembered her heart leaping out at the owl as she pointed to it. Her heart had chosen that gift for Roya. She had not wanted it for herself. She understood what it meant to give something to someone as a gift, even at that age. It was a feeling of unconditional love, and she remembered what her heart had felt like before it closed for what seemed like a very long time.

Sarah's sobs overpowered her, and the tears were streaming down her face as Roya wrapped her arms around her. She could barely see through the tears. Her mother also put an arm around her, and her father, who was too far to reach, put his arm around her mother. Roya could feel every sob as if it were her own, and when Sarah finally looked up and began to wipe her eyes, everyone, including the council members, had tears in their eyes. Everyone was touched in a different way, but what Roya noticed was the transformation of something very old that she had come to recognize as a family pattern.

Sarah's reserved emotional state was a form of protection from harsh criticism, something that their mother had experienced often when growing up. As a child, Sarah had chosen to step into the reflection of her mother's inner child, to help her mother recognize her own repressed sensitivity. Sarah's soul knew that this would help her mother develop compassion toward herself so that she could let go of identifying with the pain of her own childhood.

Sarah had taken the brunt of her mother's criticism, and now Roya could feel how Sarah had made it easier for her to come here with a sensitive heart and mind. The gift of Sarah's favor was being returned as the memory of her love for baby Roya restored her own angelic heart. Recipe—reciprocation. Every soul contract leads to an awakening and a return to greater love. Truly, the recipe for love in the book contained a reflection of their friendship as sister souls.

Now, the whole room felt different. The empathy of the room had gradually penetrated all their normal defenses to create an environment of trust in their emotional vulnerability. At the same time that Sarah had opened her heart, their mother had opened hers. Sarah's emotional release had caused a chain reaction, and both mother and daughter suddenly felt free from the painful way their sensitivity had been criticized while growing up.

"Without loving and supportive parents, this meeting would not have been possible," remarked Twa'amatae. His words gently called the parents to recognize the love that they are, and not to define their sense of self with guilt about the times when they had broken from the loving character of their souls.

"These children trusted each of you as parents, in part, because you were open to the mysteries of life. They knew you would ultimately support their exploration both inwardly and outwardly, even though they would test your boundaries—and your patience," he said, smiling at Soraya. Finally, Sarah was calming down, and after wiping her eyes again, Roya saw that she was smiling, too. Sarah had been struggling to find her place, wanting to participate, but feeling awkward and unsure of her worth. Now that the group feeling of connection had reached her on a heart level, her mind was becoming clear.

"Thank you, all of you," she said to everyone in the room. "I wasn't sure if I was meant to be here, but now, I see that I had to be."

"You are very welcome," said Twa'amatae. "We are pleased to see this kind of healing. It is part of the effect of the community field you are in. Being surrounded by those who honor the full range of human emotion calls your emotional field into clarity. We see our emotional level as a place of connection, and if anything impedes the feeling of connection with others, the field of oneness we all share will naturally root it out and expose it so that it can be honored."

"I never knew that people could be this way," appreciated Sarah. "Where we come from, people are often insensitive and even violent. We learn at an early age to be defensive, or to compete for attention. Even our family is not free from this, and we are all good people," she said looking at her parents, "who try our best to stay balanced."

"It's hard when society doesn't strive to be balanced with you," added Soraya.

"That's very true," acknowledged Frank, and Raymond nodded in agreement.

"I often catch myself trying to control my daughters," Soraya continued, "instead of speaking to them like equals. I used to despise it when my parents did that, and yet, I wasn't taught any other way. I'm just grateful, because I see all of us improving."

"Now that you are here, you will all evolve more rapidly through your connection to this community field," explained Shemazae. "What you are witnessing now is a maturing process that is naturally part of how you become integrated with the community's wisdom."

"That reminds me," interjected Sarah. "You said that your people preserve knowledge so that it can become available once a culture reaches maturity. How do you know when that happens?"

"The awakening of peace consciousness globally is the sign that a planetary culture has become mature enough to handle all of the secrets of its past," articulated Shumayan. "Until then, people will make up whatever version of history suits their beliefs or agendas, whether it is true or not. When your vision of the future becomes inclusive of everyone, your access to the living records will open, and you will become like we are, able to remember the whole of history, just as easily as you can remember your own lives."

"That's really interesting," remarked Frank. "So, you're saying that the reason why our people don't remember the ancient past is that we don't include everyone in the future?"

"Yes," replied Shumayan. "Your culture is filled with exclusive identity groups. The nature of exclusivity varies from group to group and person to person, but it forms part of a blind spot that is very common among your people. When you only see a future for one group identity over all the others, your minds can't properly resonate with the singularity of human memory. When you can imagine a future that is inclusive of everyone, regardless of race, religion, nationality, or any other factor, a wealth of knowledge about history's lessons and potentials will tilt into alignment with your perspective, empowering you to create an outcome for history that is beneficial for all."

"That sounds like *The Circle and the Stars* book," reflected Ami.

"We know. We've read it," said Shumayan. "It used concepts familiar to us, but was written in your language, which is why we understood it to contain the potential of such a meeting between our cultures."

Shumayan could sense how many more questions were in the room, and yet, he also felt that some people were saturated with the information.

"We know this is a lot for all of you to take in," acknowledged Shumayan. "We don't expect you to assimilate everything in one meeting. We want all of you to feel welcome here as our honored guests. We would like to open the city to you, so you can see how we live."

"Thank you," expressed Roya.

"Yes, thank you," Frank echoed, and everyone nodded.

"Very well. One final order of business. We are aware that you recovered an artifact."

"Yes, we were wondering when we would get to experience it again. Only four of us have seen it in action," reminded Raymond.

"There are important memories and potentials connected with this artifact that we wish to examine first," explained Shemazae, "but we promise you will have another opportunity to experience it later."

Raymond placed the box with the Resonator on the table. Roya felt a sense of satisfaction having passed the test that they had apparently given her by finding the Resonator. The silent acknowledgment she sensed from the council made her feel warm inside.

"We leave you to Claire and Amaron," said Shumayan. "They will show you around and make sure your time with us is comfortable." And with that, a tone sounded from behind them, and the three council members arose and bowed slightly before turning to the opening that had just appeared again in the wall. As soon as they disappeared into the more dimly lit room beyond, the wall rematerialized.

Claire had a big smile on her face and looked like she was holding back a surprise. "Are you ready to see the rest of the city?" she asked the group. She clearly knew that many experiences lay ahead that they could not foresee.

"I'd love to!" exclaimed Roya. She did not want to wait another minute.

"We have much to explore, but feel free to ask any questions you have along the way," said Amaron as he walked through the door, waiting for the group to fall in behind him. Curiosity took over, and an exciting expectancy filled the air, as if the environment around them was just as excited as they were to explore the wonders of Lys.

12

DOCUMENTING THE TRUTH

Lex was right about needing time to process the truth. So much had happened in such a short span of time; both parties were baffled by the scope of what they had stumbled onto. Aaron's mind was more fatigued than his body. He was grateful that Zack asked him to hold off on sharing the story until they got back to his apartment, so he could film it as an interview with better lighting. Aaron was silent most of the way back, even though the group was having a lively discussion about the discovery.

It was after 4 a.m. when they got to the apartment. Andrea was yawning as they walked in the door, and Echo offered to give her and Melanie a ride home after they all talked. It did not matter how tired they were, everyone wanted to stay and hear what Aaron had to say.

Echo offered to make smoothies, and everyone found the idea appealing. Zack almost always had bags of organic fruit in the freezer. Because Zack's apartment complex had a good weight room and gym, Echo would often come over to join him for a workout and a smoothie.

Andrea and Melanie both had a change of clothes in their backpacks, so they went to the bathroom to change while the rest of the group got cozy in the living room. By the time they returned, Echo was passing around the smoothies, and Zack was setting up one of his cameras on a tripod in the middle of the room. Aaron sat on a meditation cushion with his legs crossed in front of the camera.

"I think we should all agree not to talk about this to anyone, yet," cautioned Zack. "It's one thing to keep the location secret, but we can't start talking to people about what we discovered, either, no matter how exciting it might be. It has to stay within our group."

"I agree," Aaron nodded. "This is some seriously classified stuff. We really don't know what we are dealing with in terms of authorities. If the wrong people find out, we could be in serious trouble."

"Right, so we can't tell anyone," affirmed Zack. "Does everyone agree?"

"Absolutely," pledged Dominic.

Everyone else nodded in agreement. Now that everyone was on the same page, Zack turned on the camera and started to film.

"OK, Aaron, so what did you see down there?" Zack began.

"It's massive. There's a whole city down there, but I only saw a small part of it. Time went by really quickly. They had me in that trance until we got to their apartment, but I remember everything vividly. The first thing I saw was this huge transport station with at least four other sets of tracks. Then we walked through a maze of other passageways that connected a number of plazas. It was like a network of underground buildings. We went down an elevator at one point into a residential area. Their place was small. It was really simple. But the professor they brought in was really interesting."

"What was he like?" asked Zack.

"He was middle aged, bald on top. He looked pretty fit for his age, and he was really commanding. Apparently, he had been in the military on the surface before going down there, so he knew all about where we came from, unlike Lex and Ram. He seemed genuinely interested in the fact that two of his students had discovered us. He said that it represented hope that our cultures would not remain separate, and that the secrecy that divides us could come to an end."

"What else did he say?" prompted Zack.

"He kinda freaked me out…the scope and scale of what he was talking about. I feel a bit overwhelmed when I think about it," he paused. "Ask me something else, and we'll come back to it. I'm still trying to get all my thoughts straight."

Aaron could not help feeling that something fundamental had shifted in his worldview. He did not want to frighten anyone with the more disturbing parts of what he learned before he found a way to integrate it all into something that sounded more hopeful. This would be a difficult task for any mind, but there was something hovering on the edge of his consciousness that felt inspiring: the idea that all of this was happening for a positive and empowering reason, despite the dangerous implications of what he had learned about the Gateway.

"Did they say anything about what that underground building was that we came in through?" inquired Zack, thinking carefully about where he wanted the interview to go next. He wanted to support Aaron to keep remembering while appreciating the sensitivity of his process.

"Yes. On the way back, Lex mentioned thinking that the lower levels of it might have been an old orientation center."

"Orientation for what?" asked Zack.

"I don't know. It could have been for people coming down from the surface, or maybe from other locations. Remember how we thought that part of it felt like a hospital? I bet they used to screen people for contagious diseases before they could go work down there. They said that this particular city was becoming one of the largest that had ever been built, and they were still adding on to it. They talked about it like it was their solution for surviving the breakdown of civilization on the surface, which they apparently believe is inevitable. But that just felt like something they are taught to believe to justify what they are doing."

"That makes a lot of sense," Andrea chimed in. For a moment, she was not sure if Zack was open to anyone interjecting while he was interviewing Aaron, but she had an idea that felt relevant, and Zack just pointed his hand-held camera straight at her. "If you were going to build a massive underground city, you'd want to have access to an abundant supply of fresh water. No wonder they chose to build it near Lake Michigan."

"I think they get most of their stuff from the surface," Aaron clarified, "but the professor implied that people down there take it for granted. It's a lot like how people in America buy stuff made by slave labor without even thinking about where it comes from."

"But who pays for it all?" asked Echo.

"We do," said Aaron emphatically without hesitating. "I spent a good part of last summer researching this kind of thing. You can find loads of stuff on the internet about it, but it's hard to tell how much of it is reliable. Basically, the government has been building these secret underground military bases for decades. They probably started out as some kind of Cold War project to make sure the government could survive a nuclear war. At least, that's how they might have justified it in the budget."

"Then, they began developing them more for permanent habitation, and linking them all together with high-speed rail tunnels like the one we saw. Some researchers are saying that a whole new civilization has split off from the surface culture, and that's *exactly* what we discovered. It's all paid for through shadowy government contracts and corrupt accounting practices. A lot of the money is siphoned off the defense budget, and they have their hands in everything from the banking industry to the illegal drug trade."

Aaron was happy to focus on a topic he had spent a fair amount of time researching. Feeling knowledgeable about something was more comfortable than feeling overwhelmed by the revelation of what the professor had disclosed. Under the surface, though, his mind was racing with the impact of all that he now knew.

"So, you're saying this is all some kind of secret government project?" asked Dominic.

"No!" he said emphatically. "I don't think this belongs to *our* government. Not anymore. I doubt any part of our official government has a clue how far this has gone. There might be people working *in* the government that are part of this, but they don't answer to Congress. They operate as a secret society...part of a shadow government that links the resources on the surface with the plan of these subterranean cities. They place people into key positions of power to serve their own interests."

"What are their interests?" asked Echo. "They must be into more than just survival. Why would so many people choose to live underground like that?"

Aaron's thoughts about the professor were becoming clearer, but he realized that he was struggling to feel safe. After all, he was not supposed to have this information, and there might be powerful psychics capable of noticing that he was at a new level of awareness. Only the support of his friends allowed him to have the courage to open up about it.

"Whatever this thing is, it's really big. This isn't just some plan for survival. It's a whole secret plan for controlling the course of history, and if what the professor said is true, it's more devious than any of us could have imagined."

"I feel like I'm still in shock from all of it. The professor said that they were using frequencies on the surface in an attempt to change the resonance of our consciousness so that we would become more compatible with their whole system of control. He called it *the Gateway*. It's designed to make us more receptive to the Frequency of the Superminds. They're actually training people to manage us psychically so that we lose the ability to think for ourselves and give our power over to them. It's like they want us to stay distracted with things that aren't important while our freedom is gradually eroded behind the scenes. He talked about all of this like it was a highly developed and well implemented plan that he didn't seem to think we could do much about."

Everyone was silent, shocked by what Aaron was saying.

"They want to manage all of the world's resources for their plans and have us all working for their agenda without even knowing it. I kinda felt a loss of humanity just thinking that so many people could be complicit in such a plan, but there was something that felt hopeful and inspiring about the connection between all of us, like our fate wasn't decided yet. This Frequency thing is real, though. We could already be affected by it without knowing. It's like how children today growing up in the cities don't even know what clean air is. They're slowly changing the resonance of humanity over time so that we don't realize what's happening until it's too late, like the frog that doesn't know the water is heating up until it starts to boil. Oh, and he even said that they might try to use some kind of personal technology as the next step."

"You mean like cell phones?" asked Andrea. "I always wonder what all those frequencies are doing to people's brains. What if that's part of their plan to alter our consciousness?"

"Maybe. I think he was talking about something else, though. He didn't know any more; at least, he didn't want to risk saying anything more. He kinda cut the conversation short after that."

"Man, this sounds like science fiction," said Dominic.

"Yeah, but this is real. I felt it myself when they put me in that trance to mask the signature of my mind. He said people down there are losing their emotional range to this Frequency. The most interesting part was when the professor said that a lot of the young people down there are trying to reject the Frequency. They can move in or out of it, and they want to know about the surface culture. Lex and Ram were really concerned that these super psychic people might find out about our meeting, but they seemed pretty confident that they could mask their memories somehow to stay off the radar. They didn't elaborate much about the Superminds, but there was something ominous about them. It's like their version of Big Brother."

"Big Brother? You mean like the reality show?" said Dominic.

"No, I mean like in *1984*," replied Aaron.

"What happened in 1984?" asked Dominic.

"No, not the *year* 1984, the *book*. It's one of the greatest science fiction books of all time. You should really read it. It's classic."

"Ohhh, *1984*," remembered Dominic. "My bad."

"Yeah, we studied George Orwell in my Honors English class, senior year," said Melanie.

"Hey, it's not like I haven't hit the classics, I just haven't read *that* book," defended Dominic.

"Even *I've* read *1984*," bragged Andrea.

"What's *that* supposed to mean?" retorted Dominic.

"I'm not really into sci-fi, but it's more than a science fiction book. When someone writes something that's really relevant to the world we live in, it takes on a life of its own. And if what Aaron says is true about this Frequency, George Orwell was barely scratching the surface," emphasized Andrea.

"OK, I'll read it. Anything else I should add to my reading list?" said Dominic sarcastically.

This was one of Aaron's favorite questions. He was an avid reader of science fiction and various fringe subjects, and he loved to give his recommendations, but he knew Dominic was joking. "I think everyone should read up on these deep underground military bases. We all know for a fact now that *something* is going on down there."

"You know, the thing I can't figure out," wondered Melanie, "is why this entrance was just left there for someone to find."

"It was covered over, though," countered Echo.

"But not good enough," said Melanie. "For something that is supposed to be so super-secret, it sure was easy for us to get in there."

"Yeah, how did you say it was covered?" asked Andrea.

"Well, you saw all of those cinder blocks," Zack reminded them. "There were tons of them piled in the corner completely covering over the door. Some were also stacked inside the room, like a wall had been built—except they didn't cement the blocks together very well. When we pushed, there was movement, so we pushed harder until it just fell and collapsed."

"I imagine that someone was supposed to seal off that door," speculated Melanie, "but they did a sloppy job on purpose. They sealed up the entrance to the building from the subway station at the bottom, but they left the top open, like someone wanted it to be found."

"But who?" contemplated Zack.

"You have to wonder how all of these underground bases and cities got built in the first place," said Melanie. "What if a lot of it was done through slave labor? It would make sense to me if the people who left it open at the top were not as committed to keeping it a secret. Maybe they wanted to leave themselves a way to escape."

"That's an interesting point," said Andrea.

"I don't know, but I think you're right, Melanie, this feels like a secret that wants to be revealed," added Aaron.

"So, what do we do about it?" asked Echo, starting to yawn.

"I think we should go back," suggested Zack, "explore it some more and take more video, maybe this time without any of our faces. I feel a little conflicted about what we shot tonight. It's amazing, but I don't know how we could use it and still protect our identities. If this is all secret government stuff, we have to be very careful. I don't want any men in black knocking on my door, if you know what I mean."

"What about your idea to create some sort of secret art installation?" offered Dominic. "That sounded really cool. Couldn't you still do that part of the movie and just not say where it is?"

"I don't know," replied Aaron. "I think we should try to expose this thing."

"Expose what, exactly?" asked Echo.

"The whole thing!" proclaimed Aaron. "The building, the city, the whole secret underground! This is really serious. This isn't just confined to the underground, it's impacting everything on the surface. Our whole society is being shaped by the agenda of these secret cities, and they're even trying to program how we think and behave with mind control frequencies. Someone has to fight this!"

"And how do we do that without giving ourselves away?" asked Zack. "We could get killed."

"If Martin Luther King Jr. had thought like that, where would the civil rights movement be?" declared Aaron. "Don't you realize how big this discovery is? Researchers have been writing books about this kind of stuff, and there's lots of wild speculation. But these secret cities are so tightly secure that no one really knows how big they are, how they operate, or what they're doing there... but *we* found a way in! I think we *have* to do something."

"I like the energy of what you're saying," admitted Melanie, "but Martin Luther King Jr. had a whole movement behind him before he gave his life for the cause. And we're only six people."

"What about Wikileaks?" suggested Andrea. Aaron's head was nodding in agreement toward Zack, knowing he would make the final call on how the footage was used.

"OK, I think I see where you're going with this, but there are some hurdles here," explained Zack. "First of all, think of all the ways people might try to discredit the video footage. They might say that this could be anywhere—just some abandoned building somewhere—and that we just used some creative editing to make it look like it's all underground. They will say that we entered one building from above ground, and the rest of the footage is from some other building."

"But a building without any windows?" remarked Aaron. "There *are* some unusual features to this building that lend credibility to the story."

"True, I see your point, but how do we prove that there's a hidden city down there? We don't have any proof of that besides your story," said Zack.

"Wait a minute," Aaron paused, reaching into his back pocket.

Aaron remembered the map that Ram had given him in case he had to escape on his own. He pulled it out and unfolded it on the ground in front of everyone. It was a little smaller than a state highway map. Zack's eyes opened wide, and he panned down with the camera. Everyone leaned forward, marveling at the size of the underground complex laid out before them.

"Wow!" marveled Andrea. "Is that the city?"

"No," said Aaron. "It's only just now coming back to me. Remember when they mentioned sector nine? Well, this is it, but it's only a small part of the whole city. They said they're working on sectors ten and eleven that are even deeper and larger. There could even be more than that, because they aren't told everything."

"You've got to be kidding!" exclaimed Echo. "You saw all of that?"

"Only a small part of it," answered Aaron. "Ram marked the major turns we took so I could find my way out if we got separated. Here's the main transport station," he said, pointing to it on the map. "They led me all the way to this area over here where we took an elevator down a number of floors. I'm sure this doesn't show everything though, just the main connecting routes between structures."

"This is amazing! And you said this was only one sector?" questioned Melanie.

"Yeah. They said this is where all of the students and workers are," explained Aaron.

"I don't know how this helps in terms of exposing the city," said Zack. "People would just say that we created the map ourselves to go along with the story."

"I think you are forgetting something really important though," said Aaron.

"What?" asked Zack with interest.

"It's all true. The truth is more powerful than any of the stuff people might say to debunk this. Truth resonates like nothing else, so if we just tell the truth, then all the people who are really seeking truth will know. Who cares about the debunkers? Some people just want to prove their illusion, because they're afraid of a greater reality."

"He's got a point," stated Melanie. "If everything we present is the truth, it will be explosive."

"This is not just a matter of believability. Just feel this for a moment." Aaron paused and took a deep breath, like he was winding up to say something important. He had this wild look in his eyes and suddenly became more animated. "We have a moral duty here. In fact, it would be a crime *not* to expose this. These underground cities were created with *our* resources that should have gone to schools and health care and the poor. There's all kinds of financial fraud tied into how this is being funded, and who knows what kind of dark secrets are being hidden down there. We're as close as anyone has ever come to exposing this massive secret government that's trying to deliberately control the outcome of history. Look at this map! People have known for years that there's a black budget used for secret government projects but imagine if we could show people where it's all going—if we could show people how massive it is."

"And what would happen if we did?" questioned Dominic.

"Yeah, what exactly do we hope to accomplish by exposing this?" asked Echo.

"Listen, based on what Lex and Ram said, they are as much prisoners of the system as we are on the surface; in some ways even more so. I mean—did you see them?! They're just like us. They love to explore. They want freedom. But they live in a highly controlled society. There's a whole generation of young people being raised down there who don't know the truth about their world. What if we could open the doorway for them?"

"But how?" contemplated Zack. "I'm not doubting the possibility, but practically speaking, how do we accomplish such a goal? We need to think about our political aim. Who are we reaching out to and why? How do we want people to respond, and how do we protect ourselves in the process? Are we trying to start a revolution or just stir up the controversy so that others will find a way to do more than we can?"

"I'm not so sure we should be trying to figure out how to expose this *without* revealing our role it in," replied Aaron. "We need to expose this so widely that *everyone* knows who we are. We might be *more* protected that way, because if we all died in mysterious accidents before anyone knew about it, our sacrifice would accomplish nothing. We only need to keep this secret until we launch."

"I don't know. That sounds like a pretty big gamble, if you ask me," said Echo.

Aaron was really fired up now.

"Echo, this is bigger than our lives," he insisted. "If we do nothing, we might risk the best opportunity anyone has ever had to expose the truth behind all the corruption. Think about it. The government, the economy, and the media are all being used against us to serve these massive hidden agendas. We owe it to the whole human race to help expose what we've discovered."

Even as he spoke the words, in the back of Aaron's mind, he was thinking, *what am I getting myself into?*

"You're really serious, aren't you?" Dominic realized.

"Absolutely!" affirmed Aaron, defying his own fears and reservations. "Zack, when you first started talking about doing this movie, didn't you have a feeling that you could do something really big and meaningful; something that would blow people's minds? That's the kind of film you wanted to make, right?"

"Yeah, that's exactly right," admitted Zack. "This is more than I could have dreamed of. It's almost kind of scary that something like this landed on my doorstep. I don't know if I could really do it justice, though. This is too big: exposing a conspiracy this vast? Why would something like this come to me?"

"It came to *all* of us," stated Melanie. "I don't believe in coincidences. We should assume that we are exactly the right people for a purpose like this. Like it's our destiny."

"Right. This is not just about making a film that's entertaining anymore. It's about a cause," expressed Aaron.

"But from a film making standpoint," said Zack, "I still need to answer some basic questions about how we want people to respond. What do we hope to accomplish?"

"Disclosure," declared Aaron. "There's already a movement to expose these kinds of black budget projects. Our discovery could be just the right thing at the right time to help push that movement over the edge. We could finally get enough people demanding truth that they won't be able to control the global conversation anymore. Maybe we could trigger an avalanche of people coming forward with more information. We could even catalyze a betrayal within the secret webs of power that tie into these underground cities. What if we could inspire a revolution from the inside?"

"A mutiny?" questioned Dominic.

"Yeah, this could really rock," said Echo.

"What if there are loads of people just waiting for this to happen?" added Aaron. "Like the balance of power wants to tip the other way, and people are just waiting for a catalyst. There must be more people like the professor on the inside who feel there's a better way. And there has to be a way to wake people up on the surface before we lose even more of our power. What if we could create a future that's inclusive of *both* civilizations?"

"So how do we do it? What's the plan?" asked Melanie. There was a pause, and then everyone seemed focused on Zack. After all, he was the filmmaker.

Zack was still pondering the issue of security, trying to find the balance between artistic direction and the new and more far-reaching goal of achieving disclosure while being safe. At first, it was a question of whether one priority would have to be sacrificed for another, but then it struck him that the artistic approach might help open some doors.

"What if you did the artwork inside the underground building," he said to Aaron, "and we filmed it as part of a sequence of launch videos for the rest of the film? Then we could hype it up on social media and get a lot of interest about our secret location. We just tease people about an exciting discovery, but we don't say anything too revealing. We build a following first, and then we release the film on the web for free."

"And what if we camped inside the structure and explored it more while Aaron does the artwork?" suggested Echo. "We might find something more we want to use for the film."

"That's another idea," said Aaron. "We should think about mapping this thing out more. Do we have anyone that could create a 3D visual model for the web?"

"I might know someone," said Zack as he pulled out a notebook and started making a list. "I have a friend at film school who would be into this. We should consider...wait a minute. That's it!"

"What?" asked Dominic.

"We should let other filmmakers into this!" presented Zack. "That way we can make sure that no one can silence this project. Once we have what we need for *our* launch, we leak the location to a bunch of other explorers and filmmakers. Let them explore the structure and create their own films. We would be the first—the discoverers—but the more exposure, the better. That way, no matter what happens with the media, we have an alternative set of witnesses that will have their own footage. This could help protect us."

"Or put them in danger," countered Andrea.

"No, that's brilliant," validated Melanie. "I actually feel there's more light in that idea. If we are working for the light, we'll be protected."

"How much time do you think it would take to put all of this together?" asked Echo.

"It takes time to do a mural," said Aaron. "I would only do a section between the entrance where we came in and the hallway with the first staircase. I could do that in a couple of days."

"If you started on that pretty soon," said Zack, "I could have a rough cut of the film edited by next weekend. It depends on how much more footage we get that we want to use. I could at least have a short version, or a part one. I imagine we'll keep documenting the whole project so that there will be a part two."

"Andrea and I could help with social media," offered Melanie.

"We can help with the art, too," added Andrea.

"Excellent," said Zack. "Let's see if we can launch this in one week."

"Hey, is there any way we could continue planning this tomorrow night? I'm ready to crash," Andrea yawned.

"Absolutely," replied Zack. "This is going to take a lot of planning, so we should get some rest and meet up again tomorrow night."

Zack offered the futon in the living room to Aaron who was grateful that he did not have to make the drive across town to their dad's house. Aaron sometimes stayed over on the weekends, because it was closer to a lot of their favorite hangouts. He appreciated living at home, though, because it allowed him to save more of the money he made from painting murals. It had taken Aaron months to convince their dad that he would be more productive selling his art after graduating than going straight to college.

Aaron had always been artistically talented, but the inspiration to do street art only came to him after he started high school. One night, a couple of high school kids tagged the walls surrounding the rear entrance to the school. It was mostly dumb, offensive stuff, according to Aaron, who was unimpressed by the lack of artistry.

"If I were going to do renegade artwork," he bragged to his friends, "it would be something cool that no one would want to paint over." He almost considered sneaking onto the school grounds to paint something better over the tags, but there was an increased security presence around the school for the rest of the year, and after a little practice with some spray paint he found in the garage, he realized that he had a lot to learn about can control. His interest in street art solidified when his brother Zack graduated from high school, and their dad took them on a summer trip to Europe. Aaron was captivated by mile after mile of artwork along the railways.

While Zack's digital camera was filling with pictures of historic landmarks, Aaron's was filling with pictures of graffiti. His favorite site was the Berlin Wall, where he found many inspiring images, some political and some spiritual. He could not help thinking that a higher standard of quality was upheld in much of the European street art than what he had seen in Chicago. It was rare to meet Chicago street artists who were dedicated to improving the cityscape, but as a visionary artist, he was determined to elevate the practice.

After they returned, he began to study the craft by watching videos online and then practicing in places that nobody cared about. By the time he was a senior, he had started showing off pictures of some of his better pieces, and then someone offered to pay him to do some artwork for a new café. After that, a whole new world opened up to him. On the café's opening night, he was the celebrated artist that everyone was talking about. The people loved the atmosphere he had created, and the owners were very pleased and offered to refer his work to others. In one night, he had become known, paid, and recommended.

Even after getting several more commissions, his dad had still pushed him to apply for college in the fall, but Aaron was certain he had found his calling. The fact that he had graduated a year early made a strong argument for delaying college. He would probably still attend in another year, after turning 18, he thought, but not until he had firmly established himself as an artist. In just one month, he made over $3000 and only had to work eight days, but that still did not convince his dad, who preferred to see his sons with a busy schedule of either work or school.

Aaron's goal was quite different. He was not working for money, but for time. His idea was to be good enough and sought after enough that he could be choosy about who he worked for and get paid enough to have lots of free time and resources for his private projects. Fortunately, Aaron's dad came around when he saw that his son was becoming more organized and professional. Aaron had invested in some new airbrush equipment and was starting to hone his talents even further while mastering the ability to market his work online.

Since graduation, they had barely discussed his direction in life. Increasingly, Aaron's dad would leave to go on business trips to consult with various technology companies. He was a physicist with an engineering background, but he rarely talked about his work. Sometimes, he even seemed secretive, but Zack and Aaron never made an issue out of it.

By the time Zack and Aaron had both taken showers, the sun was just starting to rise. Even though Zack was exhausted, he could not help reviewing some of the footage from the night before; he was too excited about it. Aaron was eager to get some rest. The futon in the living room wasn't the most comfortable place to sleep, but that didn't matter. He was gone as soon as his head hit the pillow.

Sometime later, Aaron began to feel a sense of alertness, like he was starting to wake up, but he did not quite feel like he was in his body. At first, he became more aware of his breathing, but then, he began to hear the sounds of people talking, far away in the distance. As he strained to hear what the voices were saying, he began to feel movement, like he was being sucked through what seemed like a tunnel, until he found himself sitting in some kind of a classroom with about thirty other teens. For a moment, he was afraid that someone might see him, but then he realized that he was not in his own body. It was Lex! Their mind-link was still working from the night before!

Lex sat up with his spine straight and seemed to be aware of Aaron's presence, as if he was engaging their connection deliberately. Aaron could feel Lex's intention to show him something through his awareness of the room he was in. Subtle communication was happening between their minds without the use of words. Slowly, Lex panned around the room, revealing a dimly lit classroom somewhere in sector nine. There were boys and girls present, and everyone was chatting quietly until a teacher walked in.

Aaron was hoping for a moment that he would see Professor Alton again, but this man was younger and wore a military-style uniform. The class instantly became quiet when he entered, and it was very noticeable how disciplined their response was. Everyone was facing forward, like soldiers that had snapped to attention.

The instructor looked around, ready to criticize any flaws that he noticed in the appearance of the classroom, but he found none. Aaron noticed that the response of the class was not just physical, but mental, too. The teacher expected everyone's minds to entrain with his through the Frequency, though his abilities were not as strong as most of theirs. He was merely an instructor, carrying out his part of the program.

"Today, I will be presenting the latest research concerning the evolution of the human eye. For thousands of years, our species lived on the surface of the planet, and our eyes were more adapted to seeing in the brightness of sunlight. This was before we began to develop mind-viewing techniques for seeing beyond the limits of visual perception."

"Since making our home underground, our ability to see with less light has been tempered by the new environment, and our ability to see with the mind has greatly improved. Last year, you will recall that we ran phase-three of a citywide experiment that involved reducing the brightness of all light sources. The latest research suggests that the structure and function of the human eye is continuing to adapt to less light, and as we continue to develop mind-viewing abilities, our visual and mental awarenesses are integrating."

The instructor pulled out some kind of memory card and inserted it into a port on his desk, causing a briefing report to appear on screens that were embedded into each student's desk.

"Given that the efficient structure of our cities is becoming part of the memory map of our brains, the ability of individuals to navigate the cities blindfolded was also tested with extraordinary results. Our scientists expect that in less than a year, we will be able to move to a phase-four reduction in brightness, which will save the city an enormous amount of energy. If this phase is successful, we will soon roll out phase-four in all the adjoining colonies. We are already testing a new generation of supplements designed to improve vision, and the energy we saved from the last phase reduction has supported the process of adding sectors ten and eleven. Are there any questions?"

Aaron was so excited by what was happening that he almost snapped back into his own body, but Lex's control of the mind-link kept the connection stable. Across the room, a girl raised her hand, and after the instructor looked in her direction, she asked, "If we keep adapting to less light, won't this make it more difficult for our people to ever visit the surface?"

"We are not concerned with visiting the surface," said the instructor in a dry tone, expecting her to agree with his position. "We have a highly trained organization of surface dwellers that are adapted to work in that environment. They carry out all of the orders we give them to protect and supply the operations of the colonies so that we can build a lasting civilization down here."

"And why does this organization remain separate from us?" asked another student, trying to sense if there were any pathways for connection with the surface that could be discerned.

"It is a simple matter of risk management," explained the teacher. "The best way to protect our civilization from disease is to limit exposure to the surface."

"But what if we wanted to work for the organization on the surface?" asked another student.

"That's ridiculous," said the instructor. "We have left all the risks of working on the surface to the least valuable people. Those who remain on the surface are a race apart from us now. They are lucky that we provide them with enough structure and organization to serve the noble purpose of these cities. Down here is where humanity is making a fresh start. All of the best people are here."

Aaron knew through Lex's mind that this was not the answer the students were hoping for. Their curiosity about the surface was noticeable, but it was partly hidden from the mind of the instructor. Aaron could tell that something inside of these teens made them ignore what they were being told about the order of things, but Lex was not yet prepared to tell any of them what he had learned.

Aaron wondered if his presence in the room through the mind-link with Lex was somehow feeding their collective curiosity, confirming for them in some subtle way that there was more to the story.

We are working on him, Lex said mentally to Aaron, and instantly, he became more psychically aware of the other teens. Aaron could sense a coordinated effort to direct the focus of the instructor's mind to the subject of the surface culture, so they could read his thoughts about it, not his words. They would ask questions and then read the response with a level of discernment that was invisible to the instructor. There was even a feeling of empathy in the room for the condition of his consciousness. Was he merely controlled by his superiors, or was he consciously invested in the effort to obscure the connection to human history on the surface?

Aaron could feel some of the students sending energy to the man very subtly. They were trying to find a doorway into his emotional self, to help reconnect his mind with his heart. On some level, the students knew they were not expendable like many of the other groups they had heard about, so they were more fearless about testing the boundaries, even though they kept their intentions well-hidden. They pretended to agree with the program while using their considerable psychic abilities to probe for ways to erode it by getting their teachers and managers to question reality. Their goal was to break down the compartmentalized secrecy that had stratified human society, to prevent history's potentials from becoming too limited; something that felt unwise to these young, open minds.

They knew very well that the colonies needed them to advance their agenda of control. It was their collective psychic power that was so valued. They had been chosen—some of them even bred—for this purpose, to create a future with their thoughts that served the plan of the controllers. The idea was to implant a vision of the new future and the new society into their minds, under the guise of education, so that they would create with their thoughts the reality they were told was true.

For many decades, the cities had advanced their plans through the manipulation of a simple piece of universal knowledge: that our thoughts create our reality. Knowing the power of this one simple truth, a vast propaganda machine was implemented, acting on both the surface culture through the mass media, and on the underground culture through the education system, to achieve a global effect that favored the expansion of the cities and the consolidation of power in the hands of the few.

Aaron could sense the attitude of superiority that was part of the program underground; how they were all taught to think of themselves as better than the people on the surface. They were being taught to have a sense of entitlement around the resources that they were taking, as if all of the resources on the surface—human and material—were owned by the colonies as an unquestionable fact of their existence. It was not unlike the way Americans are taught to worship America's military power, Aaron observed, as if this is a part of the American identity that must remain sacrosanct in the U.S. budget, never to be undone. The constant transfer of power and resources from the surface to the underground was being protected through a marriage of beliefs on both ends that had established an insidious river of thievery.

They underestimate us, Lex said to Aaron mentally as the instructor switched on a screen that covered the wall behind him. Aaron then realized the obvious mistake of the controllers that resonated from Lex's mind to his. By pooling together the psychic resources of these gifted teens, they had not considered that they would become conscious that their thoughts create their reality. They had not considered that they would become discerning enough to see through the propaganda, or powerful enough to tilt the balance of power by choosing a different reality. The missing ingredient, as Lex saw it, was not knowing what else they could choose. *There must be other potentials for history*, they thought, and Aaron could sense what they were all thinking. They were looking for a doorway, and this was all the confirmation Aaron needed.

"All right, class, prepare yourself for a mind-viewing exercise," resumed the instructor.

Without warning, Lex released Aaron's mind, and the scene began to grow distant. For a moment, Aaron tried to hold the connection, but he had no mastery over this state of consciousness, yet. He almost felt a sense of having arms that were trying to grasp something as images of the city's structures rushed passed him, but then everything went dark, and he became aware of his breathing again. A second later, he opened his eyes.

Across town, Andrea tossed and turned in her sleep. She, too, was still exploring the hidden structures, but her connection to them was not as pleasant. At first, she thought she was dreaming, but something about it felt all too real. She found herself inside the underground building, looking for the rest of the group, but they were nowhere to be found. Then her headlamp went out, and it was completely dark. She was lost, and she did not know the way out.

"Help," she yelled. "Can anybody hear me?"

Her heart was pounding, and she began to panic. *Where is everyone?* she thought. She started feeling along the walls, but she kept coming to a dead end. She was trapped. Terrified, she called out again, "Help me! Somebody help me!"

The throbbing continued to grow, pounding in her head until the sound began to change. It was not just her heart this time. The sound became sharper, like metal striking concrete until it became almost deafening. There were others—pounding, pounding—trying to find a way out. She could hear them, through the walls. She could feel their terror, and then she heard their cries for help.

"Help!" she yelled in her sleep, and the sound of her own voice woke her. For a second, she thought it was over—a nightmare that had passed. But then, she felt gripped by a suffocating force that had a hold of her mind. Her throat tensed up like it was sore, and she could still hear the voices.

There's no way out, they said, over and over again. *There's no way out. We are all going to die.*

Andrea sat straight up in bed, trying to shake away the feeling of terror. She realized on some level that this feeling was not her own. She was being tormented by a terrible unrest that had poisoned the walls of the secret building, and somehow, it had followed her back home.

13

THE FRUITS OF KNOWLEDGE

Standing near the center of the map room, the two families soaked in the unusual sensation of the air, which felt charged with living energy. Every breath felt refreshing and restorative.

"I want all of you to feel this connection to the sound of the waterfall from a distance before we go to the viewing platform," invited Amaron. "This room was designed to capture the sound, just as the flow of the water beneath this structure was designed to help charge the air energetically. You will find that a lot of the structures in Lys were created to complement how sound and natural forms of energy can work together to amplify the presence of a field that can support expanded states of consciousness."

The sensation of the sound did indeed feel hypnotic and seemed to add to the impression that the air was alive, as if the air itself was exhilarated by the sound. From a distance, all they could see was darkness beyond, but as they approached the viewing platform, they gradually began to perceive a soft ambient light radiating from an unknown source. Amaron stopped at the entrance, as if to allow each of them the opportunity to step into discovery without being led. Claire's eyes were beaming with excitement in anticipation of what they were about to see.

Roya, Ami, and Mandy walked forward to the safety wall which came up to their chests. The edge of the platform extended beyond the wall of the map room in a semicircle. Looking over the edge, they saw the most magnificent sight they had ever beheld. Their jaws dropped open as the rest of the group fanned out on either side of the girls.

Before them was a vast cavern. On the far side, they could see tall cliffs with spectacular twin waterfalls flowing down to the bottom of the chasm many stories below, forming a river that flowed in their direction. An even bigger surprise were the numerous slanted buildings on either side of the waterfalls which connected the floor of the cavern to its ceiling. They were the size of skyscrapers, with windows, balconies, and elegantly etched patterns of light in the stonework.

Roya leaned cautiously over the edge of the safety wall, stretching to see the building beneath them. It appeared to be carved directly into the rock walls of the massive cavern. She saw many other windows and balconies and determined that the balcony they were on was about eight stories above the base of the cavern. They were right at the center of a building structure that opened as a semicircle toward the waterfalls. With a gasp of surprise, she realized that one source of the ambient light was the water itself. The falls appeared to be slightly luminescent, and the same was true of the river that flowed from the pool at their base. The river appeared to flow right into the lower level of the curved building.

"I can see why you thought we would not be in a hurry to leave once we got here," admitted Frank to Claire. *I wish I had my camera*, he kept thinking.

"This place is amazing!" squealed Mandy, twirling around in a little dance of happiness.

"Are you glad that you came?" Raymond asked Soraya, his eyes shining with delight as he wrapped an arm around her and drew her close.

"I had no idea. How could I have?" she replied. "I feel like I'm inside a dream."

Raymond took that as a yes.

"OK, if I end up losing my job," Sarah conceded, "it was worth it."

Claire and Amaron both knew that the longer the group stayed in Lys, the easier it would be to release their fears and start feeling more connected to the Earth and to each other. It was a silent agreement between them that they would carefully observe what needed to happen in each moment to support the healing process. For now, that meant giving each of them space to process the experience in their own way and letting them breathe in the air, which they knew had healing properties.

Claire's awareness was sharp, and she knew that it was important to observe the group's integration process taking place before their very eyes. At the same time, she was also deeply in tune with Amaron, and could not help feeling drawn into the heightened feeling of excitement that she felt with her partner by her side. She could feel his great relief that she had returned to him safely after such a dangerous mission.

Amaron departed the balcony early, letting Claire know that he would go ahead to prepare some food for the group. Most of them hardly noticed when he left, because they were so enthralled with the spectacular view. Only Roya happened to look over her shoulder a split second before he disappeared from across the floor of the map room. She had to blink to make sure her eyes were not playing tricks on her. One second, he was there, and the next, he was gone. It was as if he had just dematerialized into thin air. She thought about asking Claire what had just happened, but something told her she would find out soon enough. It seemed like the mysteries of this place never ended.

Down below, they could see people walking around the bottom of the cavern near the banks of the river. Then, something quite peculiar happened. A sudden glint of light caught Roya's attention out of the corner of her eye. She turned her head and saw a little orb of violet light about the size of a baseball in front of Claire's face. It appeared to Roya that Claire was watching it pulsate as it hovered just a few inches in front of her eyes before disappearing a few seconds later. She imagined that it must have communicated something to her, because Claire then called for everyone's attention.

"It's time for us to make our way to the temple. Please follow me," she announced.

Claire began leading them back into the map room, and Roya naturally gravitated to the front and center of the group, lining up with Claire as they walked. She really enjoyed soaking in Claire's attention, because she felt a sense of recognition between them as souls, a sense that had grown increasingly stronger since their arrival. She could not help wondering who they had been to one another in previous lives. Claire, too, enjoyed periodically connecting with Roya in a deeper way, though she was very skilled at balancing her attention among everyone in the group.

"I want you all to know how impressed I am with how well you made the transition to being down here," congratulated Claire with a smile as she turned around and walked backward so she could face the group. They were almost to the middle of the room.

"From our first meeting, to the boat, to the process of entering the city; I am really amazed at how well you surrendered and accepted all these new experiences. If you were being graded on the process of integrating with such dramatic change, you would all receive high marks." And with that, she stopped.

Roya was the first to look down and notice that they were standing on an image of a bird with its wings outstretched, landing on a rock. The picture was etched into a large metallic disc that encircled the group and was embedded into the stone floor. Looking around, she noticed that everyone else was now observing the disc as it was beginning to gently glow from within. Roya and Mandy looked at each other and smiled brightly, knowing that something exciting was about to happen.

"Because you are all so trusting in me as your guide, I'm sure you're ready to experience the way we travel down here," said Claire. Everyone was looking up now, waiting for her instructions. "Please make sure you are inside the disc, and keep your eyes focused on me for now. You may feel a slight tingling sensation…"

She was right. First, they felt a gentle vibration that tickled the bottoms of their feet, and then, a wave of warmth passed over them. They were all struck by a sudden urge to stand up straight, which they did, and then there was a flash of light so quick it was almost imperceptible. In an instant, the scene changed. They were in a different place entirely!

Soraya gasped and nearly fell backward, but Raymond quickly put his arm out to steady her. Claire looked completely unphased by the shift; though it took everyone else a moment to orient themselves and process what just happened.

"Did we just *disrem*?" asked Roya, recalling Amaron's instant disappearance earlier.

"Yes, that's exactly what we did," acknowledged Claire with a smile. "We are now at the ground level of the building."

"Teleportation?" inquired Frank.

"*Disremming* is a little different," replied Claire. "Teleportation is projection, or the sending of information from one place to another. Here we just change our memory of where we are standing with a little help from these discs, which act as memory markers."

"And that glow from the disc…the flash of light?" asked Frank.

"That was a little help from the beings that operate the transport system. Almost everything you see is alive and can communicate with you if you are open to receive," explained Claire.

Were it not for the opening messages of *The Circle and the Stars*, they would have thought they just witnessed an extraordinary form of magic. It would almost have been easier to accept that explanation, but gradually, the experiences of the city were producing a broadened awareness of humanity's spiritual and technological potential.

They were now standing in a large oval room with a high ceiling. A number of other people were scattered throughout the space, some of whom began to take notice of the newcomers. Looking around, they noticed four openings leading out of the oval room. Behind them was the entrance to the caverns, and they could hear the waterfall in the distance again. Roya was hoping to explore the caverns with the waterfalls, but Claire began to gesture for them to follow her in the opposite direction through a giant archway.

"This city is known as Sharindaya. It's a city of purification, and that is the purpose of the main temple before us," explained Claire. "Many healers work here to serve all who enter. Feel free to talk with anyone you are drawn to. Our people know all about your visit, but they are very respectful and will not approach you unless you signal receptivity."

"Are they curious about us?" Frank asked, as they reached the entrance.

"Oh yes," replied Claire, "but they can absorb a great many impressions without interacting with you directly. We are a very polite people and always respectful of one's inner experience."

They were all walking behind Claire now as they entered a vast room with stone pillars and large mandalas etched into the stone floor. The room was lit with gently glowing designs that were applied everywhere, again filled with liquid light that seemed to flow and pulsate to make the whole temple look alive.

Just then, a little orb of blue light zipped passed them and into the temple, disappearing around one of the pillars.

"What was that?" Mandy's eyes widening as several more colored orbs of light zipped by them overhead.

"They are *Formelle*," explained Claire, as if excited to introduce them, though she was speaking softly to respect the silence of the temple. "They're similar to Flavors, though it would be more accurate to say that Flavors are a class of Formelle. The Formelle are present wherever beings seek to co-create with the living intelligence of matter and light. They are a bridge between the consciousness of the whole unified field and the realm of human creative thought."

The whole group remained in silent awe as they looked around, hoping to spot some more colored orbs of light. As they first entered the temple, they walked along a raised dais that extended far into the space like a grand hallway. Flanked by rows of large stone pillars on both sides, it reminded Roya of a giant cathedral. Several orbs of colored light whizzed by as they proceeded.

As they walked deeper into the temple, they began to perceive subtle tones vibrating through the air. Sometimes a single tone would resonate through the space and then fade away, and then another from a different direction. They did not appear to be connected in a melodic way, but at times, a beautiful harmony emerged when multiple tones coincided simultaneously.

From atop a few stone steps at the end of the dais, they could see across a vast square room with even higher ceilings, where many small groups of people were gathered. As they watched, more of the little orbs of light danced around the temple, interacting with the various groups. It was like watching hummingbirds zipping up to a hummingbird feeder and then zipping away. Mandy could not help herself, and suddenly threw her hand up in the air to try to touch one of the orbs as it whizzed by. Her reflexes were quick, but not quick enough.

"I'm going to let you wander from here," said Claire. "I have a feeling that this temple holds a special message for each of you. Just be respectful of what others are doing. If you are invited to participate, don't be shy. Once you feel complete with what you are here to receive, just meet back at these steps."

Roya was excited by the possibilities, though her first impulse was not to explore, but to find a place where she could talk privately with her friends. Despite recent improvements in her relationship with her parents, she still felt inhibited around them, and she knew that Ami felt the same way. Mandy had no problem blurting out whatever came to her mind, but Roya could tell that Ami's first thought was the same as hers. She just hoped Sarah wouldn't feel left out.

The group had already started to fan out slightly, looking around at all the options. Claire did not make any suggestions, as she wanted each person to follow their intuition about where to go.

"We're going this way," Roya said to her mother, pointing toward the far left corner of the room out in front of them.

"We are?" asked Mandy.

"Yes," insisted Ami. The choice seemed random, but Ami knew Roya's intention.

"OK," responded Roya's mother, "just be careful." She said that every time Roya went anywhere, as if Roya was still a little girl.

They broke away without any resistance, and Sarah seemed to be happily discussing options with everyone else as they left. The direction didn't matter. They just wanted some space to talk. Suddenly, it was like a bubble had burst inside each of them, and they could not stop talking.

"This place is amazing!" whispered Mandy excitedly, trying to keep a low volume to respect others in the space.

"No one's ever going to believe us," said Roya.

"Yeah, but at least we're all here together," replied Ami.

"How long do you think they'll let us stay?" asked Mandy.

"I don't know," replied Roya. "I just wonder if we'll ever get to come back once we leave."

"What did you think of the Council?" asked Ami. "I had like a million more questions."

"Yeah, like where do they get their clothes," added Mandy.

"I was so shy," admitted Roya, almost giggling. "You know, sometimes when Claire looks at me, I feel like she's looking straight into my soul, but it feels a lot different when a man does it."

"You mean like Shumayan?" agreed Ami, giggling. "He has a really powerful gaze."

"Yeah, I'm glad he didn't focus on me as much," said Mandy. "What did you feel?"

"I could feel his heart…his love," reflected Roya, putting her hand to her chest. "Not like it was personal for me or anything, but I could feel him sensing me emotionally. It made me nervous at first, but once I relaxed, it felt more natural, like people are supposed to feel this connected."

"Yeah, I feel like I'm ten times more vulnerable down here," said Ami.

"Yeah, I'm like vulnerabillion!" Mandy laughed.

"Do you think the younger ones are as open?" Ami considered.

"I don't know, but I was thinking we could walk around to see if anyone here is closer to our age," suggested Roya. "Do you think everyone here really knows about us?"

"I guess we'll find out. Let's check out some of these groups and see what they're doing," suggested Ami, veering toward one of them.

As they approached the nearest group, they saw three people standing around an attractive young man who looked close to their age. He was lying on a large, thin, rectangular platform that was suspended in mid-air. Then, one of the people struck a large, clear, crystal bowl that was placed beneath the platform, causing it to produce a deep and long lasting tone. Incredibly, they were beginning to see the sound waves as ripples in the air, and the platform seemed to be catching them and directing them into the young man's body. The people were focused intently on his bare chest.

"What are they doing?" Ami whispered with excitement.

They were still inching closer but maintaining a respectful distance from the group. Mandy had the best view from her angle and saw that the vibrations were causing the young man's chest to radiate an X-ray-like image of his insides. Not only could the group of people see what was happening inside his body, they could read the energy of the organs to discern their health status.

"It's like an X-ray," whispered Mandy.

"Let's not get too close," said Roya. "We don't want to disturb them," but Mandy kept inching a little closer. At first, it looked like they were doing some kind of a medical exam, but there appeared to be something that concerned the group. Then, one of the women on the far side of the platform raised her hands out in front of the young man's chest. Her aura began to concentrate in her arms, and then, several violet colored orbs of light appeared and merged with her hands, causing them to glow more powerfully from within.

She was taking slow, deep breaths as energy from her hands began to flow into the young man's chest. Ami was just beginning to lean closer to study the way the energy was flowing, when one of the other women turned and looked directly at her. She had short dark hair, and her light complexion slightly reflected the violet light of the energy they were working with. Ami was startled and almost took a step back, worried that she might be intruding, but she felt embraced by the woman's welcoming gaze. It was a look of recognition, inviting her to join the group. She was being respectfully called forth.

"Ami, Claire said not to be shy if we're invited to participate," reminded Roya.

"Will you come with me?" Ami asked.

"I think this invitation is just for you," encouraged Roya, placing a supportive hand on her shoulder.

"I don't know if I'm ready for this," Ami whispered. "I didn't expect to be invited into anything so quickly. We've barely had a chance to talk."

"We'll have plenty of time to talk later. Go and see what they're doing."

"Yeah," said Mandy, wanting her older sister to go first to see what would happen.

"OK," Ami shrugged. She cautiously began to walk forward. Almost instantly, the woman turned her head again and smiled warmly at Ami. Her gaze guided Ami right into the group as the woman moved aside to make room. The two others on the opposite side of the platform also greeted her warmly with their eyes, and she began to perceive their telepathic messages.

"*Watch and remember,*" they said with one voice. Then, the other two women raised their hands, holding them out with their palms facing the young man's chest. Their hands were about six inches away from the focal point. Ami could now see that a dark region in one of the young man's lungs was causing stress in several other areas. Her mind linked right into their field of group consciousness, and she understood what they were doing.

Just then, they rang the crystal bowl again, and out of nowhere, a number of Formelle came zipping toward the group. They immediately merged with the hands of the other two people who were starting to send energy. She could feel that the orbs of light were amplifying their healing intentions.

"*Use your hands*," said the mind of the woman who had invited her. "*The sound vibrations create a bridge that makes it easier for Spirit to work through us.*"

Ami raised her hands and began to focus on sending energy. At first, she noticed a feeling of alignment with the energy of the group. Then, she felt the energy beginning to flow through her body. As it concentrated into her hands, two little violet orbs of light instantly appeared within them, activating her connection to the temple's field of healing energy. Startled, she pulled her hands back to examine them.

Around each hand, she saw an orb of light connected to the very center of her palms. As she looked closely, she had the impression that they were reflecting the presence of a violet flame somewhere, as if the orbs of light carried a part of the flame with them, though the energy felt cool and tingly. Placing her hands back into position with the others, she began to breathe deeply and focus on the young man's chest just like they were doing.

He was well-built and quite handsome, with short brown hair. His eyes were closed, but Ami had the feeling that he had become aware of her presence. Her heart and her compassion engaged, and she was surprised at how intimate her connection with him felt through the energy. She could not help wondering who he was, though she was guided to focus on the task at hand. The dark area in his lung felt old and stagnant. With a little focus, the energy began to flow through her hands like a current into his chest, which was beginning to glow more brightly. Ami could feel his body repairing itself with their love and support.

Roya and Mandy looked on with great interest. Mandy pointed out the unusual clothing they were wearing. Most of them were wearing pantsuits that were made of the lightest, almost sheer, white silky material that flowed with their movements. Over their shirts were delicate shawls that draped down in the back. They were decorated with beautiful symbols and intricate images. The patterns looked a lot like those found on the wings of the most exotic butterflies.

Just then, a bright pink orb of light appeared far behind where the group of healers was standing. Roya and Mandy both saw it at the same time. It was hovering near a row of pillars that encompassed the perimeter of the main room, forming an open hallway.

"Look! I think it sees us," gestured Mandy.

Roya, too, had the sense that it was looking at them.

Suddenly, the pink orb of light accelerated toward them, stopping only a few feet away. They both stared at it in wonder, feeling like the orb was reflecting back their expressions, and then it zipped backward about forty feet.

Mandy started to walk forward first, wanting to get back in touch with the orb, and Roya followed. When they were only a few feet away again, they felt the connection grow, and they started to notice a face appearing inside the orb of light.

"Do you think it's a Formelle?" asked Roya.

"No. It's not like the others," said Mandy. "See?"

The face was starting to become more distinct, but then the orb shot backward another forty feet.

"Let's follow it. I think it wants to take us somewhere," Mandy realized. When they approached it again, they were near the pillars where they could see several torches with golden flames. This time, the face became clear.

"Mandy, it's you!" exclaimed Roya.

Mandy's eyes got wider and so did the eyes of her face in the pink orb, and then it smiled at her. Roya watched as the same expression struck Mandy's face, and then the orb started to move backward again, gradually speeding up. Mandy was already trotting after it when she said, "Come on, let's see where it's going."

The orb kept accelerating until both girls were in a full sprint trying to keep up. It moved into the hallway on the other side of the pillars and sped away to the left. The hallway stretched into the distance, pillars to the left and a solid wall to the right. Roya was a few seconds behind, but she was starting to feel less interested in closing the distance—slowing down to notice what she was feeling.

The orb was outpacing Mandy, but it had grown brighter to light the way. Even as it rounded a corner and left the room, its pink light was still shining from the passageway it entered. Just before they reached the passageway, Roya noticed an opening into another room that instantly caught her attention. She stopped as soon as she saw it, while Mandy disappeared running after the orb. Roya was now still as a statue, transfixed on a large pool of water that glimmered as if in the light of a full moon.

The room was dark, except for the light reflecting in the water. As she entered, she noticed a few wisps of an eerie, blue, glowing mist floating in the air. She could now hear the gentle sound of water trickling from an opening in the far wall. The water filled a pool formed by a rock enclosure that came up about three feet from the ground. The room looked natural, like it was part of one of the caverns. The floor was level, but the walls and the ceiling were made of unfinished rock with a few small crystals here and there that glistened in the glowing mist.

Roya walked forward quietly, her mind touched by the tranquility of the sound. She approached the rocks that surrounded the pool, trying to see where the light in the water was coming from. Looking into the pool, she was astonished to see the full moon and the stars reflected in the water. For a moment, she was tricked, thinking that she was outside, but when she looked up at the ceiling, all she saw were rocks. The illusion was remarkable. The water carried a perfect reflection of the night sky.

Next, Roya leaned forward and looked at *her* reflection. The surface was smooth and undisturbed, giving her a clear image of herself, though once in a while, the water would trickle in unevenly, creating small ripples across the pool. She reached into her pocket for a hair tie to pull her hair back, so she could see into the pool more easily.

For a moment, she wondered if her reflection would do something like the pink orb did with Mandy. She waited for a wink or a smile that was not her own but saw nothing except the occasional ripple wavering through her reflection. Then, something unexpected happened. The position of the stars began to blur toward the moon, and the moon began to change until it was merely a glowing ring of light.

The Circle and the Stars, she thought, *but what does it mean?*

The light from the stars blended with the ring as it grew brighter. Then, the ring began to rotate to reveal that it was the rim of a chalice—a chalice made of starlight. Somehow, it felt like a symbol of love.

My cup runneth over, she mused.

The whole pool of water now seemed symbolic of an all-encompassing Spirit that flowed from the chalice as it gradually drifted toward her reflection in the pool. Every ripple of water moved it a little closer until it found its place, right in the center of her chest. The water was showing her a vision that was much more than a reflection. Roya's own heart opened wide, and she felt a deep feeling of wholeness with the water through the vibration of the chalice. She could feel the chalice at the center of her whole being as if it had become a part of her.

This must be why I am here, she thought, taking a deep breath. *I came here to find this.*

Never before had she felt such deep love. It seemed to expand within her chest with each breath. She could not tell where it was coming from but began to experience that she was one with the water as a pool of universal love. It was a love that seemed to come from the stars themselves.

Roya heard the faint sound of footsteps behind her, but she could not yet take her eyes off her image in the reflecting pool, which now had a gentle glow, like embers in a fireplace. The form of the chalice had blended into her image, and she could feel it in her heart. Around the edges of her reflection was a sparkle, like the twinkling of stars.

"It's beautiful, isn't it," came a soft voice from behind her.

Roya turned around to see Claire and smiled broadly, happy to see her. "I see you found your reflection," acknowledged Claire, gazing at the mirror-like surface of the pool.

Roya felt that she had found much more than that.

"These are the Waters of Truth," said Claire. "They say that if you come baring your soul, then the water will bear a reflection of your soul's essence back to you."

Roya turned back around to see her reflection again, and it was still sparkling. *This is my soul's essence*, she thought, trying to feel into it. The feeling of connection was stronger than ever.

"I saw something else, but I don't know what it means," Roya began.

"You found the Grail," acknowledged Claire, surprising Roya. "It means your soul's desire is for the oneness of all life—a very noble wish."

Claire seemed impressed, which greatly pleased Roya.

"Is this unusual?" asked Roya. "Has this ever happened before?"

"Yes. You are not the first, but it might interest you to know that a great many of your people have searched for it and not found it." Claire explained.

"What is it, exactly?"

"The Grail represents the balance of love that forms the unifying Spirit of the Living Water in all dimensions. It is a symbol of wholeness. The idea of drinking from the Grail is metaphorical. By honoring all forms in which the water of life is found, you align with the universal balance of love. Honoring all life makes you worthy of the gift," she said with a smile. "The symbol makes it easier to attain the balance of universal wholeness in your consciousness, because you can merge with the alignment of those who have held the balance of the Grail before. Thus, to drink from the Grail is to drink in the living knowledge of oneness."

"But I thought the Grail was some kind of religious symbol," said Roya, remembering references to it in movies.

"Ah yes. We know about your stories. From our perspective, the Grail is a living technology that was brought to this world by a family of advanced teachers." She paused to let this new awareness sink in. "Your ancient people were not ready to understand this though, so the knowledge of such gifts had to be encoded into a number of spiritual stories."

"Wow! I never thought that technology could be something like that," she expressed.

"What is truly amazing is how few people from the surface have found it."

"Why so few?" she asked.

"Most do not yet have the will to seek or know what to look for. Some have searched for it, but were really only looking for wealth, power, or fame. Mostly, it's because people think of the Grail as something that is outside of them. Now you know the secret of where the Grail is hidden. *It is hidden in the waters of the Earth,*" she said more softly, sounding like she was quoting an ancient text. "Only people who seek an experience of human unity can find it within themselves. You cannot find such a sacred instrument by looking for it externally. You can only find it by seeking the wholeness that it represents. When that is what you truly desire, the Grail finds you."

"Wow! I feel like I'm becoming one of your people, if you don't mind me saying," said Roya. Her aura was still glowing like the embers of a fire.

"You already *are* one of our people, Roya. We live with the Grail in our hearts. It's part of the reason why we live so long. We identify more with the Living Water in our bodies than we do with the world of form, and time doesn't age water in the same way that it ages the structures of the world."

Claire was now scooping some of the water with her right hand and then pouring it back out into the pool.

Like the fountain of youth, Roya thought, admiring Claire's youthful appearance.

"Our people flow through time," she said, "without forming attachments that can trap the body's consciousness in the conditions of the past. When your people identify less with the past and more with the greater medium of memory, the future of memory will open before you, and your expression in the body will become more defined by the light of what you are becoming."

"That sounds exciting. How long do your people live?" asked Roya, drawing her fingers back and forth through the water at the edge of the pool.

"Many hundreds of years. Sometimes as much as a thousand."

"Can I live that long?"

"That remains to be seen. We would like to see your people on the surface become aligned with the frequency of longer lifespans in your DNA, which is a very real possibility, but just connecting with the Grail in the way that you have does not guarantee it. What it *does* do is make it easier for you to awaken into greater states of wholeness and oneness. What you are feeling now is just the beginning."

"What about everyone else? Could they find the Grail, too?" wished Roya, flicking the water off her hand and watching the ripples in the pool.

"They are also on a Grail quest without knowing it. They have all begun the quest for greater wholeness. You are a way-shower for your family, though. In time, they will grow to integrate with what you hold. But you must be patient with each person's timing. See the Grail as part of their potential. You are a keeper of its frequency now, but remember, the Grail is just another piece of a larger puzzle. It is a reminder that we come from wholeness and will return to wholeness. Time is just a dream between wholes."

"Can I tell them about it?"

"You could," she said, "but you would be speaking about an experience they may not be able to relate to, yet. If you want to support them to *be* in the same awareness, there are other ways of doing it. Perhaps the best way is to honor them as part of the whole and embrace them with the frequency of wholeness. You can practice focusing your attention in this way. When you do this, you may draw from the strength of others who identify with wholeness, and together, we can help you change the resonance of those who are open to receive the gift of the Grail's vibration."

"I see." Roya was making a leap in understanding. "So, it's not the symbol that's important, but the vibration it represents."

"Exactly! The whole point of creating a tiny container for the awareness of the whole is to make everyone equal with a single relatable form. This way, all can find the resonance of that form within themselves. That is not dependent upon having a spiritual vision like you just had, though. Everyone will make the connection to wholeness in their own way, to receive the gift of the Spirit that the form represents."

"I feel like there's something more to this vision, though," continued Roya. "Like there's something I can do with it that will activate transformation. Is it possible to use this energy to change people that are really stuck?"

"Roya, one of the great challenges of being a Guardian of Knowledge is that you can't just share the knowledge because you are excited about it. You must respect where people are at in their experience and not push them further than they are willing to go. You will have to trust that eventually everyone will share in the same oneness identity, but for now, you have leaped ahead of most people. That means you must be patient and respectful of those who are choosing to remain in duality a little longer. You carry the light of the future, which will remain invisible until humanity reaches the right time reference."

"I understand," responded Roya, who was listening very deeply, opening to receive what felt like a transmission of consciousness that accompanied Claire's words. She could feel how Claire was transferring her awareness of what it means to be a Guardian. It was much more than any of the fictional concepts that she had read about, or seen in movies. It was part of the blueprint and purpose of being human.

"There are many others like you on the surface that also carry the light of the future," Claire continued. "And in time, you will all become activated in your roles to help shift the planetary consciousness. But until you recognize yourselves as a group consciousness, there is a danger for some who have begun to awaken very rapidly. Without being in a community like ours that shares in this awareness, some might naïvely think that they're the only ones, or that they have some truth or perspective that everyone else needs to integrate with.

"A little learning is a dangerous thing, drink deep or taste not the Pierian spring," remembered Roya.

"The quote from the library wall," acknowledged Claire.

"Yes, I looked it up. It's from an old poem warning that tasting a little knowledge can make you intoxicated, thinking that you know a lot, when you really know very little. The Pierian spring was said to be the spring of the muses in ancient Greece. If you drink deep, you can gain enough knowledge to humble you into realizing you have much more to learn."

"It's very true," agreed Claire. "And you will see this play out in humanity's awakening. Many people awaken just enough to think they can be teachers to everyone around them. They have a vision, or begin to taste the beginning of psychic perception, and they think this makes them special. The idea of spiritual superiority clouds the thinking of a great many people. The ego has no problem using visions and spiritual experiences for validation. Remember, the simplest, most universal truths do not need visions to back them up. When they are lived and modeled as a way of being, they resonate like nothing else."

"Oh, don't worry about me," said Roya. "I won't let any of this go to my head."

"Of course not. I wasn't concerned about you," explained Claire, "but I want you to be aware of this kind of spiritual confusion, because you are bound to meet people who need help to understand that they're not alone in having this kind of awakening. What is happening on Earth is universal."

"What exactly *is* happening?" asked Roya.

"There's a rare convergence of energies taking place that have the potential to realign human consciousness with its original blueprint. But this same convergence of energies is also challenging humanity, causing parts of it to deeply resist becoming an integrated whole."

"Think of it this way. On the surface, most human beings feel small and separate from the whole. This experience eventually leads some people to seek a return to the vibration of wholeness from which we all came. And then, a great quest begins which inevitably leads to a revelation of humanity's potential to awaken into oneness. Many people call this revelation *their* awakening, but in order to become truly whole, they must work to transcend the conditions of the ego, with all of its fears, attachments, desires, and insecurities."

"The process then becomes one of self-purification, and this eventually leads people to groups that are engaged in such healing processes. Eventually, the heart awakens to the path of selfless service as an instrument for the force of love that is gathering everyone into wholeness. This is the work of every great master that has ever walked the Earth. The difference now is that the process is accelerating toward a mass awakening."

"How do you gather people into wholeness?"

"It begins by serving people unconditionally, so they will not feel alone. This breaks down the illusion of separation to reveal that we are all one. Gradually, you are working to create a world of compassion and community instead of a world of fear and competition. When enough of your people resonate with a vibration of wholeness that is inclusive, a change will occur that will start to marry you to wholeness as a collective vibration. This can become a movement to create a shift in consciousness."

"Eventually, your people will be strong enough with this vibration to extend it as a frequency that embraces others into wholeness. At that point, you will be guided by the part of humanity that is already living beyond the shift. We've seen it happen on other worlds this way. It involves surrendering to something that is greater than your sense of self—trusting in a future that is guiding you all back into wholeness. Sometimes it means making the path of serving others more important than your own life."

"What an inspiring vision! Why don't our religions teach this?" questioned Roya.

"In their purest essence, they do. But before the present age, your religious movements needed structures to preserve the knowledge they were stewarding. In the present age, however, those structures are getting in the way. Now there is a new process unfolding that can bring the world into unity. But your people will have to sort out what is more important: identification with religious structures or identification with the emerging unity consciousness of the one heart."

"Do your people have a religion?" asked Roya.

"Our religion is listening," answered Claire.

"Listening?" said Roya. "How is that a religion?"

"We listen to God, and to each other's hearts, and to the wisdom of the angelic realms, and to the knowledge-keeping spirits of the natural world. How is that *not* a religion?"

"Ohhhhhh…"

"Roya, most of the wars that are raging on the surface of the planet began because of a breakdown in communication. Our culture lives in peace with each other and the natural world because we made listening more important than proving who is right. When I listen to you, I don't just listen to your words; I listen with my heart to receive the presence of the soul who is speaking, and this is what aligns our communication with the plane of the soul. When enough of your people learn how to do this, you will become a telepathic race."

"What's it like, listening to God? What do you hear?" inquired Roya.

"I hear the Voice of the One within me, and I treasure every word," Claire responded.

Roya immediately thought of the angel that spoke to her in the tree and wondered if this was similar.

"Let me give you an example," offered Claire. "*The gift of matter is motion. Therefore, celebrate your freedom to move and breathe endlessly, and realize this gift forever depends on the One who remains still.*"

"That's beautiful," Roya admired. "It's poetic."

"When the One speaks to you, the words have a way of unraveling over time to continually inspire you. I have pondered these words endlessly, and sometimes, they just remind me to breathe and to love breathing…and to be grateful."

Just then, Mandy came skipping through the hallway and stopped between two pillars. "There you are!" she exclaimed. "You will never guess what happened to me—wow, you're really glowing!"

"So are you," admired Roya, laughing, as she and Claire turned to greet her. Mandy had a pink glow around her and looked as happy and playful as ever.

"Wow! I didn't see this place before," she said while looking around. "Is this where you've been the whole time?"

"You ran right past it, but I had a feeling I was meant to come in here."

Mandy walked into the room, noticing the wisps of glowing mist near the ceiling. She went straight to the water, standing right between Roya and Claire and looked over at her reflection. Roya and Claire were both smiling brightly, observing how Mandy had changed.

"You'll never guess what happened," Mandy mentioned again, looking at her pink glow in the reflection of the water.

"What?" asked Roya.

"I was running after that orb of energy, and I followed it into this huge domed room where it was hovering in the middle. At first, I was really cautious, but then I walked right up to it, and it split in two. The pink one was still there, but there was also a blue one, and they looked like two bubbles that were joined together. Then it happened again, and there was a third one that was green. It reminded me of the symbol on the cover of the book, actually. Then it just kept multiplying and forming this pattern, like a matrix of colors. The colors were so rich and deep, and the more I looked at them, the more I felt like I was looking at something that was inside me. I felt connected to them somehow, and then…" she hesitated, searching for the words to describe the experience.

"Then the colors formed into a person that was walking around me and smiling. Sometimes it looked like me, and sometimes it even looked like you, or even Ami. It kept changing its appearance and especially the clothes it was wearing. I've never seen such amazing designs. It was like it was not just wearing colors, but it was wearing *emotions* as clothing. It was like a dream seeing how a design could reflect a person's soul energy like that. It gave me so many ideas."

"That's incredible!"

"You met your muse," Claire beamed.

"My what?" asked Mandy.

"*Muses* are masters of creativity. They nurture human creative energy and help you realize your potential. They command the Formelle by inspiration and can teach humans to do the same. *Your* muse obviously works a lot with Colors."

"It's going to help me design new clothing," Mandy said excitedly.

"That's right," confirmed Claire, "and I have a feeling this is just the beginning."

"So how do you work with muses?" asked Mandy.

"Your muse is very playful. All you have to do is tune into its excitement about working with you, and the creative juices will start to flow."

"This is sooo cool, right?" gushed Mandy.

"Mandy, you amaze me," Roya smiled at her.

"That's funny," Mandy laughed. "I was just thinking that I amaze myself. I'm getting lots of new ideas of what to make us. I can see it all now."

Roya put her arm around Mandy and said, "Let's go find Ami, shall we?" It felt like it was time to reunite the group.

"So, what made *you* glow?" said Mandy as they exited the room. They could see Ami still standing with the group of healers, and there was a beautiful violet aura around all of them.

"I had an experience that opened my heart," shared Roya.

"I can tell. So why don't we see these kinds of things on the surface?" Mandy asked Claire who was walking beside them.

"It's partly because you were raised in a culture that focuses its attention almost entirely on the physical world. There's a strong denial of the energetic world in the surface culture, but your families are proof that it's waning," Claire explained. "You'll find no shortage of subtle beings on the surface, though. You live surrounded by invisible communities of energetic beings. If you had been raised to pay attention to them, you would be able to see them more easily."

"So why has it been so easy for us to see them down here, since we weren't raised that way?" asked Roya.

"Right now, we are at a higher vibration, so your senses are more in resonance with the plane of reality where these beings dwell. Plus, when you have a large enough group of people who already perceive reality in a certain way, it is easier to entrain the minds of newcomers to perceive in the same way. I think part of the reason you are here is to remember that this is part of your natural state of being."

Just as they began to approach the group of healers, Ami turned and broke away to meet them. Her eyes were wide, and she appeared to be taking in the details of their auras as she realized that they had all been through a shift.

"Guys! I can't believe what's happening!" Ami shared excitedly.

"What?" asked Roya.

"They said that the temple recognizes us and that our knowledge is returning. It's like remembering things that you didn't know that you knew," said Ami.

"Like what?" asked Roya, thoroughly intrigued.

"Like that I'm a natural at transmitting healing energy! It's all coming back to me. We just worked on this young man named Feather. Apparently, he's connected to another soul from down here who was born on the surface. Whoever it is, she has some form of lung cancer, and Feather was able to take a form of her energy into him so that the healers could help her re-pattern the disease. Feather's also a healer."

"Whoa! Isn't that kind of dangerous," asked Mandy, "taking the energy of someone else's disease into your body? What if it stayed stuck inside him?"

"He wasn't really taking in the *physical* disease, just the emotional level of it. He was reflecting her through his empathy. I asked about it, and they said that cancer just isn't possible down here because of their unity consciousness, and because their food, air, and water are pure. What he did was to hold compassion for the denial of life that was in the woman's cancer, but it wasn't only *her* denial. It was a pattern in her whole family. It was like the woman had empathically absorbed their energies into her body until it manifested as cancer, just like Feather did as he was reflecting her. It was too much for her to handle by herself, so she called out for assistance to help shift the pattern. They say it's easier to transform stuck energy when people feel things together."

"So, did it work?" asked Mandy. "Is the woman going to heal?"

"Yes! And not only that, but everyone connected to her on the surface is also healing through a shift in consciousness. It's amazing! Every time they do healing work, they don't just work on the person who's sick. They work with everyone the person is connected to so they can heal the whole dynamic behind the disease. They actually see our diseases as mirrors that reflect larger patterns of discord in our society. I just never thought of it like that before, but they said it's a key to ending all disease."

"That's right," added Claire. "There's a connection between the manifestation of disease and the state of separation and duality that most of humanity experiences on the surface. The *gift* of disease is that it's helping humanity to evolve compassion, so you can begin to collectively lift each other out of the vibratory levels where disease manifests. Once humanity learns to vibrate with oneness, it can release the plague of separation and become immune to duality."

"Empower others, and you will be empowered," quoted Ami. "It's one of the first things Feather said he learned about how to work with energy. If you focus on empowering the other person, the collective immune system strengthens inside both of you. That's part of why this healing just happened.

They're transferring their knowledge of the healing process to the surface through these connections."

Feather was now sitting up on the platform, wrapping a long swath of red cloth around his upper body in a sophisticated manner, forming a kind of shirt. He then hopped off the platform looking vibrant and walked over to the girls. Ami's words must have cued him, because he had something to add.

"It's true," he said in a deep, rich voice. "We empathize greatly with those of us who have taken bodies on the surface, and sometimes the drama there is so intense it sparks these connections. Naturally, when this happens, we see it as an opportunity to support those who are suffering."

"You must really care about this soul to feel her disease like that," said Roya.

"To be honest," said Feather, "I didn't know I had it in me, but we are being tested in many ways to integrate with your culture, and I just learned a lot."

"I'm Roya, by the way, and this is Mandy."

"Nice to meet you. I feel like I already know you through your friend here," he said, gesturing to Ami.

"How did you get the name Feather?" asked Mandy.

"Feather is the English translation of my name, but I like it just as much," he said.

"So, you're named after a bird feather," Mandy, burst out, perplexed. "I didn't think there were birds down here."

"Oh, you haven't been to the gardens," said Feather, with a gleam in his eye.

He then looked at Claire, and they were both silent for a moment. Roya thought they must be talking telepathically, and then Claire said, "He would like to show you the gardens, while I find the others."

He could tell that the three girls were also keen to explore, and he was more than happy to be their tour guide. Just then, that little violet orb of light appeared in front of Claire again. She looked at it for a moment, and then it snapped away so quickly they could not see where it went.

"Hey," Roya noticed. "I saw that same orb of light when we were on the balcony."

"Oh, that's my messenger," replied Claire. "Everyone down here has one. It's a little like your version of a cell phone, but it's a Formelle, so it's alive. Just now, I told Amaron to meet us at the entrance to the gardens. He's out there gathering food."

"That's so cool," admired Mandy. "Can we get one, too?"

"I don't see why not," supposed Claire. "I'm sure they will be happy to work with you. I will go find the others now and meet you in the gardens."

Claire looked each of them in the eyes as a way of saying goodbye, and then she was on her way.

"Follow me," said Feather, gesturing to an opening in the far wall. Roya, Ami, and Mandy all looked at one another, holding back nervous giggles. As they walked together, Roya could tell that Ami was proud of herself for establishing a friendship with another healer their age, and a good-looking one, too! Feather was just shy of seventeen and was just a few inches taller than Roya. As they walked, each girl was trying to formulate the right question to make the conversation interesting, but Feather was one step ahead of them all.

"There are lots of other teenagers in Lys, you know," said Feather. "I suppose I'm the lucky one." He was trying to be flattering to break the ice, and it was working. "Please tell me if my English sounds OK."

"Oh, it's great," giggled Mandy.

"Yeah, you're doing just fine," said Roya.

They were almost to the opening, and as they got closer, they could see a staircase leading down.

"Most of my friends would be shy," said Feather. "We've never tried our English with the surface culture. I'm just glad I studied it well. I had no idea I'd get to meet people like you."

When they reached the entrance, Feather continued to march down the stairs, which were just wide enough for all four of them to walk side by side. When they reached the bottom, they were standing at the beginning of a long hallway that led to the gardens.

"I have a question," Roya began. "What are your schools like?"

"Schools?" repeated Feather, pondering how to answer the question. "This whole place is a school. We are all students of each other."

"But don't you have teachers?" asked Mandy.

"Oh sure, we have lots of teachers," said Feather. "My friends and I often travel to other cities to visit them."

"Do you travel with your parents?" questioned Ami.

"I travel with my pod. There are nine of us. We are all really close friends, but that's normal for pods."

"What's the purpose of a pod?" asked Ami.

"It's part of how we learn," explained Feather. "We finish basic education when we are about eleven years old. By then, our learning pod has formed, and we are allowed to go wherever we want with our pod to learn and explore. That goes on for about ten years, and then the smaller pods start to gather into larger ones that have a shared purpose."

"Let me get this straight," said Mandy. "You are allowed to travel to other cities…without your parents …as long as you're with your friends?!"

"I was twelve when my pod took our first trip to another city," Feather explained.

Mandy was in shock. The idea of having that much freedom seemed exciting and scary at the same time. Roya could not help wondering what she would do with such freedom. It was beginning to dawn on her that perhaps since they were down here, they might be able to stay for more than just a short visit. She wondered what her friends would think of the idea. Up ahead, they could see a lot more light, and the cavern they were entering looked expansive. Reaching the entrance, they came to a stone platform that extended from a great wall, and before them was the most magnificent garden they had ever seen, completely lit as if it was in the morning light.

"Wow!" said Roya. "It's like daylight."

"This is amazing!" exclaimed Mandy.

"I had no idea!" added Ami.

It was more than a garden, in fact; it was a forest with fruit trees and flowering plants. Everywhere they looked, the forest was thriving in the light, which seemed to vibrate in the air as if it came from everywhere at once. The light made the caverns warmer than the temple, and it was bright enough that it took a minute for their eyes to adjust. Magnificently large crystals grew out of the rock walls, and some even grew from the cavern ceiling.

"How did all of this get here?" asked Roya.

"We brought a lot of the plants and animals with us when we came down here, but some of the species developed more recently. Look closer at this crystal," invited Feather, pointing to one nearby.

They all looked, and within a few seconds, they noticed several colored orbs of light coming out of the crystal. They flew right down into the forest and disappeared from sight. Roya stared intently into the trees, certain that she might spot more of the orbs, and sure enough, she began to notice some unusual movement. It took a moment for her eyes to focus in on them, but she could now see about five little orbs near the top of a tree. The more she concentrated, the more they came into focus, until she could see that the forest was filled with little orbs that were flitting around and interacting with the environment. Just then, a number of them came together in a group and flew into a nearby crystal and disappeared.

"The crystals are home for some of the larger Formelle that can bridge dimensions," Feather explained. "And the smaller ones use the crystals to transport lifecodes from many other realms, to program the matrix of life here. That's how our gardens became so diverse. Once these crystals were activated, the Formelle started coming through them into our gardens to work with the plants and animals."

The caverns stretched as far as the eye could see, and the air was filled with the sweet fragrant smell of flowers.

"That's the same river from the waterfall in the city cavern," Feather pointed out. "It flows beneath the heart of the temple and comes out here."

"Is it always light like this?" asked Mandy.

"Yes," replied Feather. "These caverns are always light, and the ones with the waterfalls are always dark. But our lighting preferences vary from city to city. For example, my pod just returned from a city that is lit by rainbow colored mist."

"Oooh! Maybe can we join *your* pod!" hinted Mandy with a hopeful grin.

Ami and Roya both looked at each other with knowing glances, confirming that they were both musing over the same possibilities. Meeting Lyssian teen boys and exploring the Inner Earth had just become a source of endless fascination.

Just then, Amaron emerged from the garden with a basket of fruits and nuts for all of them to eat. Behind them, on the platform, Claire was approaching with the rest of their families. Roya could not tell if it would have been nighttime or morning on the surface, but she was definitely hungry, and she was also ready for a deeper rest. Something told her that they would soon be shown to a place where they could sleep, but for the moment, it felt good to share a fresh meal together, deep beneath the surface of the Earth, in a garden of perpetual summertime.

14

CLEARING THE PATH

Something was changing in the fundamental nature of reality. A shift was taking place, and everyone was affected in some way. But the change meant different things to different people. For some, it was something to fear: the end of the world as they once knew it. For others, the change held the possibility of greater freedom and the birth of a new and more promising vision of human potential that could bring civilization back into balance with the natural world. The heart of humanity was beginning to reveal itself, accelerating the process of connecting everyone together. But without recognizing what was occurring, many people, groups, and even institutions resisted the change—still clinging to a sense of identity separate from the greater whole.

Even the survivalists hiding deep underground were affected by the change, which was not part of their plans. For them, the increasing technological interconnectedness on the surface only accelerated the implementation of the next level of control. They could not imagine the possibility that a new kind of human energy might emerge to challenge their plan for history. One thing was certain: the change could not be stopped. For better or for worse, the change would remake the world. But not without a struggle.

Some aspects of the struggle remained invisible to the masses as hidden webs of power tightened their grip on the world, fighting to maintain control of their desired direction for the shift in reality. Other aspects of the struggle were being played out for all to see as people worked to expose the corruption and reclaim power that had been misplaced in the institutions that run the world. But the key to ending the struggle for power was not in overthrowing corrupt regimes, nor was it in simply exposing the culture of secrecy. More and more, the struggle to define the new reality was unfolding as an *inner* experience, and that is where the necessary breakthroughs would occur; for the struggle was not against any one person or group but between humanity's denial of oneness and its profound oneness potential. For the heroes, the struggle was one of finding the courage to take a stand for the cause of human unity.

This was the cause that was beginning to stir in the hearts of those who were now in the unique position to help catalyze the change. Aaron had been struck by the truth of his own words the night before when he said, "this is bigger than our lives." He really meant that, and he knew that his friends had felt the power of it, but that was only the beginning. Because of his mind-link with Lex, he now believed that his commitment to help break down the barriers would empower Lex to strive for the potential reintegration of his people with the surface culture. Now that Lex had revealed that his peers *knew* they were being lied to, this was ultimately a matter of justice. Aaron could no longer deny his calling to make a difference in the unfolding drama.

For Andrea, this was not just about exposing big secrets. More than one kind of barrier was collapsing, and she was becoming aware of the unrest in the invisible world. Like it or not, she knew that peace could not be achieved without healing those who had become lost there.

"I feel like I'm under some kind of psychic attack," she said to Melanie over the phone with a tone of panic in her voice. "I was having nightmares all this morning after we were dropped off, and now I feel like I'm being drained of energy."

"Has anything like this ever happened to you before?" asked Melanie.

"I've always known I was sensitive to people's energy; like if there's negative energy around, I can feel it, even when I don't see where it's coming from. But this is more than just bad vibes. I feel gripped by something terrible that's making me feel helpless. I think that place really *is* haunted."

Melanie was deeply concerned. She had never heard Andrea sound so distressed but did not know what she could do to help. She was unfamiliar with this kind of thing, so all she could do at first was try to learn more about it.

"I didn't think that a haunting could just follow you home," said Melanie.

"I didn't think so, either, but one time, my cousin's family did this tour of Alcatraz. My cousin was only three at the time. They let him go inside one of the jail cells, and after about a minute, he had this terrified look on his face. After that, my aunt and uncle said he cried for weeks. Sometimes, he would scream like a caged animal. They had never seen anything like it, and we figured out that he had picked up some kind of entity, like a disturbed fragment of someone's soul that had been imprisoned there. It must have latched on to him, and he was channeling its energy."

"Whoa! That's freaky!" exclaimed Melanie, having never heard such a story. "How'd they get rid of it?"

"After a few weeks, it seemed to just go away, but I'm sure our prayers must have helped. God, I hope this doesn't last that long. I feel awful."

"So, do you think you picked up something similar from inside that building?" Melanie asked.

"Yeah. I saw them when I went to sleep. I think a bunch of people died in there, but they don't know that they're dead, and they're still really upset." Andrea almost had trouble completing her last sentence as she felt the energetic grip in her throat grow tighter. The oppressive energy was entering her field in waves for which she seemingly had no defense. The pain and fear sensations of the beings were strong enough in her nerves that some of the muscles in her neck were starting to seize with the tension.

"I wish there was something I could do to help," expressed Melanie.

"Just keep talking with me. The sound of your voice feels soothing," Andrea replied, feeling like Melanie was literally a lifeline. "Do you know how to send people energy?"

"You mean like distance healing? I don't think I've ever tried."

"I think you're doing it a little right now. I can feel you. It's just your nature, but if you intend to do it more consciously, it will help. These beings feel cut off and alone, and our connection is the exact opposite, so it's helping me feel a little less stuck inside their drama."

"OK, what should I do?" Melanie was poised and ready.

"Just pick a color of light and see it flowing to me and filling me up and surrounding me."

"OK, I'll try my best," said Melanie, focusing more intently on feeling the connection between them with an intention of love. A moment later, she began to visualize a blue light, seeing it all around Andrea. "Wow, I think I'm feeling more of an energy flow now. Like, as soon as I focused on sending energy, it felt like it started flowing on its own. Can you feel that?"

"Yes. It's very comforting," Andrea said with a sense of relief in her voice. "I think Archangel Michael is helping us. I've been asking for him, and I know he wants to help us heal this. Let's just try to stay connected. It's really helping. I feel like I can breathe a little better now."

"I wonder why you didn't feel attacked before," said Melanie. "You felt all right when we were there, didn't you?"

"I think it was because we were all together. Something about the group energy must have protected us. But after we split up, I started to feel drained. I thought I was just exhausted at first, but then this feeling came over me like I was suffocating. It feels like sadness, and rage, and even terror. Mostly, it just feels like there's something or someone pulling on my energy, like I'm being gripped by something I can't see."

"Do you still feel it?" asked Melanie.

"Yeah, it's still there, but it's a little better. Before talking to you, I couldn't tell the difference between me and them, but *our* connection is helping me find my focus on my own frequency."

"Do you want me to come over?" Melanie asked in a reassuring voice, feeling more confident in her ability to help. "You know I'm just a few miles away."

"Yes, could you? I'd really appreciate that." Andrea sounded even more relieved. "Maybe your being here can help me think straight so I can figure out what to do. The gripping energy is still so strong."

"Done," said Melanie. "I'll be there in a few minutes."

Melanie did not know much about the phenomenon of lost souls or the astral plane, but it felt good to show up for her friend. She felt committed to making sure Andrea did not feel alone, as if the very act of choosing to support her would begin to heal the situation. Only a few minutes later, Dominic left a message on her cell phone to say they were all getting together later that evening. Apparently, Aaron had something new to share that was really important.

When Melanie arrived, she could see the distress in Andrea's face. Melanie started by making some hot peppermint tea and then cooked them both some dinner while Andrea was relaxing on the couch. Andrea began to explain over dinner about her ancestry and how her grandfather was not only a full-blooded Mexican Native American, but that he had come from a lineage of shamans and had studied many Native American cultures. He had passed away several years ago, but she was certain that he would have known what to do.

"He taught me something about purification once," Andrea mentioned, "but I don't know how it applies to this. It had to do with clearing negative energy before going into battle, but it feels like I'm already in battle."

"What if this is happening because you're supposed to share this with the others? Maybe it's a sign that we all need better protection."

"I think you're right," agreed Andrea. Melanie always had a knack for making sense of things. She was usually not the first to speak, but her insight proved that she listened thoughtfully for the highest potential, and she always liked to say that there's a message in everything. Were it not for Melanie's presence, Andrea would have stayed in for the evening, but she was beginning to think it was important to share her feelings with the rest of the group.

That evening, they all met back at Zack's apartment where Aaron was going through his art supplies. He was just as energetic as he had been the night before. Usually, he was fairly reserved in his expression, but for the second time, Andrea got to see him light up about something as he explained how he experienced the mind-link with Lex. No one had expected that they would be moving into the next phase so soon, but Aaron was convinced that whatever they were going to do, they should act quickly. He did not want to leave time for doubt to creep in.

"I had such a clear connection to Lex!" he explained emphatically. "And he showed me with his mind what one of their classes is like. Most of them are probing for some kind of way to access the outside world, and they're psychic enough to do it, but the people in charge are totally blocking their thinking. As far as they're concerned, surface dwellers are just a bunch of dumb slaves. What's amazing is that Lex found what they're all looking for through us. It's just not safe for him to say anything about it. But luckily, it doesn't seem like any of their authorities know about us."

"Well tell him to keep quiet until we're done filming," joked Dominic.

"I'm sure he'll be cautious," said Aaron. "In fact, this whole connection with him is what could make it all work. If there's any danger headed our way, I think he will be able to warn us. This is the green light we need to take the next step. That's why we're going back tonight."

Melanie and Andrea both looked at each other, apprehensive about what the group was planning to do.

"Before you do anything, I think you need to hear what Andrea has to say," Melanie prompted her to speak.

"Remember when you said that building might be haunted? Well, you were right. There's something in there, and somehow it followed me home," she said, pausing a second to gauge their response. "That place has some serious disturbances, and they've been attacking me since early this morning."

For a moment, Andrea worried that everyone would think she was crazy, since she was apparently the only one feeling it, but they all seemed open-minded and supportive.

"So why are they attacking you and not us?" asked Echo.

"I think it's because I'm more sensitive in some way," considered Andrea, "or maybe I was the first person to notice them, so they honed in on me."

"Who exactly are they?" asked Dominic.

"They're lost souls, stuck between worlds," Andrea surmised.

"Do you mind if I film this?" Zack asked. "This is fascinating."

"No, I don't mind," approved Andrea.

"OK, just start at the top," directed Zack after grabbing one of his video cameras.

Andrea explained about the nightmares and everything she knew about the astral plane, starting with her cousin's experience at Alcatraz which had prompted the family to seek the advice of a psychic. According to the psychic, sometimes, people can become lost in transit from the physical plane to the vast light-filled realms of the Afterlife. This can happen when their release from the body is sudden or traumatic, and especially if the person is still holding on to life in the physical. A person with a lot of unfinished business is likely to resist surrendering to physical death when it occurs, even to the point of denying that it has happened. They live on in a dream-like purgatory, processing their unresolved memories until they are ready to let go. To make matters worse, the region of the invisible world that contains these types of reality is also home to all sorts of parasitic entities. They roam around seeking to exploit lost souls, causing them to vibrate with fear.

The psychic, who had extensive experience with clearing spaces of such disturbances, explained that lost souls often dwell in a particular area, usually the place where they most recently lived. Although there are exceptions. Apparently, some places on Earth act as exchange points between many layers of reality, where energy flows back and forth more easily. Lost souls and astral entities are often drawn to such places, which function as portals into the physical plane where it's easier to get the attention of the living.

Andrea was not sure if the abandoned building was such a place, but she was certain that they were dealing with something similar to what the psychic had described. She was beginning to believe that her background had prepared her for exactly the situation they were now facing. She could still feel the lost souls focusing on her, but the energy of the group was helping her feel less drained.

"This kind of freaks me out," voiced Echo. "What if somebody did this on purpose? Didn't you say that in your nightmare, they were pounding on the walls, looking for a way out?"

"Yeah," replied Andrea.

"So, what if this is some kind of psychic security system?" suspected Echo, who had been following the story more closely than Andrea realized. Security was an ongoing concern for Echo because of his experience with urban exploration. "If the people who run the underground are super psychic, they would know about the astral plane, too, right?"

"I suppose so," Andrea hesitated, "but how could this be part of a security system?"

"Suppose they deliberately confused and trapped those people to create some kind of psychic security web? This way, an intruder would draw the attention of these beings, and the handlers who set it up would detect the disturbance. What if they're counting on these beings to attach themselves to any intruders so they act like a tracking device? At the very least, the way they attack people would scare people away from the area. Remember how that homeless man said that none of his friends would go in that building because it was haunted?"

"Great," grimaced Andrea. "So, you're saying these government psychics might be able to trace these beings right back to me?" The very idea caused her to feel like there was a knot twisting in her stomach. "Guys, we have to find a way to stop this."

"How could we disarm an astral security system?" asked Melanie.

"We'll use our positronic accelerators!" joked Dominic, to ease the tension in the room.

"Maybe you could disarm it with laughter," Zack smiled.

It was hard for Andrea to think of these beings merely as part of a security system, because she was beginning to empathize with their plight. She felt a rage bubbling up inside again, but she could not tell if it was her rage about being the subject of such manipulation, or theirs for being exploited.

"I don't know about the security system, but I feel like we have to help these beings," expressed Andrea, "so they can move on."

"How do we do that?" asked Aaron.

"Maybe it's like that movie, *The Sixth Sense*," suggested Zack. "If we listen to them, we can help them find a resolution to their lives, so they can be at peace."

"That's easy for you to say," said Andrea. "You're not the one who's hearing them." She was growing less fearful and more agitated. Over the last half hour, she'd been trying to close down her receptivity to be less vulnerable, but that seemed to limit her connection to the group vibration.

"Maybe we just need to support you more," Melanie suggested. "You said the group energy was helping you feel better."

"True. I've been remembering what my grandfather taught me about the purification ceremony, and I think we could use it in this situation."

"Is it something we can just do from here?" asked Echo. "I'm feeling a little uneasy about going back to that place."

"Yeah, what if this *is* part of a psychic security system?" Zack was concerned.

"Guys! Let's not lose focus," encouraged Aaron emphatically. He could feel the group vibration begin to drop, in fear of what they were about to undertake. "We've come too far. I feel like Lex will keep an eye on us. I'm certain that we will have fair warning if there's any real danger. Remember the sense of purpose we felt last night! We have to stay in touch with that feeling."

Again, Aaron felt like his words were being guided by a calling, and he knew that no matter what appeared as an obstacle in their path, they had to overcome it. Fortunately, his confidence resonated with the group and pulled them back together.

"He's right," agreed Melanie. "There's something about this that feels like destiny. We shouldn't just let our fears turn us around. And we need to do whatever we can to clear this for Dre." Fortunately, Melanie's devotion to Andrea helped focus the group back to their mission.

"So, are we going, or can we do this thing from here?" repeated Dominic.

"Well, based on what that psychic told us about clearing work, it might be better to be at the location where the disturbance originated. And since we want to go down there again, it makes sense to just do the work on-site. As long as you guys are there with me, I'm willing to go back," conceded Andrea. "All I know is, whatever this is, we have to clear it."

Although this was a personal plea, everyone knew it was essential to overcome this obstacle before they could move forward as a group. If there were any danger of being traced, they had to set aside their fears and act quickly.

Two hours later, after dark, they were parked near the building complex on the same street they had used before. This time, they all wore regular clothes, but some of them had extra supplies in their backpacks. They were prepared to spend the night inside the structure, if necessary. They had food and extra water along with Aaron's art supplies. Aaron was not sure if they would go ahead with the installation, but he wanted to be prepared in case they all felt the coast was clear. Although the security issue was foremost on his mind, the artist in him was pondering what to create.

Andrea was feeling a little better since they had started the journey. She had begun to form an intention in her mind to help these lost souls, and the support of the group was keeping her energy level up. When they entered the underground complex, they decided to explore it a bit further to sense any hotspots that might be connected with the disturbance. Andrea had a feeling they were looking for a specific place that could help unlock the story of these beings.

Because they had found the stairs so quickly before, the first level was almost completely unexplored. This time, they all stuck together as they systematically checked every room and hallway, periodically pausing to feel into the energy.

"What exactly are we looking for?" asked Dominic.

"I don't know," answered Andrea. "Some kind of vibe that tells us something about what happened."

"So, are you psychic?" he asked.

Andrea hesitated, not feeling comfortable with that label, even though she *did* feel in tune with her inner senses. "That psychic my family talked to said that everyone is psychic, but it's like a muscle that most people have forgotten how to exercise. Have you ever felt good vibes or bad vibes?"

"I suppose so," responded Dominic, poking his head through the doorway of another empty room.

"You know how you can tell almost instantly when you walk into a party if it's a good vibe or not?" asked Melanie, who had this conversation with Andrea before.

"Yeah," replied Dominic. "You're telling me that's all there is to being psychic?"

"No, but can you remember any times when there was a really good vibe all night?" she prompted him.

"Yeah."

"Well, didn't you have a sense that it was going to be a good night, even before you got there?"

"Yeah, I suppose I did," said Dominic. "So, what does that mean?"

"It means that people are always broadcasting their vibes out into the universe," explained Melanie, "and we all have the ability to pick up on the broadcast, because we are all connected. Most people just don't pay close enough attention to the energy."

"You sound like you know what you're talking about," said Echo as they rounded another corner. The sound of water dripping from the ceiling could be heard in the distance.

"I'm just connecting the dots," said Melanie. "I always just called it intuition, but I didn't really associate it with psychic perception until Andrea started to explain what she knew about it. This astral plane stuff is new to me, though."

"Man, I can't tell if I'm feeling bad vibes or if I'm just chicken," joked Dominic. The humorous inflection in his voice never failed to make them laugh.

"Shhhhh," Zack hushed them, trying not to giggle himself. "Try to laugh silently," he urged in a quiet voice, but it was no use. The very act of trying not to laugh caused the group to explode with laughter for a few seconds. Dominic was eager to push it further just for the stress relief, but he held back. One of Dominic's favorite things to do was to figure out what made his friends laugh and get them into a fit of hysterical laughter. Though he did not realize it, his own intuition was honed around the humor potential of situations.

Just around the next corner, they entered a strange hallway that stretched only ten yards before ending in a brick wall.

"That's weird," observed Zack. "It looks like this originally went somewhere, but somebody walled it off."

Just then, a wave of terror struck Andrea, and she began to back away from the dead end hallway. For the first time, she had a waking vision, and her heart was racing. For a split second, she had an image of a group of people pounding on the other side of the wall, screaming for help.

"What is it, Dre?" asked Melanie.

Andrea had backed up against a wall and looked disoriented.

"This is the place. Can you guys feel them? I think they were trapped on the other side of that wall." Andrea shivered.

Zack walked forward and placed his hands on the wall, and Echo followed cautiously behind him. Dominic and Aaron hung back at the entrance to the dead end hallway, watching both Zack and Echo while paying attention to what was happening with Andrea.

"I *can* feel something," Zack shivered. "It's cold. Like something died here, and all the good was sucked out."

"Yo, I've got goosebumps, ya feel me?" asked Echo.

"Yeah," said Zack. "Dre, are you OK?" he asked with concern as they turned and started to walk back.

"Something's watching us," Andrea half whispered. "It can see us."

"Who can see us?" asked Aaron. "You mean the lost souls?"

"No...not them. There's something watching them, too," she said. "I think we should go back. This is even darker than I expected."

"What is it?" questioned Echo, looking back at the wall.

"I don't know, but we need to leave *now*," insisted Andrea. "This is not a good place." And with that, they all started to walk briskly back the way they had come.

"Aaron, are you sure you would get a warning from Lex if we were in danger?" Zack worried. "Did you feel that just now? What if we just tripped a psychic alarm?"

"I don't know what I just felt," said Aaron nervously. "Let's just get to a better position. Then we'll figure out what to do."

The group was silent as they made their way back, making sure they did not miss a turn. The level they were on was much larger than they previously thought, but they had used pink sidewalk chalk to mark their path back to the exit.

"Let's duck in here for a moment," suggested Zack as they reached the room that was closest to the exit. This was the very first room they had all entered the night before. Somehow, this room felt safer, like it had more of their own energy in it.

Zack took off his backpack and sat down with his back against the wall. "Whew," he sighed. "What was *that* all about?"

Seeing that he felt relieved, Andrea and Melanie sat down and started digging out their water bottles from their backpacks. Echo stood near the entrance to the room to listen for sounds and his self-assumed security role allowed everyone to relax a little more.

"I had a flash of a vision," explained Andrea.

"I think I had one, too," added Melanie, "or maybe I was just picking up on yours. What did you see?"

"I saw what happened," Andrea's voice quivered. She paused, covering her eyes with her hands for a moment. Her eyes were still closed when she dropped her hands and began to describe what she saw. "Those people that died in there were slaves."

"That's what I was feeling!" exclaimed Melanie. "Go on."

"These were the people that cleared out this whole building complex. They had to work, moving everything out, and then, after they were done, they were knocked out by a group of soldiers. That flash I had…it was of a bunch of them being dragged into that hallway, unconscious, by a group of military people. And then they walled them in. Those people died in there, starving and suffocating."

"That's cold-blooded," said Dominic.

"Who would do that?" asked Echo, disgusted. "They must be heartless."

"That's not all," continued Andrea. "While they were screaming and pounding on the walls after they woke up, they attracted a lot of astral energy. Something is there with them, like an astral entity, and it's big. It's keeping them trapped there by tormenting them with fear images. It uses their fear to keep them distracted so they don't turn inward and realize their predicament."

"Wow," interjected Zack, "you got all that from one flash?"

"No, but I can feel that entity watching us now," she shuddered.

"Yeah, me too," agreed Melanie. "It's worried that we might disturb their illusion."

"What did *you* see, Mel?" asked Andrea.

"I just got that they were slaves who were involved with closing out this building. Their superiors didn't want them to live with the knowledge that it was here. They wanted to prevent them from telling others that might try to escape."

"They must have been the ones who didn't finish sealing the exit properly," said Zack. "Maybe they were planning an escape."

"I think so," presumed Melanie. "I feel like they had someone on the outside that was going to help them, but the plan was foiled."

"Do you think that entity is part of the psychic security system?" Echo wondered.

"I don't know," replied Andrea. "This is even worse than I thought. Hey guys, let's all just focus on each other for a moment. Whatever you do, don't think about the entity, or that place. Just think about right here, right now. Let this room be our sanctuary."

This was the first piece of valuable guidance that came through, and they all immediately gravitated to the idea. They formed a circle, sitting on the concrete floor, and each of them began to focus on their awareness. Zack was hoping Dominic would say something funny, but he looked a little freaked out at the moment. Then Melanie pulled out a large vanilla candle from her backpack and placed it in the center of the group. As soon as it was lit, they all turned off their headlamps and removed them.

"How are you feeling now, Dre?" asked Dominic.

"I'm OK. I think I was really drained from the attack before, because I was taking it personally, but as soon as I realized that these lost souls were in trouble, I started to find my center of power again. I think that's the key. If you take it personally, you get caught up in their drama, but when you focus on helping, it becomes less scary. I can still sense them, though. It's like they think I'm a doorway out, and they're trying to pull at my heart energy."

"Maybe you *are* a doorway out," Melanie considered. "What if our love could change their vibration so they stop being afraid?"

"Seriously?" asked Zack facetiously.

"She's right," remarked Andrea. "Let's try to strengthen our connection with each other first. I want to share something my grandfather taught me about purification before going into battle."

Suddenly, Andrea's words were followed by a kind of stillness that came over the room. She felt the presence of her Native American ancestors, many of which she assumed were from her grandfather's shamanic lineage. Everyone else began to sense a change in the energy of the room, though they did not know what they were feeling. Andrea knew it was a sign and was immediately more inspired about what she was sharing.

Though she had not expected this, the very intention of sharing the ritual blessing had invoked a powerful force of protection that embraced the energy of their circle. The angry stare of the entity felt less intimidating, and the pulling Andrea felt seemed to fade. The room was starting to feel clearer, and she knew they were being supported.

"My grandfather said that some of the Native Americans practiced a form of warfare that began internally. Their intention was to meet the enemy inwardly first, in a sacred ceremony, to remove the struggle for power by making peace with the source of the conflict. This way, they could resolve the conflict before ever meeting the enemy in battle. Nine times out of ten, the enemy would choose not to fight, but to negotiate instead."

"Whoa! That's way cool," exclaimed Dominic. "Does it work on parents?"

"Yes," she said bluntly, not wanting to get sidetracked. "He also said that all people share a connection through Divine Oneness, no matter how different they may seem. We are all mirrors for each other. That's a key to understanding how to change the reflection of the enemy. You see, usually, if someone attacks or offends us, our tendency is to fight back. When we don't acknowledge them as equals, we just end up reflecting each other's power struggles. Whatever we judge in them will draw us into conflict until compassion awakens, and we forgive what we judge."

"If we start by respecting their feelings and power, we can elevate the relationship toward a potential for harmony that is always seeking to emerge. So, the insight is to focus with compassion on the equality of all beings and recognize how connected we are. When we appeal to the oneness potential of our enemy, we can change the conflict into an opportunity for spiritual growth. The goal is not to win the battle, but to end the conflict with a mutual acknowledgement of oneness."

"Wow!" expressed Echo. "Your grandpa taught you all that?"

"It works, too," explained Andrea, nodding. "When he first told me about it, I didn't think much of it, but it actually got me out of a fight at school once."

"What happened?" Echo prodded.

"This girl wanted to fight me after school, and she was saying nasty things about me to provoke me. I was really offended at first, and I didn't know what to do. I was scared, but mostly angry. I found myself arguing with her over and over again in my mind during class, until I realized that I was just arguing with my own projection. So then, I tried to imagine that she was me. It was like the whole image reversed, and suddenly I felt compassion for her need to get attention—just like we all have that same need sometimes, right? So, I stopped judging her need, and then I started to pray that she would feel her own power without needing to steal it from others."

"Acknowledge your enemy's power, I could hear my grandfather say, and so I did. By acknowledging her power, it strengthened my own power to hold a vision of a peaceful outcome. By the time we met after school, she seemed less invested in harassing me. I just kept holding compassion for the fear in both of us, and it kept the tension from turning violent. We actually ended up liking each other after that day. I wouldn't have believed it could work if I hadn't seen it for myself."

"That's dope," remarked Echo.

"Yeah," said Aaron. "I had no idea you were so deep."

"Thanks," responded Andrea, smiling. "I take that as a compliment."

"So, how do we do that here?" Aaron wondered.

"The ceremony begins by recognizing that we've become connected with a group of others in a disempowering situation. Maybe they feel threatened, or maybe *they* have violated us and *we* feel threatened. Either way, we go around and honor each other's connection to spiritual power so we can start to unplug from the power struggle. It makes it easier to let go of taking things personally."

"How do we honor each other?" asked Zack.

"We compliment each other," replied Andrea. "My grandfather said the ancestors often did this first within their group, and then they would practice extending the feeling of being honored to the others. If you guys are ready, I'll go first."

"Sure," said Dominic.

"OK, then I'll start with you," said Andrea. She became very present with him, looking him in the eyes and honoring his presence. Then she remarked, "You have a great sense of humor, and I can tell that you really care about your friends."

Dominic's face lit up with a smile. Melanie could tell that he had really received the compliment on a feeling level, and everyone began thinking of what they could contribute.

"You're one of the best dancers I know, and you've really inspired me to keep learning and practicing," added Melanie.

"Wow, coming from you, that's a huge compliment." Dominic's good vibes were contagious. The whole room was basking in his glow, and the power of the ceremony was effortlessly revealing itself.

"I admire your dedication," shared Aaron. "You're really amazing to watch."

"Yeah," said Zack. "Even when you're not dancing, you have a rhythm to the way you move. And you really appreciate everybody's differences, like how we all have a different style."

Dominic nodded to Zack and Aaron, giving thanks.

"I love how quick you are," admired Echo. "You can move quick, react quick, and your humor is quick-witted. That shows real intelligence."

"Thank you," said Dominic warmly. His voice was filled with gratitude, and that was the whole point of the practice, to leave everyone feeling grateful.

"Now you pick the next person," guided Andrea.

"OK, Zack," began Dominic. "Only someone with an imagination as big as yours could dream up a movie like this. You're truly adventurous."

"Thanks," responded Zack, who had his camera out to film their dialogue.

"You're the best older brother I could ever imagine having," Aaron said, reaching out to place a hand on Zack's shoulder for a moment.

"And you've been like a brother to me," acknowledged Echo. "I will never forget the way you lifted my spirits when I was struggling. I feel like we've known each other our whole lives, even though it's only been a year."

"You're a really thoughtful person, Zack," expressed Melanie, "and I love that you look out for people. I feel like you're the kind of guy that doesn't put himself first."

"Yeah," Andrea nodded. "You're a leader, but in a way that's really inclusive. And you're brave."

Zack smiled big.

"Talk about bravery," said Dominic. "This is the bravest bunch of people I've ever known! I mean, we're sitting down here in some kind of secret government building with entities hunting our souls, and you guys are just a bunch of happy campers."

Everybody cracked up laughing.

"You might as well break out the marshmallows," he added. "And this dude snuck all the way into their secret city and made it out with a map," he said laughing at Aaron. "That was *seriously* brave."

The energy of the group was really high now, and the pace of the dialogue had increased.

"You *are* really brave," said Melanie to Aaron. "And you're the best street artist I know."

"You're really thoughtful like your brother, too," added Andrea.

"Yeah, and I'm impressed by your ambition to take on this whole conspiracy thing," said Echo.

"It's an honor for me to film anything that you do," remarked Zack to his brother. "You're an artist with paint *and* an artist of thoughts and words."

"Same goes for Echo," said Aaron. "You are a true artist of thoughts and words, and I would be honored to include some of your poetry in my installations."

"Awesome," expressed Echo. "I'm already working on something."

"This is truly a powerful combination of forces," asserted Zack.

"This feels good," said Melanie. "Let's keep going."

"Let's switch gears," suggested Andrea. "I'm going to share some things about Melanie, and I want all of you to just honor the connection between us. I will honor her, and you all focus on honoring us."

"Mel. You are my best friend," she said as tears started to well up in her eyes. "When I met you, there was something so pure-hearted about you. You made me feel like I was important. Because you value yourself, you helped me to value myself more, and I wouldn't be the same without you. I used to feel like I didn't fit in, but your friendship took that feeling away. There've been times when you put your arm around me, and it felt like an angel's wing. You have a big heart, and I wouldn't be here without you. You bring out the best in me."

In that moment, Melanie's eyes began to water, too, and they embraced. The silent appreciation of their connection seemed to amplify the love in everyone's heart. That was when everyone began to feel the flow.

"Can you feel the connection between our hearts?" asked Andrea.

"Wow!" exclaimed Aaron. "I've never felt so connected to a group of friends before."

"Yeah," agreed Echo. "It's like normally when I hang out with people, we relate on some level, but this is a lot deeper."

"We're making room for the true expression of our souls to shine through," explained Andrea. "That can only happen when the heart is being honored. Now, let's continue the process silently. Everyone focus on Echo, and share your praises with him. And Echo, you just allow yourself to feel it. You're looking for a feeling that is blissful inside, like you're celebrating how connected you feel with us."

"OK," said Echo. He was sitting cross-legged with his back straight in a meditation posture. Intuitively, he felt to go around the circle and take a long look into everyone's eyes. Five hearts and five minds were receiving his presence and reflecting back their appreciation. Echo realized that he had a guard up that he just now began to notice. His focus on the safety of the group had kept him occupied with their surroundings. The presence of praise helped him relax his guard into a more receptive focus. And so, with a single breath, he opened up and allowed the group energy to flow in. For the first time, it felt like the others were protecting *him*.

Gradually, he allowed the feeling of appreciation to connect with his heart until he truly felt touched. It felt really different to be aware of how much power human attention has when used in this way—to convey love and sincere admiration. He could almost hear the compliments and praise each person was speaking silently as they gazed.

Then Andrea said, "now focus on me," and the attention shifted to her. There was a divine synchronicity to this order that she had not planned on, but it was profound. Other than Melanie, most of them did not know her well enough to appreciate what was unique about her, but the ceremony itself had given them a window into her soul. She could feel their praise and recognition of her as a true spiritual warrior.

This was the moment they all began to recognize love as the source of their spiritual power. Melanie did not feel the need to say anything yet, but she was beginning to have the impression of a large group of Native American spirits surrounding them and offering protection. She could almost see them, and she sensed one of them moving around the circle, offering each of them a blessing.

"OK, can everyone feel that vibe that's between us?" asked Andrea.

"Totally," responded Melanie.

"This is the coolest thing we have ever done," expressed Zack. "It's like everyone has this power that can amplify the power of others, and when you're focusing on it, there's a flow of energy that comes right from your center."

"That's exactly right!" agreed Andrea. "Now the goal is to extend that same sense to the others by inviting them into the circle of power. Let's start by imagining a circle of light that is expanding out around us and see all of the ancestors and higher beings that are supporting us as a part of the circle."

They all instinctively took a few deep breaths, feeling the circle that connected their hearts. After a moment, Andrea continued.

"Now, let's think of the dead end hallway and extend the circle to those who are lost."

Everyone closed their eyes for a moment, thinking of the hallway and inviting all of the beings to join the circle. Immediately, a wave of energy moved through the group, and then the ominous presence of the entity showed up. At first, it tried to focus on Andrea as it had before, but her field was too strong and too interlinked with the others. They could feel the anger of this being who was afraid of losing its power, but they remained focused on the balance of the circle.

"Can you feel that?" Melanie whispered.

"I feel an angry presence," replied Echo.

"Yeah, that entity is pissed," Aaron agreed. "I can almost see its eyes, like it's trying to intimidate us with its stare."

"Just stay focused on each other and on the circle," insisted Andrea. "Hold the invitation for all beings that are present to join with the circle and align with our higher power. Don't judge this entity's anger. It will probably leave when it no longer has fear as a food source. Just keep expanding and ask for the angels and the ancestors to help these souls cross over and go to the right place."

A few moments passed, and they each felt as though the energy of the circle was guiding them, as if the circle was a being unto itself. There was a palpable feeling of unity, and the energy of the lost souls began to relax a bit, as if they were becoming more aware of the present opportunity.

"There's something else," noticed Melanie. "It feels like they're still holding on, even though they can see the light. It's like they need us to do something for them."

What do you need? Andrea asked the beings telepathically, extending her inner senses to feel their response. Another moment passed, and then a wave of clarity moved through the field.

"We need to forgive the people who did this," said Andrea. "If we can forgive their ignorance, and then apologize for what these beings experienced, they can let go."

"Yes, that's it," affirmed Melanie. "Just intend forgiveness for all that occurred here, and we can be like the mirrors of the forgiveness that these beings need to express to the human family." She was in a state of prayer, and her words were felt as a force of guidance that channeled the healing power of the circle.

They all felt the shift in the field when the trapped souls released and moved on. It felt like a great relief, and the remaining pressure that Andrea had been feeling inside was gone. For a few more moments, the room remained deeply silent. The flicker of the candle was hypnotizing them into a deep state of peace. The constant focus of unity could not be broken, and the angry stare of the entity turned away as it disappeared.

It's gone, thought Andrea, and then she opened her eyes.

"Did you just say, *it's gone?*" asked Dominic.

"Yeah, but I didn't say it out loud. You heard that?"

"I think we both said it," remarked Melanie. "I just thought the same thing when I felt it leave, or maybe I was just hearing you."

"Wow, it's like we're becoming telepathic," said Echo. "Even the sounds of our voices feel different, like there's a resonance there…more of a connection. I can't explain it."

"Yeah, I feel it, too," agreed Zack. "It's like you're all inside me. How are you doing, Dre?"

"Great! We did it, guys. We cleared the path. It feels safe now," she responded. "I don't think that entity was part of some psychic security system. It was just a parasite feeding off their fear. Once we cleared the path for those souls to go home, it had no reason to stay."

Everyone looked around, faces smiling in the gentle light of the candle, and Aaron seemed to have an unusual glow around him, like he was beaming with excitement about something.

"Guys, I just had an incredible idea for the mural. You're gonna love this!"

"Wow, you're really glowing," Melanie pointed out.

"I know, I feel really inspired!"

"No, no, no…I mean you are *really* glowing," she persisted. "Can anyone else see it?"

"I don't know if I am seeing what you're seeing," said Echo, "but you do seem brighter."

"You *all* seem that way to me," acknowledged Aaron.

Andrea reached in her backpack and pulled out a camera.

"I want to see if it shows up on the camera."

"Good idea," said Dominic. "You have to see the look on your face." Dominic pulled out his phone and snapped a picture just after Andrea, and then he looked astonished as he stared at the screen.

"What the heck is that?" he exclaimed, turning the camera around for everyone to see. There, in front of Aaron's forehead, was a large orb of white and blue light.

"That's probably the flash reflecting off something in the air," supposed Zack.

"No," replied Andrea. "Look at this," she said, turning her camera around. There on the display screen was the same blue and white orb, just a few inches in front of Aaron's face. "That's the same thing from a different angle!"

"What do you think it is?" asked Aaron.

"Maybe it's one of your guides," replied Melanie.

"Here, take another one," Aaron suggested.

Andrea and Dominic both snapped a couple of pictures of Aaron and then started taking them of everyone else. By then, Melanie had her phone out, taking pictures as well.

"Look, there are orbs everywhere!" said Dominic with surprise.

"And there's Aaron's again, just over his right shoulder," Andrea pointed out, turning her camera around again to show the group.

For a few minutes, they kept taking pictures and examining them. The mood had shifted to one of magic and wonder.

"What do you think it means?" asked Echo.

"It means we're surrounded by good spirits that want to help us," Melanie brightened. "Doesn't it feel that way?"

"Yeah, it feels like we've claimed this as *our* territory now," asserted Aaron. "I think we can begin the work."

"Let's do it!" declared Zack. "What do you need from us?"

"I've got a brilliant idea, and I brought enough chalk for everyone. Follow me," gestured Aaron, as he stood up and walked out into the hallway, noticeably unafraid.

15

THE PROPHECY

The two families had been in Lys for less than a day, and already, their sense of time was shifting. Even as they slept, the natural rhythms of the body were going through some kind of adjustment. The people of the Inner Earth had an entirely different sense of time, which pervaded the atmosphere. Their sense of night and day was not dependent on a cycle but was rather something that was chosen according to one's preference of environment.

As the hours rolled by, this new sensation of time was having a relaxing effect, removing any sense of hurry. For Roya, this became the most relaxing sleep she had experienced since she was a baby. It was like remembering what life was like before there were any demands on her time; before school, before homework, before chores, and before there was anything else to plan.

The idea of living for *several hundred years* had echoed in Roya's mind ever since Claire had spoken the words. Even as she slept, the idea continued to unravel, trying to find its expression in her dreams. She could not help thinking how much more she could do with her life if she could live for hundreds of years. Was such a thing even possible for her on the surface, or could it only happen down here?

For the first time in a long while, she was not in a hurry to grow up. When she was younger, she could not wait to be old enough to have adult freedoms, but for now, she felt perfectly content just being sixteen. Finally, she did not feel like she was waiting for her life to begin. *This* felt like a new beginning.

At some point, Roya began to hear the sound of the ocean in the distance. She knew it was the calling of a dream, as the sound was filling her inner senses. Suddenly, she found herself standing on a rocky shoreline, looking out at the churning sea. The water was turbulent, and out in the bay, she could see a number of whales with long tusks extending from their heads. They were narwhals! Just like the picture in *The Circle and the Stars*. The strangest feeling came over her, like they were aware of her presence and were joyfully laughing. It was not that they were making laughing sounds, but there was a giddiness to their presence that Roya could feel.

They seemed like proud creatures, and several of them broke from the group and swam a little closer, as if to greet her.

She was standing on an outcropping of rocks that met the water, which was deep enough for the narwhals to make a close approach. As three of them swam by, one of them sprayed water in the air, and she reached her hands out to feel the mist.

"Wow!" she said out loud, noticing how aware she was of her dream body. Seeing her hands in front of her prompted her to look down to see the full length of her body with her feet planted firmly on the rocks. In that moment, she knew that the whales had called her there for a reason. Her gaze was then drawn to the right where she saw one of the narwhals lying on the rocks just above the waves. This was a highly unusual sight. She wondered how it had made it out of the water and what it was doing there. Looking along the rocky shore, she noticed a clear path over the rocks to the whale, so she headed over to get a closer look. As she began to walk, she could feel the narwhal's excitement about meeting her. Before this moment, she had never realized that a whale could relate to her like a human being, but this one recognized her as an old friend.

She could feel his sense of humor and good nature. There were clearly many unique qualities to his personality, and she could feel that these narwhals were keenly interested in humans, particularly in her. For a moment, she wondered if it had been beached, but then she realized that everything this whale did was very purposeful.

As Roya approached, she noticed that this one did not have a tusk. Instead, there was an opening that looked like a natural orifice where the tusk would have been. Had it lost its tusk, or was this whale just made different than the rest? The narwhal seemed to invite her telepathically to examine its features more closely. And then she was struck by a vision.

In a flash, she could see the annual hunt of the Inuit people, who killed some of the narwhals for food. The Inuit would shoot at the narwhals with rifles from the edge of the ice and then attempt to snag the dying whales with a grappling hook, often losing many more whales than were successfully landed. It was shocking to think that a being so conscious and with such a great interest in human culture would be seen only as food or a source of income from the sale of their tusks. Then the vision shifted to the feast, and Roya heard the whale's telepathy in clear English, adding commentary to the vision.

"It's ironic that the Inuit people believe that ingesting our meat can give them power. If only they knew how to ingest the gift of our living consciousness, their relationship to us would evolve."

Roya was taken aback by the light-hearted tone of the whale's comments. She would have thought that the narwhals would be terribly sad or angry about being hunted by humans, especially when so many of their lives were wasted due to ineffective hunting techniques. She was surprised that they did not seem to be highly offended by watching humans eat their people but were rather calm and gentle in their attitude. The whale looked right past the injustice and focused instead on all of the lovable qualities of the humans. The contrast was shocking to Roya. They truly held a love for humanity in their hearts, but they longed for more humans to become conscious enough to know them personally.

It was now apparent that the vision Roya was having of people eating the narwhal meat while laughing and telling stories was something the whale had seen through its psychic abilities. Now she understood why the narwhals had such a love of human culture. Even though they dwell in the arctic seas, their minds could travel the world, observing everything that is happening on land. And more than other whales with similar abilities, they had grown exceedingly fond of human beings.

They loved our stories and our humor. Like the Guardians of the Inner Earth, they had chosen to document our achievements by recording psychic impressions of our history, which were passed down as part of their racial memory. Over many thousands of years, they had stored up a great deal of memory that we could learn from, if only we did not destroy them before we became conscious enough to receive the gift. Like so many other hunted species, the narwhals were patiently waiting for humanity to wake up.

As soon as Roya understood, the vision ended, and she found herself standing in front of the narwhal again, but then something strange happened. A thick, milky, white substance began to ooze from the orifice where the tusk would normally be.

Without words, the whale seemed to be asking her to ingest some of the substance. If this had not been a dream, Roya might have thought this was gross, like licking snot from someone's nose, but her heart told her this was a precious gift. She reached out and collected the smallest amount on two of her fingers, and without even thinking, she placed both fingers in her mouth. The substance tasted sweet, and she felt an instant zing of sensation zip through her body. The substance, she now knew, was a psychic ethereal secretion connected with the brain chemistry of the whale. It was not a physical substance that could actually be found in the anatomy of the whale, but a symbolic form of energy that appeared like milk to nourish the mind. She had just ingested knowledge of its abilities.

What happened next was the strangest thing that Roya had ever experienced, and after all that had happened in the last week, that was saying a lot. Suddenly, an exciting sensation drew her attention to her forehead where it felt like a narwhal tusk was beginning to grow. At first, it was only a foot long, but it kept growing and growing until it was a full six feet. The speed and the power of the transformation was a little frightening, but it soon began to feel natural.

The dream abruptly ended, and Roya became aware of her body, lying on a sleeping pad in a room with her sister, but the process continued to unfold. The feeling of a whale body came over her, and it was like being in two places at once. Her heart expanded into the feeling of being a narwhal, swimming with a pod, and yet she was lying in bed and feeling her human body's connection to the dream tusk.

Roya lifted her hands up to her head to feel for it, but all she felt was her normal head—no tusk—and yet, the sensation felt incredibly real. Then it dawned on her *how* these whales had developed such strong psychic abilities. The tusk told her the story quite clearly. It acted like a tuning fork to pick up subtle vibrations, and over time, they had developed a practice of extending their field of consciousness along the form of the tusk. This elongated the presence of a psychic center known as the third eye, transforming the narwhals into powerful natural psychics. The same practice they developed to extend their consciousness to the tip of their tusks was now used to project their minds over great distances. In essence, by exploring their bodies, they had developed a focus of attention that had opened the doors of perception.

Roya relaxed into the sensation of the whale body and breathed. Even being fully awake, she could still feel the tusk for several minutes until the feeling gradually began to fade. She felt like she had just been accepted as a member of the pod and began to wonder, *why me?*

"*Now we can better protect you,*" answered the whale telepathically.

"*Protect me from what?*" Roya communicated back with her thoughts. No reply.

Roya searched her mind and could not think of any reason why she would need such protection or what kind of protection the whales could provide, but the connection was real. There was a lingering sense that the narwhals would be keeping an eye on her. It was a warm feeling of safety. Her heart expanded with a feeling of gratitude toward them.

While the families were resting, Claire walked briskly through the hallway to the meeting room where a number of other leaders from the Council of Lys had gathered. Shumayan was there with about fifteen others, some of whom had been summoned from other cities. Claire was eager to hear their assessment of what was unfolding, but perceived a nervous energy among the leaders, even before she arrived. She had not expected to see such a meeting take place so quickly after her return, but the arrival of the two families was an unprecedented event, especially given that originally, they had only expected one emissary from the surface.

The doorway to the room was open, and she was the last to arrive, sensing that a part of the meeting had already unfolded before a messenger had called her to attend. As she took her seat, many warm smiles and acknowledgements greeted her from the men and women that had gathered. On this occasion, they had chosen to hold the meeting in spoken English, to imbue the language with their consciousness.

"Let me say on behalf of everyone here," one of the elders began, "that we are all very grateful to see that you have returned safely. Your courage is inspiring, and we have already learned much from your mission."

"Thank you," said Claire. "I agree, now, that it was worth the risk. And I am so grateful for our team on the surface."

"How is everyone?" asked one of the women.

"They are all fine," informed Claire. "I was skeptical at first that surface dwellers could be trusted with our lives in this way, but they took care of every detail to create my identity and provide the support that I needed to integrate with the culture. The group is ready if we ever need to send another."

"That is one of the matters we are debating," presented Shumayan. "We are very aware that the attempts to find our cities have escalated. There seems to be a concerted effort in many locations to tunnel with the intention of targeting us, and now they are using seers to guide their efforts, as well. Some of *our* seers have reported witnessing forms of psychic penetration into our cities, but it's unknown if they have discovered any real intelligence regarding our locations."

"As you know, our collective vibration, in the past, was out of phase with their culture, but that seems to be changing, somewhat. We always assumed that this collapsing of density was how the prophecy would be fulfilled. Their vibrations would rise with that of the Earth during her time of initiation, and ours might become slightly denser as the energy of duality is cleared from the consciousness of the surface culture. We have expected for some time that we would see more of *our* consciousness beginning to awaken within theirs. But the emerging bridge between these two densities also means that we've become more vulnerable to elements of greed and duality that are still running rampant."

"We are interested to know," said another woman, "how did the opening arrive to bring *two families* here? When did you know that more than one person was involved?"

"Is everyone aware that the intended recipient of the book is only sixteen years old?" mentioned Claire. Clearly, this was a surprise to some, but she also noticed looks of confusion as to the significance of this statement, given that teens in Lys were able to travel more freely without their parents.

Claire continued, "Let me say first that I am certain that we found the right person. She may be young, but it is clear that she carries the bridge between our two cultures, as do her friends. I first learned there were three of them when Roya approached me about her experiences with the book."

Claire began to recount the whole story from her first connection with Roya in the library to her experience of how the book and the seer technology had brought the two families together. She explained her realization that Roya was part of a group of three, and that the bridge had extended to both of their families, uniting them in a shared purpose to support the girls in their journey to Lys.

"This has to be a great blessing that the bridge opened to seven people and not just one," recognized Claire.

"It is unexpected for sure, and it might be a sign, but it doesn't make us feel any safer regarding the security of our cities," explained Twa'amatae. "We still know very little about how the other bridges will form if the Prophecy of Integration is true. Their military culture that dwells underground has begun to seal portions of itself off from the surface entirely, and the wall of secrecy that separates them from the surface now feels more like an all out denial of their connection with the rest of humanity. How can we ever expect to bridge consciousness with people who see us only as something to be conquered and exploited?"

"We can't," said one of the men emphatically. "This situation has no solution. It's unrealistic to expect every civilization we bond with to make it. We have to accept that some civilizations fail. We've seen it happen on other worlds, and we are looking at another failure happening right now. We have to begin preparing to evacuate our people before any more of our cities are compromised."

Claire could feel the man's negative tilt trying to pull the energy of the room toward his view of reality. It was unusual to feel this much fear in a Lyssian, and she could feel several others beginning to resonate more with him. Nothing had polarized her people like this before—at least, not in her lifetime.

"We have always seen that such planetary events contain the potential of multiple timelines," reassured Shumayan, "some that show a path toward higher evolution and others toward failure. We must not forget that our most discerning seers have described a shift in the field of matter itself. They see the increasing presence of unpredictability in all of these events, and they say that new probability fields are arriving all the time that have made them less and less certain about the final outcome."

"Which means they may not be able to see if an attack is coming!" the man warned forcefully.

"True," said Shumayan, "but they also could not foresee that the Formelle would manifest an artifact that would send Claire to the surface. *And* they could not see that she would return with seven people."

Shumayan was always good at finding the balance, and Claire was grateful for his ability to hold receptivity to the diverse perspectives of the council. This was often what allowed the creative process of the council to flow with such ease. All around the room, Claire could see that a consensus had not yet been reached concerning how to relate to the opportunities present, or even what they were. She sensed many other troubling things happening in far away places that the council was pondering from their earlier meetings.

"What if these families are a bridge between all three cultures?" inquired Claire. "If it was just one person, they would likely be doubted by their people, but with seven of them, they could help us send a message to the world. They could bring the issue of these attacks out in the open so that their governments could start to address what their military is doing in secret. It could humanize *us* to *them* and start a dialogue on the surface that might be part of the path to Integration."

"That's an excellent point," agreed Shumayan, "and we should consider what we could do for them to prepare them for such roles."

The question of how long the two families would be allowed to stay was one that Claire had been wondering about from the very beginning of her journey with them; especially since she had already formed a strong bond with Roya. She had been waiting for the issue to be resolved, but it seemed that the attention in the group had begun to shift toward an elder, who was regarded as one of the wisest of the seers. The older woman wore a maroon robe with gold trimmings, and her hair was a silvery grey.

"We must assume that we do not yet have all the answers," she said slowly, as if she had to think carefully to construct her sentences in English. "Claire, we ask you to continue to observe what is happening in the field of these people and support them to awaken. There is a great mystery here, and it would be wise to attune to the subtle way that the light of the future is interacting with these events. Go and be with them, and we will speak again. Let us trust that the hand of the Supreme Creator is at work and remain alert for opportunities."

It is an honor to serve, thought Claire, and the room remained in silence, as was customary when such an elder had spoken, to give their messages space to have their full intended impact. Claire arose and gestured with her right hand, slowly opening her fingers before she turned and walked away.

Roya's eyes were open now, and she was lying on her back. For a moment, she began to play with her psychic senses more. The memory of the tusk gave her the feeling that she could extend her mind outside of the body more easily, as if her mind had become loosened from the restriction of the body. Then her attention was caught by the sound of laughter in the next room. It was Mandy and Ami, and they sounded like they were having a blast.

Just as Roya sat up, a little green orb came zipping into the room and stopped a foot in front of her face. Being a tad more psychic was perfect timing because the orb immediately began to connect with her energetically, and as she tuned in, a message resonated into her mind.

"Hey Roya, come on over," resonated the orb in Mandy's voice, *"we've got company."* And then the orb zipped back around the corner. Sarah was still asleep, so Roya tried to leave quietly so as not to wake her. In the next room, Roya found Ami and Mandy both sitting cross-legged on their sleeping pads, facing each other with their backs to the wall. Hovering in the middle of the room was the green orb along with another one that was blue.

"What are you guys doing?" asked Roya quietly, letting them know with the volume of her voice that others were still sleeping. "Is that what I think it is?"

"Yeah. They're messengers like the one Claire has," Mandy bubbled. "Watch, I can change its color." Mandy stared at the green one that was hovering closest to her, and after a few seconds, it changed to yellow. "You see? It responds to your thoughts. Now you try it," she said to Ami.

"OK," said Ami, staring at the blue one.

Roya sat down cross-legged with her back against the wall closest to the entrance while Ami concentrated on the orb.

"You have to *visualize* the color," instructed Mandy. "Don't just think a name, visualize it."

"OK, give me a second," said Ami, still staring. Then she closed her eyes for a moment, trying to settle on a color, and when she opened them, the color of the orb started to shift. For a moment, they could see Ami's indecisiveness reflected in the orb as its hue shifted up and down the color spectrum until it began to settle in the violet range.

"There!" she exclaimed as the color locked into place. "It's violet." She seemed satisfied with the outcome.

"You see?" said Mandy, "Now you can name the color. They don't know what violet means to *you* until you show it the color with your imagination, but now it will remember."

"How do you know so much already?" asked Roya. Mandy was already shifting the color of her orb again, with noticeably more control.

"I think it's from when I met my muse," speculated Mandy. "All those colored orbs. They gave me a sense of how to work with them. It's a lot like using Photoshop, except you just change the colors with your mind." Now Mandy's orb was a vibrant pink. "So, you got my message."

"Yeah," said Roya. "I heard your voice in my mind. I was just coming out of this wild dream when it showed up." She paused, trying to put her thoughts in order so she could explain the vision, but curiosity took over instead. "So, how did you get them?"

"They just appeared as we were waking up," answered Ami.

"I think it's because they heard us talking in the temple about wanting our own messengers," said Mandy. "I remembered what Claire said about them, so I thought I would try sending you a message, and it worked."

"So how do I get one?" Roya asked just as Ami and Mandy burst into laughter.

"OMG, did you see that?" Mandy could barely contain herself.

"What?" asked Roya, and then she noticed they were looking just over her right shoulder. As she turned her head, she saw a bright red orb just a foot and a half away. It had appeared just outside of her peripheral vision at the entrance to the room.

"It showed up right when you said, *so how do I get one,*" said Ami, smiling.

The red orb floated around in front of her, and now all three orbs were just a couple of feet apart from each other near the center of the room.

"Maybe one of us should send a message to Claire," suggested Ami.

"Let me try," offered Roya. She focused into the orb and spoke to Claire with her mind, *"Claire. We are awake. Please come join us and tell us more about these messengers."* As soon as she finished, the orb disappeared.

"I guess we just…whoa!" said Roya as a violet messenger orb appeared right in front of her. It was Claire's.

"I'll be there shortly," it said in her voice. They all heard it in their minds perfectly clear, and then the little orb changed from Claire's violet back to Roya's red.

"Wow!" said Roya excitedly. "It's like they're all connected."

"Cool," remarked Mandy.

"What shall we try next?" Ami questioned.

"Well, if they're alive," Roya began, "maybe they can tell us how to work with them." Just then, all three orbs began to vibrate with enthusiasm. Gradually, they moved closer together until they merged into one pearlescent orb. It was nearly white, but with many colors shimmering lightly across the surface, and then it began to speak to them telepathically.

"We are Formelle. Our purpose is creative unity. As long as your minds are in unity, our services are available to you. We welcome the opportunity to co-create with the human imagination. Through our communication services, we can help synchronize the frequencies of your minds with the emerging collective brain of one humanity. We are a messaging system for the new human being. Through the new telepathic communication web, you may send and receive messages, thoughts, feelings, memories, and living information. Think of us as the training wheels for telepathy. Together, we can bring humanity online with a new knowledge sharing system of pure energetic communication."

The girls' excitement glowed in silent awe for a moment. The pearlescent light filled the room and subtly revealed the hidden unity of their minds. Seeing their personal messengers merge into one made a statement about the oneness potential of their consciousness.

"Did both of you just hear the same thing I did?" Roya wanted to know.

"I'm pretty sure we did," said Ami. "I don't even need you to repeat it back to me."

"This place is full of surprises," replied Mandy. "It feels like a dream."

Gradually, the color of the orb began to shift, and it split back into the three messengers. Ami's was still violet, Roya's was red, and Mandy's was now a swirl of blues and greens.

"How are you three?" greeted Claire from just outside the door.

"Wow! That was quick," exclaimed Roya.

"I wasn't far away," said Claire. "Looks like you've met your messengers."

"You've got that right," said Mandy with a huge grin.

"We just saw them merge into one," explained Roya.

"They are a many-in-one consciousness," said Claire. "They have assisted many worlds to awaken into unity."

"Yeah, they offered to help align our minds with some new kind of communication web," said Roya. "Can you tell us more about it?"

Claire now entered the room fully, walked right through the messengers, and sat down cross-legged with her back against the wall, opposite of Roya. Her body passed through the messengers, and they did not budge. Claire smiled, and then said, "Why don't you tell me everything they said, and I will fill in the blanks."

"Hang on," requested Roya. "Let me get my notebook, I wanna write this down."

Roya quietly snuck back into the room where her sister was still sleeping and pulled her notebook from her backpack, along with her favorite pen. When she returned, Ami recounted the message perfectly as Roya wrote it down, and Claire seemed unexpectedly surprised.

"Training wheels for telepathy?" she repeated with a note of curiosity in her voice. "I never thought about the possibility that you would integrate with our communication system while you were down here."

"Is that how *your* people became telepathic?" asked Roya.

"Well, when my people began using Formelle as messengers, we were already telepathic, though our telepathy was more emotion-based than mental. Gradually, as our society absorbed more of the complexity of other cultures, their function in our consciousness evolved. The Formelle helped us develop other levels of mind so we could reflect the consciousness of all those upon the Earth. Now it seems that my people have been stewarding a unique relationship with the Formelle that was meant to pass to your people, to help you develop your telepathy."

"But how will billions of people integrate with this way of communicating without coming down here?" asked Roya.

"They don't need to come down here," answered Claire. "The

consciousness of our communication system could just transfer to the surface. We've known for years that some of your people are starting to communicate with each other telepathically the way we do. We just didn't know exactly where it was all going. We have to tell the council about this. You three are living proof of the Integration that was predicted long ago."

"What exactly was predicted?" asked Roya.

"A prophecy has resurfaced a number of times over the centuries, and each time it stirs up a lot of conversation and debate about where our history on this planet is going. The prophecy speaks of three phases: Convergence, Integration, and Emergence. These are the three phases of a transformative event in planetary history that my people believe is now well underway. But what it all means is still a subject of debate."

"Convergence, Integration, Emergence," repeated Roya, writing in her notebook.

"The prophecy spoke of a great Convergence of historical forces, some opposing each other, and others more unifying. The unifying forces of oneness and wholeness would connect everyone together in a way that confronts people inwardly with how their fears, attachments, and beliefs obstruct their own awakening. But this was never about just *my* people. This was about the world we left behind on the surface, and how the many families of consciousness sharing this planet would come together as an integrated whole."

"The prophecy states that the Convergence was destined to catalyze a great change, challenging all of the forces present to achieve Integration with each other through a unified field of being. It also states that more and more people would achieve this Integration and model it for others until a new world emerged from inside them."

"We believe the Emergence is connected with the arrival of timewaves from a new future of wholeness. These timewaves will inform the world of a purpose that includes all the families of consciousness connected with the Earth. In essence, the Emergence is connected with the realization of a Divine Plan that will give all of humanity a shared vision of its infinite potential."

"That's really inspiring," expressed Ami.

"Yes, it is. But the prophecy said it would not be an easy process. It would involve integrating with opposing forces to achieve balance, as well as facing one's fears of reconnecting with the greater whole. *The Circle and the Stars* describes this in its own terms, but we tend to think of it as a birthing process, which can be both painful and ecstatic. Wisdom tells us that surrendering represents the path of least resistance. But even now, my people are debating our role in this birth process, and not everyone agrees with the prophecy."

"What's not to agree with?" asked Mandy.

"Some believe it's quickly becoming an unrealized historical potential—a failed process that is becoming more dangerous. Others debate whether we should have a passive or an active role as midwives. Humanity is clearly struggling, and that struggle could end in disaster, or it could become a universal success story."

Claire spoke as if her words were being directed not just to Ami, Mandy, and Roya, but as if she was speaking for the benefit of all who were not physically present to witness this revealing. She had a way of regarding human interaction that continually intrigued Roya, as if each conversation was being enacted for a vast field of attention that others were tapping into. It gave Roya the impression that destiny was unfolding in such a way that it produced events designed to reveal wisdom, and that they were all actors in a series of performances that animated the wisdom for others to sense. She wondered if this feeling was connected to what the council said about how their people could gain impressions of them without directly interacting. Perhaps the people on the surface were being affected in some subtle way by what was happening to her and her friends while they were in Lys.

"Could the Formelle help us fulfill the prophecy?" asked Roya.

Just then, their messengers brightened slightly, as if to acknowledge Roya's question. Claire was already tuning in to see what the Formelle might like for her to share about how to work with them.

"That was a *yes*," said Claire. "They want me to tell you more about them." She paused for a moment, and then she suggested, "Let's try something different. I'm going to share with you our memories about how we discovered the Formelle, and *they* will help attune your minds so you can see the memories inwardly. Is everyone OK with that?"

I see inwardly, remembered Roya. *The book had known.*

"I'm ready," said Mandy, and Ami smiled, nodding her head yes. Roya's eyes were already closed. She sensed what was coming. What she did not see was that all three messengers were drawn to Claire's forehead, synchronizing with her memories. Each of the girls felt the movement of their messengers as if they were invisibly tethered to their minds. Clearly, a bond had formed, and the messengers were starting to feel like extensions of themselves.

Claire appeared to be squinting her eyes for a moment as she focused inwardly, and it looked like there were subtle wisps of energy flowing from her forehead into the messengers, which hovered as a single pearlescent orb. She had become more focused on her breathing, and then, with one deep breath, she exhaled, sending each messenger to its receiver. Roya felt a gentle wave of energy penetrate her forehead, and she began to see light streaming into her inner field of vision, as if it was coming from far away.

The orbs were now touching each of their foreheads, synchronizing their brainwaves with Claire's. At first, Roya struggled to find her focus, wondering if the others were any further along in the process. Their brains wanted to cooperate with what Claire was intending, but an unexplainable resistance was coming from somewhere deep inside their minds. Despite their hearts' intentions to receive, something inside them was holding on to a less connected state, contemplating this new step in evolution from a place of uncertainty.

Claire sensed this apprehension as something collective; a primordial attachment to a more dormant state of being that still felt comfortable to the ego. She could feel the willingness of all three girls, and yet, they were burdened slightly by a fear of becoming too different from the rest of their society on the surface. For a moment, she considered that this was too big a step too soon, but then a force of guidance compelled her to command them into the new state. A single word then appeared in their minds. It was Claire's inner voice saying, *"Illuminate!"*

The resistance instantly abated, and their minds became aligned with the command. Everyone was choosing illumination, and the scene quickly began to open up in their inner field of vision. They could all see a strange looking vehicle that was floating on the ocean somewhere. It was a submersible that had surfaced, and several unusual looking people were poking their heads out of a large hatch of some kind, looking at the sky. The surface of the craft glistened in the sunlight with an iridescent glow. It looked less like a hard substance and more like living tissue, and energy was pulsating along a number of pathways that formed a beautifully intricate pattern across the surface, like a nervous system.

Everywhere they looked, dolphins were swimming around the craft, attracted to its energy, which seemed to mesh with the natural environment. And then the meaning of the vision became clear. The people were at one with the craft through some sort of symbiotic relationship. They were in touch with its living energy, and the craft itself was communicating with both them and the environment.

As the people descended back into the craft, closing the hatch behind them, the craft submerged and then sped away, cutting through the water with little resistance.

They were underwater now, seeing what looked like a city under the ocean near a great island. The water was clear to a depth of more than a hundred feet. Other craft were coming and going from some kind of underwater seaport, and many building structures glowed with lights that complemented the bright colors of the beautiful tropical fish that swam everywhere, undisturbed by the activity. It was then that they began to hear Claire's inner voice, narrating what they were seeing.

"Long ago, during the time of Lemuria, our people made a commitment to ourselves and the Earth: that we would only develop and use technology that was in harmony with the natural world. This was a social agreement that attracted the interest of many other families of consciousness that hold wisdom concerning the right use of resources. We became bonded to all the families of the Earth, so they aided us in developing our technology. We took inspiration from the natural world, from the living forms we saw, and from their electrochemical response to the environment. We created living vehicles that allowed us to inhabit the life of the ocean, entering into a symbiotic relationship with a field that is shared by all living things."

Suddenly, the scene shifted to a vast city on the surface. Numerous tall people were busily walking about, going into and out of the buildings, many of which were made of a transparent glass-like material. Among them were a number of shorter people with round faces like the ones from the submersible; some of them sitting together on the marble steps leading up to one of the buildings.

"When we became part of the Atlantean civilization, we brought them knowledge of the field that exists between plants and animals, which could be used as a great source of knowledge and power. But the Atlanteans were too focused on their individuality to pay attention to the communion that is always occurring between non-human life forms. They were enamored with the emerging powers of the mind, and their hearts were not open enough to fully receive the gift of our wisdom—or our presence."

The Lemurians looked very focused on sending conscious energy to the Atlanteans, imbuing them with the field they carried. And though the Atlanteans received a benefit from this field, they did not seem to acknowledge the contributions of their shorter friends. From the small group of them that sat together on the steps, a beautiful field of love radiated out to everyone that was passing through the large grassy open space between the buildings.

"Our love and support persisted through many stages of their development. Unfortunately, their hearts did not yet have the capacity to register a love so unconditional, but our people passed the test of delivering this gift without needing to be recognized. We knew that we were imbuing their DNA with a gift that would not be discovered for many ages. Now this gift is in your DNA, like a present that is waiting to be opened. We gave humanity a unified body of love that holds a deep attunement with the natural world."

Roya, Ami, and Mandy could feel each other's excitement about this information as the scene shifted again. This time, they saw a large Atlantean temple that reminded them of the Parthenon in Greece, though it was round. It was elevated on a rocky hill at the center of a city, and the white stone pillars were immense. In the center stood a large crystal where a gathering of people had come to witness something. The vision zoomed in on the crystal where they saw a light begin to emanate from inside it. The light grew brighter and brighter, and scientists were standing nearby, measuring the energy with some kind of handheld devices.

A group of light beings emerged from inside the crystal and began to speak as one. Eight of them hovered just above the ground, encircling the crystal. They appeared in the most beautifully glowing humanlike forms and were many times taller than the Atlanteans. Even though the beings spoke in the Atlantean language, the first expression translated into the girls' minds as something familiar: *"We are Formelle."*

"The Formelle first appeared when the Atlanteans began experimenting with the electromagnetic field of the Earth. They came to participate in a grand collaboration and might have helped our two cultures to achieve integration on a different timeline. The Formelle are beings of light that hold the subtle blueprints for all things, and they are gifted in developing forms of living technology— even technologies of pure light. They construct subtle systems of consciousness that can potentially amplify the power of human thought, a gift that was eventually abused by the Atlanteans—part of what led to their destruction."

Roya, Ami, and Mandy could sense even the nonverbal thoughts that Claire was sharing. It became clear that she would not show them the horror of the destruction, and they knew she was being gentle with their minds since this was such a new experience. In the next scene, they moved forward to a time when relations between the Atlanteans and the Lemurians were breaking down.

Before them was a great council chamber, reminiscent of a senate committee where hearings were taking place. A group of Lemurians was seated before a panel, and many Atlanteans were in the room. This new group was clearly different; though they had the energetic signature of the Lemurians, they were genetic hybrids of the two civilizations.

Several of them were standing before the Atlantean council speaking about the imbalances that were arising in the field of the crystals. They were concerned about the unequal distribution of power and where it would lead. They were asking for permission to work more closely with the Atlantean government to help them integrate more with the love vibration. This speech was silenced before it could be completed, and a tall, intimidating man who was seated at the center of the panel pronounced a judgment that had apparently been made before the meeting had convened. The Lemurians were to be expelled from attending any more of the council's meetings, or any government meetings for that matter. The Atlantean rulers were saying no to love.

Next, they saw the Lemurians leaving the building, some of them with tears in their eyes. Then a call came to them telepathically from the oceans that seemed to soothe the ache in their hearts. The call was from their brothers and sisters who dwell beneath the water, and it reached out to all of the Lemurians living among the Atlanteans across the surface of the planet. It was a call to return home, for their mission was complete. It was time to let the Atlanteans go. Many groups had completed a genetic transformation that had assimilated the DNA of the Atlanteans, and now they were to join the part of the Lemurian civilization that had been developing beneath the surface of Earth.

"The Formelle taught us that matter is alive; that it is made of energy that responds to imagination. For a time in Atlantis, our people entertained the illusion that material forms are solid and unchangeable by human thought. But as we became more integrated with the Formelle, we discovered that solid matter was only behaving according to our perception. The illusion of solidity is actually just a pattern inside the brain, and matter is governed, in part, by our root assumptions about the nature of reality."

"As soon as we realized this, we began an evolutionary process that removed these filters. Our desire to know the Formelle empowered them to work with our minds to deconstruct the limitations in thinking that we had adopted when we began to incorporate Atlantean DNA into our makeup. We then understood how matter was designed as a clever and persistent illusion that challenges physical beings to evolve beyond such limitation. We were meant to evolve a capacity to co-create with the living intelligence of matter through the unified field of love."

Next, they saw the early people of Lys exploring vast networks of caverns inside the Earth. Roya could feel how Claire had deliberately skipped past a sad time when many of the islands on the surface had to be evacuated, before becoming submerged. The world beneath the surface would be their new home for many ages, and the Formelle would remain present as companions and guides.

"*The Formelle taught us to view physical resources not as commodities like the Atlanteans did, but as conscious partners who have a say in how they are handled and what they are used for. We had already seen through the Atlantean civilization how living energy was abused in warfare, and rare materials were coveted as a form of personal wealth; so we decided to humble ourselves to the Formelle's perspectives about how to co-create with the Earth's resources. We found that they were willing to help us further our civilization, despite the failures of Atlantis. By partnering with us, they gain something that fulfills their creative purpose, and we gain the benefit of co-creating almost anything imaginable with them. They call us the Architects, and we call them the Builders of Form.*"

Next, they saw a group of Claire's ancestors being guided by the Formelle to a specific cavern, deep within the Earth. The Formelle appeared as a number of glowing orbs, and they led the group to a chamber of giant crystals. Next, they led another group to a large deposit of palladium, and the discoveries continued, one after another.

"*The Formelle specialize in living technology. They provide energy and assistance with large service projects that facilitate co-creation between all members of a society. Because our goal was to connect everyone together inside the Earth, and to make life easier for everyone, they began to bring forth gifts from the field of matter to help us achieve our dreams.*"

"*When we first began to ask them how these resources were to be used, they told us to dream of the civilization we wanted to build in an unlimited way. Only then would we realize that everything we needed had already been provided. The energetic blueprints for the new technology were already attached to the resources themselves. The Formelle had foreknowledge of our intentions and had already planned for the ingredients we would need.*"

"*With the crystals came a new conduit system that connected our cities with a powerful resource of living energy. The Formelle inhabit the crystals and use them to bridge the dimensions. The Formelle have a special relationship with the palladium, enabling them to create a transport system that links our cities through energetic pathways of resonance. Now their intelligence is integrated with our whole knowledge system. Eventually, there will be no more tilt between their realm and ours. We will share our forms with them, just like the nature spirits of the Earth, and the Formelle will share all of their creative potential with us. This is the goal we aspire to by humbly serving the potential of our co-evolution."*

At this point, Claire relaxed her focus. That was enough group-mind for the girls to integrate with. She could feel that they were still filled with questions as the dreamfield between their minds began to fade. Gradually, they returned to their awareness of the room. Mandy was the first to speak.

"Can we do that again? It felt like I was flying around to all these places, but it was more instantaneous, like leaping from one reality to another. How did we do that?"

Claire smiled, feeling lucky to witness part of the prophecy of Integration unfolding right before her eyes. "The same part of the brain that dreams is also capable of viewing other people's memories. In this case, I was sharing some of the memories of my race, and the Formelle were assisting our brains to link together in a natural way."

"Was that *your* voice I heard?" asked Mandy. "Your words are so precise."

"It was more than my voice," explained Claire. "I was channeling the voice of my people. I might suggest that you could do the same. When you intend to speak as a representative of your people, the collective oversoul will tilt into alignment with your frequency of expression, and your speech will become more filled with light."

"I feel like I'm learning so quickly," expressed Ami. "It's like drinking knowledge from a fountain when you're that connected." She was breathing quite deeply, the scenes still resonating in her mind. Roya was still taking it all in.

Claire's heart was glowing with gratitude at the opportunity to share in this way. This was more than she had hoped for. The council would be very pleased with this development, of that she was certain. She was already rolling up a ball of memories to send with her messenger to the council as a group message. Silently, the orb received its instructions and whisked away, barely even becoming visible.

Roya looked as if she was waking up from a deep sleep, though she was still reviewing the visions internally to make sure she remembered everything. Once her eyes were fully opened, she noticed that their messengers had disappeared, but the experience had left the feeling of a ring around her head. It was a very subtle feeling, but somehow it felt like it was a part of her.

"Wow," Roya opened. "I felt reluctant to surrender at first, but then I thought I heard you say, *illuminate,* and suddenly, I was flooded with all this information. What was that all about?"

"I gave you each a choice that you were ready to make," said Claire, "the choice to let go of secrecy." With that, she paused to see if her students might make the leap in comprehension to understand what she meant. This was a classic move that her teachers had often employed, knowing that she had all the information she needed to decode their cryptic statements. They would often relate a new perspective as if it was already familiar, challenging her to expand her perception to integrate with whatever they were holding silently as an awareness. Now she was doing the same.

Because Claire had spent more than a month on the surface, she had closely observed a strange phenomenon that the Council of Lys had discussed with her before she departed.

"Your tendency will be to learn from them in our normal way," they had said telepathically, *"by merging mental spheres and sharing memory, but do not attempt this in the surface culture. You will most likely encounter great resistance from the minds of those you meet if you do not reserve your presence. We have studied this resistance for a long time and have found that they value the ability to hide their thoughts from each other. There's a fundamental distrust of the intentions of others that contains an echo of the old Atlantean war, so we suggest that you try learning about them more passively. Practice sensing their thoughts casually without focusing on them directly. Learn to look without looking, and you will learn all you need to know."*

The council was right. When Claire first arrived on the surface, she had an encounter with a man that shocked her into her new environment. She had met him while exploring Watertown, and in the beginning, she thought he was open-minded enough to handle more of her presence. He was drawn to her at first, curious and helpful. He wanted to guess at the origin of her unusual accent, and she was trying to figure out what to say, but then the conversation shifted gears. He started talking about his family, and Claire saw some of his memories bubbling up into the forefront of his mind, but when she mistakenly responded as if it was an invitation to commune more deeply, the man freaked.

She was just beginning to merge with his memories, when he forcefully broke the connection and excused himself. "That was weird," he said before he walked away. To him, breaking the mind-link was as automatic as flicking away a stinging insect, but to Claire, it felt shocking, like there was an unconscious resentment of unity that struck her on a heart level.

It took several days to integrate with the experience before she was ready to go to the library, where she discovered that a volunteer position was open. Luckily, she had an experienced Lyssian emissary to stay with who had lived on the surface for more than a year with the help of other supporters. He was able to complete her orientation by teaching her how to conceal her presence inside her form. This involved a great deal of focus with the addition of eating some of the lower vibrational foods of the surface culture.

Roya was still pondering Claire's statement about secrecy, while Ami and Mandy looked like they were waiting for someone else to speak. Claire was certain that Roya would be the first to get it, and so she was very present with her, empowering the shift in her thinking by focusing again on the bridge between their minds.

"Are you saying that our ability to experience collective memories is connected with how honest we are with our presence?" Roya surmised.

"Go on," said Claire, giving her a look of approval.

"Then secrecy is not just concealing information, it's concealing presence."

"Yes," responded Claire enthusiastically, clapping her hands together once, startling Mandy out of a daydream. "Sharing memory telepathically is natural to your people as well, once you choose to move beyond secrecy. It was so strange for me, I have to say, seeing how many of your people struggle with feeling alone, and yet a mechanism deeply implanted in your minds fiercely guards your attachment to remaining in separation. We call it the anti-mind."

"What's the anti-mind?" queried Ami.

"Almost everyone on the surface has it to some degree," explained Claire. "It's a collective pattern that maintains the state of separation in human consciousness. What you call the mind contains what we call the anti-mind, which is a form of resistance to universal mind. You think your mind is who you are, but its very nature is a betrayal of sorts. Without the anti-mind, your bodies would be more like containers for a resonance of universal mind."

"But would you still have a personality that way?" asked Mandy.

"Look at our people," said Claire. "Do you think we have personalities?"

"Absolutely," agreed Mandy.

"Yeah," said Ami. "It's interesting. I can tell your people are in a state of oneness, and yet, you're still unique individuals."

"An important observation, and quite contrary to the philosophy of the anti-mind. The anti-mind believes it is protecting its individuality by remaining separate from the universal mind. Ironically, your individuality would be greatly enhanced without it. It is impossible to understand the value of your uniqueness without understanding who you are to the oneness of being."

"What I noticed about your people when I was on the surface is that you deny the shared medium that connects all memories into one. The anti-mind prefers to possess its own memories, which are then used like a shelter from the group mind. You do this, so you can have the power to keep secrets from each other and to hide whatever you fear for others to know. But in doing so, you inadvertently deny knowledge of your oneness and the vast resources of *collective* intelligence. When I saw some of this resistance coming up, I gave you each a choice to align with the way my people relate to memory. Now you are beginning to understand what you can do when you are not attached to owning memories."

"Well, what would we base our sense of self on if not on our individual memories?" debated Roya.

"Your unique frequency," explained Claire, "and potentially the whole field of humanity's creative energy collectively." She was focusing intently on everyone's betweenergy, as if to acknowledge with her consciousness the answer behind her words. "My people see all memory as part of one field of consciousness. We are all unique flavors of the love frequency that co-create with the memory field of the One. So, our sense of self is based a little less on our personal memories and more on the collective memories that we create by sharing the gift of our frequency with the community. There is also a greater incentive to be kind to others when you experience their memories as an extension of yours."

"Oh. I get it," said Ami. "Your people have mastered the golden rule, but it's like you seem to understand it on another level. The collective memory thing is really a key."

"Right," Claire acknowledged. "Eventually, your people may come to understand such insights collectively. For now, an evolutionary process is unfolding that will awaken these insights throughout the world. The prophecy says that the increasing energy of oneness will begin to supersede the resistance of the anti-mind. People will become more sensitive to how they make others feel. Behaviors that previously made sense to the anti-mind will be revealed as fear-based, selfish, and unnecessary. Eventually, this kind of awakening can connect your people collectively with the realms of illuminated truth, allowing you to see yourselves through the eyes of the community. In this way, people can become aware that their real potential lies not so much in what they create for themselves, but in the memories, they create for others. That is the real inheritance of the present life."

"Be kind to others, because their memories will become yours," reasoned Mandy.

Roya had been wondering how well Mandy was following the conversation, because she looked like she was daydreaming again, but her comment proved how alert she really was.

"Well said," praised Claire. "The anti-mind does not recognize that the will of the One is for you to experience both your individuality *and* your collective nature. The two are not at war with one another, but the anti-mind fears annihilation by the collective."

"Is there any truth to its fear?" wondered Roya.

"No, the philosophy of the anti-mind is flawed. It is merely a residual resonance of the original wound of separation that occurred through the destruction of Atlantis. In a more ancient time, well before the destruction, some people on the surface of the planet experienced connection with each other through a form of group consciousness. They were identified with the presence of a field that had the potential to guide them as a collective through a connection to humanity's infinite future. But then, a secret war developed between various factions that wanted to control the power of the field to manipulate reality on a mass scale."

"The anti-mind first began to develop because of a power struggle between the masculine and the feminine that imbalanced the harmony of the field. This made it difficult to fully trust in the connectedness of the field, and it led to patterns of avoiding intimacy. You can always recognize the presence of the anti-mind by the way it prefers distractions to avoid facing its fears. The anti-mind will always throw out excuses for not surrendering to greater states of connection."

"This kind of aversion to the connectedness of the field grew stronger in Atlantis because of a growing environment of suspicion and paranoia that degraded the field significantly. The government was always spying on its citizens and seeking to exploit them. The anti-mind used separation as a defense mechanism against the government's psychic spies. The rulers of Atlantis did not want people to remember or align with the unifying potentials of the field, but the more they sought to scare people and dumb people down, the more they dumbed themselves down."

"Finally, the anti-mind solidified as a pain reaction to the destruction itself. People didn't want to feel the pain and suffering of others through the field, so they withdrew their awareness and hid their presence within the container of the body. In your natural state, humans are radiant beings that can emanate a field of awareness that extends far past the body, connecting you with each other and the natural environment. When you are really open, you can even feel the movement of the planets."

Wow! thought Roya. *The movement of the planets.*

"Most people on the surface, though, identify more with the forms of their bodies than with the living field of consciousness that unites all souls. Subconsciously, they are hiding from a level of connection that would take them beyond humanity's ancient fears about how that kind of interconnectedness was abused in Atlantis."

"I feel like I have always had less of this ability to hide my presence from others," confessed Roya.

"It's true," Ami agreed. "She wears her heart on her sleeve."

"It's harder for me to hide my feelings than to share them," Roya explained.

"Which is exactly why this shift in thinking was easy for you. The reason the three of you fit together as friends is that your expressions are authentic. You enjoy reflecting each other and do not hide what you are thinking. There was only a tiny residual fear about becoming lost when we started, but you were ready to break free from the resonance of the anti-mind...to see without its control."

"The ability to hide what you're thinking, and feeling is a really powerful tool in our society though," related Ami, "especially when so many people are looking to take advantage of your fears and weaknesses. I don't know if I could have surrendered to this kind of experience on the surface; but down here, I feel safe enough to let go."

"That's right. You are much less guarded down here. The anti-mind is relaxed, because you are not surrounded by fear or greed or prejudice. The oneness of humanity never went away, though, just because your people chose an experience of separation. It's still there, hidden and obscured by the illusions of the anti-mind. The potential of human unity is always present in the field all around you. It's part of the awareness our people are working to restore in human consciousness to help you realize that you have a choice. According to the prophecy, everyone will face a choice between attachment to the anti-mind and integration with an emerging resonance of human unity. Without the anti-mind, you will all resonate with the revelation that: Everything is Love and Light."

Just then, Claire's messenger appeared as a violet light upon her forehead, and she connected with it briefly before it disappeared.

"We have just been called to a very important meeting with the council. They are ready to reveal some greater truths about your purpose here."

16

THE SECRET WAR

On the way to the council chamber, Roya was considering again what life might be like if they stayed in Lys. Having her two best friends from the surface with her and both of their families present seemed ideal. They could all just choose to stay and begin a new life, at least for a few years, she thought.

Of course, they would eventually want to return, but not before they had thoroughly explored the wonders of the Inner Earth. Her father always talked about wanting to take the family on a world trip as an educational experience for her and Sarah, but this would be a million times better! Lys had no crime, no expenses, and no pollution. It was literally an unexpected paradise culture filled with amazing sights to see. And they were considered honored guests here.

Most of all, Roya thought about the education they could receive and the freedom they would have. Perhaps she and her friends could join a pod of Lyssian teens and travel to other subterranean cities to learn from the great teachers. She was already considering how to present the idea to her parents, but first she would have to talk to the council to see if it was even an option. It was too soon to be presumptuous about what they had planned, but somehow, her wildest dreams seemed possible. For the first time in her life, she felt like she had freedom to expand, and it felt amazing.

When they reached the well-lit chamber, Shumayan, Shemazae, and Twa'amatae were already seated inside, and the Egg was placed at the center of the round table. Each person took the same seat they had before, exchanging smiles with the council members. This time, Roya was determined not to be bashful, so she opened herself to allow the council to feel her. She looked each of them directly in the eyes with her full presence. When Shumayan looked at her, noticing how much more open she was, she could still feel a slight quiver in her emotional body. For a moment, she just tried to feel her nervousness without reacting to it, and then it passed.

There she was, proudly unafraid to be noticed as an emotional being. Until then, she had never realized the extent to which she had hidden her presence. It felt like she was rediscovering an energetic aspect of her nature, with a mind that could surf new channels of perception and a heart that could open and close like a flower, basking in the radiance of other heart-centered beings.

When they first met the day before, she did not understand what she was feeling when Shumayan gazed at her, but the feeling of nervousness had faded once she could read his intentions. He had intended all along to engender a feeling of equality between them, even though to her, he felt far more powerful and masterful than she.

Before then, she was fairly conditioned to expect men, and even some women, to be rather insensitive to the feeling level of things. But Shumayan's gentle gaze of acknowledgement had steadily penetrated the defenses that her mind had placed before the gateway of her heart. She was disarmed, yet relieved to feel safe enough to be completely herself. Even though the others were equally acknowledging, her heart enjoyed radiating a special gratitude toward him for the way he had helped her achieve a new level of openness.

"I trust you are all well-rested and nourished," began Shumayan.

"Yes," said Raymond. "I think I speak for all of us when I say that we are grateful for your hospitality."

"We are honored," replied Shumayan. "Tell us, did you receive any messages from your experience with the temple?"

"We got a lot more than messages," Mandy expressed without hesitating. "I met my muse." The council members all understood and looked pleased.

"I worked with a group of healers and remembered how to work with healing energy," added Ami after their attention seemed to precognitively shift to her.

Roya looked at Claire, wondering how much to share about her experience with the Grail, but Claire's eyes told her it was OK. The attention had already shifted to her, and the council seemed intent on opening the floor to the younger participants first.

"I visited the Waters of Truth, and when I looked at my reflection, I had a vision of the Grail, and I felt our potential for wholeness," said Roya, pleased with how well she was articulating her experience.

"Do you understand now how families and communities form a container for the energy of a greater whole?" asked Shemazae.

"Yes," Roya answered. "I can see how we are all part of each other."

"Very good," Shemazae said supportively. She seemed pleased that Roya was holding this insight in her consciousness, as if she had been waiting for this to emerge in some form since their arrival. For the Council, this was a sign that the whole group was integrating with the community field.

"That's very interesting," said Frank. "May I say something?"

"Please," encouraged Shumayan.

"When I was in the temple, I received a message that our two families shared a special connection, and that we were meant to do something together. I just heard this in my mind, and I felt the truth of it. I don't know what it is we are meant to do, but I feel committed to it."

"We will be able to tell you more about that soon," informed Shumayan. "Would anyone else like to share?"

"I spoke to a woman who told me something special about my future," said Sarah, "but she suggested not to share it until I know it's the right time."

Roya looked at Sarah, surprised and curious. She could tell that whatever the woman had told Sarah, it was exciting. She was just glad that her sister had also received something unique from her experience of the temple.

As each person shared their experience, Roya noticed how the focus of their hosts would energize each speaker to bring out the best in them. Their collective focus seemed intent on generating what Roya was beginning to think of as a contribution spiral. She could almost sense the presence of a spiral-like energy that was opening the space to connect them with higher vibrations. The focus of the room then shifted to Soraya.

"I got my message in the garden. I realized how alive we can feel when we're not distracted by computers and cell phones. Our people have forgotten what it feels like to be truly immersed in nature. You've taught me that the natural world still holds many mysteries, and we should be seeking them and protecting them."

"Spoken like a true Guardian," said Shumayan, whose attention began to shift to Raymond next.

"I was amazed by how your people practice healing," acknowledged Raymond, "and when I heard how easily Ami integrated with doing energy work, I had an epiphany about transforming health care. Are the Formelle connected with the healing work being done on the surface as well?"

"Yes. There are many such hidden resources that are beginning to reveal themselves to humanity. We think this is part of the reason you are here," recognized Shumayan on behalf of the council. "It is no coincidence that your people are already in touch with the use of energy medicine. The ancient healing arts are being restored to the surface, but we expect your guides will explain more about this. For now, we have a more pressing matter to discuss."

"So much more could be said about the meaning of each of your experiences, but it is time to bring you into the conversation we have been having about the potential integration between our cultures. Everything that has occurred through your visit contains the seed of that potential. We will certainly be reviewing these memories for some time to learn more about how the integration might occur. But if action is not taken, we are greatly concerned that this potential may be entirely lost."

Suddenly the mood of the room shifted.

Lost, thought Roya. *How could the potential be lost?*

"What we are about to share with you may be difficult to hear, but it's in all of our best interests to acknowledge the truth about the challenges we face. More than ten years ago, your people discovered and attacked one of our subterranean settlements in the mountains of Colorado."

"What?!" exclaimed Roya, not expecting the conversation to go in this direction.

Everyone expressed a look of surprise and a feeling of concern.

"How can that be?" asked Frank, distressed. "Who would do that?"

"Your military has built a number of secret underground bases in those mountains that are part of an extensive network of such bases that spans the continent. During one of their construction projects to create a transport tunnel between two of these bases, they stumbled onto a more ancient tunnel that was once used by our people."

Roya began to sense a series of visual impressions that accompanied Shumayan's words. Having just experienced viewing some of the Lemurian memories with Claire, she began to focus on seeing inwardly to view the presence of the collective memories.

The tilt medium, she recalled. *A shared medium of memory…let their memories be mine,* she invited as she aligned with Shumayan and signaled her willingness to see. It was like opening the container of the mind so that it could be filled with another's thoughts. The impressions became more vivid as she closed her eyes until she began to see the memories like a movie playing on a screen that accompanied Shumayan's words. *I see inwardly,* she asserted.

"Almost immediately after they discovered the ancient tunnel, they sent a team of soldiers to explore it and found an entrance into one of the caverns we populate. This was a large and beautiful cavern with a deep fresh water lake, and our people had a small settlement across the lake from the entrance they came through. This was completely unexpected, and most unfortunate. They came across the lake in boats and attacked our people, raiding the settlement and looking for our technology. Though most of our people managed to escape, a number of them were killed, and we had to seal off this sacred place to protect our other settlements. Ever since then, the military has increased its efforts to try to find our hidden cities so they can be raided for their secrets. For this reason, we call these people the Raiders."

"Have they found any more of your cities?" Frank worried.

"Unfortunately, yes. For some time now, your navy has been using high-powered sonar systems to search for some of our ocean-based settlements. They have the general location of a couple of these, but they are too deep to be reached by your submersible technology. It is far more likely that they will find their way into some of our mountain cities. But right now, they are drilling blindly, hoping to hit another tunnel."

"I must say, I don't consider that we are part of such people." Raymond clarified. "You said 'your people' and 'your military,' but these people that attacked you do not represent most of us on the surface. These secret military bases are part of a separate culture that we know little about. On the surface, those of us that have researched this call them the breakaway civilization. We literally have no access to what they are doing down there, and our official government has no oversight. So how can we be responsible for the things they are doing in secret?"

"We understand," said Shumayan, "but now you know. Now you can be responsible."

"How does knowing make us responsible?" Raymond questioned.

"Your people often deny knowledge so that you can deny responsibility. Knowledge and responsibility go hand in hand. The great dilemma from your angle is that your people have denied knowledge of a greater reality for so long that you have left yourselves vulnerable to exploitation. You are ignorant of both the dangers and the opportunities in the greater reality, and this has allowed the greed and fear of an elite few to have a great deal of control over you. Now you must tread a dangerous path to reset the balance."

"What can we do to help?" asked Roya. She knew in her heart that this needed to be the next question.

"That is precisely what we have been reflecting on since you arrived. Do you recall the symbol of the three circles on the cover of the book?" asked Shumayan.

"Yes," replied Roya.

"We think it represents a peaceful integration between the three human civilizations that now share this planet. Our people lovingly refer to your people on the surface as the Explorers, because you have entered an age of exploration that has the potential to take you to the stars. You gaze at the stars in a way that was familiar to us in our ancient history, but now we have learned to explore the galaxy inwardly, through the hidden channels of the body."

"You mentioned three civilizations," Soraya prompted.

"The third one is the one we call the Raiders. We see them as a part of you, even though they behave as a separate civilization. They are inextricably linked to the surface but are developing the means to control you from underground. As we see it, they are waging a secret war against their connection to a more inclusive reality. Their minds are at war with their hearts, and with the essence of knowledge itself. Because all knowledge is sourced in oneness, the more they seek to suppress knowledge in your culture, the more they separate themselves from the Source of all life within themselves. That being said, the potential of an awakening seems to be stirring in some of them, which means that anything is possible."

"If we are the Explorers, and they are the Raiders," asked Sarah, "who are you in this equation?"

"We are the Guardians," replied Shumayan. "We have preserved the knowledge of humanity's oneness with each other and the Earth through a unified field of consciousness. We protect your potential to remember the original blueprint for humanity in the galaxy—to remember who you are. What concerns us, though, is that some among us in Lys have lost faith in your culture's ability to remember."

"Is it because of the attack that happened?" asked Frank.

"That is one reason. We are also concerned about the slow pace of progress on the surface toward forming a more symbiotic relationship with each other and the environment. You are lagging in this area, but we cannot ignore the out of control agenda of the Raiders to steal what they can from both our cultures."

"This has led many to believe that the potential of the prophecy has been lost, and they fear that the Earth could become a hostile environment for us if the Raiders become more powerful. It has come to our attention that the suppression of knowledge in your culture has brought you dangerously close to the tipping point. If this goes much further, you may lose your potential to achieve a lasting balance that would allow a peaceful integration to occur. We are here in part to preserve the knowledge and achievements of this world. If you stop progressing spiritually, there would be nothing more for us to preserve."

"What would happen if the prophecy were not fulfilled?" Soraya worried.

"Our people would leave and return to the stars," said Shemazae.

"But if you leave," Roya said pleadingly, "we would lose access to everything that you've been holding for us."

"True," acknowledged Shemazae, "but the situation is very complicated. If it becomes more dangerous for us, some believe we must evacuate to protect ourselves. Others maintain that we must not abandon humanity, and that certain sacrifices on our part are necessary to help humanity awaken. We have entered a time of unpredictability, and we cannot see for certain what will happen."

Roya's heart began to sink. She did not know if anyone else felt the same, but as the council reflected on the potentials, it was as if she could feel two different timelines appearing in her heart. One of them felt brighter and more expansive, but the other felt extremely dark. Strangely, she did not feel fear about the prospect of living through the timeline of a potential failure of civilization; rather, she felt a deep sense of loss for what everyone would miss if the prophecy were not fulfilled. It would be devastating, as if the whole point of our existence on the Earth had been missed. Something about this feeling touched a deep wound inside Roya's heart that she could not seem to trace, as if this had all happened before.

She looked at Ami as if to convey her emotions, and Ami looked back and seemed focused on reading her for a moment, silently responding to Roya's need. Then something inside Roya told her to just take a deep breath, and as she did, she turned her focus back on the council.

"We know now that you can feel our concerns," recognized Shemazae, "and we believe you can do something to help."

Everyone was poised to listen.

"We have been looking at many of the historical potentials regarding the surface," said Twa'amatae, "and one man in particular seems to hold a key to the balance. He is a scientist and an inventor that is on a path to many breakthroughs, but he is in danger of losing focus on his work. He does not yet understand the value of what he has discovered, and without support, many important historical potentials could be lost."

"Can you tell us more about him?" asked Frank. "Could we find him and help him?"

"Yes. This would be the answer to a prayer. And we are certain that our meeting here contains such a potential," explained Shumayan. "When you return to the surface you should try to connect with this man and share with him all that you have witnessed. Tell him about this Resonator. This may be exactly the confirmation he needs to stay focused on what is shifting in the global scientific paradigm. As we see it, you are already connected with this man by your resonance and the nature of the path you are on together. You do not need to know any more than that. The invisible world will help you make the connection."

As exciting as it was to know that there was a way to help, all Roya could think about is that Shumayan had just mentioned their return to the surface. She had been wondering when she could ask about the possibility of staying, but it did not seem like her desire fit with the agenda of the meeting. Still, she did not give up hope.

"Can we do anything else to help while we are here?" asked Roya.

She was feeling ever more confident as a speaker and wanted to find a reason to extend their visit longer. In her own way, she was searching for a key to integration that she hoped she would find in Lys.

"I have an idea," offered Amaron in response, who had been sitting quietly the whole time. "What if we took them to Adinai?"

The council members immediately understood what was being suggested and began to ponder deeply what the others could only guess at. A silent discussion appeared to be going on as they looked each other in the eyes. Roya noticed that the mood seemed to have shifted in a positive direction.

"Thank you, Amaron," Shumayan said out loud for the benefit of the others. "This is a most welcome suggestion."

Roya looked over at Ami and Mandy to see that they looked equally excited. She could feel Ami telepathically giving her a high five.

"What Amaron has suggested," explained Shumayan, "is that we seek to include you in a special gathering where your presence could have a highly controversial, yet beneficial effect."

"Another city is hosting a public debate about the prophecy and the intrusion of the Raiders," explained Shemazae. "Adinai is a place where many of our people go to work on the process of integration through practicing the English language. If you went, it is likely that you would be able to address the forum for these debates. You may be the sign that some need to revive faith in our purpose here."

"What would we say?" asked Frank.

"That might depend on what is happening at the debates, but just your presence would be enough to allow the people there to feel the potential of integration through their connection to you. Based upon the way you have integrated with the energy of Lys since you arrived, you are well prepared to represent this potential."

"It might help if we knew a little more about these debates," Raymond prompted.

"They are quite engaging," said Amaron with enthusiasm. "And they can go on for days with very few breaks. Adinai is one of many cities in Lys where we practice speaking one of your languages. We find it highly entertaining to watch our people debate out loud in a foreign language."

Roya looked at Claire to show her excitement about getting to go with her, but Claire seemed deep in an inner dialogue with Amaron as they gazed at each other silently. Roya assumed they must be using telepathy again by how present they felt with each other. She could almost feel the subtle impressions flying back and forth and wondered if they were talking about the journey ahead. How fun it would be if she could master the ability to chat with Ami telepathically during class without texting.

"We know you have many questions, but before you go to Adinai, we would like to offer you the opportunity to experience the Resonator again. Some of your questions can best be answered by your own guides."

Ami, Mandy, and Roya all looked at each other with tremendous excitement. For Roya, this meant that her mother and sister would get to see what she and her father had seen before, bringing them all to the same page.

Without hesitation, Shemazae lifted her right hand with her palm facing the Egg at the center of the table. It immediately began to glow even more than when they first experienced it in the cave. The vibrations quickly began to increase until a gentle hum with many subtle tones filled the room. Soraya looked at the Egg in astonishment, and Roya knew her mother could feel it.

Without any discernible command from the council, the lights began to dim until they were completely out. Roya sensed that the Formelle had read what was happening and knew exactly what to do. The energy from the Egg began to expand and blend with everything around it until the walls appeared to give way to a larger and less visible reality. It felt as though they had entered a vast cavern filled with beings that were looking on with great interest. This time, the shift happened quicker.

Roya and her dad were both focused on expanding their awareness with the contact field, trying to sense the presence of the guides, but then their attention was drawn to a wispy smoke-like energy that began to appear around the Egg. It was a subtle glowing plasma that Roya figured was the same as the ectoplasm that her dad had witnessed in some of his paranormal encounters. As the field grew stronger, they could feel a dimensional pillar of energy arising from within the Earth to assist the formation of the bridge.

The glowing smoke-like substance continued to appear until it became even more luminous and began to take the shape of two people whose lower bodies were not fully formed. This time, their faces looked more defined, and Roya knew at once that it was Houston and Lance. Houston had a clearly discernible mustache and beard, and it added to the sense of what he had looked like in his most recent lifetime. He had an aura of mindfulness, and his eyes were bright and inquisitive. Though skin tone was not as readily apparent, Roya could tell from the details of their faces that Houston was more Caucasian, whereas Lance's voice and facial features seemed more African-American.

Lance's energy communicated a feeling of joyful expectancy even before he spoke. His eyes were also more defined this time, and his gaze contained a feeling of warmth that regarded everyone in the room as spiritual family.

"*I see a look of surprise on some of your faces. Did you not expect spirits to be this good-looking?*" joked Lance.

He was clearly trying to break the ice with Sarah and Soraya, and it worked. They were both now smiling.

"*It's true,*" said Lance, responding to some of the silent questions in the room. "*We do reside in what you would call the Afterlife, though that's not what we call it here.*"

"*We just call it home,*" added Houston.

Their words were resonating through the bridge of acoustic and electrical energy generated through the Egg, using the subtle harmonic tones of the field as their vocal cords. Somehow, they could modulate the harmonics of the bridge with their thoughts to make the sound of words from the vibrations.

"It's nice to hear from you both again," said Raymond, who was not shy about being the first to respond back. "I'm sure you already know everyone here."

"*We do indeed,*" agreed Houston. "*Your lives have become an entertaining topic of discussion over here. We are both excited and concerned for what lie ahead.*"

Raymond looked around at the others, not wanting to talk over anyone, but it seemed that everyone was content to let him engage the conversation further.

"We would be grateful to learn more about how you see things. What excites you, and what concerns you?"

"We overheard the conversation about the three circles, for instance," Houston continued. *"Three civilizations and three potentials for integration. We would like to suggest that the very fact that we are having this conversation represents yet another potential of integration: integration with the invisible world of Spirit. Your colleagues here in Lys operate within a state of conscious connection to the invisible world. As you integrate with the field of consciousness they are holding with you, their connection to Spirit may strengthen yours. You see, in our realm, we live in a state of unity consciousness, whereas in your realm, you are greatly affected by a resonance of duality. The more you transcend duality in your consciousness, the easier it becomes to hear the voices that are always speaking to you from within a plane of unity."*

"Could this kind of resonance technology be rediscovered and made widely available?" asked Frank, wanting to jump in and participate.

"That is one possibility," offered Lance. *"Many researchers are working on developing the means technologically to open the bridge for the masses. But the technology can only work when the bridge is also present in human consciousness. The bridge between dimensions does not require technological assistance as much as it requires a sincere desire among more of your people to listen to Spirit for guidance. Eventually, the bridge will be present in the world as a multidimensional communication field, like what you are experiencing here."*

Listening is our religion, thought Roya, remembering Claire's explanation from the temple.

"The most powerful form of communication technology that can bridge the dimensions, however, is your own DNA," continued Houston. *"Your DNA is multidimensional, and your brains are already evolving and remembering how to function as multidimensional antennas. Just like the people of Lys, you can learn how to focus your attention on living energy to experience a deeper and more intimate communion with the invisible world."*

"It's easier to imagine that happening, though, if more people could have experiences like this," suggested Frank.

"True," agreed Lance, *"But more of your people are now learning to quiet the mind and commune with the angelic realms inwardly. We see this especially in the younger generations who want to break free from the separation between worlds and unite the dimensions inside their own bodies. Some of them are literally jumping out of their own skins to make the connections. They despise the idea that there is anywhere their consciousness cannot go. They are defying the secrecy that has created so much separation and compartmentalization in your society—shattering the barriers with their thoughts. These brave souls are*

rewriting the software of the human brain and restructuring the matrix of physical reality for everyone. They will literally dream a new world into being."

Raymond was enraptured with inspiration and looked to Frank to see if he had caught the significance of how this related to their own children. Frank smiled back in recognition. There was a pause for a moment as everyone was feeling into the truth of what they were beginning to collectively see as a grand and inspiring new vision of human potential.

"I have so many questions," said Frank. "You mentioned concerns, though."

"*Yes,*" replied Houston. "*We have great concern about the crossroads that you have now reached as a civilization. The breakthroughs you can potentially make in consciousness can guide the evolution of technology and define its role. But you must be careful not to make technology so important that it defines the evolution of the human brain. Other worlds have gone down that path and have lost a great deal of their creative and spiritual potential. Many influential minds want to trap humanity in an addictive relationship with technology, so they can manipulate and control that version of reality. You must be very careful at this stage. While technology may be helping you become more net-worked in ways that support the global awakening, dependency on electronics also inhibits your view of what your brains and minds are really capable of through natural conscious evolution.*"

Roya really wanted to say something, but was feeling apprehensive about speaking up, because her dad and Frank were doing all of the talking. She was determined to find her place in the conversation, though.

"I just keep thinking," she said, a little forcefully, at first. "It's not right that we're the only ones hearing all of this. This just seems like really important stuff that everyone needs to know. But if I told anyone on the surface about this conversation, nobody would believe me. I just don't know how we could even share this with anybody."

Sarah gave Roya one of her big sister looks, as if she was disrupting the pecking order, but she was actually envious, because she had been feeling too shy to speak up herself.

"*Here is where you must trust in the journey you are on,*" said Lance with a soft tone. "*In your journey, you will face problems and situations that seem unsolvable at first, just as humanity is experiencing the same. You must learn to see the opportunity that is hiding in every seemingly unsolvable problem—to see your evolutionary potential instead of assuming limitations. If you look for the gift in every situation, you will always be gifted by whatever happens, and the path of grace will continually open before you.*"

"Wisely spoken," remarked Claire emphatically, intending to note the relevance of this statement to the Council of Lys regarding the great dilemma before them. Roya was pleased that her comments had yielded another key, though the focus of the energy was already shifting back over to her dad.

"The council said you could tell us more about the Formelle and our potential to co-create with them," requested Raymond.

"Sure," said Lance. *"In our awareness of the universe, the whole construct of matter is made of Formelle. They are what your physicists call superstrings, which are tiny vibrating rings of consciousness that are self-aware as a collective within the unified field. These tiny Formelle are a form of living code that can reflect and hold the instructions of higher beings, but they are so tiny that the human mind can hardly conceive of their existence. For that reason, a part of their presence appears in the form of beings that work to bridge humanity into a creative relationship with the living intelligence of matter and light. Formelle have been witnessed this way on every living world with intelligent life. They hold the subtle blueprints of all things, from atoms to apple trees, from planets to galaxies, as well as subtle structures of light that your senses are not yet attuned to perceive. Every blueprint is a being in the realm of the Formelle. In worlds like yours, they bring forth blueprints for living technology that can guide civilization down a technological pathway that is more in harmony with nature."*

As if to confirm what Lance was saying, the whole field began to tingle with the presence of the tiniest, sub-atomic Formelle, sending a zing of energy that said *"hello"* from that subtler layer of reality. Roya could feel Mandy silently giggling through the field.

"Could they play a role in our healing work on the surface then?" Raymond asked.

"Yes, of course." confirmed Houston. *"This is an exciting time when many of the human potentials you are witnessing in Lys are beginning to appear on the surface. From our vantage point, we can see cosmic forces working to amplify the community field of Lys so that it can arise to share its gifts with the surface culture. For example: the potential of a new telepathic communication system is taking shape, and the Formelle are working with you in subtle ways by weaving connections and supporting you to discover your own natural telepathic abilities. As people discover how to tap into this emerging telepathic web, the field will teach them how to engage the community in a new experience of inner dialogue."*

"And with regard to the healing potentials you are asking about," added Lance with excitement, *"we've been tracking a new development that could be revolutionary! The Formelle are weaving another network within the emerging*

*web that is connecting all healers together as a single resource. Plus, every time
someone heals by changing their DNA, the Formelle record these changes in a
library of healing codes. Eventually, anyone will be able to access these resources
of healing knowledge and energy from the global presence of the healing field.*

"That's fantastic!" declared Raymond. "It's even better than I imagined!"

"We know that you have many more questions," said Lance, *"but there is
someone else here who wishes to speak with the Carter family. We would like to
offer them the opportunity to have a little privacy for this reunion, so we will
be phasing back now."*

Mandy instantly had tears in her eyes, and Ami looked at her dad to
share her feeling of elation.

"Thank you from all of us," Raymond bowed slightly in respect. "We are
grateful for all that we have learned from you."

*"Be well, and rest assured that this dialogue will be furthered in many other
ways."*

Claire and Amaron arose from their chairs as part of the wall behind
them disappeared, providing an opening. At nearly the same time, the
three members of the council arose as an opening appeared behind them
as well. Roya smiled at both Ami and Mandy, knowing they would have
a lot to share when she saw them next. There was a moment of silence as
they all acknowledged Lance and Houston who were just starting to fade.
The bridge remained open, and, just as Roya and her family began to leave,
they could feel a feminine resonance beginning to enter the room.

"We would like to take you to a special place nearby while we wait for
the others," said Claire quietly, gesturing for everyone to follow. As soon
as they were outside the room, there was a quick buzzing tone and the
wall rematerialized. As Roya walked away, following the group down the
long hallway back to the map room, she was intimately aware of her
betweenergy with Ami and Mandy. The power of the bridge to the spirit
realm had accelerated the presence of interconnectedness, and she could
feel some of her friends' emotions resonating through the field between
them. By the time they reached the map room, the sensation began to fade
as her attention shifted toward what laid ahead.

After walking along the perimeter of the map room, they entered a stone
archway that led into a large domed room with three other openings into
rooms beyond.

"This is what you might think of as an art museum," introduced Claire.
"Each of these rooms contains living memories from the surface of the planet.
Some of our most skilled artists created these murals. Feel free to explore. Each

of these circular rooms will have openings to other rooms. If you get lost, we will send you a messenger to guide you back when it's time to reconvene."

Roya immediately sensed an opportunity. She looked at Claire and beamed with her eyes that she wanted to talk one-on-one. Amaron sensed what was happening and signaled to Claire that he would stay with Roya's family.

"Mom, I'm going to go with Claire to one of the other rooms. I'll come find you in a bit," informed Roya, knowing that Claire understood. Her mother nodded, and her family began to walk toward the doorway to the right.

"Claire, I wanted to ask about the possibility of a longer stay down here, but it seems like the plan is to go back to the surface right away."

"I understand," Claire said with compassion. "If it were up to me, I would be happy for you to stay. Many of us would."

"Who is it up to, then," Roya asked a little demandingly, "the council?"

"It's up to the Greater Force that brought us all together. The council only seeks to understand and interpret the creative forces that are guiding history."

"Are they ever wrong?" asked Roya. "What if it would help the integration of our two cultures for us to stay here longer?"

"You are worried that you won't see me again," Claire recognized, and instantly Roya knew that Claire was reading her. "You want to learn more and grow, and you've never had a teacher before that can show you this much of your hidden potential," Claire empathized. Roya could not have said it better. "Roya, sometimes the best way to tap into your hidden abilities is to be in a situation that challenges you to use them. And one thing I am certain about is that you will be more challenged on the surface."

"Really? All I can think about is how much I could learn by being down here."

"From my perspective, you already have the knowledge of our culture. You are just in a process of remembering, and you don't have to be down here to do that. The opportunity to come here was a great blessing that has accelerated the remembrance of your soul's knowledge. I am quite certain that the integration that wants to take place between our cultures will best be served with you on the surface. *Your* role is to be a bridge."

"I've never known anyone who understands me like you do. I don't want to lose that," Roya paused, as a tear welled up in her eye. "Will I ever see you again... after we return?"

"I don't know," admitted Claire, "but we will always be connected. From the moment we met, I knew our time together would be short. I've been training you from the very beginning to know you can be in touch with me no matter where you are. Remember when I taught you how to channel Mandy's artistic abilities?"

Roya nodded.

"You can also channel *my* awareness by focusing on our bond."

Roya was not fully confident that she could do this on her own yet, but she was determined to learn.

"Can you tell me more about how I can develop these abilities? I really want to stay connected with this awareness."

"Sure, let me show you something," Claire said as she invited Roya into one of the adjacent rooms. They walked together into another well-lit domed room, the walls of which were covered with a beautiful mural of a rainforest. "You see this image?" Claire pointed to a place on the mural where a beautiful blue butterfly was poised on the edge of a leaf. The detail of the image was amazingly clear.

"These images are not made of paint or ink of any kind. They are made from pure memory. Each of these murals is actually a living being, another kind of Formelle. They are record keepers that hold living memories for others to experience. If you focus on the forms, you will only see what is on the surface, but if you focus into the resonance of the imbued memories, you can experience the awareness of the original observer."

Roya studied the butterfly for a moment, looking at the little drops of water on the leaf until she started to notice that the water was glistening. Something was changing in her perception of the image, and it began to appear more three-dimensional. Then light began to stream from the image, and the wings of the butterfly began to move. With a sudden rush, the image extended out of the wall to fill the space around them. Roya sensed that Claire was assisting her connection with the living memories. Now it felt as if they were standing in the middle of the rainforest.

Slowly, she began to look around and even listen to the sounds of the forest. She turned her head to look at Claire and saw that she was just as absorbed in the scene but was looking up. As Roya followed her gaze, she could see that the rainforest had filled the entire space. Birds were flying overhead, and even monkeys leaped from branch to branch.

"Wow! Is this how your people stay in touch with the surface? With living art like this?"

"Yes. It is one of the ways. It might interest you to know, however, that there are just as many natural wonders *inside* the Earth as there are on the surface."

"Oh, like what?"

"Well, there are layers of reality that are even less dense than Lys, and in some places, it would not seem like you are underground at all."

"I would like to see that," Roya wished, still casting her vote for a longer stay.

"Perhaps one day you will," Claire hoped.

"There's something else I've been curious about."

"I know. You've been wondering why my hair looks so different than everyone else's."

Roya nodded with an innocent smile.

"There are places inside the Earth that you cannot go in bodies like ours. To go there, you have to merge with other beings from those realities. It's like putting on a diving suit so you can walk on the bottom of the ocean."

"Have you ever done that?"

"Yes, but very few of our people have. Some have gone and never returned, and among those that *have* returned, sometimes the experience changes their appearance. In my case, my hair developed these colors. I was very lucky that I didn't get lost, though. It was a dangerous mission."

"Why did you go there?"

"To seek lost knowledge. Thousands of years ago, part of our culture was in communication with Ancient Egypt. Toward the end of that time, something went missing that I believe may be a key to the integration of our worlds. I went to find it."

"So, did you?"

"Unfortunately, no. And when I returned, I was forbidden to continue the search. The council never did agree with the mission. But I now believe that the courage I demonstrated is part of why I was chosen to go to the surface. The Great Forces of Creation know that I would do anything to heal the split between our worlds."

"And you've got the hair to prove it," quipped Roya, and for the first time, she succeeded at making Claire laugh.

Just then, Roya noticed light coming from another room. The moment her attention shifted focus, the rainforest scene began to fade until it disappeared.

"Go ahead. Try another room," encouraged Claire. "This will be good practice for you. Just focus on the resonance that the forms contain, and they will speak to you and show you their living memories."

Roya began to walk into the next room with Claire right behind her. What she saw there was something she did not expect. It was a window into the age of the dinosaurs!

"No way!" Roya exclaimed. "How did your people capture such ancient memories?"

"There's no limit to what you can see when you know how to collapse time with your focus of attention. Our people have just as much fascination with the ancient Earth as many of your people do. We've just learned to explore it with the mind."

This time, Claire allowed Roya to practice focusing on her own. At first, it was difficult to align her mind with the resonance of the memories. But she was determined to succeed and kept staring intently at the baby triceratops depicted on the wall. After a moment, the energy began to flow from the image. The dome overhead began to fill with the deep orange color of the sunset until the whole mural came to life around them. Claire joined with Roya's focus only after she could feel that Roya had done it on her own. Together they stood in an expansive meadow, watching a herd of triceratops.

"You can do this on the surface, too," said Claire.

Roya's eyes were wide with wonder as she looked around with great interest. "You mean, looking into the past, like this?"

"Yes. What we are doing is a form of dreaming. Right now, the field of consciousness we hold down here enhances the dreaming area of the brain. We don't separate dreams from physical reality in the same way that you do on the surface. As long as your people separate dreams from reality, your brains cannot grasp the hidden intelligence within matter and how to co-create with it. Our dreaming minds and our conscious minds are more integrated. That's why the Formelle can do so much for us."

"Will it still be this easy when I return to the surface?"

"You will never go back to the way you were before. Once you experience an opening like this, the brain will not forget. But without the support of a community field, you will have to practice extending your consciousness to keep progressing."

"Any suggestions?"

"Yes," replied Claire, realizing that she had little time left to pass on what she knew was critical information for her student. Roya's desire to learn brought Claire's knowledge into focus, which began tilting into alignment with Roya.

"Practice blending your consciousness with other things, like trees, animals, water, or stones. Consciousness lives inside everything. Focus on holding a more expanded state of connection with the environment, and it will reciprocate your intent. Take slow, deep, conscious breaths while opening to receive the living presence of everything around you. Be alert for hidden messages sent to guide you. And learn to become a blank slate so you can reflect the living intelligence of the universe."

"Spend some time lying on the Earth, and allow yourself to meld with her, integrating with the Earth as a whole living being. This will strengthen the bridge in your consciousness that links our civilizations together."

Claire's awareness seemed so vast to Roya, but she was soaking it up like a sponge. She wished to bring as much of Lys back with her as she could. It brought her comfort to know some ways that she could practice staying connected when she returned to the surface.

After a long period of silently gazing into the scenery, Roya heard conversations in the distance and knew that the group had started to come back together. As the meadow around them collapsed back into the wall, she had a strange feeling of finality, as if Claire had just energetically said goodbye. She was starting to accept that she would be returning home.

Everyone was talking excitedly when Roya and Claire returned to the entrance of the gallery.

"Roya," beamed Ami with a smile on her face.

"We got to see our mother," bursted Mandy excitedly.

"Yeah, it was amazing," sighed Ami. "She looked just like I remembered her, and she told us she's been watching over us. I always knew I could feel her."

"It was really emotional at first," added Mandy, "but then we were all laughing like a family again."

Frank still had a tear in his eye when his gaze first landed on Roya, but he quickly wiped it away and smiled. "Thanks for waiting for us," he said gratefully.

"It was no trouble," assured Roya emphatically. "Seriously, I could spend days wandering around in here."

While everyone was talking, Amaron waited patiently for the group to sense that he was commanding their attention with his presence. Roya was the first to notice. She always found it interesting how Claire and her people could bring the group energy into focus without speaking. One by one, they all fell silent and listened.

"I know you are all excited, but we need to prepare you for what lies ahead. This debate will be intense, and though you will all be treated with the utmost respect, you may encounter some among us that hold strong opinions about the surface culture. You are going to stand out, and a lot of attention will be focused on you. This may feel quite intimidating, but just relax and know that we will be right there to support you. Is everyone feeling ready to do this?"

"Yes," proclaimed Sarah, who seemed poised for the next experience.

"We are ready," said Raymond, and everyone nodded their heads in agreement.

"Good. Then it's time to show you how we travel between cities. You're going to love this next experience," hinted Amaron, with a gleam in his eye.

17

THE GREAT DILEMMA

The two families had no idea what to expect when they reached the transport room. Claire and Amaron had deliberately waited until they were standing right in front of the portal to explain. They wanted to enjoy the look on everyone's faces as they made this new discovery.

Before them stood an immense, silver-colored metallic ring, some 12 feet in diameter, embedded into the stone wall, whose base sunk just below the floor. The ring encircled a flat gray surface that hummed with energy, and something about it gave the impression that it was not entirely solid. At first, the surface was not reflective, but after a few moments, its appearance began to transform. As they stood in front of it, a feeling of connection began to open, sending a subtle zing of energy through their nervous systems. Their reflections were suddenly visible, giving the surface the illusion of depth.

Mandy was overcome with excitement and could not contain herself. She immediately exaggerated her initial surprise at the energetic connection to entertain Ami and Roya. It was her favorite game of pretending to be zapped by energy, but this time, her reaction contained an element of truth.

Roya and Ami started giggling with Mandy, but Roya was also poised to learn something new. She gazed at their reflections and could even see the soft glow of their auras. The more she focused, the more it began to suggest a mirror-like force field instead of a solid surface. She began to sense that Claire and Amaron were doing something energetically to support their attunement with the portal, and she knew that whatever happened next, it would be amazing.

"This is part of our transport system," explained Amaron. "In some of our larger cities, we have transports that would be more familiar to you, like a levitating train system, but those are a remnant of an earlier time.

We now work more with the Formelle to collapse the distance between our cities through these memory portals."

Amaron reached out to touch the surface as some of the energy reached out to connect with him in response.

"We discovered that the Formelle can bend and stretch space and time to create a system of energy tunnels that connect these rings together in most of our cities," added Claire. "Oh, and you might want to step aside for a moment."

Just then, they experienced a gentle vibration of energy coming from the portal that seemed to announce the arrival of a small group of people. They emerged from the force field, landing on a series of geometric shapes etched into the floor, and kept right on walking as if nothing had happened, even though it looked like they had appeared out of nowhere.

"All you have to do is focus on remembering yourself on the other side of the ring you want to emerge from," continued Amaron, "and the Formelle will do the rest. In this way, they assist our people in mastering the art of disremming so that eventually, as our vibrations increase, we will outgrow the need for the portal system. They're like the training wheels for anchoring the soul's natural ability to travel by thought. Since you've never been to Adinai, though, just focus on Claire, and you will end up where she goes."

Claire approached the ring and walked forward, stepping right through the reflective surface. The field appeared to stretch and open, forming a new space where she was now waiting on the other side of the ring. Mandy enthusiastically volunteered to go next, marching right through with her arms swinging wide until she was standing next to Claire with a big smile on her face. They both remained visible to the group, and this made everyone feel at ease.

One by one, they stepped into a dark cavern-like space with no visible barriers that felt distinctly different from the transport room. The air was humming with energy, and a very gentle electrical current was zinging through their auras. Once they were all through, Claire turned to face the darkness, and they saw what looked like a tunnel of bluish-white light begin to stretch out before them.

Roya tried to find her focus on the ground, but all she could see was the energy. The surface she stood on seemed to have some elasticity to it. Whenever she walked, she noticed that her steps had a bounce to them, as if there was a little less gravity here, making her movements effortless. It was beginning to feel like an invisible tether was pulling her along, right from her center of gravity.

Claire was getting further ahead, and Amaron was bringing up the rear. The tunnel continued to stretch out in front of Claire, and the color began to shift into many different sparkling hues. Looking out to the sides, she could not see anything but the energy of the tunnel and sometimes a hint of their reflections. Up ahead, she could see that the tunnel tilted slightly down and stopped where Claire was now standing. As they all arrived, the tunnel started to collapse until the light was gone, and they were all standing together on a flat, stone surface.

Looking around, they saw an incredibly vast cavern surrounding them. They were standing at the center of a platform so large they could not see the whole of it. Below them was a subtly glowing mandala etched into the stone. High above them, another large ring emitted a soft glow, illuminating part of what looked like a vast dome. Around the edges of the spacious cavern, they could see numerous glowing rings that formed a perimeter in the distance, more than the length of a football field away in any direction.

"This is what we call the Switch Room," said Claire. "All of those rings that you see represent portals to other cities that are all over the world."

"How is that possible?" Frank marveled. "If the other side of each of those portals are anywhere in the world..."

"It's possible because our people collectively understand the connection between memory and the very fabric of space and time," clarified Amaron. "This room is like a shared thoughtform that is part of our collective memory now. What you are standing in is part of a living technology. Our brains are connected with this construct as an extension of our bodies. And that tunnel of energy we were traveling through is not generated by technology in the way you think. It's another type of Formelle."

"You mean, that energy tunnel is a being?" asked Ami.

"That's exactly right," Claire smiled at her. "The Formelle create the pathways that we travel through. Though the more we use these pathways, the more they become established as pathways in our brains. As long as we are in harmony with the Formelle, our bodies are compatible with the way they can collapse distance."

"So, you didn't even have to invent teleportation," Frank realized. "Is that right? You just integrated with some already existing technology of being?"

"You catch on quick," praised Amaron. "Your people normally perceive space as a barrier to travel, but when you identify with the sacred geometry that unifies all of space, you can integrate with the resonance of forms that are reflecting everywhere in the universe. That's what allows us to reflect from place to place through these pathways of light. The Formelle are part of the living intelligence of sacred geometry."

"So, is it the same on other worlds?" wondered Ami.

"Different worlds have different forms of living technology," Amaron explained, "but the path to achieve such spiritually advanced technology has always been the same. Prioritizing oneness with each other and the natural environment, before material pursuits, gave us access to the Formelle and all their intelligence and power. The Formelle are connected across all worlds, so they know of every kind of blueprint for civilization. They are the gateway through which awakening worlds become married to forms of living technology."

"That's incredible!" exclaimed Soraya. "Could the same happen for us on the surface?"

"I don't see why not," said Claire.

"The next level of technology for you might be different, though," suggested Amaron, "because our civilizations are at different stages. You would have to become more connected as a unified whole before you could integrate with the Formelle to this degree. But as your people awaken further, you will experience your own unique revelations about how you can co-create with the technology of living light."

"Could a technology like this be used to travel to other worlds?" asked Frank.

"Only locally within the same star system," replied Amaron. "The Raiders have even experimented with an artificial version of this. It's one of the reasons our people are so worried about your people. If you were using science only for peaceful purposes, we would be celebrating your discoveries. But right now, some of your brightest minds are being used to develop technology for greedy and militaristic purposes. To answer your question, though, travel between star systems through beam technology is still limited by Einstein's relativity. While you are traveling, time is still passing inside the construct, so enormous time gaps still occur between visits for those who travel. That makes this kind of travel impractical for people who want to stay connected to the timeframe of their own civilization. The next time we travel to the stars, we will do it as one."

"You know about Einstein?" Roya was surprised.

"It might interest you to know," said Claire, leaning in, "that Einstein's work is celebrated on many worlds. Now come, let's keep moving. One of those portals will link us with the path to Adinai. Just follow my lead."

Claire had barely turned her head to face the darkness when a procession of ring-like standing waves of energy began to arrive and align with her focus until a new tunnel of light had formed. As they all began to step behind her into the light, it felt as though they were being slightly lifted off the ground, and this time, they began to move at a quicker pace. They accelerated right through one of the glowing rings and into a space that vibrated even more brightly. Each step contained a leap through space, like walking forward on a speeding train. For Roya, it was a little like skating, and Mandy was experimenting with a bounce that grew longer and longer. They each discovered that they could slide or bounce their way through the tunnel of light, and it felt like a rush just to feel the currents of energy moving with them.

Up ahead, they could see that Claire was closing in on another ring, and this one appeared to have more of a gold color. She stepped through and landed on solid ground, and the rest of them followed. Stretching out before them was a wide hallway with a high ceiling and many orange and red tapestries draped along the walls.

"This is the Welcome Hall to the city of Adinai," pronounced Amaron. The hall was empty, but it looked very majestic. After walking about a hundred feet, they came to a large stone staircase that opened wider as it went down. Before them was a vast cavern with a small, but well-lit city at the center. It was filled with stone buildings interspersed with wide walkways where many people were strolling about. The main complex was surrounded by open space and green grass, with a number of tranquil waterways. In the distance, they could hear the sound of a river rushing by at the edge of the great cavern.

Again, there was a gentle ambient light without a detectable source, though lights were also coming from the windows of some of the buildings. The round features of the architecture lent a sense of interconnectedness between all of the structures. This was the first time they had seen anything that looked like a normal city underground, and it was impressive.

They followed Amaron as he led them down the main pathway that went from the base of the stairs into the city center. In less than five minutes, they were standing in front of a large circular arena where they could hear people speaking inside.

A number of people standing at the entrance took notice of them, but Amaron and Claire guided them straight into the arena where they saw as many as a thousand people seated in ascending concentric circles of stone benches. They quickly found a seat a few levels up from the bottom. From there, they could see a panel of eight speakers seated in a designated area near the opposite side of the arena.

Mandy noticed that the white clothing that Claire and Amaron wore was similar to that of most of the others sitting in the lower levels, while the people in the rows above wore all sorts of colors. The panel of speakers wore red and orange, like the tapestries from the Welcome Hall.

"What do the colors mean?" asked Mandy.

"The people in white are representative speakers and teachers from the different cities, and the others are spectators," described Claire, "except for the council that you see wearing the colors of the city. Because of who we are, we may have a chance to speak."

This was the first time that the two families had seen such a large congregation of Lyssians together. Their auras beamed brightly, and Roya noticed the palpable presence of a group resonance field. The space in the forum felt charged with a dynamic energy.

A lively debate was already in progress, and Roya was surprised again at how well they were all speaking English. There did not seem to be any order to the process, and yet, each person seemed to know when it was their turn, as if an invisible moderator guided them.

"We have spent a long time debating about the future of the surface culture while the Raiders continue to threaten our way of life. We cannot continue to waste time and risk allowing more people to be killed, or more cities to be compromised," emphasized a man who seemed irritated with the pace of the proceedings. "We have fulfilled our purpose here on this world. Let us now return to the stars and preserve this knowledge for a time when the Earth will be safe again, or perhaps we can find a new world that is ready to house the frequency of our knowledge."

"Yes, how can we trust that the prophecy accounted for these violations?" posed a woman in white. "It speaks of a great Convergence, but our lines of evolution have been completely divergent from the surface for more than thirteen thousand years. We've done our part to fulfill the potential of this prophecy, but what if they have become too corrupt to fulfill theirs?"

As Roya began to attune her inner senses to the flow of the meeting, she could feel a connective energy that would concentrate around the presence of each speaker. The more she paid attention to the field, the more she could feel the balance of the field shifting from one speaker to another as the meeting unfolded. She could almost guess who would present next as the flow of collective attention responded to the presence of each person with something to contribute.

"Perhaps we have been living beneath the surface too long," proposed another woman. "It would be arrogant to place ourselves at the center of this prophecy and think that our risks are greater or more important than those of anyone else. We should not assume that we know so much about how the prophecy wants to be fulfilled."

"Yes," agreed another man. "And what about the new children on the surface? More and more departing souls from our people are incarnating on the surface to bring knowledge. And what about the emissaries of love and light from all over the galaxy who continue to incarnate on the surface to help raise their vibration? Are they not helping to bring them out of duality with one another? The prophecy speaks of an Integration that is much wider than that of just the surface culture and the people of Lys. We are here to be witnesses to the miracle of a new birth, not to decide the fate of humanity before completing the circle first. If we leave now, it may affect whether or not the birth occurs. It makes sense to wait. If humanity fails to enter the upward spiral of evolution, then we will be free to leave knowing that we did all that we could."

There was a brief space of silence, and Roya could feel the energy beginning to concentrate around a younger man whose aura was brightening up with something to say.

"And what do the Immortal Masters have to say about all of this?" asked the man, directing his question to the council.

"They have been silent for more than a thousand years, and no one has seen them nor travelled to their sanctuary beneath the sands of Egypt," answered a woman from the council.

"Then perhaps we should send someone to contact them," replied the young man. "Are they not also vulnerable? If they are in the dreaming trance, they might not be aware of what is transpiring on the Earth. Their spirits could be far away in another galaxy, while their bodies lie unprotected."

"They are protected for now by forces even greater than those which have protected us, and besides, we do not have access to their sanctuary," said the woman from the council. "Those tunnels were sealed long ago, and no one can enter unless the Immortals themselves allow it. We must respect their work and trust in their silent partnership with us for now."

"It is pointless to try to answer these questions," interjected another man. "The only way the questions can be answered is to live through the experience of these changes."

At this point, a number of people were taking notice of the two families, and it felt like there was a silent conversation happening about them in the energy of the space. Roya could not help feeling that their presence was starting to influence the flow of the room's attention.

"I posit that these questions have already been answered," asserted a man sitting just below the two families. "Humanity has already passed the point of no return. We have seen this level of corruption before, and no matter how many emissaries of light incarnate on the surface, it does not mean their purpose is to fulfill the prophecy. They are operating just as we are, to preserve knowledge. The Family of Light has done the same on other worlds, incarnating to act as witnesses and record even the fall of great worlds for the Living Records. Their service is to be commended, but we should not assume that their presence in the surface culture is a sign that the prophecy is being fulfilled. We've already been forced to evacuate and seal off some of our mountain settlements that are even more vulnerable than the cities here. We are simply awaiting the decision of the council to move forward with a full withdrawal."

"Will you hear, then, the testimony of the surface dwellers?" Claire spoke loudly as the field of attention shifted toward her.

Suddenly, all eyes were on the two families, and Roya could feel an intense increase in the energy around them. She could tell the crowd was being respectful energetically, but she felt uncomfortably exposed, both inwardly and outwardly.

"Clairadinda! We are happy to see that you have returned from your mission to the surface," said a woman from the council "And these are the people you brought with you?"

There were several gasps from the crowd and many people were looking at each other with an expression of surprise.

"Yes," she acknowledged. "I believe there are forces at work here that are part of the prophecy." The energetic reaction of the room suggested that some of the people viewed this as a violation, while others experienced a flash of hope.

"Before we hear from these surface dwellers, please speak of your mission," requested a man from the council.

"This forum was not aware of the full nature of my mission," said Claire, standing up, her voice echoing through the chamber. "I was sent to the surface to deliver a book that was manifested for us by the Formelle. With the help of our supporters on the surface, I was able to blend in and deliver this book to a library where it connected me with this young woman."

Claire placed a supportive hand on Roya's back as she continued talking. "She was successful in passing a test given by the Elders, and she, along with her companions, retrieved one of the living artifacts of the previous culture. We did not expect that this seeker would be so young, nor did we understand that the plan was to bring both of these families together, but that is exactly what happened. What we have witnessed since they have been down here is truly remarkable. Look at their fields. They have begun to Integrate with the group energy body of our people, and the young ones are Integrating very rapidly with the Formelle. Surely, this represents proof that the prophecy of Integration is being fulfilled. That, in itself, is a message that bears great relevance here."

"And what is the nature of this book that the Formelle gave you for this mission?" asked a man from across the forum. "I have never heard of such a thing. Do you have it here?"

"Yes," replied Claire, "but I will let Roya speak, for she is the one that the book called to first."

Claire gestured to Roya to stand up next to her and speak. "Do not be afraid. Just share your experience with them," she encouraged Roya softly.

Roya had never felt such an extreme mix of emotions. Part of her felt terrified, and yet the adrenaline pumping through her veins told her that she was going to stand up and speak. She looked over her right shoulder at her dad sitting just behind her.

"Don't worry sweetie, I'm right here," he said in a reassuring tone.

Roya could feel her pattern of shyness flashing through her mind, but none of her old patterns of avoiding attention could take root. She looked at Mandy and Ami momentarily to draw from their strength, and intuitively, they each knew to send her energy.

Roya gathered her wits, determined not to stay stuck in fear. She reached down into her backpack and produced the book. Standing up, she held it against her chest as if to shield her heart somewhat from the powerful presence of everyone's attention.

"My name is Roya Olivia Sands," she started, noticing how well the acoustics of the chamber broadcasted her voice.

"It is a great honor to be here. I know my friends and family feel the same," her voice started to quiver.

She paused for a moment, still gathering strength to match the presence of everyone focused on her, but her emotions became more intense until they spilled over, and she burst into tears. Something was happening that she could not control. As she clutched the book to her chest, something told her silently that she did not even need to say anything more at this point. The tears just flowed out as she began sobbing in earnest.

Roya's mother started to reach a hand up to Roya in support, but Claire quickly gestured to her as if to say *no, just give her space.*

Roya had no words for what she was feeling, but she did not need them. Her heart was transmitting her soul's energy so powerfully that she could feel herself addressing the forum with her whole being. A feeling of compassion for everyone and everything surged through her and flowed through every tear, and then it became apparent what was happening. They were all listening to her heart empathically, and her heart was speaking. While the purpose of the forum was to practice expressing everything in spoken word, Roya was stepping into the natural communication method practiced by the people of Lys.

She took several deep breaths as the emotional waves continued, and her sobbing began to subside somewhat. Roya's heart could not hold back the feeling of awe and wonder at this incredible hidden world. All of her hopes and fears about the future of her own people on the surface were mixing with newly found hopes and fears about the people of Lys and their dilemma. She could feel that everyone was perfectly patient with her process, and she began to relax into an indescribable state of connection with the whole forum.

Gradually, she dropped the book down from her chest and allowed herself to feel completely disarmed. Her aura was glowing even more brightly now, and she was leaving her shyness completely behind. She was holding connection with everyone in the room, feeling into the experience of having no masks whatsoever. She had transformed before their very eyes, demonstrating exactly what they hoped the surface culture might become. Finally, the words came, and she began to speak.

"Before yesterday, we didn't even know that you existed. And now we are here, and we want you to know that we mean you no harm. We had no idea that any of our people were trying to hurt you. I've been listening to this dilemma, and I feel so sorry for what has happened. I'm afraid for our people on the surface and for yours. We are destroying ourselves and the Earth. But I also believe we can awaken. If there is anything we can do to help... Please, we don't want you to leave. Meeting you has given us all hope. And I believe we have the potential to heal this world together."

The reaction in the room was mixed. Roya could clearly feel a supportive energy in the field around her, and her heart continued to flow with her empathic connection to the whole forum. It was a shocking feeling to be so emotionally naked without any way to hide, but having her parents and friends with her helped her feel safe, and there was something else. She could feel Claire's presence in her heart, extending a feeling of added support.

"Thank you, Roya," appreciated one of the women from the council. "Your heart has spoken clearly. We can feel that there is more to the surface culture than many people here have considered. If you will remain open, we will allow others to comment."

Roya continued to stand as a dance of living energy was silently working within the field, playing with the opportunity to weave more connection between everyone through her heart. She could feel her friends and family opening into this higher level of interconnectedness with her.

"Her heart is like ours," observed a woman sitting nearby. "Perhaps she is part of the bridge that has been forming. Clearly, her heart does not resonate with secrecy like the Raiders. She is an open book."

"Yes, but these people cannot help us with the problems we face," announced another woman. "There's no denying the connection that's building between our consciousness and theirs. It's the whole reason we've been learning their languages—to strengthen this bridge. But this bridge has had no effect on the consciousness of the Raiders. They are continuing to break away from the surface culture they come from, and they are dangerous. We must also consider the dangers of having surface dwellers here. They could be changing the resonance of every place they visit, making us more visible to their seers."

"They are not the same as the Raiders, though," countered another man. "These people are more like us."

"Even so," followed another man quickly, "they have no power or influence in the world to stop what is happening beneath the surface."

"That is merely an assumption," responded a woman from the council who was clearly still inspired by Roya's offering.

"Maybe they are not here to stop the Raiders from intruding," offered Amaron. "Maybe they are here to stop us from leaving. What we are witnessing here is written in the book that Roya holds. Its message is reminiscent of the prophecy."

Amaron gestured to Roya to read from the book, and she knew exactly which part was most appropriate. The energy of the room shifted back to Roya as she opened the book and began to read.

"*The Secret Ingredient,*" she started, briefly looking at her mother with a little smile.

> Love is the secret ingredient that makes every recipe for history into
> a winning formula for even greater love. The key to following the
> recipe is to remember that love was actually the first ingredient. It

is more than a bonding agent. It is the very essence of creativity. It came before everything, and so, everything is made from it.

No matter what kinds of identities are formed within the field of matter, the energy that gives them form comes from love and must eventually return to love. And no matter how much the players of history resist love's unifying power, love is always reminding everyone that the recipe for freedom is inclusive. All are equal players in love's plan for the shared outcome of history.

Before awakening into love, the citizens of the universe see the forces of physics as something apart from love. But behind all of these forces is a hidden doorway into a realm that accelerates consciousness until you can see that love is the only force.

In every universe, it is the same. Time is created backward from the beginning and remembered forward—as an awakening out of identification with matter and into identification with love and light. The unified cycle of time is always folding back into the integration point to birth new loops of universal memory. Awakening and transformation is a common theme to the experience of time and history. It is happening everywhere. The potential to awaken into greater love is embedded into your DNA. It is in the air that you breathe, and even the air knows this.

The key to overcoming your fears is to remember that your awakening into love and light has already occurred. You are simply remembering the script that you wrote from beyond time and experiencing the adventure of transformation.

Roya paused for a moment, having the stunning realization that she was experiencing exactly what the book described. It seemed to speak to something bubbling up from inside her, as if the living intelligence of her body was confirming the words were true.

Your DNA knows this, she thought, as if she was speaking the truth of her body. Her waking consciousness was starting to become congruent with the hidden knowledge of the body, and she sensed the presence of a doorway.

"Thank you, young emissary," a member of the council respectfully acknowledged. "You have spoken these words as if you wrote them."

Roya didn't know it, but the man was giving her a high compliment. In Lyssian culture, to articulate another's expressions with the same tone is to be a transmitter of their original truth.

"But what does the author of this book know about our dilemma?" questioned another man. "At this very moment, the Raiders are searching endlessly to find a way into our cities. Are we to just greet them with love and hope they will be transformed?"

"This book references the great cycles of renewed creation," stated Amaron. "The concepts and symbolism in its messages seem to contain the reflection of *our* knowledge but written in *their* language. Is this not a sign of the Integration that is beginning to occur?"

"It takes a long time for a universe to awaken," commented a man nearby. "And civilizations do fail. Worlds fail. It has happened before. We must act to preserve the knowledge that we have, so that one day it may help awaken other worlds that are ready. Perhaps some from the surface can make the journey with us, so that more of their knowledge can be preserved."

Clearly, some were not yet convinced that they should remain with the Earth, but the council appeared to align with an optimism that was brightening the energy of the forum.

"Where did this book originate?" inquired a woman from across the chamber.

Roya could feel everyone focused upon the book, almost as if they were beginning to read it telepathically.

"It came from right here in this city," Claire replied.

There were even more gasps from the crowd and looks of astonishment.

"This book came to us from the Formelle," Claire continued. "We were meditating in the crystal temple with some of the Elders when the book appeared before us in a flash of light. They said I was chosen to take the book to the surface, and the book is what connected us all together."

"This is a remarkable occurrence," expressed a man from the council.

"We will continue our investigation of these matters in the temple. Let us complete the circle and see if the Formelle will reveal something more about the meaning of these events."

What Roya did not yet know was that in Lyssian culture, completing circles was something akin to a religious duty to many. They understood the circular patterns encoded within the universe and believed that whenever a circle was near its completion, it was important to bring it to fruition.

Without another word, the council arose with Claire and Amaron, who gestured to all of them to follow the council to the exit, and the rest of the participants stood up and began to fall in behind them. Everyone felt the exact moment to stand up and enter the flow of movement so that the whole forum began to gracefully exit the building in an organized fashion.

Just outside the chamber, the eight council members led everyone along a walkway, until they entered an open field. Claire and Amaron walked side by side, following the council toward a wide set of stone stairs that led to a small cavern. Roya and the two families followed with many hundreds of others who formed a wide procession behind them.

The stone stairs gradually narrowed as they neared the entrance where two large pillars stood about seven feet apart. Just inside the dark entrance was an expansive chamber. It took a few seconds for Roya's eyes to adjust, but plenty of light was emanating from a large, upright crystal standing at the center of the cavern temple.

The crystal appeared to be quartz and stood about seven feet tall and more than two feet wide. The eight members of the council fanned out forming part of a perimeter around it, with four of them on either side. As everyone filed in, Roya could feel the book beginning to vibrate with energy as she held it to her chest.

"What do I do?" she asked Claire.

"That crystal is one of the places where the Formelle channel energy between our level of physical reality and the more refined dimensions of pure love and light. It is also a gateway to the invisible realm of the Formelle. Just present the book to the crystal, and we'll see what they want us to know about it."

As the crowd filled the room, the two families stood just behind Roya, who stepped forward into an open space around the crystal. She looked at the four council members on either side, and then a familiar feeling came over her. For a moment, she clearly remembered her favorite daydream of watching the two lion statues bow to her as she walked into the Flower Memorial Library.

Faith and Courage. She heard these words as if someone was speaking them to her telepathically, encouraging her to trust her place in the unfolding plan. There *was* a circle coming to completion, and it was not just the return of the book to the temple. It was something far greater.

Everyone was perfectly silent as Roya took a step forward. A warm glow began to arise within her as she presented the book to the crystal. Almost immediately, the crystal brightened, and its energy reached out to embrace the book. And then the energy began to envelop Roya.

She felt guided to take another step closer, and the energy grew brighter still. Both Roya and the crowd felt increasingly uncertain about what they were witnessing, and yet a deep feeling of serenity entered the field. The energy felt so peaceful and clear. She looked around for a moment, though she did not turn back to see her family. She then noticed that the three golden circles on the book were lighting up.

Roya's mother was feeling quite nervous and wanted to ask Claire if she knew what was happening, but she felt frozen with the noble silence of the room. Something told her to trust, though a fear was arising within her that she could not explain.

The light around Roya began to increase dramatically, and a number of the people had closed their eyes, focusing inwardly on the vast presence of the light. Many were expecting the Formelle to manifest in some form, but the glow just kept getting brighter. Then, a gentle tone began vibrating through Roya's whole body, and suddenly, the words of instruction she had decoded from the library had a whole new meaning. It was like hearing the words for the first time.

Drink strong oneness vibrations in lungs, she recalled, and yet it was as if the light itself was instructing her.

The words resonated in her mind with a reassuring tone that made her feel safe to breathe in the light. And after exhaling fully, she drew in a long slow breath with the intention of pulling light into her body. The sensation of the light flowing past her lips and filling her whole being was extraordinary.

Drink deep or taste not… the words challenged her to go deeper.

Roya exhaled forcefully and drew in another slow, deep breath, this time, feeling a profound sense of oneness with the Earth. Another breath, and her heart opened wider than ever before. She did not even think it was possible to be more open, but the joy of surrendering to the light was taking over.

Images and words from the whole journey began flashing through her mind. Every moment of synchronicity stood out and felt connected in the presence of the light, until she realized that the glowing book in her hands had been a recipe for creating this very moment.

This is a recipe for transfiguration.

A feeling of stillness came over her like a force, and her body seemed to slow down while the connections accelerated in her mind, crystallizing the opening of a doorway.

The toned bridge… It's in our DNA!

She was beginning to hear what sounded like faint voices in the distance. Some of the voices seemed to be saying her name, and with each breath, she focused even more purposefully on her connection to the light, trying to discern the source of the messages.

Roya. Roya. We are over here ...beckoned the voices. She wondered if anyone else could hear them.

The book was even lighter in her hands, almost floating. It felt as if the whole room was breathing with her as the light continued to expand ever more rapidly. The crowd was poised with anticipation to witness what might appear, and then... FLASH!

She vanished!

There were loud gasps from the crowd, and Roya's mother fainted! Luckily, Raymond caught her before she fell to the floor and eased her down gently. People were frantically looking around at one another as the glow of the crystal subsided. Ami and Mandy looked at each other in shock.

"What just happened?" pleaded Ami, breaking the silence.

Claire turned to her as if to respond, but she was still speechless herself and was reaching for an explanation that wasn't there. "This has never happened before," she confessed. "I don't know what it means."

Claire could feel a barrage of questions arising that were directed at her, but before anyone could say anything, they heard the sound of yelling in the distance. They began to sense a great commotion stirring in the city beyond the temple. Some of the crowd started to leave to see what was happening, and then everyone's messengers began to appear.

Hundreds of little communication orbs of every color materialized in front of people. Some were brighter than others, but everyone had the same reaction. Only seconds after the orbs appeared, they began heading quickly for the exit.

Amaron's orb was bright orange, and almost immediately, he turned to the two families and said, "There's been a breech! We have to evacuate."

"Raiders!" warned Claire. "We have to go, now!"

"We aren't going without Roya," Raymond insisted, kneeling over his wife. Claire knelt down and placed her left hand over Soraya's forehead, gently sending her energy until she started to come around.

"We can't stay here," implored Amaron. "They could capture us or kill us. There's no telling what they might do."

"Can you stand up?" Claire asked Soraya.

"Yes, I think so. What happened?"

"We have to go. The city is under attack."

"But where's Roya!?" Soraya's eyes looked around wildly.

"She is safe," Claire said more slowly, feeling that less urgency in her voice was needed to help Soraya stay calm. "Trust me, the Formelle would not have done this if it were not safe."

"But how do you know!?" demanded Raymond, nearly yelling. "What happens if she comes back and we're not here? She will come back, won't she?"

"The circle is complete. I can't predict how or when she will come back, but I am certain the Formelle know what they are doing. We will consult the council, but first, we must get to safety immediately."

People were quickly funneling through the exit between the two pillars, and the two families began to move with the crowd. One of the council members walked over and placed her hand on Soraya's shoulder as they were walking, sending her an energy of reassurance. Both of Roya's parents kept looking back at the crystal, hoping that she might reappear, but the crowd was beginning to close in behind them, pushing them forward.

When they reached the staircase, they could see some kind of eerie light in the far distance, and everyone seemed to be fleeing away. They were all headed toward the Welcome Hall. Some of them were running, but as people neared the stairs, they were forced to proceed more slowly as the path narrowed.

Ami and Mandy both kept standing on their tiptoes in curiosity as they walked, trying to see past the crowds to get a look at where the intruders were. The Raiders did not appear to be advancing on the city yet, but there was an ominous feel to their presence that cut through the field like a knife. It was the antithesis of feeling the loving presence of the Lyssians. It was like the presence of the Raiders wanted you to be afraid.

18

THE LIVING LIBRARY

For a moment, Roya felt frozen in time. She was perfectly still and at peace in the light as it continued to raise her vibration. That moment seemed to stretch into an eternity, and she had never experienced such a deep level of trust. The light was her companion and she felt *completely* unafraid.

She sensed the field of light spinning both in and around her body. It was like she was moving, but not moving, at the same time, as the field of light folded the space around her into another location. Her body then began to resonate with a place that had unique characteristics of vibration. The spinning began to divide into a myriad of forms that she felt connected to. Depth and contrast began to appear. All at once, she felt an opening inside her that allowed her to exhale the breath she had been holding.

As she drew in the next breath, her body released from stillness. She could feel the contours of a large room taking shape around her. As the light began to fade, she felt her feet firmly planted on a shiny marble floor. A final wave rippled across her field of vision, and then, the whole scene came into focus. She saw the crystal from the Temple of Adinai suspended in midair under a large, white, domed ceiling.

"She made it through!" a voice resonated within the open space. There was a tone of delight and relief in the words suggesting that getting her here had been an experimental, but successful, achievement.

Roya found herself standing at the edge of a large balcony that encircled the crystal, which was suspended high above the floor below. Looking up into the domed ceiling, she saw something familiar: the muses from the Flower Memorial Library. The dome was larger and brighter, but all eight muses were there, and they looked slightly animated, as if they were happy to see her.

"Where am I?" she said quietly.

And then she heard: "*Welcome to the Living Library.*" It was not a single voice this time—it sounded like many voices speaking as one.

There was something familiar about this place, and it was not just the dome with the muses. She was certain that she had been here before, in a dream, perhaps. Roya began to wonder if the unconscious memory of this place is what had attracted her to spend so much time at the library. The building felt alive and self-aware, like it knew her personally.

"*Do you like it?*" said the voice in a deeply caring tone.

"It's beautiful. It feels like home."

"*The rooms here can change to fit the personality of the visitors.*"

Looking around, Roya noticed that the walls began to shimmer slightly wherever she focused her attention. At first, they appeared to be white, but as soon as she began to wonder what was beyond them, they started to become transparent. Roya was captivated by the rich and colorful scenery outside the perimeter of the room, but momentarily, began to play with her ability to make the walls appear solid versus transparent. The room seemed to be the highest point of a large building surrounded by a vast landscape.

With the walls now fully transparent, the room reminded her of a lighthouse. It was raised well above an expansive rooftop park where luminous people were walking around. The whole roof of the building was filled with walkways, gardens, benches, and fountains. Other buildings beyond the library appeared to have a gentle glow, and she could see trees and mountains in the distance. The sun was directly overhead, casting beautiful rays of colored light through the stained glass window at the top of the dome, which fell onto the softly glowing crystal, hovering at the center of the room.

Roya felt connected to everything. Something fundamental had shifted in her awareness. Before, she had always felt as if everything in reality existed outside of her. But now, she felt a profound sense of reflectivity within her, and in everything around her. It went beyond just what she could see; it was a state of connection with a much greater reality.

Roya walked around the perimeter of the room, noticing how light she felt as she was looking through the walls. There was slightly less gravity here, and her movements felt more graceful to her. She began to swoop her hands through the air as she walked, mimicking the way Mandy had moved through the light tunnels. Gradually, she took longer strides until she developed a bit of a bounce. After completing a circuit around the room, she walked back to the edge of the balcony, smiling.

If this room reflected her personality, she knew that the transparent walls reflected her desire for expansion.

Looking over the side to the floor below, she first expected to see the twelve signs of the zodiac, like at the Flower Memorial Library, but instead, she saw the twelve symbols of living knowledge from the map room of Lys. They were glowing with a golden light that reminded her of the letters from the book. Only now did she realize that the book was no longer in her hands. It seemed to have disappeared at some point in the shift between realities. This was beyond her wildest dreams. She was on the surface again, but it was more like Lys!

"Where is this place?" Roya wondered.

"At various points in history, certain forms of time travel are permitted in accordance with the Divine Plan. Your journey here has been anticipated for hundreds of years on this timeline. You are currently in a land that used to be known as Colorado, but as a multidimensional construct, this library is also a living model of what is awakening in the DNA of the 21st century. Before such places came into being, they first awakened within humanity as a spiritual blueprint. This new knowledge system was designed to teach humanity about the nature of the Earth as a Living Library, and who you are in relation to it. You are considered by the people of this time period to be one of the Founders."

Roya felt deeply honored by her invisible hosts as they regarded her in some way that she could not fully comprehend. Once again, she felt awash with questions, and the answers could not come fast enough, though she sensed they were responding to more than just the simple ones she was asking.

"When are we?" she asked, deliberately attuning her mind to the consciousness behind the voice this time, trying to discern something more about her hosts.

"An interesting question, given how many different time references are interacting with this space simultaneously. Generally speaking, we prefer to count from one global shift in consciousness to the next. In the time that you come from, you are just living through the first global shift. The radiant people you see outside have recently lived through the second great shift. Some of them are guiding you from your future along this probable timeline, just as we are guiding humanity from beyond the third shift. Beyond the fourth and final shift, humanity is called to journey to the stars."

The idea of one global shift was amazing to consider, but *four?!* With a little effort, Roya found that she could move her awareness backward and forward in time to sense the resonance of what was happening in different parts of the timeline. In this new state of connection with light, this felt like a normal and natural way to explore, as if the body was always meant to be a gateway for human consciousness to co-create with the whole timestream. Through her body, Roya could now feel echoes of all four global shifts as one interlinked progression of evolutionary events, and beyond each of these thresholds, she could feel how humanity's joy had increased.

"How did I get here?"

"*You came here by traveling inward and embracing the light of wholeness, which is the light of humanity's collective future on this timeline. This learning center reflects the inner landscape of the new human being. Your journey here represents part of an energetic opening that is taking place in the DNA of your time period—unlocking the potential of a future where humanity has become a unified, knowledge-sharing culture.*"

"Who are you?" asked Roya in an increasing state of wonder.

"*We are the librarians. We are here to assist you. We are guiding you from a future where all human beings have assumed their divinely appointed roles as librarians and stewards of the vast wealth of knowledge that is stored on Earth. We represent a model of what humanity is becoming.*"

"Is this one of the libraries of the future that the book talked about? Is this where it came from?"

"*Yes, the book was created here so that you would find your way back to this place. It contained a script that was agreed upon by all the participants.*"

"So, we created it in the future...using knowledge from the future...to give it to ourselves in the past. How is that possible?" Roya was perplexed.

"*Those who became conscious enough to enter the library were allowed to alter their own past, as long as they were willing to live through the changes that they introduced. The rules of the game enforce an incentive to improve reality for the greatest number of people, so there is little danger that such power would be abused.*"

"Are you saying that I was here before on another timeline, and was allowed to change my past?"

"*She's very sharp,*" a male voice commended, and there was a twinkling of light that rippled around the room, which registered as a feeling of excitement. Roya was beginning to sense quite a large gathering of invisible beings around her, so she became very still, opening her inner senses to feel the librarians.

After a moment of waiting for them to say more, she thought to prompt them again. "What would I have changed about my past?" The room was still silent, but there was a feeling of expectancy in the air, like their lips were sealed until she asked the right question. "What would I have changed about my past," she whispered to herself again, pondering the idea more deeply. "If I had come from a past with a lot of negatives, I would have tried to make things more positive," she said, thinking out loud. "What would I have changed...about humanity's past! That's it! We must have connected things together that had remained disconnected before...We?...There must have been others!" she realized.

"You are so very close to remembering, but we cannot give you the answer in this way. What we can tell you is that you were allowed to change the timing of when you first discovered the library, and as you are about to realize, timing is everything."

"May I see what you look like?" requested Roya.

Instantly, the air became more luminous, and she saw the outline of many forms reflecting in the light. She was surrounded by subtle light beings, but they could not increase their radiance too much. They did not want to overwhelm Roya, so they chose a form that would be familiar. Out of the ethereal essences of being that shimmered around her, a single person began to materialize. Roya could actually feel the group of light beings breathing life into her form and filling it with their grace and intelligence.

"Claire? Is that you?" recognized Roya in astonishment. The person in front of her looked exactly like Claire, but there was an even deeper gentleness and elegance to her presence. Even though she looked physically real, Roya could tell that she was made of pure living light.

"We thought you would like to see this form again," said the librarians. *"Claire is a part of us."*

"What is my purpose here?" she asked Claire. Seeing her face brought Roya's thoughts into greater focus. Claire smiled at her with that same pleasing look she had whenever Roya was asking the right questions. She then pointed to the crystal, saying, "look."

As Roya turned to face the crystal again, a light began to radiate from it, forming a window that expanded into a holographic vision. The space around them became filled with imagery, and a story began to unfold.

Before them was a small African village where a group of children were playing. The village looked very poor, and the vision directed their attention to a schoolhouse that was far too small. It was old and did not have nearly enough chairs and desks for the children, so they held their school meetings outside.

The scene shifted to a school session where the children were asking a lot of questions. They had almost nothing to use for school supplies and very few books to work with, but the children had an insatiable curiosity about the world. They desperately wanted to learn, and the teacher felt overwhelmed with the lack of support to feed their hunger for knowledge. She was not adequately trained or educated herself and this was a cause for some of her grief. *These children deserve better,* she thought.

Later that night, a presence began to appear to three of the school children, who were sleeping under the stars. It was the librarians. At first, they contacted the children in their dreams, but then their dreams expanded into a shared vision where they saw several luminous people standing in front of them, smiling. As soon as the children acclimated to their presence, the librarians began to speak.

"Do not be afraid. We are here to connect you with the Awakening Hearts throughout the world. Your hearts have prayed for education, and now it has come to you. We will give you the ability to learn faster than you have ever dreamed possible, and your minds will have no more limits. Together, your brains can evolve as one."

They felt trust for the librarians, who represented the potential of what they could become. Their hearts opened to receive the gift, and the symbol of a book appeared in each of their hearts. The Book then opened to reveal the gentle glow of humanity's oneness, as if this was the essence of every page.

"This Book is a symbol of the great Living Library that is awakening within you. Through it, you can learn from the sacred knowledge of the Earth and co-create with the world as one community. Just look within your heart and ask a question, and the Book will open to teach you from the resources of one humanity. Soon, you will master the ability to remember the knowledge of the great Living Library as if it is your own."

The next day, the children talked about it endlessly. They shared the vision with their friends, and most people that heard about it felt a feeling of hope. From that moment forward, the evolution of the village began to accelerate. The children wondered how they could improve the life of the village, and the Book began to feed them with knowledge of the hidden potentials of the region. As the children followed the guidance, they became increasingly intuitive, and their lives became more synchronistic and meaningful. It was not long before a number of other children and even adults felt the connection as well. The presence of the Book and the Awakening Hearts had begun to pulse within those touched by the vision. The Book was beginning to teach them how to set a field of intention that expanded far beyond their perceived limitations.

Next, the vision shifted to a church somewhere in America. A man from the congregation requested to speak. The Book was clearly open inside his heart, and it had connected him to the people he was destined to help.

"I know that our church has done a lot of good for our community," he began. "But I believe people in faraway lands may need our help even more. I feel like there's a whole new level of inclusiveness that wants to shift how we all relate to the world community. And it's not about finding more ways to include people in our beliefs; it's about inspiring people through our actions to have faith in the oneness of the human family. We *have* to think bigger about the difference we can make. We have to keep reaching across borders to create bridges between cultures. We have to demonstrate that we are one global village until *everyone* on Earth shares this vision. This is a key to humanity's future."

As the man spoke, a feeling of connection was stirring in the crowd that reflected his inspiration. It was the answer to a prayer, because many had felt hungry for more spiritual growth. But they were not sure how to access the next level of religious experience, nor were they sure how the setup of their religion could take them there.

Many believed they were waiting to enter a new world, and yet the act of waiting was turning into a feeling of stagnation. They did not realize that the very spirit of the new world was calling them to help create it through acts of love and compassion. What they could not see is that their experiences were a reflection of a collective pattern. It was not just their congregation. A growing feeling of discord was arising everywhere about humanity's own dysfunctional behaviors and the need for courage and leadership. Something needed to shift, and the man's inspiration was opening the doorway to the world of compassion that people had been searching for but had not known how to enter.

"If humanity is ever going to realize a shared vision of our purpose," the man continued, "then we have to empower everyone to share their gifts with the world, and not leave anyone behind. I feel a calling in my heart to connect with other communities that are hungry for the kind of change we can bring. If any of you are willing to join me, I'm planning a journey to Africa to explore what we can do for some of our neighbors there."

Behind the man's inspiring words was something even more profound that he did not express aloud, something he could not explain. The Book in his heart had spoken to him about what he was meant to do, *in the past tense.*

"You spoke to the people and inspired them. You guided them to Africa and formed a bridge of peace that changed the lives of people from both lands. You helped connect humanity together as one global village, and hearts were forever changed."

This was the answer to the man's prayers. He had prayed about how he could best serve humanity, and the Book had appeared within him as a guide. The records of the future had revealed his role as a catalyst. Never before had this man felt so guided, knowing that he was destined to make a difference. He had entered a path where he was being intuitively led by the calling of his potential.

From there, the vision shifted to an area of the Middle East where another group of children were aligning with an incoming field of oneness. This time, Roya felt an even deeper connection with the scene, as if a part of her own presence was stepping forward to share her inspiration with the children about their potential. She felt her compassion join with an emerging global force of awakening. It was the energy of One Heart that spoke to the children and opened the Book within their hearts. The whole Living Library of the Earth's knowledge began to speak to them through the form of the Book and the vibration of the One.

They began to learn at an accelerated rate, their inner education working in tandem with their outer education. Opportunities for change that were invisible before became visible. The children felt more empowered than ever before to speak the wisdom and guidance they were receiving. Although their lives were deeply affected by war, they expressed an unshakable faith in the goodness of humanity that was contagious. They demanded for humanity to awaken and transcend the consciousness of war. Their voices were like angels, inspiring people to improve the life of their communities. The people who heard the children speak were inspired to pledge their hearts to peace.

Roya began to feel a powerful force of compassion swelling inside her chest, reflecting the compassion awakening throughout the world. There were many regions experiencing the chaos and despair of war, economic hardship, and starvation. But the messages of the Book foretold that a great awakening would bring helpers to every corner of the globe to shift people out of the struggle for survival.

Something incredible was beginning to happen. The Book had connected the helpers in a visceral way with the plight of the most impoverished communities. Scene after scene unfolded where Roya saw people respond-ing intuitively to the needs of others as compassion became a guiding force throughout the world, inspiring them to step out of their comfort zones and demonstrate bold and courageous action. The Awakening Hearts were linking together to find new ways of sharing resources with the global community. The Book spoke of humanity's potential to experience a collective revelation of its shared purpose. But first, it would have to know itself as One.

As Roya watched, the voice of the librarians explained: *"The Book is a living symbol of humanity's new collective DNA. It represents the DNA of a shared reality with which you are learning to co-create. It is the means for you to share new evolutionary codes of choice with each other as you practice listening for guidance and showing up to be the change. Together, you are evolving the resonance of humanity toward a global harmonic expression of joy and radiant living."*

The vision then accelerated, and Roya saw scenes all over the world of connections lighting up between people who were aligning with the reflection of the One Heart in their betweenergy. The resonance of humanity was changing! A Spirit of Oneness was entering the world and linking people together through a unified field of being.

As the vision expanded, it became apparent that the *Earth* was consciously involved in the process of awakening humanity. Surges of unifying Earth energy began to arise like currents of living light to play a role in connecting together emerging groups of awakening human beings. The vision showed people lying down to sleep at night and feeling the gentle surges of Earth energy connecting them with others throughout the world. The Earth was teaching the Awakening Hearts that her frequency is a unifying principle in humanity's spiritual evolution.

People began to come together in groups to practice channeling the new currents of Earth energy. The power of the Earth was amplifying their intentions of world unity through the heart. The rise of this sacred power was even becoming strong enough to change the resonance of humanity's oppressors. As the surges increased, more and more groups began to practice lying on the Earth together, allowing a transformation to take place. People were becoming married to the Earth in their consciousness, and the Earth was helping to shift humanity into a higher expression of being.

As the field of connection grew, people began to receive spiritual downloads of their evolutionary potential and purpose as co-creators. Kindness and love began to take root as a way of being in many places, accelerating the global awakening process. The resonance of this emerging oneness collective was becoming strong enough that people could simply choose to join with it and find it in their hearts.

At one point, the vision zoomed out, and Roya could see a change happening to the whole of the Earth. Waves of cosmic energy were impacting the world and connecting everything together. As time continued to accelerate, she saw the consciousness of Lys transferring to the surface through this new multidimensional field of connection. People everywhere were integrating with the new telepathic messaging system, while hosts of angels worked to connect everyone with an angelic vibration of peace. The bridge between humanity and the invisible world strengthened as the potential of becoming an integrated whole drew near.

The light in the world was increasing, linking everyone into a growing field of interconnectedness that could do amazing new things with human intelligence—far beyond what the internet had made possible. A time of rapid evolutionary change had arrived, offering humanity the opportunity to unite in a way that most had not imagined. Through the field of the vision, Roya could feel an emotional tremble building globally as humanity approached the moment of collectively realizing its shared purpose.

Roya was so caught up in the vision that she hardly noticed the tears that were streaming down her face. Her heart was overwhelmed with joy, inspiration, and relief. It was as if all her questions had been answered, and she knew, at last, that there was a plan for humanity.

As the vision completed, the light window retracted and closed, as if pulled back into the heart of the crystal. She was silent for a long time until she turned and looked at Claire. "Is this why I'm here?" she asked, "to help with this vision?"

"This is a vision of humanity's potential, but there is a real danger that it may not come to pass. This is why those of you who made it here before agreed to alter your own past. You wanted to gain the upper hand, because some do not want this potential to be realized."

"The secret war," Roya stated. "This is what they are trying to suppress? But why?! Why would anyone want to suppress such an inspiring future for humanity?"

"Give me your hand!" Raymond called out to Sarah who was falling behind. It was a stampede for everyone to reach the portal, and the closer they got, the thicker the crowd became. They had arrived at the bottom of the wide stairway that led up to the Welcome Hall and were careful not to move too fast. No one had ever seen the stairs or the hall so jammed with people.

Luckily, the soldiers could not see the entrance to the Welcome Hall. From their angle, at the edge of the city, the stairs to the hallway were hidden behind a series of buildings. The soldiers did not appear to be advancing quite yet. They were still developing a strategy for how they would cover the most ground in the shortest amount of time. Apparently, the nature of how they arrived made their mission time-sensitive, and the territory was unfamiliar. They did not want to waste time with a bunch of prisoners. What they wanted was to raid the city for its technology.

Frank, Mandy, and Ami were right behind the others as they reached the top of the stairs. They were among the last few thousand people to reach the hallway. Up ahead, people were stepping into the portal in great numbers and disappearing.

"When you reach the portal, focus on the City of Sharindaya, and it will take you directly there," instructed Claire as the two families moved within a hundred feet of the giant ring. "When you know where you want to go, you will skip the Switch Room."

"Are you sure Roya will be all right?" petitioned Raymond once more.

Soraya looked at him, grateful that he asked again. She was still deeply worried. It took all of her strength to keep moving forward, feeling as though she was leaving her precious daughter behind.

"I am certain that she is safe," Claire reassured, "but if we want to find out what to do next, we must speak with the council."

Claire truly believed what she said, but she had honestly never seen anything like this before. No one had. In all the years that Claire had visited the temples, the Formelle had never done anything of this nature. She was perplexed, as were the rest of her people who had witnessed the spectacle. It was one thing to materialize a fully written book, which also had never happened before, but to pluck a human being from physical reality and take them into the realm of the Formelle—*that* was truly a paradigm-shifting event. If this had happened to someone from Lys, it might have meant something different, but whatever kind of rare honor this was, it had been given to an outsider. It was as if the Formelle wanted to further the debate that had been going on about the prophecy.

Right now, thousands of people were beaming into the other cities of Lys with news of this anomalous activity, which would instantly stimulate a global conversation within the Inner Earth. The Prophecy of Convergence was being forced upon them by the arrival of the soldiers, but the presence of the two families and Roya's disappearance into the realm of the Formelle would insure that people stayed open to the mystery and would not jump to conclusions.

If that was what the Formelle had intended, the timing they had chosen for Roya's disappearance was perfect. Until this event, only a handful of people in Lys had even known about Claire's mission to the surface. Now, in a matter of hours, everyone in Lys would know of Roya and her friends.

Claire took the lead saying, "Just follow me through the middle. You will likely see several other pathways splitting off as you enter. Don't be afraid. When this many people are using the system, this is just how the Formelle handle the flow."

She was right. As Raymond, Soraya, and Sarah stepped through just behind Claire, they saw a tunnel of light stretching out before them. Several other people had entered almost side by side with them and were accelerating into tunnels that seemed to split off to either side.

Raymond gripped Sarah and Soraya's hands tightly as he walked forward, staying focused on Claire. The other tunnels faded away, and it felt like they were gliding. Raymond even had the sense that the Formelle were shortening and lengthening the tunnels to adjust the timing of the arrivals, so people did not run into each other.

Just behind them, a surge of people who were all going to Sharindaya had entered with Frank, Ami, and Mandy. As they walked along through the flow of liquid light, the energy of the tunnel rippled and wavered as it stretched out to create more space between the travelers. They were traversing hundreds of miles in a matter of seconds, when Ami began to hesitate. Until that moment, she was committed to returning to Sharindaya with her family, but in her heart she felt a different calling. The tunnel seemed to stretch out before her, positioning her father and Mandy further away. People were starting to brush past her, and then the field of the tunnel collapsed, at least for her.

Suddenly, she found herself standing in the Switch Room, alone. There might have been thousands of people passing through the space she was in, but she did not see them. She was right in the middle of the platform, surrounded by numerous city portals in the distance. She could see the portal for Sharindaya out in front of her, some 100 yards away, and was certain that her family was already there. She felt conflicted for a moment, but deep down, knew she had to go back to the temple. She could not leave Roya behind. *What if Roya returns and no one is there to guide her or tell her what's happening?* she worried. She hoped her dad would understand.

Ami turned, panning around the room to see if she could locate the portal to Adinai. At first, she started to wonder if she would know how to engage the transport system on her own. She walked toward the edge of the platform, wondering if there was a way across.

Looking into the distance at the many transfer rings around the perimeter of the Switch Room, she almost did not see the edge of the cliff she was walking up to. Her heart raced as she looked down to see what appeared to be a dark and endless abyss surrounding the massive rock column under the platform. For a moment, she felt stuck as she backed away from the edge. The thought occurred to her that if she didn't know what she was doing, she might just drop right into the darkness, but she chose to believe she was safe.

Ami began to focus on her memory of the temple with Roya, and almost instantly, one of the rings blinked at her from across the room. She turned slightly to align herself with the ring and a stream of liquid light began to reach out toward her. Every step she took was a leap of faith, but she tried not to think about the black abyss that might be beneath her as she entered the transfer tunnel. The light pulled her forward ever so gently, as if it was not just her will to return, but the will of something greater that was guiding her into position. Only a moment later, she emerged into the Welcome Hall. It was completely empty.

Roya had no idea what had begun to unfold in Adinai just after she disappeared. Her whole presence was absorbed with protecting the potential of humanity's awakening that she had just been shown. At the moment, she could imagine no greater purpose for her life.

"I would do anything to protect this world," declared Roya.

Her soul was crying out in selflessness. It was not just a statement that she was making to the hologram of Claire. It was a prayer that her heart spoke to the universe saying, *I am ready to serve!*

"You have said those words before," illuminated Claire, "and we are ready to help you."

Claire then gestured to the marble railing of the balcony as it disappeared. It felt like a gate had opened, and yet there was only open space before them.

"Walk forward," invited Claire.

"But there's nothing there," Roya hesitated, looking over the side, certain that there must be some misunderstanding.

"Trust me," encouraged Claire.

Roya proceeded forward cautiously, pausing at the edge of the marble before the open space. She looked at Claire one more time to see if more instructions were coming, but she realized that only her trust was required.

Taking the first step forward in midair, she felt her foot come to rest on an invisible platform, which activated the presence of a barely visible crystalline staircase made of light. The staircase spiraled down like a funnel, until it reached a gold disc in the center of the floor, just beneath the suspended crystal. Stepping down, she noticed how the outline of the stairs closest to her lit up slightly, as if they were happy to serve her. Her heart was beating with exhilaration as the whole environment responded to her presence as if it were alive. She felt more trust with each step that she took.

"Always remember," instructed Claire, "the path you need may sometimes be invisible at first, but it will always be there. Doubt, fear, and impatience: these feelings can obscure the path. They disrupt the flow of guidance that connects your intuition with the highest possible future. Learn to trust in your path, and it will always reveal itself."

"I understand," acknowledged Roya as she reached the bottom of the stairs. As soon as she stepped onto the gold disc, it began to vibrate, activating a pillar of light between the disc and the crystal above. Around her, the twelve symbols on the floor became more illuminated, and Roya felt a connection to the stars pouring into her pillar of light. For a moment, she had the sensation of being in many places at once. The consciousness of the twelve symbols washed through her like a shower conveying a vast meaning, beyond words. The download happened in an instant, and Roya felt touched by an awareness of her soul's blueprint.

Claire then pointed to a set of large wooden double doors in front of Roya. "There is a book inside we need you to see."

The doors opened, and she saw a vast temple-like space filled with towering shelves of books. Her connection into this new space came with a rush of energy, and the whole scene felt alive.

"How will I know which one?" asked Roya. The library seemed like a labyrinth before her.

"Just follow your intuition," instructed Claire. "You will know."

Roya walked through the doors and down a set of stone stairs that fanned out into a wide aisle between two rows of shelves. A slight tingling sensation remained from her connection with the gold disc, and her vibration was even higher now. Only a short distance in, she came to an opening where she could look out at the expanse of the floors below. There she saw numerous floors and platforms with intricately carved stonework that vibrated with living energy. Some places were filled with books and others were more garden-like, with plants and flowing water that poured from openings in the wall to create an elaborate system of irrigation throughout the entire living structure.

Walking to the right, she descended down another flight of stairs, deeper into the library. Shelves of books towered over her, and she could feel some of the books she passed as if their titles and subjects announced themselves. This felt like a normal part of the awareness of the library, expanding upon the sense that everything around her was also within her. *Finding the right book should be easy with this awareness,* she thought.

Then, she noticed light coming from behind the aisles in front of her and saw luminous people like those she had seen in the courtyard above. Most of them looked fairly young, and she would occasionally see children. A golden energy surrounded each of them, encapsulating the colors of their inner auras.

As she rounded a corner, she saw an open space where a number of people were standing around a large hologram of the Earth that was hovering over a crystalline pool of water. The people were using their thoughts to access the living records of history that flowed from the hologram into their awareness. It was like they were drinking from a fountain of knowledge with their minds.

She approached quietly, noticing how perfectly silent everyone was. What captivated her most about the hologram was the fact that the geography of the world had changed significantly. Clearly, the ocean levels had risen and the coastlines were completely different, though she could also see islands and other land masses that had appeared, which did not yet exist in her time reference. She also noticed that some of the vast areas of desert were now green.

Her curiosity drew her closer, and with a few more paces, she found herself nearly looking over a young girl's shoulder. Suddenly, the girl turned and asked Roya with her eyes if she wanted to watch, too. She was accessing a memory portal about the forests of Antarctica and the history of civilization there since the 21st century. As Roya looked on with interest, the portal expanded as if to invite another viewer. Roya became entranced with the moment, realizing that she was seeing part of the living records of the world. But she was determined not to become distracted from her mission. A sense of urgency spurred her on.

The girl sensed Roya's directive and seemed to encourage her with a smile before turning back to the hologram. It was enough for Roya just to know that such a thing was possible. She hoped to come back and explore further after she had found the book that was calling her.

Reaching out again with her inner senses, she began to scan the area around the Earth Hologram, feeling for intuitive signals. Across the room, she took notice of a pathway that led down another set of stairs. A tingling sensation in her solar plexus seemed to signify that she was on the right path.

At the bottom of the stairs was an expansive arena that reminded her of the map room from Lys. Several more luminous people walked by, smiling as they looked over at her. Their expressions were so joyful that Roya sensed the people in this time period had moved beyond all forms of emotional pain. For a moment, she basked in the wondrous feeling of having so much knowledge and human creativity within reach. But then, she picked up the trail again. She felt her body turning toward the entrance to a large spiral ramp that wrapped around an open space, connecting all of the levels above and below.

As she reached the ramp, peering over the edge, she could finally see the bottom of the library many floors below her. Beautiful flowering vines draped from the outer edge of the spiral ramp at every level. The midday sun shone through a glass ceiling that refracted the light in certain places, allowing rainbow colors to reflect into the scene. At the bottom of the space, a beautiful fountain gushed, surrounded by many radiant people.

She began to walk briskly down the spiral ramp, noticing a sweet fragrance in the air from the flowers, until she came across a floor with an unusual feature. A stonework path led to a circular area that was slightly sunken. The stones were grey and rough, giving the impression that she was walking along a trail outside. Roya felt mysteriously drawn to this place, experiencing a connection to the stones as if they recognized her.

The sunken area at the end of the path contained a stone pillar at its center which displayed a single book. Behind the book, a stone wall enclosed part of the circle. It was adorned with more of the flowering vines, and water trickled down the stones and into the floor. She appeared to be alone as she approached the book, feeling a silent reverence for it that connected her with the invisible presence of angels in the space. She could feel how the library had accorded a special place for this artifact, because it had come at such a great price. This was all the knowledge that was left of a lost civilization, but it was not a civilization of the ancient past.

As Roya stepped up to the book, she heard the voice of an angel command: *"Read."*

The book was similar in size and shape to the *Circle and the Stars*—a fairly thin, midsized book with a smooth hard cover. The book represented a form of communication that went beyond written words. Appearing across the white surface of the cover, golden letters began to illuminate the title.

The Book of Aaron: How We Lost Our Way, Roya read silently.

As the book opened before her, she instantly felt connected to it, and it spoke to her in a man's voice saying: *"Behold! I am among the last surviving witnesses to the destruction of humanity and the raiding of the Earth. The year is 2037, and soon, there will be no place left for those unwilling to submit to the technology."*

The man's voice sounded strangely familiar, and it also gave her the chills. There was a finality to these statements that rattled her to the core, because the man sounded like he had accepted a painful truth that he was powerless to fight against. She had expected a scene to open holographically, but instead, she felt surrounded by the ominous feeling of an elusive and menacing presence, gradually creeping in on the world and interfering with it. This was part of the record of Aaron's experiences. Somehow, he had been able to sense something happening in the world behind the scenes that eluded almost everyone else.

Roya knew that this man's words were sacred, and they begged to be regarded with a sobriety that stretched her mind into an expanded awareness of Aaron's world. As the pages of the book began to turn themselves, she heard Aaron's narrative inwardly, and instantly felt compassion for the plight of this man and his companions.

For many years, my friends and I fought against the suppression of knowledge, trying to educate people about what we had learned... but even those of us who knew about the alien presence could not imagine the grand scale of their plans—until it was too late. Every step in the progression of events appeared benign on the surface, but humanity was being manipulated in very specific ways designed to erase our freedom and sovereignty.

Step by step, the new system of reality was phased in, packaged and sold as something innovative, entertaining, and beneficial to the world. The technology was said to give us new freedoms and make us more secure. Little did we know, our freedom and security was being defined by our captors.

The aliens were patient and persistent in pursuit of their agenda and took great care to mold our field of attention into a focus that fit with their plan. All they needed to do, at first, was to nudge an undiscerning government down the right technological pathway. The idea was simple: get the military addicted to alien technology to entice them to enter into a secret alliance. The benefits of advanced technology were obvious to any organization that wanted to maintain military and technological superiority.

Roya began to see images of military officials passing around pieces of alien technology. The people were mesmerized by the possibilities and became instantly addicted to acquiring more. Some of them were afraid of the alien influence, while others were formulating plans for what they could achieve with it.

"This is the future," she heard many of them thinking, an idea that the aliens were intent on implanting. Thus, began a process whereby the aliens could secretly lead us away from the historical potentials they were competing against.

The field of the vision then sharpened Roya's inner senses to reveal something profound that none of the military people could see. Unbeknownst to all of them was an invisible glow that surrounded the technology. The objects carried the resonance of the alien civilization they came from, and Roya could see the subtle effects it had on everyone's consciousness. They did not know it, but they were holding a technological Trojan Horse in their hands, making it easier for the aliens to influence them telepathically from afar.

Many discerning people suspected an alien influence in the rapid technological advances of the twentieth century. But the greatest breakthroughs related to the study of alien technology remained highly classified during this period. More relevant to this stage of the alien plan was the creation of a vast propaganda machine. In order to get their hands on more alien technology, the officials had to weave a web of lies around their involvement and comply with the alien agenda to keep the public guessing about their existence.

Ultimately, it didn't matter how we had achieved the age of electronic information. Looking back at the history of the alien intervention, the early phases had a single discernible goal—get humanity to bond more and more with technology than with each other until we could only imagine unity through a technological interface. Thus, the advent of personal technology provided the perfect opportunity to trap humanity in a concept of its progression that distracted us from more spiritually unifying potentials.

The keys to a timeline of spiritual awakening had been seeded in human consciousness anciently. But the aliens must have known this, because their strategy was based on distracting us from this very potential. Over the years, dependency on electronic technology dulled humanity's senses, making us more susceptible to invisible forms of psychic and technological interference and less invested in developing our natural abilities.

Manufactured wars, forced poverty, and all kinds of psychological manipulation created a feeling of powerlessness that pervaded the air. Most people were distracted with so many problems and so much disinformation, that they no longer felt empowered to discern the truth. And the alien presence was very effective in creating a puzzle that could not be easily solved.

The constant display of lights in the sky created the impression of a mysterious ET presence that was still investigating us from out in space, while secretly, this was a way to divert our attention from the bases being constructed underground. Curious truth-seekers were manipulated into wanting the elusive ETs to come closer, even holding UFO summoning events. At the same time, other forms of propaganda promoted fear to reinforce humanity's denial of the ET subject. The plan was to prevent humanity from becoming alert enough to collectively discern the dangers and form a unified response.

As the pages of the book continued to turn, Roya's awareness began skipping through scenes that showed some of the hidden impacts of the emerging technology culture. What seemed fairly innocent on a small scale looked very different on a larger scale. The enormous amounts of time people were spending on various types of electronic gaming and entertainment was syphoning away part of humanity's collective brainpower, and the newer trends were even more addictive. The visions revealed how people were more becoming entranced with technology and less connected to the natural world. Roya felt shocked at the accelerating loss of collective potential.

Many decades had been spent on developing and introducing ever more advanced gaming systems. It took more than a generation for enough people to become hooked on video games so that the next level of the progression would seem logical. Augmented Reality would simply be adopted into the culture without any rational thought about the evolutionary potentials being derailed.

The aliens wanted us to become integrated with the idea of immersive technology that blends physical reality with the digital environment. That way, the alien level of brain/mind interface technology would appear normal—or like the next step. The quest for ever more advanced forms of Augmented Reality and Virtual Reality was creating a culture of users that cared nothing for the environmental and social problems of the world outside of the new gaming life experience. The plan was to wait until we reached a certain stage of dependency on electronics, and for enough people to have become married to the idea of immersive technology, before introducing the next level of enticement.

Engineers and programmers thought they were designing a visionary new kind of reality that was radically innovative. They believed they were enhancing our ability to connect with each other. They lacked the discernment to know that they were aiding the plan of control by introducing the precursor technologies. They simply could not see that they had been raised since childhood inside a controlled system that had limited their imagination and shaped their thinking about humanity's future. The idea that we could all be naturally and empathically connected through pure love and light was completely missing from their programming.

With the introduction of thought-sensitive Augmented Reality and Virtual Reality, many assumed that humanity was becoming a truly advanced civilization. The mainstream media naïvely presented mostly positive views of these innovations, while framing opposing views as the product of an older generation that was out of touch with the new reality. The airwaves became filled with technology pushers who enthusiastically embraced the technological prison being designed for humanity as if it actually held the keys to our freedom. By the time the alien technology was introduced, the propaganda had cleverly programmed us to accept it as the gateway to our evolution.

Suddenly, Roya felt transported right into the body of Aaron. His memories were showing her the technology. This was the day that he first tried it himself. It looked like a type of headgear. He took it out of the box and placed it on his head, adjusting it to fit. He walked to a mirror to see how it looked. Roya noticed that he was an attractive looking young man with a fair complexion and short, wavy, brown hair. She could see the gear wrapping around his forehead, positioning four small cubes the width of quarters just above his brow. These contained very sensitive receiver/transmitters. Each of the cubes that touched his skin had a smooth disc that connected the user's brainwaves with the technology. Other smaller transmitter/receivers were positioned on the top, back, and sides of the head and were embedded into the rest of the architecture.

Roya was aware of Aaron's thoughts as the device began to switch on. It recognized the bioelectrical presence of the human brain and began to run diagnostics. She could feel a gentle frequency penetrating his brain. At first, it did not feel particularly unnatural, but the real effect would take hours to achieve for a first time user. As Aaron read the instructions, he sat down and relaxed with the feeling. First, the device had to build a brain map of the individual user before it could develop a unique handshake that could engage the mind.

After almost an hour of the mapping procedure, the first image tests began to project inside the brain. The device used the frequency of human thought to entrain the brain into a conscious dreamstate. This enhanced the user's ability to see the images that were being projected. The image testing was also part of the mapping procedure while training the user to focus on the internal imagery. New users were told to try the device in the dark, first, until they had learned how to focus on the images. It was like learning how to use a new set of senses, but the brain adapted rapidly to the presence of the system.

Time flowed by very quickly in the vision. After learning how to focus on the images and form the first mental commands, the holographic interface opened up and offered the first set of games. This was the next generation of virtual reality. The technology bypassed the eyes and caused the brain to see a frequency that contained holograms that the mind could interact with directly. The first gaming options were also designed to further train the new user's brain and mind to integrate with the new experience so that it felt increasingly more real with every session.

Roya knew something right away that gave these memories a powerful context. When she first found *The Circle and the Stars,* she had experienced seeing inwardly, like dreaming while she was awake. It was more powerful than just remembering something vividly, or daydreaming, because her inner vision became engaged as powerfully as the input from her physical senses. This was a natural ability; one she had begun to develop further through her experiences with the people of Lys.

Now, she was doing it again naturally in the Living Library, but the technology Aaron wore was designed to create similar experiences *artificially.* The deception was obvious. People who had not yet developed insight would think that this technology gave them something that they would not otherwise have. But in truth, the technology was designed to trap the human imagination, imprisoning it inside a limiting structure before it could awaken to the next level.

The agenda was to hijack the human brain before humanity could discover its natural ability to consciously evolve as a unified telepathic culture. Roya felt sickened by the idea, and then somehow, she reached up and pulled the device from her head. It was not her, though, but Aaron. He just had a similar insight as if he had been touched by a higher level of discernment. He was not fascinated with it. Rather, he recognized that this technology was incredibly dangerous to human freedom. He did not plan on ever using it again.

> It was hailed as a breakthrough in modern technology. Formally, they called it the Neural Link Interface, but in social media propaganda it was simply called "The Embrace". Among the resistors, however, it became known as the CyberCell. While this conveniently referred to the product's status as the next generation of cellular technology, this term also described how the technology was a prison for the mind.
>
> We remember watching our friends trying it. At first, it was introduced as a next generation gaming system. They used it to play a variety of multiplayer games that involved interacting with a shared holographic platform that could be manipulated directly by their minds. Even those of us who distrusted the influence of the technology had to admit that it was ingenious. The technology enhanced the human ability to see with the mind in a purely digital environment, while also expanding upon thought-sensitive AR and VR experiences that used the eyes. People thought it was like being psychic. They had no idea that using the technology destroyed the sensitivity needed to develop real psychic abilities. The aliens wanted to interfere with the natural evolutionary potential of the human brain in a way that captivated the imagination. In this way, people would think they were unlocking the brain's potential and would quickly lose their discernment about what was really happening.

The vision skipped into a number of scenes where people were trying the technology. Roya saw a couple of boys in a locker room somewhere, playing one of the multiplayer games before class. They wanted to show it off to their friends. While the game they were playing was not visible to anyone else, the two sat on a bench facing each other, immersed in a joint experience of the holographic game environment. Their eyes were open, but they were focused on the inner imagery shared between their minds that made the game seem like it was visually all around them. All the while, they were describing their experience to the others, making it seem incredibly enticing.

> People thought it was amazing to be able to control the games they played with thought alone. Being able to manipulate a virtual reality with the mind made physical reality less interesting. Users became entranced with the power they felt to create inside this digital environment. Whole virtual worlds were developed for the mind to explore, and people said it was like lucid dreaming. It was truly a clever and innovative way to capture the human imagination and imprison it inside an artificial reality. The technology was an instant hit with gamers all across the world, and soon, CyberLink Towers were as common as cell towers.
>
> The technology quickly became integrated with the most popular forms of social networking. People wearing the device could look at others passing by and see their public social media profiles and avatars. In this way, people could use their physical presence to automatically advertise their online persona. They called this the Wearable Web Presence. Gradually, more and more of the most popular networks and data streams became integrated with the CyberWeb so that people could surf social media networks with their minds.
>
> In the beginning, it was touted as the next level of Augmented Reality, and every feature that was added was called a Reality Enhancement. When people were not gaming in the virtual worlds, they were interacting with a digital environment that completely overlaid their perception of physical reality. This made people want to wear the devices all the time. After a while, newer generations of the device looked like nothing more than a fashion accessory.

As the scenes progressed, Roya saw increasingly more people walking around with the gear on their heads. People would often wear their CyberCells out on the town, looking for more people to game and network with. She overheard people talking about it and saying things like, "Yeah, I even wear mine to sleep. It's like a part of me."

The scene flashed to a group of teens at a mall, sitting around a table with their gear on, when they noticed another group nearby that was also wearing the gear. They looked at them, thinking a series of commands, and suddenly the gamer profiles of the other group popped up in their minds.

"This is so cool!" said one of the boys. From there, they used a feature that allowed them to ping the others and message them. They invited the other group to join them in a virtual game. Everyone was eager to show off his or her cyber identities in the gaming world. That was just one example of how the technology began to create a new kind of addictive social experience.

By far, the most destructive feature was the buzz stream. Even in the beginning, users talked about the interesting bodily sensations created by the technology, but the more advanced versions had the ability to stimulate the pleasure centers of the brain in ways that became addictive. Some of the more popular forms of artificial reality allowed users to buzz each other in a way that quickly began to replace human intimacy. People using the technology became distracted from real emotional exchanges, and instead, became nothing more than cyber thrill seekers. The idea of forming lasting relationships with people based on genuine emotional rapport began to fade from human culture. All users cared about was staying buzzed and entertained—anything less equaled boredom.

Through a planned series of upgrades, people were being enticed on a regular basis to value and crave the next level of enhancement to their new technological prison. They were also told that their electronic senses could be expanded if more people joined the rapidly growing global network. Users were constantly bated through the promise to gradually increase the intensity and variety of sensations they could experience. All across the world, people were joining the CyberWeb in droves.

A number of other methods were also being used to deliberately disconnect people from their natural state of being. The pervasive use of antidepressants and other prescription drugs paved the way for a new generation of mood enhancing pharmaceuticals that flooded the mass market and became synonymous with the cyber culture.

At the same time, the technology being used to create the network was entraining everyone with a planetary-wide frequency fence that blocked humanity's senses from any form of cosmic intelligence that could expose what was happening. CyberLink Towers beamed whole cities with a frequency that interfered with people's ability to access their emotions.

These methods were designed to disrupt humanity's connection to the wisdom of the Earth and the discernment of the heart. Without these two human faculties intact, it would be difficult to receive any form of guidance coming from the Angelic Realms or the natural world. This technological frequency was also set up to make people susceptible to the minds of the controllers themselves.

Throughout the world, hidden outposts were established for the aliens where they used thought amplification technology to project their mental energy into the population. Through telepathy, they sought to contact people and influence their thinking in ways that indoctrinated them into the new hierarchy of leadership. The ultimate goal was to program humanity to respond to the mental will of their new masters. Eventually, hybrids were introduced that looked human, but were part of the alien world management team. They were phased in to positions of leadership in every sector of society and quickly began to accelerate the plan of control.

People made such naïve assumptions about the alien agenda, having been gradually programmed to think that their involvement was beneficial. Hardly anyone realized that humanity was being tricked into welcoming a level of interference that would remain clandestine until it was too late.

The aliens needed us to choose the control of our own accord. Otherwise, their activities would be in violation of a galactic system of law that we were prevented from knowing. The technological interference blocked us from receiving the telepathic warnings and teachings of more spiritually evolved worlds. As far as the general population knew, the government had good reasons for keeping its knowledge of the alien presence a secret. What people did not suspect is that the aliens themselves were among the architects of the secrecy.

By the time it was officially announced that our government was working with ETs, no one seemed to realize the significance of such a statement. The media/propaganda machine cleverly distorted the admission by suggesting that we had known all along that ETs had been helping us with our technology—as if this could only be beneficial. They just began introducing talk of the alien influence one day as if this was the new normal, and people were too plugged in to care about what it really meant.

Not long after this, a number of massive projects were introduced that involved gathering natural resources to give to the alien nation in exchange for more technological enhancements. They tricked us into paying for technologies that would make us even more resourceful as a collective of cybernetic workers.

Humanity was being transformed into a manageable workforce, who valued alien technology and entertainment over the resources that were being taken from the Earth. With every new enhancement that was offered, it catalyzed a more forceful effort to convert others into the new workforce to meet the demands of our alien leaders, who never revealed their physical presence directly. The new human collective saw the obvious advantage that more workers would bring more enhancements to everyone more quickly. With only the pursuit of new technological enhancements on humanity's collective electronic brain, humanity barely noticed how much the Earth was being plundered.

The goal of civilization had changed. As long as people obeyed, they were allowed a place in the new world order. Eventually, the frequency of the electronic collective overtook the resonance of natural human thought, permanently erasing the sense of having a human identity outside of the cyber system. Humanity's ability to express itself through language diminished, having been gradually replaced by the commands used to interface with the digital environment. The only freedom left was found in the virtual world, which was actually a prison for the collective soul. Eventually, an identity shift occurred that involved bonding with an artificial intelligence that was introduced to manage the whole system of slavery.

The technology had changed the resonance of humanity and the functioning of society so that eventually, most people assumed that the only way to survive was to submit to the technology. In the end, we had lost our way because of an addiction. In a matter of years, we had become unrecognizable to our former selves.

When there was no place left for the Resistance, we retreated into the mountains where our journey became invisible to the authorities. We were protected by a mysterious presence that sought to guide us to safety so that I could make this record as a warning to other worlds. I leave this Earth knowing that this record is preserved by the angelic stewards that guard the little knowledge that remains here. My spirit goes with these words to wherever knowledge needs to be protected.

Do not let humanity's fate become yours! Value the natural world! Value your natural senses! Value your natural emotional connection with each other! Value love and creative freedom! Beware of an alien presence in your skies! Be discerning! Do not barter freedoms for the illusion of security! Believe in your purpose as stewards of the living creation! Listen to the Gaia of your world! Unite yourselves to protect your sovereignty! Unite yourselves and remember that you are One!

In the last scene, Roya saw Aaron in the mountains somewhere, sheltered from the pervasive effects of the Frequency. He was kneeling in prayer, and as the image zoomed out, she saw a group of angels that had appeared before him. They had asked him to make a record, and they held before him a book of light, which Aaron was imbuing with his words and memories. There was no need for him to make a physical record in this time, for there would be no one left in the future to read it. This was a record collected by angels to serve a multidimensional plan—to be preserved as an artifact from a potential timeline that Roya knew had to be averted.

A million thoughts were racing through her mind. She knew now that she had to return to the temple and tell everyone what she had learned—but she needed more information first. *How do we prevent this from happening?* she thought, wondering if Claire and the librarians might answer her. But no one responded.

The book closed by itself, and the imagery faded from her awareness. Looking around, she hoped to find someone to talk to, but then a wave of light passed through her unexpectedly. She felt connected again to a source of light that gently embraced her from within.

Just then, she noticed someone standing across the room that appeared to be observing her. The woman stood at the edge of an aisle and seemed to have been deliberately hiding her face in a book, only showing her eyes. Roya was sure that the woman was now aware that Roya had seen her, but before she could investigate further, another wave of light wrapped around her.

A deep feeling of peace came over her as she relaxed into stillness. Her body then began to fill up with light from within, and it quickly overwhelmed her senses. The room grew brighter as if light was streaming from inside of everything around her until the Living Library disappeared.

19

THE ALIEN NATION

When Ami had not emerged from the portal in Sharindaya, there was an immediate reaction of panic.

"Where's Ami?!" yelled Frank.

"I don't know! She was right behind me," said Mandy frantically. By now, they were all staring at the portal in disbelief.

"Just wait a moment," responded Claire as a few more people emerged, "she might have fallen behind. There were a lot of people that entered right when we did."

Claire wondered at first if Ami had gotten distracted by some of the other people and ended up aligning with someone else's pathway, but after another minute went by, she knew something else must be keeping her. After several more people entered Sharindaya through the portal, the activity ceased.

"Wait here, and stay together," instructed Claire.

For a moment, Amaron resisted her intent to go back, but he sensed she knew what she was doing and let go. Claire stepped into the portal, intending to go to the Switch Room where she could better sense Ami's location. She expected this would be a safe place to investigate, but when she got there, she noticed something strange. Across the vast, cavernous room, she could see that the portal to Adinai had gone dark. She tried engaging an energy link with the portal, but the transfer tunnel would not completely form without a connection to the other side. Instead, without moving, she focused her awareness on the portal, collapsing the distance in her mind's eye until she could see it up close. Scanning the whole structure with her mind, she perceived nothing but a rock wall inside one of the large palladium rings. The portals to either side were working fine. Each of them glowed a different color, but this one was inactive.

"The way is shut," said the collective voice of the Formelle. *"This is for the safety of Lys."*

"Did Ami return to Adinai?" asked Claire telepathically.

"Yes. She is safe. They are both safe."

This was not a welcome message, even though it was reassuring. She was not looking forward to explaining to the families that Ami was somehow safe in an inaccessible cavern filled with soldiers. For a moment, she scanned her memories for any alternative way into Adinai, but she realized there was no way back. Her mind raced to find an explanation to what she knew they would see as a problem. She reasoned that if the Formelle were conscious enough to protect Lys by shutting the portal, they were also conscious enough to know for certain that Ami and Roya were safe. Ami would not have taken this risk unintentionally, and Claire trusted that the Formelle would not have allowed her to return if she had no purpose in being there. She must have been following her soul's guidance, but she did not have time to discuss it with anyone. Still, this would not be easy to explain.

When Claire returned, everyone was staring at her with great expectancy.

"Where's Ami?" pleaded Frank desperately.

"She returned to Adinai," stated Claire.

"What!" Mandy reacted in shock. "Why would she do that?"

"I don't know," answered Claire emotionally, feeling empathetic to how everyone was receiving the news. "The Formelle assured me that she and Roya are safe. We can only assume there's a reason why she felt called to return."

"Well, can't we go back to get her?" cried Frank frantically.

"The portal to Adinai is now closed, but I'm certain the council can give us more information. We should inform them immediately about what happened."

They were all silent for a moment, processing what they had just been told. All three parents had looks of astonishment and disbelief on their faces.

"I don't like this. I don't like this at all!" worried Soraya. "First Roya disappears and now this!"

"Well, come on then," insisted Mandy, not wanting to waste any time.

She tugged at her dad's arm, pulling him back away from the portal, feeling his resistance to surrender.

Even as Ami reached the stairs at the end of the Welcome Hall in Adinai, she was still sorting out what had compelled her to return. It was not just

Roya. It was a calling. She felt guided. It was as though her mind had taken a backseat, allowing her intuition to move her body without thinking.

This was a strange new feeling. She should have been scared. From the top of the stairs, she could see soldiers holding some kind of weapons to the far left. Two of them were entering the main building complex. She was cautious, but unafraid, as the guidance was overriding her concerns for safety.

At just the right moment, she felt an impulse to creep down the stairs quietly and head to the right. A minute later, she was out of sight behind some buildings, and she could see the stairs leading to the temple far ahead. After another long pause, she began to walk right through the open field before the temple. Although she was noticeably visible, something told her not to be in a hurry—just to be quiet and trust in her vision. She had clearly seen an image in her mind of Roya reappearing. Something told her that the soldiers would be busy for some time searching the buildings, and Roya would need her to be at the temple when she returned.

Ami tried sending a thought to Mandy to let everyone know she was OK, but it was not very strong. She was more focused on the temple up ahead, obeying the force of guidance that seemed to be pulling her gently along. She observed how it felt to be in this no-mind state. A point below the center of her chest felt like it was opening, and she was trying to recall what the book had said about it; something about her center of gravity being a center of consciousness.

When she reached the stairs to the temple, she did not even look back to see if she had been noticed. With every step, she felt more invisible, and somehow, she felt protected. Inside, the crystal was glowing with a soft white light. Roya was nowhere to be seen, but Ami had the strangest feeling that Roya had never left the room. She walked to the place where Roya had been standing when she disappeared, but she felt nothing. Then, she felt guided to walk around behind the crystal, so she could gaze at it while having a view of the entrance. It was here that she began to realize that it was the crystal that had called her to return.

For a moment, she felt frantic as she feared that she might be ill-prepared to deal with what lie ahead. Surely, the soldiers would eventually come to the temple, but would Roya return in time, and how would they escape?

"Do not be afraid, Ami," said a voice from the crystal.

Ami was surprised, not as much by the voice, but by the way it sounded. She wondered if it was the Formelle, but the voice sounded more like that of an individual being. It was more personal, and had a gentle, feminine quality to it.

"Who are you?" she whispered.

"I am a gift, and you are one of my bearers."

Ami was fascinated. She felt honored in some way but could not brush aside the need for more answers.

"I don't understand. Is Roya coming back?"

"Yes, and when she does, she will need your courage—the same courage that brought you here. There's no turning back now. We need you to perform a task for us. Events are accelerating, and there is a great need for courageous action. We thank you for answering the call."

"What call?" questioned Ami quietly, impatient for more answers. She was not sure what she had gotten herself into. "I thought I was coming back to get Roya when she reappeared so we could go home. What kind of task are you talking about?"

"The way is shut. Another way home has been provided. We know it will be difficult to trust without having all the information, but you are both ready for this. You will know what to do when the time comes, but for now, we must ask you to meditate. Receive the gift inwardly, and do not doubt that you made the right choice to return here."

Ami was beginning to break down, realizing how separated she was from her dad and Mandy, and yet, a soft and comforting glow of peace was forming around her. She knelt down on the floor and began to relax, her fear and apprehensions fluttering away as the energy of peace began to embrace her. She could not help wondering when she would see everyone again, but the thought of being there for Roya kept her centered.

As the peace deepened, the iridescent white light of the crystal began to reach out to her. She sensed the presence of a being arising from within the crystal until she saw a graceful human form appear. She was made of light, wrapped in a cloak made of light, and her eyes glowed with a radiance that pierced Ami's soul. Her grace and beauty were captivating.

Ami's eyes opened wide, and instantly, the presence of this masterful being began to cause a shift in her breathing. Just like Roya's experience, Ami was learning to breathe in the light and raise the vibration of her body. The woman continued to move forward until she knelt down before Ami, radiating a deep humility that penetrated Ami's heart and completely disarmed her. She took a deep breath in unison with Ami, and it felt like a part of her presence was reflecting into Ami's body. Gradually, Ami surrendered more, until it began to feel like the woman was breathing for her, showing her how to take in more light with each breath.

She placed her right hand over the center of Ami's chest—the light pulsing into her as they continued to breathe together. Her face was full of kindness, more beautiful than any Ami had ever seen. She was ageless and timeless, and her presence filled the room. Every move she made was silent, and Ami could feel her as if they were one.

"You are made of Light!" said the woman telepathically; her lips did not move. *"You come from the Light, you were made to serve the Light, and you shall return to the Light. The Power to create with Light is in your name!"*

My name? thought Ami, pondering the message, until something began to shift. She drew in another slow, deep, conscious breath, and felt her whole sense of being shifting into alignment with the hidden code of her name. "I AM," said Ami out loud. *My name is an anagram of I AM,* she realized.

"Any intention that you place after these words will contain the manifestation power of I AM. Remember this, and you will align with the pathway to safety."

A deep silence hung in the air after these words had resonated into her mind. Next, the woman lifted her hand away from Ami's chest and touched her on the center of her forehead. Ami felt the light streaming into her mind and closed her eyes. With each breath, she felt more at peace in the light until she seemed to center on a single affirmation: *I Am Safe.*

Several moments must have passed before she felt guided to open her eyes. The room was empty again, but she could still feel part of the being's presence within her. The glow of her own aura was brighter than ever, and she wondered if the being was just invisible, or if she had returned to her own realm through the crystal. Either way, the experience of connection with the light had expanded her field of consciousness tremendously.

Ami tried not to react to the sense that the soldiers were getting closer. She could feel them, like a dark cloud on the horizon of her mind, but the empowering light of the being, still resonating in her body, kept her focused. Several times, she started to feel fear on the very edge of her consciousness, but the light told her without words that she had the power to remain safe. Even as she felt them approaching the side of the city closest to the temple, she continued to ignore any fear thoughts as they arose. As far as she was concerned, this was all a test of her wits and an opportunity to learn the power of I AM.

"I am safe," she whispered to herself. "I am safe, and I am fearless."

For a moment, Ami felt the power of her affirmations as an impenetrable shield, as if nothing could have moved her from that place. Then, a shift in the field of the temple caused her to become more alert. She could feel

Roya's presence entering the field and could see the outline of her form appearing just around the right side of the crystal.

Waves of liquid light washed through Roya's form like water, pouring her physical presence back into its place. But something was different. Even before Roya had fully arrived, Ami got up and walked around the crystal to get a better view. Roya was standing in the same place she had been when she disappeared, but without the book in her hands. Ami could feel how Roya was perfectly integrated with the same light that she could still feel resonating through her own body.

A quick series of light pulses flashed through Roya's form, and then she was fully back. She looked startled and did not immediately realize that Ami was standing next to her. She first looked down at her feet, and when she turned her head in Ami's direction, Ami could see a look in Roya's eyes that was angelic.

They both had a shimmer of white light around them, and their minds were very clear. For a moment, their exchange was non-verbal as the field of light between them seemed to synchronize them into a perfect state of connection. To Roya, Ami's eyes looked just as angelic, and they both shared a sense of timelessness that enveloped them.

"Where is everyone?" asked Roya out loud as she suddenly reacted to the unexpected scene of the temple's emptiness.

"Shhhhh," warned Ami. "After you disappeared," she whispered, "a group of soldiers entered the city, and everyone evacuated." Ami paused for a moment, because Roya looked like she was still processing whatever had happened to her before she returned.

"I came back for you," Ami said after a while, intending to bring Roya into focus with the present situation. "Claire was certain that you would be safe, but I felt called to come back and wait for you. And now I don't know what's supposed to happen. The soldiers are here, and the transport tunnel is now closed."

Suddenly, Roya was overcome with a feeling that she needed to tell Ami everything before she forgot. Something was happening inside her. The memory of her journey to the library seemed to be fading, or at least parts of it were. Her sense of the order of events was starting to become mixed up. Listening to Ami explain the current situation was interfering with all she was trying to hold in her consciousness. But Ami was insisting that they become more alert to the situation outside the temple.

"We have to talk. I just learned something really important!" pressed Roya.

Her eyes began to well up with tears just thinking about it all. Her body could not fully handle the immense feelings evoked by the memories of what she had seen.

"Can't it wait?" pleaded Ami, realizing that Roya still did not comprehend the full extent of their dire situation.

"I don't know," said Roya, still in a daze. "I feel like I'm starting to lose touch with part of it. How long was I gone?"

"About twenty minutes, maybe more. I'm not sure," replied Ami hastily.

"That's all?! It felt like I was gone for hours."

Roya was starting to notice Ami's sense of urgency. Ami kept looking over to the temple exit, and Roya could tell that she was concerned about the soldiers, so she decided to follow Ami's cues, even though a part of her felt oblivious to any danger.

"Let's see if we can spot them," prompted Ami, pulling Roya along with her. "If the coast is clear, we should find another place to hide. I'm sure they'll check in here."

Roya followed Ami as she led them to the exit. Peeking around a pillar, they could see soldiers converging after having completed their search of the surrounding buildings. Then, they clearly saw one of them pointing in their direction. They were now proceeding across the field between the main building complex and the stairs to the temple.

"Oh no!" Ami cried.

"What should we do?!" exclaimed Roya. "We're trapped!"

"No, we're not," asserted Ami. "We must never believe that we're trapped." She remembered clearly being told that there was another way out. "I know this looks bad, but I think we can handle with this."

"There's hardly any place to hide in here," said Roya, looking around. The room was completely open with nothing to hide behind—except the crystal, but that would surely make them vulnerable if the soldiers were to come far enough in to see them.

"Look!" Ami pointed to the two pillars that formed part of the entrance. Each pillar stuck out about six inches from the inside wall so that you could hide behind it. Of course, once the soldiers walked in far enough and turned around, they would be exposed, but that part did not bother Ami. "When they enter, they'll probably head right for the crystal. So, if we hide behind these pillars, we'll just wait 'til they're in far enough, and then we'll sneak out. They probably already searched the buildings, so we should be safe there."

"That's brilliant," said Roya.

Both girls were adept at playing hide and seek as children. Sometimes, when there was not a good place to hide, they had to rely on other skills, such as remaining completely still and silent until the seeker had passed, even pretending to be invisible. For this reason, both girls shared a silent understanding that they could just imagine they were invisible and escape anyone's attention. Ami's plan needed no more explanation. Roya knew that they would both hold the focus of blending in with their surroundings.

"OK, you take that side," Ami pointed to the right as she ducked behind the pillar to the left.

They caught a glance of the soldiers getting closer to the temple before they backed into their positions. Both girls stood close against the wall, arching shoulders back and sucking in their stomachs. They tried to be as thin as possible and adjusted their breathing, so they could be quiet. The adrenaline pumping through their veins did not make it easy.

Roya felt supported by the stability of Ami's presence as they heard the soldiers approach the steps. They were bonded together in a way that felt comforting, and it allowed Roya to trust what was unfolding. She did not know what she would've done if Ami had not been there to guide her. Ami was on hyper alert to sense when the window of opportunity would open, expecting Roya would follow her cue. She was certain that Roya would see or sense her movement. They were counting on the light of the crystal to be a distraction, but Ami was a little worried about the noise factor. Fortunately, the soldiers were talkative.

"I can't believe we haven't found anything," one of the soldiers grumbled. "I thought these people were supposed to have all kinds of tech."

"It's obviously hidden," said another soldier. "Keep your eyes peeled. If we don't find *something,* the commander's gonna blow his lid."

"Yeah, like he did when we lost Kravitz on the last mission. Hell, I didn't know the bridge was gonna close. I thought we had another ten minutes."

"That wouldn't happen to us, would it?" worried a soldier from the rear of the group. The first two were just reaching the top of the stairs before the entrance.

"No, this is different," explained one of the leaders. "Time tunnels are trickier than the energy bridge we just came through. Since we came here from the same time reference, the connection is more stable. Besides, even if it did close, they'd be able to locate us and open another one after the machines have cooled down. Kravitz wasn't so lucky, but I don't blame the team. Those psychics are trained not to value us and to close the bridge at the first sign of trouble. I think one of 'em just got jittery."

"Well, I'd like to know which one it was so I could teach him a lesson. No one should get left behind like that, especially in the age of the dinosaurs."

"Whoa!" exclaimed one of the last soldiers to reach the top of the stairs. "Is that what I think it is?" said another.

All six of the soldiers entered the temple in pairs and spread out in front of the glowing crystal, their backs still facing the entrance. They continued to talk excitedly, and several of them pulled out electronic instruments that were taking some readings from the crystal. Ami knew this was their one shot.

Without hesitation, they moved together at nearly the same moment. They quickly disappeared through the exit, creeping silently down the stairs. The coast was clear. There was no one in sight. When they reached the bottom of the stairs, they both began to walk more briskly toward the nearest building. Roya noticed that Ami was heading to the right, when she seemed to remember that the Welcome Hall was around the buildings to the left, but she felt intuitively that Ami knew what she was doing.

They were nearly to the buildings and were prepared to look for a hiding place, when suddenly, two soldiers rounded the corner of one of the buildings to their left. Ami and Roya stopped in their tracks. The soldiers were 30 yards away but did not appear to have seen them. Very carefully, the girls began to creep toward the corner of the nearest building, praying that they could quietly sneak behind it before they were seen.

Just then, one of the soldiers glanced up and said, "Hey, look."

"Let's get 'em!" shouted the other.

Suddenly, both the girls and the two soldiers broke into a sprint. They had only a few seconds lead on the soldiers before they would round the corner. Their only hope was to lose them inside the building complex, but by the time they reached the next intersection, the soldiers had spotted them, just before the girls disappeared around the next corner.

Ami and Roya ran at top speed, hoping they could disappear around another building before the soldiers had them in view again. After making two more turns, Ami stopped them both. She wanted to peek back to see if the soldiers were still behind them.

Roya stayed hidden while Ami cautiously peeked around the side of the building.

"Do you see anything?" whispered Roya.

"No," said Ami. "That's weird, I thought they were right behind us."

"Do you think we lost them?"

Ami had the same question in her mind and remained optimistic, but something about the silence bothered her. She expected that she would be able to hear their footsteps. They had not been far behind. Then, suddenly, Ami felt the shocking jolt of an electrical charge and dropped to the ground in front of Roya. For a second, Roya didn't know what happened, but she quickly noticed the two soldiers walking toward them from an unexpected angle, holding some type of energy weapons.

They must have doubled back around. For a split second, she wondered if she could still make a run for it, even though she did not want to leave Ami. But before she could even complete the thought, she saw one of the soldiers' weapons light up and she was struck by a jolt of energy that literally knocked her to the ground. Both girls were out cold.

"Nice shot!" said one of the soldiers as if they were playing a video game.

The other soldier was lost in an observation.

"Hey, Gordon," he said, as they approached the girls. "Do you notice anything strange about these two?"

"Yeah," he replied, leaning over to pull back the collar of Ami's shirt, revealing the tag. "They're both wearing surface clothing," he said, perplexed. "How do you think they got down here?"

"I don't know, but that means there must be another way in from the surface. Chief's gonna love this."

"Whoa, do you see that?" Gordon pointed out. "They're glowing, just like the others."

"What do you mean? I don't see a glow."

"Just take your eyes out of focus a little and look more closely. I'm telling you, Vic, there's a glow."

"Hey, you're right. I think I can see it. How can that be if they're from the surface? I thought Chief said only the people down here were like that."

"What he said was that the people down here were semi-physical and semi-etheric. They can phase-shift into another vibration where they are less visible to us, but they have a glow when they are dense enough to see. That's why we have to use electromagnetic weapons to stun them so they drop out of their own frequency."

"That's weird about these two, though," remarked Vic as he was admiring his weapon.

"I know. Definitely interesting, but the clock is ticking. You get this one, and I'll get the other. We need to get them back to the bridge. I'm sure they'll want to interrogate these two on the other side."

Roya and Ami remained unconscious during the trip across the energy bridge the military had used to infiltrate the caverns of Adinai. They were oblivious to being transported into a deep underground testing facility for exotic technology.

The testing facility was one of several that involved the use of experimental psychic technology—or psy-tech—that artificially amplifies the power of human thought. It was here that a group of psychics used the 'tech,' as they called it, to open a physical channel of energy—or energy bridge—between distant places, and even between distant times. The process involved projecting one's mind to a target location to link with its physical resonance. The machines then assisted by amplifying the presence of entangled particles until they formed a connection big enough for people and objects to move through.

Once the link was established, the bridge would stay open for a certain amount of time. By trial and error, they had learned to take into account a number of factors. There was always some uncertainty, but everyone involved on a trip knew the risks.

For years, the secret project had tried to remote view into the hidden cities of Lys, but something had kept them cloaked. Even the most advanced psychics could not gain a clear percept of them, but that did not stop them from trying. What they did not fully understand was that the whole population of Lys was at a higher vibration. Even capturing several of their people in the Colorado caverns had not revealed the secret of their civilization's seeming invisibility, which was not entirely physical, but also emotional.

The Lyssians were a joyful people, light-hearted and clear of mind, which made their energetic signature hard to locate for those who do not resonate with joy; but joy alone could not protect them forever. The Earth itself was changing, collapsing the dimensions together in an attempt to bring many different vibratory levels of existence into harmony and integration with a shared reality of oneness. The very heart of the galaxy was overseeing this monumental restructuring, nurturing whole worlds into oneness with a growing galactic community. Not every living world, however, had evolved to respect the freedom and sovereignty of other planetary cultures. Though the seed of galactic unity was present in every world, in too many of them, this seed had remained dormant.

Roya and Ami remained unconscious for the medical evaluation. They had been injected with a sedative and then scanned for pathogens. All of the examiners were fascinated by the results and were debating how the girls had come to develop the same type of glow they had witnessed around the people of Lys. There was very little time with which to explore the subject as the commander had ordered the evaluations in preparation for a highly classified meeting. They had to be sure that the girls had not brought any contagions from the surface that could contaminate the sterile environment they would be taken to for interrogation.

Though both girls remained connected to each other through a field of oneness, they awakened in a state of fear. The long rectangular room they were in was dark, with only a few very dim lights that were embedded into the table. Both Roya and Ami were seated at one end, and their hands and feet were tightly bound. As their eyes began to find their focus in the dark, they could just make out the form of several people seated along the sides of the table toward the other end.

They appeared to be in a boardroom of sorts, but the dimly lit room had an ominous feeling to it. As Roya strained her eyes, something about the people on the left felt off to her. She kept blinking, hoping her eyes would clear, but they were still blurry for several minutes. Then, she saw something that made her heart start pounding even harder. Ami saw it nearly at the same time that Roya did. The three people seated to the left, toward the other end of the long table, *were not human.*

To the right were several people that definitely looked human, wearing some type of uniforms, but the beings to the left had thin bodies and large heads with big black eyes. Their mouths were small and they had two little slits that appeared to be nostrils, and no discernible ears. Their presence was cold and unsettling. These beings were clearly emotionless.

Both Ami and Roya began to panic inside, and at the same time they felt paralyzed. Some kind of pressure held them right in their place, even beyond their bindings, and once they were fully aware of their surroundings, they could not even muster the will to look away.

At the very end of the table, they saw another being with a large head and black eyes lean forward from the shadows into a light that was faintly shining up from the end of the table. It was another alien, and this one was staring straight at them. Strangely, the others were just facing forward toward the humans opposite them, but Roya sensed that they were still looking directly at her and Ami through their peripheral vision.

"How did you enter the caverns?" demanded the alien leader telepathically.

Both Roya and Ami were silent, but their thoughts were racing. They were not prepared to resist the power of the leader's mind, or any of them, for that matter. The alien leader seemed to have complete control of the mental environment, causing their memories to spill into the room. The three men on the right were as emotionless as the aliens.

Roya could feel intuitively what was coming next. She knew that the alien's probing would trace the story back to her finding the book, and she would become the target. She seemed to have no control over the interrogation process. The alien's mind was subtly questioning her telepathically in ways that produced streams of thought from her subconscious mind that he could read. Roya could sense that he was getting closer to something he was searching for as memories of the whole journey flashed through her awareness uncontrollably.

The Flower Memorial Library, the journey with Claire into the Inner Earth, the Council of Lys; Roya wondered how dangerous it was to the people of Lys that so many memories of them were falling into the wrong hands. Then the process seemed to stop on a single moment; the moment when Roya had disappeared from the temple. Roya felt the interest of the alien suddenly pique. What happened next came as a shock to all her senses.

It was like the striking of a cobra, and all at once, the full force of the alien leader's mind gripped Roya's consciousness. She sensed a dark energy closing around her that emanated from the alien's brainwaves as he probed even more intrusively into the depths of her mind. He was seeking access to the light of the future that had come through the crystal and what it had revealed to her. His grip felt punishing as he squeezed tighter, searching for a way to gain access to it, but something was stopping him from getting past the moment of Roya's disappearance. Roya was not even sure if *she* could remember what happened at this point. A seal seemed to be in place, like all her memories of the library were shutting down, and the alien became frustrated that Roya possessed a connection to the crystal that he could not penetrate.

His psychic grip had become physically painful, her whole nervous system reeling. For a second, Roya started to disassociate from her body, her consciousness trying to find a way to escape from the terrifying grip of the alien's mind. But another thought began to arise that gave her strength. Somehow, she had been prepared for this in a most unexpected way. She began to think of Harry Potter and the Dementors and all the lessons he had learned about the Defense Against the Dark Arts. It was like the books and movies were speaking to her, and suddenly she knew that she needed to find her focus on a joyful memory.

"You can do it," she heard a gentle voice say. *"You can repel his mind."*

It was as if her soul had been waiting for this moment, had known it would come, and had invited it; because it was the only way to master the art of psychic defense. She began to hear the sound of waves crashing in the distance. The sound grew closer until it swelled around her, carrying her into a feeling of buoyancy, and then she recognized the distinct feeling of whales. It was the narwhals! As if they had known exactly what she would need in this moment, Roya's intent to find a joyful memory was instantly met by a sense of their companionship. They had arrived with a show of force that was unexpectedly powerful. What started as a memory quickly became a living connection. They were with her, swimming alongside her, in a space of shared dreaming. And then one of them swam closer and affirmed a deeper connection, merging hearts and minds with her.

Just then, she remembered the vision and the feeling of the tusk. *Like a wand,* she thought, and suddenly her heart exploded with joy knowing that, somehow, they had known her so well—had known of her love for Harry Potter—and had symbolically given her both a wand and a patronus at the same time. In her imagination, the narwhal had become her patronus—a powerful guardian and shield. She felt so loved and honored that tears of joy began to well up in her eyes. The part of her imagination that had always been able to see herself in the books had just come to life. And in that moment, Harry Potter was real.

The revelation quickly brought the situation into focus. She was slightly out of her body, but now she knew that she had to come back.

"Relax your focus," she heard the whales say. *"Do not fear his mind."*

Roya connected into the joy of the whales and began to relax her resistance. At first, she struggled to allow the alien's grip. It felt so uncomfortable, but something was beginning to happen that neither of them expected. A connection was forming through her third eye. She felt the tip of the Narwhal tusk extending from her forehead. It was like a conduit was opening within her that could feed the alien's greedy mind, and an inexhaustible supply of light was flowing through the tusk. The presence of the tusk was buffering the connection between her mind and his, allowing her to channel the light without being depleted.

At first, the alien continued to pull on the light, probing her whole energy body as if to examine what was happening and how best to exploit the connection. But Roya was increasingly mastering the new state. It helped to imagine that the aliens were Dementors that she could fend off with her joy. Gradually, the flow of light increased, tempting the alien to steal even more. He wanted the power that was in the light but did not want the connection. Roya could feel that he wanted to remain separate, but her nature was to see everything as another form of love. The two realities could not co-exist.

Suddenly, the other aliens became engaged. Sensing the unusual nature of this exchange, they began trying to suppress Roya's energy to stop the connection from growing. They all seemed alarmed by the fact that Roya's awareness was expanding into theirs, and they did not want anyone to read them or know anything about them. Their reaction was fierce, and both Roya and Ami could feel it. There was a palpable feeling of anger about not having complete control over what was happening. That is about the only alien emotion that could be sensed from the whole exchange.

Until that moment, the oppressive mental control of the alien presence had kept everyone in silence, but something had been building in Ami's consciousness, a feeling that she could not ignore...the feeling that she could not live in terror or allow herself or Roya to be oppressed. It was a sense of justice that swelled from within her, until it suddenly shifted to a sense of command.

Without warning, Ami yelled, "STOP!"

The energy of the whole room shifted, and the auras of the two girls became radiant. The courage and strength needed to speak that one word was tremendous, and the word had an instantaneous effect, breaking the psychic grip of the aliens. Somehow, the power between all of them felt more balanced. For a moment, Ami was unafraid, as if the affirmation "I Am Fearless" had conjured a hidden place of power from within her that demanded an equal place in the room.

The alien leader retracted his focus and seemed to be examining the fact that Ami's voice had broken the spell of his mind control. Both girls expected some kind of backlash, but strangely, there was little reaction. What none of them could understand was that Ami's sense of command and Roya's surrender had allowed a presence of oneness into the room that was more expansive than the oppressive force of these alien superminds. That, however, did not stop them from exercising other forms of control.

"They are no longer any use to us," said the alien leader to the commander telepathically. *"Their souls, however, are stronger than most. Use them for the machine. They might be just what you are looking for."*

Just then, Roya saw the man sitting closest to her on the right make a gesture, and out of nowhere, two men emerged from the darkness behind her and Ami. There was no time to think about what the alien leader had meant before she saw a man's hand holding a needle and syringe next to her. She swallowed hard and wished she could reach out and hold Ami's hand, but Ami was already unconscious.

Across the room, she could not help noticing that one of the men had turned toward her and was looking her directly in the eyes. He had an oddly gentle looking face, even though there was something about him that seemed alien. He had a goatee and a mustache, and long, curly, dark hair—an unusual contrast to the other men with short military haircuts. His gaze caught Roya off guard, but then she felt the pinch of the needle, and everything went black.

20

SOUL TRAP

Lex was lying on his back on the top bunk in his room, deep in thought over a plan that he had been constructing. If he and Ram were ever to make contact with their new friends again he would have to construct a narrative that could protect them both in case they were ever interrogated. He believed he had a solution, but it would be risky. First, it involved making a series of remote viewing observations of the abandoned building and the explorers inside. For this reason, he was just beginning to relax into his remote viewing focus, extending his mind into the structure to look for Aaron and the others.

They were not hard to lock onto. The link to Aaron in particular was still very strong, but he tried not to focus on it for the moment. His intent was to build a narrative around the idea of himself and Ram as informers who had first become aware of the explorers from a distance. He would scan the structure, pretending that he was just practicing the remote viewing focuses he had learned from his training. Then, he would pretend that he had sensed the explorers and decided to investigate a possible intrusion into the city. This way, if they were discovered in their next excursion, they would have a cover story that supported their reasons for going up into the building to investigate.

He was already constructing alternate versions of his memories, imagining that it was the explorers that had created the hole at the sealed entrance to the abandoned station. He had to create a completely different story in his mind, and to move through it, back and forth, until he had covered his tracks and obscured the original memories. They had to be prepared to pretend that their actions represented loyalty to the authorities, even if it was out of place to privately investigate such matters.

Lex wanted to be confident in the narrative that he was building before imprinting it into Ram's mind, but mostly he was enjoying the process of observing his new friends. With eyes closed, he focused on seeing through the field of non-local, universal mind, just as he had been taught; something that had become as natural to him as tying his shoes. In the advanced levels of his psychic development training, he had been taught to use these techniques to keep tabs on the people he would eventually be responsible for managing. Part of the idea was to give people like him a presence of psychic superiority that his subordinates would respect. If he could demonstrate his ability to see what they were doing, even when he was not in the room with them, they would be more apt to follow orders and accept the hierarchy of leadership. Lex knew this was just a fear tactic, but what his own superiors did not realize is that he was exceptionally gifted.

He had always been fascinated by the idea of an awareness field everywhere in the universe that he could tap into. Why would people only use such a gift for spying and frightening people when they could be explorers instead? To give such training to a curious and gifted mind was more than a happy accident. Lex believed that his soul had a purpose: to turn the use of these gifts toward something that his superiors had not intended— something that might actually create a shift in the direction of the secret civilization.

From the safety of his room, he zoomed in on the activity in the upper levels of the underground building. Several of his new friends were searching the structure, but the most interesting thing was Aaron's artwork. He had already covered nearly fifteen feet of wall with chalk art and had created a basic outline of almost ten more. Lex tried to get a clear percept of the colorful forms, but some of it seemed too abstract. There were forms that he did not recognize, but the colors were exciting, and Aaron seemed completely absorbed in what he was doing.

Every once in a while, Lex would retract his focus of attention to sense if any other psychics might be noticing what he was doing. When he determined that the coast was clear, he would gradually extend his focus again, like a clam cautiously opening its shell, prepared to pull back at any sign of danger. He would observe for a minute, then pull back again, trying to remain emotionally detached to what he was seeing. There was certainly a risk to what he was doing, but something told him that he was safe, and this was all meant to be. Then, something unexpected happened. He felt another signature that was different but reminded him of the energy of the explorers from the surface.

What is that? he thought to himself. The signature felt strong and attractive, almost irresistible to his curious mind. It was coming from somewhere in the city, on the levels below. He relaxed his focus again and then reached out with his awareness, allowing a connection to form. This time, the signal became clear, and he could feel it in his chest. It was not just a psychic signature. It was an emotional call for help.

Roya and Ami were awakened suddenly by the injection of some kind of stimulant that instantly brought them into the awareness of a very strange looking room. They were each lying on an examination table, hands and feet still restrained. Standing over them was a middle-aged man with a shaved head, very pale skin and glasses. He wore a white lab coat. His cold stare held a complete disregard for their feelings.

Looking around the room, they could see all kinds of computers, lab equipment, and a number of unfamiliar pieces of technology, some of which were connected to large glass tubes. Just before them was a large rectangular observation window, but from their position on the tables, they could not see what lay beyond. The lights inside the room were dim, but bright enough to see the details around them.

Gone was the suffocating pressure of the alien minds, but neither of the girls felt any impulse to speak. At least they could turn their heads to see one another. They looked into each other's eyes, focusing on the connection between them and trying to build their vibrations again. They could still feel part of the connective field of Lys, and they could both still see each other's auras, though they were not as bright as before.

"Do you know where you are?" said the man in the white lab coat.

For a second, Roya's mind took the question seriously, trying to focus on any awareness of truth about their situation, though it became apparent that the man had intended to answer his own question.

"This is one of the most super-secret labs on Earth," he said with pride. "And it's going to be your new home."

There was something twisted about the way he delivered this news. He was clearly alluding to some kind of fate that Roya could feel would involve exploiting them.

"Here," he said. "Let me give you a better view."

The man reached down below Roya's table and unlocked it, tilting its position up until she was locked into an 80 degree angle. Her feet rested on some kind of brace, but she could now feel the strap that went around her waist, holding her in place. A moment later, he had Ami's table in the same position. Together, they could now see out and down into a large room that was filled with columns of electronic equipment and huge cylinders that reminded them of water tanks. They were one floor above, looking out over a space the size of a school gymnasium.

"Beautiful, isn't it?" said the man, entertaining himself. "It's one of the most advanced computing systems in the world. And you see those cylinders? That's where the two of you are going."

"What are you going to do to us?" Ami blurted angrily.

At first, the man seemed to ignore her as he was starting to flip switches on a control panel nearby. They could hear several fans kick on behind them—part of another set of machines—and it sounded like several more computers were booting up.

"You two are different," he observed. "Your readings are different. You might be just what we're looking for, but there's no telling what will happen until we plug you in."

For a moment, he went back to flipping switches and checking the information on several computer displays, but then he went on.

"That machine you are looking at is an artificial intelligence, and now we are working on giving it intuition. We call it Harmony."

"How can you give a machine intuition," retorted Ami disgustedly, trying to find a sense of personal power again in her voice.

"By feeding it souls," sneered the man darkly, as if to silence her with fear.

Roya felt a cold shiver up her spine. The very idea that a human soul could be treated as nothing more than a science experiment was shocking and repulsive. Ami, too, felt incredibly agitated and was starting to pull at her restraints to see if she could find a weakness.

"Oh, you won't get free from those," bragged the man. "The only freedom you have left is in the machine. You see this container filled with gas?" he continued, tapping a large glass tube on one of the machines behind him.

Ami could hardly see, but Roya was closer and had a better look. The cylinder was about a foot wide, extending from a large black box with an instrument panel on the front. The gas pulsated occasionally with a pink glow.

"*That*...is the future of quantum computing," he boasted. "It's a form of gas that can store memory, but it does more than that. We can actually extract a human soul from a body and place it in this gas-like medium. You see those cylinders out there?" he pointed out to the floor below. "Those are containers for the machine's mind-matrix. The trouble is, we haven't been able to feed it a soul that has enough strength to enhance it. There's probably a few dozen test subjects in there, but they failed to boost the system. Now they are just ghosts in the machine," he laughed coldly.

Just then, Roya saw the man open a large black case that contained something he was handling with great care. As his hands became visible, she could see some kind of headgear that looked similar to the device from the Book of Aaron. The sight of it started to jog her memory of the library, but a lot of the details were still fuzzy.

He placed the first one on Roya's head, and then a second one on Ami's. Almost instantly, the technology switched on, detecting the presence of their brainfields.

"Let me give you a piece of advice," he went on. "Don't resist. Don't fight it. If you let the machine into your mind, it will become a part of you, and your essence can add something to the machine. Intuition, perhaps. A semblance of human intelligence. You may even retain some awareness of who you were before, but you will no longer be human. Your consciousness will infuse into the mind-matrix of the machine, and then you can work to expand into whatever else we allow you to have access to…maybe even other bodies. But once you are in, your bodies here will be switched off."

He said it like he enjoyed speaking about the body in this way, like it was just another piece of his lab equipment. The devices were sending a number of different energetic pulses through their brains as the man watched several computer monitors closely.

"Almost finished," he said, after only a few minutes. "You don't realize it, but you're both receiving an IQ test."

The energetic pulses quickly began to intensify, and both girls started to perceive flashes of light inside their heads. It started with a few images of shapes, but the images quickly became more complex. Numbers and words came next, but they were flashing through their brains so fast they could not hold any memory of what they were seeing. Suddenly, it stopped.

"Very good," said the scientist. "Impressive." He was fixated on the computer monitors but had a look of satisfaction on his face. "You two are definitely the brightest we have ever had. Now that Harmony has mapped your brains, it's time for the procedure."

He seemed excited, which only repulsed Roya more. They were both looking at each other again, and this time Ami said, "Don't worry. We're gonna get through this."

"How?" pleaded Roya.

"I don't know. Just stay connected with me."

In that moment, Roya realized that Ami had not needed to come back for her. She could have stayed with the others. Roya had been too distracted by everything to fully comprehend the sacrifice Ami had made by returning to be there for her. Suddenly, Roya felt a warm feeling all around her. It felt like Ami's friendship, but it was stronger. A presence was amplifying the connection between them, and Ami could feel it, too.

The words of the light being from the temple were coming back into Ami's mind again, and she knew she had to trust her decision to return for Roya. This was the deepest moment of surrender she had ever faced. Never had a situation seemed so hopeless, and yet, the reassurance of the light swelled inside her. Whatever happened, they were in this together.

"Don't worry," said the scientist. "You won't feel any pain."

It was the most compassionate sounding thing he had said, though he didn't actually know how it would feel to be put into the machine. He was just trying to keep them calm, so they would not struggle and end up damaging any of his equipment.

The scientist walked over and rotated their tables back into a horizontal position. Next, he removed the gear from their heads and slid the tables back until each of them connected with a large machine that was embedded into the wall. Both of their heads fit just inside an opening that felt cold. Then, another set of sensors automatically extended from inside the machine and latched onto their heads. With a few more switches, a light came on that illuminated a glass plate with gas swirling around behind it.

"First, you will bond with the gas," said the scientist, "and then, off you go!"

A low tone began ringing in their ears, and it quickly rose in pitch. Both their tables started to vibrate with a hum as the machines came alive and started pulsating. Roya could feel a kind of magnetic sensation beginning to pull her energy up into her brain, and then, without warning, a jolt of electricity flashed through her body. There was a searing pain for an instant, and then her body went limp.

Because Ami's head was braced by the sensors, she could not turn to see what had happened, but she felt that Roya's presence had disappeared. Her mind became frantically focused in prayer: *I AM safe with Roya back on the surface. I AM safe with Roya back on the surface. I AM safe with Roya back on the surface.* Her heart reached out to the light invoking any kind of help that could possibly reach her.

A minute later, Ami felt waves of magnetic pulses pulling all of her energy into her brain until a flash of pain and light catapulted her out of her body. The pain only lasted a second, and then, she could no longer feel her body. Struggling to understand what was happening to her, she tried to comprehend her new environment. She felt nothing but the sense of being in a pulsating, electrical field. The sensation of the gas was coming into focus around her, but strangely, she had no sense of breathing.

A minute passed, but she had no awareness of time. Next, she noticed some type of opening that began to pull on her energetically. Then, with a rush of both air and magnetism, Ami felt her presence shooting through what felt like a tunnel that was pulsing with light until she entered a noticeably vaster space. This time, she began to see light all around her in a glowing mist. Momentarily, she felt entranced with the sensations, but then, she began to focus on her own self-awareness. Like a flower opening its petals to the radiance of the sun, her presence began to unfurl until she had extended the thought-form of her arms and legs. It took a moment to reconstitute her form, but there she was as a being of light.

Focusing into the energy, she began to witness the strangest thing she had ever beheld. The glowing, pulsating mist reflected a host of incredibly complex patterns that seemed to have intelligence. It was not the intelligence of a conscious being, but that of a living machine. With every process the machine engaged in, the molecules of the gas medium could assume any structure needed for the computations. Ami witnessed that the machine was, in fact, designing new ways of organizing information with a high level of precision and at an incredible speed.

At first, she felt free to just observe. The machine was involved in some kind of process, searching for patterns in the chaos. The process almost sounded musical, with patterns of information having subtle tonal vibrations that continuously changed in her field of awareness. Ami then became aware of words, and then voices—countless recordings of human conversations being correlated and analyzed for patterns of congruence. Waves of information were passing through the space—videos, phone calls, emails. The machine was processing a vast amount of data, searching for something that she could not fully understand.

"Roya," she called with her mind, reaching out with her senses to feel for Roya's presence.

Suddenly, the machine took notice of her, and Ami felt like she was being probed. Every vibration of her presence was being scanned with thousands of processors. It felt like she was being pulled apart and plugged into the greater structure of the machine. She was beginning to lose her coherence as an individualized consciousness, until another vibration struck her.

"You can fight it!" she heard. It was Roya's unmistakable presence. *"Just focus on our betweenergy!"*

At first, she could not detect where Roya's voice was coming from, but then she saw a face begin to emerge from the cloud of patterns. As Roya's arms and legs came into focus as well, it felt as though Roya was struggling to free her consciousness from the machine matrix by focusing on the connection between them.

It soon became clear to Ami what Roya was doing. By focusing on their connection, Roya was amplifying their resonance to resist the gripping presence of the machine that threatened to assimilate them. Ami then began to focus on their synergy as well, until she felt the coherence of their forms strengthening together. Roya was clearly in front of her now, her energetic form intact. Their eyes locked, and it felt like they had solidified the bridge of energy between them. The patterns of the machine danced around them, still probing and pulling at the edges of their auras, but their connection seemed to be generating an energetic buffer that maintained the integrity of their consciousness.

"Don't lose focus," encouraged Roya telepathically. *"Just keep looking at me."*

She did not know what to do next, but she knew that she had to maintain their connection.

Though Ami was holding the focus, she was also tightening her energy, struggling to stay open enough to connect, given the uncomfortable sensation of the probing, which felt like being pricked by thousands of needles. Then, a shift occurred, and the link between them grew much stronger. A bright little pinpoint of light appeared beside them and began to expand into an opening. The energy coming through the opening embraced them, and both their auras brightened with a beautiful white light.

"Are you seeing this light?" Ami asked.

"It's helping us," replied Roya in wonder.

The light continued to grow stronger, strengthening what now felt like a shield around them, enveloping them both in a deep feeling of peace and safety. The opening continued to expand in size until a third being emerged to join them: it was the Lady of Light from the Temple of Adinai! Ami recognized her instantly.

Back in the temple, Ami did not have time to explain to Roya anything about her, but realized she was now there to help. The being of light gazed at each of them for a moment, strengthening their fields until all three were glowing with white light. With a smile, she conveyed that they were safe in her presence.

"Now focus on the others," she said to Roya and Ami.

"Others?" thought Ami, not knowing at first who the being was referring to, but Roya seemed to know immediately. As Ami followed Roya's focus into the information cloud, she began to sense the presence of other human energies. Some of them had been hiding in the machine, taking shelter in different places where the machine could not effectively probe. Others seemed to have been pulled apart, having lost the will to remain coherent. Behind the light being, the opening she came through expanded until it clearly revealed an energetic pathway to the crystal in the Temple of Adinai. The presence of this masterful being conferred the power to both Roya and Ami to help all the souls reconstitute and align with a safe pathway into the light, by way of the crystal. It was a way out!

"You must help them through," she explained.

Roya and Ami focused intently on each human resonance that they could feel inside the machine, and one by one, they presented themselves to be healed and strengthened. Dozens of them came forth, some adults, some teenagers, and even some small children. It was shocking to consider the plight of so many souls. *How long have they been in there?* wondered Roya, compassion swelling in her field.

As the Lady of Light gestured to the first several souls that approached, the pathway fully opened, and they began to flow through her grace into the light of the crystal, disappearing within it. Her presence felt like a mercy to all of them, sent from a higher realm. Roya suspected that these souls were being guided to the Afterlife, since they no longer had bodies to return to. She then began to wonder how she and Ami would be able to return to their families without their own bodies.

After a few minutes, all of the imprisoned souls had made their way through the pathway, and the Lady of Light reached out her hands to Roya and Ami, gesturing for the three of them to join hands together.

"Thank you for your bravery, young ones. Your task here is now complete."

"Can we go with you?" asked Ami.

"Your bodies are still alive. If you come with me now, you would not be able to return to your families. Just focus on the light between us, and I will send you back to your bodies."

Roya and Ami looked at each other, trusting deeply in the presence of the light around them as they deepened their surrender. The light grew brighter and stronger until the machine's probing abated completely, its power subdued by the presence of the light. Suddenly, Roya could sense her lungs. She felt her body take a breath, as the light grew so bright it completely enveloped their environment. It felt as though a tremendous charge was building, and they could feel a joyful smile radiating from the Lady of Light.

For a moment, Roya could sense far beyond the machine, her awareness racing with the energy along countless cables and connections. There were electrical generators, computer networks, and security monitors. And then, in a brilliant flash of light, the energy surged, and everything went black.

21

BROKEN HARMONY

I just had them in my focus," said Lex, still lying in the top bunk. "But then they were gone. I can't explain it. Try to see if you can find them with me."

"You know you're the better seer," said Ram in the bunk below. "I doubt I'd be able to see more than you did."

"Then just listen to what I'm saying and tell me if it feels true. There are two girls from the surface in Sector 10. They felt bright, like their energies are stronger than most, and they felt afraid, like they're in danger and signaling for help."

Ram tuned in, trying at first to follow Lex's flow of attention. They often practiced together like this. Lex would focus on the target and then share it with Ram telepathically, making it easier for Ram to find it. This involved tracing the pathway of Lex's attention until his mind began to resonate with whatever Lex was focused on. It took some effort, but he often did gain impressions this way, though sometimes, he was not sure if he was remote viewing or just imagining what Lex was describing. Ram was much better at sensing and feeling things than seeing them.

"That feels right," said Ram. "But what happened to them?"

"I don't know. I was trying to see if I could track them to their actual physical location, but something happened, and the signal broke. It's interesting, though. Because I had a target to focus on, I got a better sense of Sector 10. I saw a room full of computers that had unique vibrations. I'm sure I could locate it again if I focused on it."

"What was it like?" asked Ram, but before Lex could reply, everything went dark.

"Whoa!" exclaimed Lex. "What's happening?" he paused for a second. "Do you feel that?"

Lex was referring to a sudden feeling of stillness that accompanied the darkness, like a pause in the field of consciousness. Ram was silent, trying to feel past the walls of their room to gain a psychic impression of what was going on.

Lex jumped down from the top bunk, confident that he knew every inch of the area in the dark. Ram didn't need to guess what he would do next. Lex opened the doorway into the cavernous underground building beyond. He stepped out onto the walkway and looked out over the railing. Not a single light. It was pitch black all the way down for twenty more stories below. Nothing above either.

Listening into the dark, they could hear movement. Some people had been caught in between places and were feeling their way around, in search of a lighted area.

"Ram, check this out! It's totally dark," Lex whispered.

Ram now joined him at the edge of the railing. They could hear the echoes of voices begin to fill the open space beyond. And a few flashlights switched on.

"I have an idea," said Lex.

"Oh no," replied Ram, "not another one of your ideas. Haven't you had enough danger for a while?"

"You know the service tunnels we explored near the perimeter of Sector 10, right?"

"Oh no, you've gotta be crazy."

"This is the perfect opportunity," suggested Lex with excitement. "The power is out. This might be our one shot to get through those doorways. The security is surely disabled as well, and if we get caught, we can say we were lost in the dark. But we need to hurry, this might not last long."

Ram could almost see Lex in the dark with the dim glow of someone's flashlight from across the walkways, but he did not need to see the details of his face to know the look Lex was giving him.

"OK, I'm in," said Ram reluctantly.

Lex was quick to take advantage of opportunities, and at times, he seemed fearless, but Ram could not help wondering if Lex would be as cavalier without his participation. Ram had a hard time saying no, mostly to make sure his daring friend would be OK. He was slightly less adventurous and preferred to play it safe, though he always felt glad in the end that Lex had pushed him beyond his comfort zone.

In only a few minutes time, they had found a couple of their flashlights in the darkness of the room, but they agreed to keep them off and make their way in the dark as much as possible. Lex also insisted that they wear gloves to make sure they did not leave any fingerprints on any door handles. He quickly grabbed his backpack, and they headed out.

It was a long walk down almost twenty flights of stairs, but they did not bump into anyone in the stairwell, and the power outage was holding. Lex knew right where to go and did not miss a single turn through the complex at the bottom of the building. For weeks, he had been thinking about how to get a peek into Sector 10 from this area. The bottom of the residential building complex was technically not off limits to students, but students were rarely seen in this area, so they always tried to keep a low profile.

Sometimes, Lex had the feeling that the deeper they went, the more separated the consciousness of the people became from the surface. They had learned enough about insects in school to know that there was something ant-like to this pattern of society. With such a highly organized and hierarchical social structure, if you did not learn how to blend in and move with the pattern, you would stick out.

It might have been dumb luck that the power outage happened when most people were asleep, as the whole complex was inactive. Most of the activity seemed to be happening in the residential areas higher above. Down here, the maze of passageways seemed endless, but it was hard to tell, since most of them eventually ended in some kind of security door.

The area of their interest was a particular set of service tunnels that housed pipes along the walls that fed into Sector 10. There were only a few known ways to get into these service tunnels from down there, but Lex had found them all. Knowing every tunnel and every doorway was part of his aim. He always wanted to have an escape route mapped out in his mind if they ran into trouble, though he had not yet thoroughly explored this area.

As they walked along the inside of the service tunnel, this time with flashlights on, they felt a chill in the air. Lex was reasonably certain that some of the pipes were part of a cooling system for the massive complex of computers he was honing in on. Momentarily, he paused, trying to remotely sense the strange room he had felt the girls in. Ram just followed in silence, not wanting to interrupt the process when it seemed like they were getting close. After another few minutes of walking, they arrived at a door with a magnetic lock. Without a keypad or a door handle, the door looked like it was only intended to be opened from the inside.

Lex had seen lots of different kinds of security doors going to different areas, mostly into Sector 8 above them. Some of them used keypads, and the more sophisticated ones used a fingerprint and retina scan, but this door looked like it was used for maintenance. There was a metal plate that extended from the door over the latch area, but that did not deter Lex.

Using a screwdriver, he was able to get some leverage on the metal plate until he could slip his fingers behind it and pull the door open. They both looked at each other, shocked at how easy this was. The magnetic lock was disengaged, and without electricity, no alarm could be tripped.

"What if the power comes back on," worried Ram, feeling anxious. He was trying to think of ways to talk Lex out of doing anything more than taking a quick peek.

Lex responded to Ram's question silently by reaching into his backpack and pulling out a piece of foam with adhesive on one side. He then stuck it inside the metal plate to prevent the door from closing all the way, so the electromagnetic lock could not re-engage. Then he gave Ram a slight look of mischief, as if to coax him into the adventure, before disappearing into the darkness of the hallway beyond.

Ram was right behind him, closing the door very gently to test the security of the foam. He did not like trusting his freedom to something so fragile, but it seemed to do the job. By the time he reluctantly let the door rest fully on the foam, Lex was already half way down the hallway, headed toward the next door. Ram tried to walk a little quicker but was more concerned with being quiet. They still had no idea if any people were around, but the area seemed to be empty.

At the end of the hallway, past a number of other doors, they came to a T-intersection and another doorway. Lex had his cheek pressed up against the door, listening for sounds on the other side.

"Do you hear anything?" Ram whispered.

"Shhhh," hushed Lex. He strained his hearing to make sure the area just beyond the next doorway was clear. He must have felt secure, because he began to pull on the door, but it did not open. For a second, Ram was relieved, as if this spelled the end of their journey, but then Lex pulled a little more forcefully, and it popped open a crack.

Ram took a big, deep breath, trying to gather his wits, as Lex silently urged them on. He slowly opened the door, noticing someone with a flashlight across the massive room and up on a walkway. Ram could not tell what Lex was seeing, but gathered that there must have been some activity, because Lex had suddenly stopped. It was hard to see the room in much detail, but Lex gradually opened the doorway more, certain that they were not visible from this position.

They were on the edge of a large room with a high ceiling, filled with columns of electronics and cylinders easily big enough to hide behind.

Lex was unphased by the presence of the man up on the walkway as he continued to inch his way into the room until he was just past the doorway.

This time, he pulled out a thicker piece of foam to jam the door, after Ram made his way inside. They both crept along the perimeter of the room away from the man with the flashlight who seemed busy looking at the columns of electronic components as if waiting for some sign of life. Lex had seen a room full of servers before, and this looked somewhat similar, but these were more advanced, and the cylinders were something new. He could not imagine what they were for.

Just then, the man abruptly turned and disappeared through a doorway that closed behind him. Ram breathed a sigh of relief.

"OK, have you seen enough?" Ram urged.

"No," beamed Lex, clicking on his flashlight so that it shined right up onto his face to reveal his look of enthusiasm about continuing.

"I'm going back," warned Ram, testing his friend.

"Just give me a few more minutes," persuaded Lex, knowing that Ram would never leave on his own. Ram disliked that Lex always knew he could string him along in such situations. He did not have the will to split them apart, and Lex often took advantage of this to ensure that he would not be alone in his endeavors.

"What are we doing here?" asked Ram.

Suddenly, they both saw the flicker of a little green light at the bottom of the column of electronics next to them. And then another. The computers were starting to reboot.

"OK, seriously, let's get out of here now," Ram insisted.

"No, wait. I'm sure we have a few more minutes. They probably have a backup power supply that's kicking in, but it'll take a while. I just want to see what's up there," his eyes gesturing toward the door at the top of the stairs.

Lex had already begun to walk cautiously up the stairs, very aware that if the man came back, he would be plainly visible, but something was propelling him forward. He could not explain it, but he was unable to resist the feeling to enter that room. Ram had completely lost focus on the fact that Lex's original motivation was to see if he could locate the two surface dwellers he had sensed earlier.

At the top of the metal stairs, the doorway was immediately on the left, next to a long observation window. The door was already open, and Lex pushed right through it while Ram waited midway up the stairs, positioned so that he could still duck out of sight if the man came back. His heart was racing.

"Ram, get in here. Take a look at this!"

Ram was reluctant, but he reached out to sense if the man was nearby, and for once, he got a clear impression that they were truly alone. The heightened emotions of the situation and the adrenaline amplified his ability to feel into the space around him. He began to focus on holding this expanded awareness to be prepared to react if he sensed the man coming back.

Ram cautiously made his way inside the room where he could see Lex standing over the bodies of two teenage girls, lying on tables. Their heads were positioned just inside two holes in the wall that connected them to some kind of machine. Lex studied the scene with his flashlight, and then he held his hand near one of their faces, noticing the girl's breath was shallow.

Ram walked over to look more closely, and Lex began to fiddle with the gear around Roya's head. With a few quick moves, he disengaged the clamp and began pulling off the other gear and sensors. He was starting to work more quickly, as if he had decided that he knew what he wanted to do. In less than a minute, he had pulled the table free from the wall and had Roya out of all the gear. He was just starting to undo the straps around her ankles when she took a big gasp of air.

Lex paused for a second, holding his breath, and Ram walked around to the end of the table to get a better look at the girl that had just regained consciousness. She was breathing deeply, and her eyes were now open. She looked dazed, and uncertain of where she was.

Lex swallowed hard as Roya locked eyes on him. "Are you OK?" asked Lex.

"Help us," she pleaded, sensing she could trust him.

Instantly, Ram knew, without a doubt, why they were there. For a split second, he considered that it had been a mistake to get involved, but the serendipity of that moment was undeniable. They were the only link to the surface that could have possibly even shown up to help these girls, and instantly the path was clear. For some strange reason, it felt like their meeting with the other explorers had been fated for this exact situation. They *had* to help them escape.

"Don't be afraid," Lex reassured the girl. "We're going to get you out of here."

He immediately began working on loosening the other restraints.

"This is insane," voiced Ram.

"Hurry, get the other one unhooked," commanded Lex.

Ami's body appeared lifeless while Ram worked quickly to remove all the gear and undo the straps that restrained her to the table. Roya quickly sat up, but before she could take a look around, her head began throbbing with pain. For a moment, she was in shock and felt disoriented, but she quickly composed herself. She had to get to Ami.

Lex helped Roya off the table and noticed that her legs were a bit wobbly. He helped her stand as she quickly pivoted over to lean on the table where Ami was. She started trying to nudge her, but Ami was unresponsive.

"Ami, wake up," said Roya desperately.

"Not too loud," whispered Lex. "We need to get you out of this Sector as quickly as possible."

"Who are you?" asked Roya.

"I'm Lex, and this is Ram. We're not even supposed to be here, but we know the way out. You're from the surface, right?"

For a moment, Roya struggled to place the context of that question, but then she remembered that they were deep underground.

"Yes."

They all stood around Ami's table as Roya continued to nudge her, waiting for a response. She appeared to be breathing very shallowly, and it was clear to Roya that she was not all there yet.

Suddenly, Ram sensed something that gave him an even greater feeling of urgency. The man must be thinking about returning, because he could feel his flow of attention coming back into the room. Ram's awareness had never been this clear before.

"Guys, we need to get out, like NOW!"

"We're going to have to carry her," said Lex.

Ram did not like the sound of that, but he didn't hesitate. Whatever it took to get them out of that room, he was ready for it. Though he and Lex were physically very fit, he was glad to notice that Ami was not very heavy. Her slender build made it easy to lift her off the table and Lex was ready to lead them out.

"Get the door," signaled Ram, and Lex quickly moved to open the door wider, so Ram could get through with Ami over his shoulder.

Lex was helping Roya while she struggled to regain her orientation. It was clear that they were in danger, and she knew she had to escape and get back to the surface, but her body and memory were buzzing with so many sensations, it was overwhelming. Only the rush of her adrenaline kept her focused on the present moment. Just down the stairs, they entered what seemed like a maze of columns and cylinders spread out across the vast room. Without speaking to each other, everyone matched Lex's quiet but brisk movements as he guided them straight toward the door.

Then, without warning, a whole row of columns lit up with little green, red, and blue flickering lights in front of them, and they stopped in their tracks. Lex paused to listen for any human activity. He switched off his flashlight, letting his eyes adjust for a moment. Ram was considering how he could manage to switch shoulders or get some help from Lex, but then something unexpected happened. They all heard the unmistakable sound of a doorway opening from behind some of the columns as two men entered the room with flashlights.

"They should never have allowed such an experimental machine to manage so many systems," said one man. "Someone's going to be in serious trouble."

"This wasn't supposed to happen. The system was perfectly stable, but there was some kind of freak power surge. It doesn't make any sense. We don't even have anything connected to this system that can generate a spike that big."

"Well, we can investigate that later. You check the containment system to see if it's still holding a charge. It's designed to hold for several hours, even if the power fails, but only if the temperature is right. I'm going to check the primary processors."

Both men split up and began examining the readouts on the columns. Lex became even more careful with his movements, realizing that their chances of escaping undetected had just become more challenging, but it was a large room, and there were only two men; plenty of places to hide, if they were quiet.

Lex inched his way around the side of one of the large cylinders, and the others followed. The flashlights from the two men revealed approximately where they were. They were both still a safe distance away but were moving in their direction.

Ram was starting to breathe more heavily as he struggled to hold Ami up, but it was not a good time to discuss what to do. It was only a matter of minutes before the security system reactivated. And if the foam pieces were still in place, the magnetic locks could not engage, and it might set off an alarm.

Roya leaned up against the wall of the cylinder they were hiding behind, waiting for a signal from Lex. For a moment, she was able to feel the relief of being back in her body but standing still in the dark increased her sense of disorientation. In her confusion, she wondered if Ami was still inside the machine, and her mind began to drift back into the buzzing sensation of the machine matrix. The sensation began to overwhelm her brain, as if she was phasing in and out of the machine's consciousness.

But how? she thought, wondering why she could still feel the machine if she was not hooked into it anymore.

Her whole nervous system tingled with sensations from the machine's processors, and for a moment, it felt like she was still floating, disembodied in the gas matrix. She began to extend her inner senses, trying to find Ami's signature, but then she felt a hand on her shoulder as Lex signaled her. Her eyes opened, and she could just barely see him gesturing to follow his lead into the dark.

Roya knew what Lex and Ram also recognized; that it was only a matter of time before someone entered the control room and found their bodies missing. When Lex reached the door, he did not hesitate to open it wide enough for Ram to get through with Ami. He quickly removed the piece of foam, careful to avoid making noise, and quietly closed the door behind them. Ram continued to move forward into the dark toward the next door until Lex switched on his flashlight. Within seconds, they made it through the second door and were safely inside the service tunnel. Ram lowered Ami down off his shoulder, and Roya was quick to help balance her as they gently laid her on the floor.

"How much farther?" asked Roya quietly. Even at low volume, their voices carried down the hallway.

"It's too far," insisted Ram. "We'll never make it before the lights come back on. We have to try to hide them down here."

"No, we can make it. I'll help you carry her. We may never have this advantage again with the lights off, and we only need to get to the transport tunnels without being seen. We can do that in twenty minutes."

"It's going to take more than twenty minutes just to get back to our own level, especially if we're carrying her," argued Ram. He knew Lex could be overly optimistic, and this was not the time.

"Then let's try to wake her," suggested Lex.

Roya was already leaning over and whispering in Ami's ear while gently gripping her arm. Almost as soon as she focused on Ami, she began to feel their connection again, noticing a familiar feeling of light resonating between them.

"Just give me a minute," said Roya.

Ram was still trying to relax his muscles in preparation for whatever lay ahead. Lex was facing the long dark hallway in front of them, scanning with his remote viewing awareness to sense if their pathway to the stairs was clear. After years of both exploring the underground and practicing the awareness, he could easily scan through the tunnels he was most familiar with to see if anyone was there. Unfortunately, he saw the presence of a congregation of people blocking their path.

Roya placed her right hand over Ami's chest and began to focus on breathing. She could still see a little shimmer of light in Ami's aura, barely discernible. Recalling how the light had taught her to breathe when she had been standing in front of the crystal, she focused on her connection to living energy. Every time she breathed in, she imagined drawing in light as if the solid structures around her were just a ghost of an illusion. There was only light within and behind everything, and her breath was the instrument of connection to the light. When she breathed out, she imagined sending the light into Ami, praising her presence as a reflection of the light.

For a moment, she thought she felt the presence of the crystal again, and then Ami took a deep breath. Roya knew that she was halfway there and maintained her focus. With each breath that Ami drew in, her aura strengthened, and Roya was starting to feel the space of connection between them filling with energy. After another moment of breathing in silence, Roya leaned over and whispered in Ami's ear again.

"Ami, we need to go. It's time to move. You need to wake up."

Ami opened her eyes and reached out to grab ahold of Roya's arm "Where are we?" she asked, feeling disoriented.

"We're in a tunnel. We're still underground, but these boys are going to help us get out. We need to hurry."

Lex turned and knelt down next to the girls.

"We have a problem," he warned. "There's a whole group of people out in the plaza we came through. We're going to have to go a different way."

"Do you know another way?" asked Ram.

"Maybe," replied Lex. "We might have to figure it out as we go."

Ram was relieved that Ami was coming around, but Lex's idea did not sound promising.

"We live down here," Lex explained to Ami, "so if there's another way out, we'll find it. You just have to be quiet and follow our lead. If we tell you to hide, then hide. If we tell you to run, then run. Do you understand?"

Ami nodded her head, quickly becoming alert to the situation.

"Once we get to the right level, we will lead you to a transport tunnel where we can leave the city and take you back to the surface. Can you stand up?"

Ami sat up slowly, and Roya put her hand behind her to steady her. "My head hurts," Ami complained.

"Mine does too," empathized Roya, "but it'll be OK once you get moving.

Just take it slow at first and try to stand."

Ami stood up much more slowly than Roya had initially, which probably helped minimize the throbbing in her head. She seemed a little dizzy at first, but she quickly oriented herself. She felt relieved to be free, and the two boys felt supportive.

"Can you walk?" asked Ram urgently.

"Yes, I think I'm OK."

"All right, let's move," urged Lex as he began to lead them away from the plaza outside the maintenance corridors. "We don't know how much time we have before the lights come back on. I'm hoping that most people will think this is some kind of an exercise. Let's just see if we can find a way into a different plaza with fewer people."

Ram knew that Lex was capable of doing exactly that, but he was more concerned about the control room they had come from. He followed from behind, trying to sense if the absence of the girls had been discovered yet. When they were in the computer room, he had felt certain that the man would return any minute, but it was sometimes hard to predict the timing of such things.

Lex was walking faster to assess what was up ahead, while Ami's movements were still gradually picking up the pace, until Ram exclaimed in a forceful whisper, "There's someone in the hallway behind us!"

Lex was close enough to hear and instantly switched off his light. Far down the long hallway, they could see the lights of several people that were walking slowly, though they did not seem to have noticed them.

"We need to turn a corner before they see us," warned Ram.

They all began to walk more briskly, trusting Lex's senses as he navigated in the dark. They naturally began to link together, holding hands to stay connected. Roya and Ami had no idea that Lex could sense things so well in the dark, but they both assumed that with him in the lead, they could keep walking forward briskly without running into a wall before he did.

"That last door I checked was the last plaza," he whispered back to Ram, "and it was still full of people."

"We must be past that whole building complex by now. What do we do?"

Suddenly, Lex stopped, and Roya ran into him, though they quickly rebalanced. He had accurately sensed the end of the hallway at a T-intersection.

"Which way do we go?" asked Ram, trusting in his friend's decision.

The air felt different here, as if there was a very slight movement, though not quite a breeze. Roya felt a little more moisture, and something else was strange. She had often noticed the unique living resonance of the places she had visited in Lys. Each place had a personality that seemed to greet her. If this place had such a personality, then it was not welcoming at all. A palpable feeling in the air told them that they had crossed into someone else's territory. The air itself resonated with an energy of extreme secrecy.

Lex had begun to lead them around the corner to the left, completely out of sight from the people down the hallway, who were still walking toward them in the distance. They would have preferred to use a flashlight, but in the absence of any other lighting, they would certainly be noticed. Lex tried to remote view ahead and was perplexed by his impressions.

He sensed a doorway at the end of the hallway they had just entered, but something felt strange.

"I think we should head this way toward where the air is flowing. Maybe there's a way around the building complex to the other side," he considered.

"Whatever we're going to do, let's just do it before any of the locks engage," urged Ram. "Our luck could run out any minute."

Lex moved forward cautiously in the dark with everyone following closely behind until they came to a metal door. It was easy to find the handle, but the door did not give way when he pulled on it.

Behind them, they were beginning to see the lights of the men who were approaching from around the corner. Ram then grabbed the door handle with Lex and they both gave it a strong yank until it opened. A gust of air rushed in, and they could feel an increase in the humidity. Darkness lay before them, but they had no choice. They all stepped through and closed the door behind them.

The whole environment was discernibly different. They were standing on a metal walkway with rails suspended above what felt like a vast, open room. A couple of times, Roya reached her hands out past the rails into the dark but could feel nothing. Walking forward into the darkness, she was again struck by the ominous feeling that they were violating the space by being there.

Lex continued to lead the way, but after walking forward a good twenty yards, something stopped him in his tracks. Somewhere below them a series of lights began to switch on, illuminating the lower levels of what they could now discern was indeed a cavernous space. One by one, dim rows of lights activated further and further away, revealing what looked like a whole other city.

Ram gasped at the sight of it, though Roya and Ami still had no idea that this place was such a big secret to them. They all stopped and looked over the side of the railing. They must have been more than ten stories above the ground level. The walkway connected the tops of two building structures that joined the ceiling of the cavernous room to the ground. The cavern was filled with such structures as far as the eye could see.

From their vantage point, they could see down numerous pathways where people were walking briskly along as if the blackout had been of little concern. To Roya, they looked like a colony of ants that were oblivious to the larger world they were a part of, busily working toward their collective goals. The whole scene gave both Roya and Ami the chills.

"What is this place?" questioned Ram in a state of shock.

"Another sector," speculated Lex.

"Sector 11?"

"I don't know," replied Lex, at a loss for words.

"There's another doorway up ahead," pointed out Ram, bringing everyone's attention back to their escape.

They quickly began moving again and found the other doorway was open. Clearly, all the lights were coming back on, but at least now they were back in the maintenance corridors that he knew would connect with Sector 9. From here, Lex extrapolated where he might find an emergency stairwell and led them onward. He was certain that the locks on the security doors had begun to engage, but that would not prevent them from exiting the corridors. When he peeked through a door, Lex could see some people with lights on the upper walkways, though the plaza in front of them was still dark.

"We're almost to the stairs. And it looks like it's all clear," said Lex reassuringly. He made this sound like the danger had passed, even though Ram knew that they still had a long way to go. It was not worth concerning the girls, though, since they appeared to be experiencing a bit of relief from Lex's optimism.

"Just follow close behind me, and if I turn off my flashlight, that means be very still, and don't make a sound. Otherwise, just try to pretend that you belong here and that what we're doing is normal. Even if we're seen, we might not be noticed. We just have to act natural, and hope for the best."

"We'll have to climb a lot of stairs to get out of here undetected," warned Ram, knowing that the girls were already fatigued. "Let's just try to set a pace and keep moving."

"OK," said Ami. "We're ready."

22

REMEMBERING THE RECIPE

Both Andrea and Melanie sat cross-legged on the floor, wearing their coveralls, as they worked on the bottom of one of the murals. They were just down the hall from Aaron who was detailing the image of a lioness on the opposite wall. Everyone was having fun, and Echo was doing beat-box to create a little bit of a soundtrack to the scene that Zack was filming.

Everyone had contributed to the artwork in some way. Zack and Echo, who were less experienced as artists, had worked on coloring in some of the larger features that Andrea and Melanie had outlined, like fields of grass or bodies of water. Dominic, being the tallest, had been drafted into working on parts of the sky closest to the ceiling. Aaron had given everyone a few lessons on working with chalk, as it was one of his favorite artistic tools.

Andrea's idea was to create an elaborate street scene that depicted all of them working on a mural together on the side of a building. It was a kind of self-portrait of the group, working and playing together. Everyone loved it.

"So, what does the lion represent?" Zack wanted to know, focusing in on Aaron's work with his camera.

"I don't know," responded Aaron. "When I'm in the flow, it's like the scene just creates itself through me."

For a moment, he stepped back from the wall to get a better look at the whole mural. A bright park-like scene with people and families playing filled the wall on the right, which transitioned into a dark scene with war and destruction on the left. In the dark world, people looked terrorized, and they appeared to be bombarded with frequencies coming from towers and dishes, though a few of them were turning and pointing toward the light. The lioness stood on the grass at the edge of where the park shifted into the scene of desolation. She was baring her teeth and had one paw raised with claws extended.

"I think she's like the protector that stands at the balance between worlds. She's a symbol of our power to declare a boundary to greed so that the world of light doesn't get taken over by the world of darkness."

"That's profound," admired Zack. "Could the green in the light world also take over the other world and make it green again?"

"I suppose," said Aaron. "Though, I kinda think these are two extremes that can't coexist. Like they're two potential timelines."

Aaron pondered the whole scene for a moment and then went back to work. Off in the distance, beyond the park, and nearly straddling the split between worlds, was an image of the Great Pyramids of Egypt. He was just beginning to add a spiral of energy opening from that scene to expand into parts of both worlds. It was the grandest, most symbolic mural he had ever created, and in his mind, it was just the beginning.

As Aaron continued working, Zack started to pan over and take some shots of the girls and their section of wall. Dominic was nearby, practicing his best shuffle moves to Echo's beat-box when he sprang forward into a handstand.

"Hey, Dominic," called Andrea. "How would you like me to draw you into this scene doing a handstand?"

"Sweet! Go right ahead, just don't expect me to hold this pose," he joked as he fell back onto all fours.

"So, where ya gonna go from there?" Zack asked Aaron. "You've got a lot of wall left beyond the apocalypse."

"Yeah, I've been thinking about that," Aaron answered, but before he could say anything, Zack had an inspiration to share.

"What if you gave the impression that this whole mural was actually like a hologram projecting out of a book? You could have an open book with light rays coming out of it that connect to the mural from the side, and then you could build a whole other scene around the book."

"Actually, I think that works," agreed Aaron with an upbeat tone in his voice. For a moment, he wished he had thought of it himself, still embracing the idea of incorporating someone else's suggestion. And then something unexpected happened.

"Hey, I could draw that," offered Andrea, and before he could object, she bounced right over and started drawing the image of an open book about five feet away from the edge of Aaron's mural.

For a second, Aaron felt a part of himself objecting. He had not realized how territorial he felt about his artwork until this moment, but he had not expected anyone would just spontaneously start adding to his section of wall. Andrea was so quick to jump in and co-create with the mix of ideas that Aaron could tell she was also "in the flow." Their creative energy had just connected in a new way. The image of the open book emerged so quickly and beautifully that he admired her artistic ability, and it was the perfect solution for how to continue the mural.

Aaron stepped back for a moment again, taking in what was unfolding. Part of him was still in a process of letting go of ownership over the space next to his mural, but in that one simple gesture, Andrea had catalyzed a shift in his thinking. Before, he had segregated the creative energy of the girls over to the opposite wall. He had imagined an invisible barrier that allowed him to be in the zone with what he was creating, but somehow, the creative energy of the group had just taken down that barrier. He could now feel the flow of the group energy, as if they were co-dreaming and co-envisioning the whole project as one consciousness.

Just then, Aaron looked over to the section that Andrea and Melanie were working on, and he saw the image of them all together creating a mural on the side of a building. It was as if Andrea had precognitively expressed a level of artistic collaboration that was still emerging, and the synchronicity of what Aaron was witnessing was breathtaking.

Andrea's style was different, but the fusion was what made it interesting. She began drawing the light rays coming out of the book that connected with Aaron's mural. Aaron had the strangest sensation that the image of the open book was connecting to something in his heart. It seemed to reflect something deep inside him, like a portal that was opening. As he found his focus on the book within, he realized that it was telling a story inside him that was reflecting into the world around him. It was a story of how people were showing up within an emerging field of oneness to inspire everyone about humanity's potential to co-create in peace. It was a vision of many hands working together that shared one heart.

"I wish you could film what's happening inside my head," expressed Aaron.

Zack turned the camera back on Aaron for a moment, waiting for him to say more.

"Just think, if we got some other artists down here, this could be like our Damanhur...you know, that place in Italy with the subterranean temples and all the artwork? We could fill these walls with art and create a virtual journey that people could walk through on the web. If we can just keep working like this, I'm not in a rush to expose any secrets. We have a chance to create something really fantastic that could inspire a lot of people. And it's totally renegade street art. You can't get more underground than this."

Zack loved the dialogue, but suddenly, everyone's attention shifted toward the sounds they heard coming from the end of the hallway.

"Do you hear that?" said Echo, who had stopped beat-boxing. Someone was coming.

Lex and Ram walked ahead of Roya and Ami and noticed the faint glow of light as they reached the top of the stairwell in the old abandoned facility. Both of them felt excitement and fear about getting closer to the surface. It was an interesting psychological game to break through the inner barriers that had been put in place.

Lex had made up his mind that he wanted to get closer to the surface, and yet he could think of plenty of reasons not to take the risk. The game he played was to convince himself that his destiny was to help the girls, and that his mission would not be complete until he had returned them safely to the surface. This meant that he could not simply guide them to the way out and turn back. He would need to take them all the way to the exit.

Lex knew that the lights ahead were from his new friends and did not hesitate to call out to them when he reached the level just below them.

"Hey, it's me, Lex," he shouted up the stairs. "Don't be afraid."

He had quickened his pace so that he could ascend the last set of stairs ahead of the others and explain that he was not alone so as not to startle anyone with the unfamiliar faces. Echo was closest to the section of hallway where they emerged, and his light fell upon Lex.

"Whoa man, what are you doing here?"

"I'm not alone," he said to Echo as the others started up the stairs behind him. "We found two girls from the surface that got stuck down here, and we need your help."

The sight of the lights at the top of the stairs felt like a relief to Roya, and the moment she heard Lex talking with Echo, she felt everything would be OK.

"Hey guys, come down here," Echo called to the group. He did not need to speak very loudly as his voice projected very well up the long hallway to the murals.

"You're from the surface?" Echo asked the two weary girls.

"Yes," said Ami. "We were captured. If it weren't for these two, we wouldn't have made it out."

"There was a blackout," Ram explained. "It was pure luck that we even got into the Sector where they were being held."

"Sounds like a crazy story. I'm Echo, by the way," he said, extending his hand. "I'm here with five of my friends."

A moment later, everyone had come together at the T-intersection of hallways, and they all began to study each other with interest.

"This is Zack and his brother Aaron," introduced Echo. "This tall guy over here is Dominic, and this is Andrea and Melanie."

"I'm Roya, and this is my friend Ami."

"You said you're from the surface," investigated Zack. "How'd you end up down there?"

"That's a long story," answered Ami. "We started out in New York."

"You mean this network of bases connects all the way to New York?" questioned Zack.

"Well, we didn't start out in one of these bases," said Ami.

"You guys are in for a bit of a journey with these two," said Lex. "They told us some pretty fantastic stuff on the way here. We're hoping you can help them get back home."

"That shouldn't be a problem," Aaron assured. Still buzzing from the epiphany, he was having, Aaron was struck by a feeling of familiarity around the two girls. The introductions seemed to continue happening energetically as they all began experiencing a state of connection with each other. It was an undeniable feeling that suddenly made everyone feel more buoyant. There was a sense in the air that the group had just become more complete, as if they had all been waiting for this moment when they would finally meet and stand in a circle. Unfortunately, they could not stay that way for long. Lex could feel Ram wanting to retreat to their safe zone as soon as possible. He was torn, because part of him felt the same, but the feeling of connection with everyone around them made them want to stay a little longer.

"We don't have much time," said Lex. "Someone is probably looking for these two, and we don't want to be out of place."

"Right," Zack understood. "You've come this far, though. Don't you want to see what it's like outside? It's not far from here."

The thought had been present in Lex's mind on the whole journey, and he knew Ram would join him if he chose to make the leap, but he also knew it would be hard enough to hide his thoughts of *this* place. A trip to the surface would permanently change their resonance, connecting together two worlds inside them that for everyone else in their society remained disconnected. It was the greatest of all temptations, and yet the answer was sadly clear. For the second time, they would choose to wait. He did not even need to consult with Ram about what to do.

"I really wish we could, but we need to go," conveyed Lex. "I trust it can happen another time. Right now, we need to protect ourselves by getting back before anyone notices we're missing."

"You have to at least see what we've been creating," invited Melanie. "Just one glance. Didn't you say that you don't have art down there?"

Lex and Ram looked at each other and instantly knew it was a yes.

"OK, but just for a moment," agreed Lex.

They all walked down the hallway toward the murals. Realizing that the girls had been through something traumatic, Melanie was already embracing them both energetically. She positioned herself next to Ami and placed her hand on Ami's back, sending her love. Her intent was to link the new girls into a sister vibe to make them feel at ease.

"Are we almost to the surface?" questioned Ami.

"It's very close," Zack reassured her as they approached the murals.

The four newcomers were captivated with everything they saw. Even though Lex had received an impression of the artwork from his remote viewing, nothing prepared him for the emotion of seeing such an expression of human creativity firsthand. It was a completely foreign sensation, and it felt like he was leaving a part of his old reality behind.

First, they saw Andrea and Melanie's mural to the right, and then they came upon the image of the open book to the left. Even though the book was the most recent addition to the mural, Aaron was beginning to imagine time differently. He imagined that the book had always come first, and that he had merely been drawing part of its living story before Andrea had made her way over to the wall to fill in the rest of the mural's invisible blueprint.

Zack's eyes met with Lex and then Ram as he told them with his gaze that the way out was just around the corner. He respected their choice and did not want to tempt them, but he was beaming with the sense that they were standing at the bridge between worlds. Lex and Ram knew that the potential was still there, and for a moment, they both shared a thought about just leaving the underground for good. The air was swirling with possibilities that were exciting, and yet, confusing. Where would they go? How would they live? Would anyone come looking for them? Would they endanger their new friends if they left with them?

They had taken another step into a larger world, and something was shifting in their awareness of what was possible. It would take time to process all of the potentials they were feeling, but for now, it was enough just to wonder.

"Just get them home," requested Lex, intent on breaking the connection before they got too lost in the experience of the artwork.

Roya turned to Lex first and said "Thank you. I know you didn't have to help us. I don't know what we would have done without you two." She drew him into an embrace and Ami hugged Ram before they switched. This somehow felt natural to Lex and Ram, even though this form of expression was rare in their society.

"It was the right thing to do," expressed Ram.

"I don't know if we will ever see you again, but I am glad that we met," said Lex.

They all took turns embracing each other, saying their goodbyes. It was hard to pull away from the group energy, but Lex could feel a force of guidance urging them both to head back. A moment later, they were walking briskly down the hallway toward the quiet stairwell to the station below. They had a long way to go, but the timing of the impulse that guided them seemed to carry with it the message that they were still operating within a corridor of safety. They just had to keep moving, and they would be able to return unnoticed, filled with a wealth of new experiences that most of their peers could not imagine.

"You heard what Lex said. Someone's going to be looking for these two," reminded Zack. "We should get them out of here ASAP."

"OK, let's grab our gear then," responded Aaron. No one wanted to just abandon the project, because they had just found a flow together that was raising the vibration of the group. Helping Roya and Ami to safety, however, was clearly the new group mission.

"Where exactly are we?" asked Roya.

"This little secret place is right under an industrial part of Chicago," shared Echo. "We've been sneaking in here to explore, and we just started this little art project."

"Do you have any water?" Ami asked. "I'm so thirsty."

"Me, too," requested Roya.

Melanie was quick to respond with a couple bottles of water from her backpack. The girls looked like they needed a lot of support to decompress from all they had been through. Melanie took turns focusing on each of the girls, sending energy to comfort them.

The whole group was ready to leave in minutes. Zack had already led Roya and Ami to the secret door to show them the way out while they waited for Aaron to pack the last of their gear. Everyone moved quietly, and it was apparent to Roya and Ami from the behavior of the group that they intended to be stealthy as they exited the building.

The fact that they were with six total strangers in an unfamiliar place, far from home, did not seem the least bit unnerving. On the contrary, they felt an envelope of safety and protection around them, like their journey underground was coming to a graceful completion. They had a sense of being with friends, and *that,* more than anything, set their minds at ease.

Roya's first thought when they exited the building was to ask for a cell phone to try to call home, but it was obvious that they still had a ways to go on their mission to leave the area. The sky looked clear, and a gentle breeze was blowing as they entered the field just beyond the factory parking lot. Zack and Echo led the way as they traversed the field and ducked into the alleyway across the street. Within minutes, they had quickly covered the distance between the factory and Zack's van. It was a tighter fit having eight people in the van, but without any seats in the back, there was just enough room. As soon as Dominic shut the sliding door, they all breathed a sigh of relief.

"I don't think I'll ever get used to that," said Dominic. "Getting from the van to the building, or from the building to the van...I always feel like I'm waiting for someone to shine a spotlight on us."

"How are we gonna know if it's safe to go back next time?" asked Andrea. "If anyone's looking for these two..."

"Good point," acknowledged Echo. "We may not be able to tell."

Everyone paused for a moment, considering the implications. Zack pulled away from the curb and headed straight for the freeway.

"Where shall we take them?" asked Zack.

"They can stay with me," offered Melanie, "until we figure out how to get them home."

Roya instantly felt more relaxed by the invitation. It was clear that Melanie intended to take care of them.

"Isn't your place kinda small?" questioned Aaron.

"Yeah," replied Melanie, "But that doesn't matter to me."

"I just want to take a shower and get some rest," said Ami.

"And maybe eat something," added Roya. "I'm starving."

Instantly, Melanie started digging in her backpack for some snacks.

"How long were you down there?" asked Aaron as he produced a plastic bag from his backpack that had slices of organic apples.

"Thanks," said Roya as she reached into the bag and grabbed a few apple slices before passing it over to Ami. "What day is it?"

"Wednesday," answered Andrea as she offered them some trail mix. "Sun should be coming up soon."

"Then we were down there for almost a day and a half," Roya realized. "We started out on Monday evening. That's when we first went to Lys."

"Lys?" wondered Aaron, who was very intent on learning more about the two girls but did not want to pressure them for information. It was clear that they needed rest, and he wanted to respect their space, but his sense of recognition had not diminished since they had first connected.

"Apparently, it's a lost civilization," said Ami, just before biting off half a slice of apple. Roya was already munching away.

"No way!" bursted Andrea. "Can you tell us about it?"

Aaron suddenly felt satisfied that the group energy had begun to penetrate the mystery of the two girls. Now he would not have to interrogate them as the conversation had begun.

"It was amazing," volunteered Roya, happy to focus on her memories of Lys and not the more recent episode. "They're very ancient and wise. They said that their people were part of Atlantis, but they've been here way longer than that."

"How did you end up down there?" asked Melanie.

"We met one of their people on the surface," said Roya. "It's strange." She paused, trying to recollect all of the mysterious events that had led up to their journey underground. It was difficult to know where to begin, and she easily felt overwhelmed with all the memories.

Melanie waited patiently for more, but Roya seemed momentarily lost.

"We got separated from our families down there," Ami continued. "If we could just try to call home. We need to know if they made it back."

Melanie quickly produced her phone. Ami leaned in closer to Roya who dialed first. The phone rang for a minute, but it went to voicemail. Next, Ami tried, but also had to leave a message.

"Maybe they're not back yet," thought Roya. "Let's just give it some time."

"Don't worry," reassured Melanie, "you're both safe with us. You couldn't have met a better group of friends to look out for you."

Everyone silently agreed with Melanie's words. She was speaking for the consciousness of the group, and they all felt she was expressing the powerful bond of friendship they shared, which now extended to Roya and Ami. Roya appreciated how everyone had instantly included her and Ami in the group energy, and it struck a chord. She knew she could share everything with them, and she was quite sure she would not feel that way about just any group of people. The thought occurred that she could share *The Circle and the Stars* with them, but then she realized that it was missing.

"Ami! The book!"

"I know. It's gone."

"What book?" asked Melanie.

"It's what connected all of us together," explained Roya. "It must have disappeared when I went into the library. It had a picture of a doorway, and I'm pretty sure it was the same doorway we came out of when we left that underground building. It must mean we were all meant to meet each other."

"How is that possible?" wondered Aaron.

"The book came from the future. It guided us. Both our families came together because of it," she said, looking at Ami.

Ami's mind was racing, and the rest of the group was just trying to keep up.

"Do you remember what it said about how the ingredients would feel a certain joy about combining?"

"Yeah," replied Roya, already following her line of thinking.

"Wait, what are you talking about?" asked Melanie.

"There must be a reason why we're here in Chicago," said Roya. "There's something we need to figure out."

"Is this something I should be filming?" asked Zack from the front of the van.

"Maybe we can at least get to a place where we can all talk," suggested Aaron.

"We're not far from my apartment," offered Zack. "We have to go there anyway for everyone to get their cars. And you're both welcome to take a shower there."

"Don't worry, his bathroom is clean," assured Melanie with a little smile.

"What's that supposed to mean?" Zack shot her a look.

"It just means you're cleaner than most guys I know. Take it as a compliment."

"As a male, I feel insulted," said Dominic, only kidding, and they all laughed.

Roya smiled, sensing that this kind of banter could go on for hours. She could tell that they all liked to pick on each other and make friendly jokes.

It was another fifteen minutes before the van pulled into the basement parking garage of Zack's building. Luckily, Zack's place was spacious enough that the main living area felt comfortable with eight people. The bedroom was up in the loft, and the main living room had plenty of space to sit on couches as well as on the futon bed.

Ami and Roya took turns showering and freshening up while the others were in a lively discussion about the risks of continuing the project. They both tried to rest a little in the loft, but they were unable to sleep. They were processing too much, and after about an hour and a half, they both came downstairs to join the rest of the group.

"Are you sure you don't want to sleep some more?" asked Melanie.

"We've just been through so much that it's hard to sleep. We're both wide awake," replied Ami.

"Well, you're welcome to join us," Zack motioned to the couch. "We all have a lot to talk about."

Zack had his camera out, but they had already agreed this was not the time to film, yet. It was important to unravel the mystery first, to see how everything fit together. The sky was getting brighter outside, but they kept the curtains drawn, and Melanie was preparing everyone a hot cup of chai tea.

"I feel like I know you," Aaron blurted out, speaking first to Roya. "How is that possible?" Aaron was usually the most reserved of the group, but he was starting to notice that the new group energy was making him feel more spontaneous.

"Something feels familiar to me about all of you, too," acknowledged Roya, and Ami nodded in agreement.

"You don't know this yet, but out of all of us, Aaron is the only one that has been all the way down into the underground city like you two," explained Zack. "So how much of it did you see?"

"Not that much," said Ami. "We were knocked out part of the time. And then, the lights went out. Lex and Ram guided us through parts of it in the dark until we got to that long rail tunnel."

"How'd they know where to find you to get you out?" asked Aaron.

"I don't know," replied Roya. "They just said they knew."

"Did they put you into any kind of trance?" Aaron asked.

"No, but we were already really out of it," Ami answered, not knowing that he was referring to the Frequency. She hesitated to say more about what happened, because she sensed that Roya did not want to go there, yet. They were both still in a state of shock. Thinking about the machine made them both feel a little unhinged from reality.

"What happened when *you* went down there?" Roya asked Aaron.

"They did something to me psychically that masked the signature of my mind so that I would seem more like their people. Then, they took me in far enough to see where they live, and we met with one of their teachers. He was someone that used to live on the surface, and so he knew a lot about the differences between us and them. Most of them are really mental with very little emotion."

Ami recalled the coldness of the scientist that had plugged them into the machine, and it gave her chills. She was happy when Zack changed the subject.

"So, what about this other place called Lys?" Zack prompted. "What did their people look like? Did they say anything about who they are?"

Roya was glad they were asking questions, because it helped her remember. Parts of the journey were starting to blur in her memory, like a dream that was beginning to fade. She did not know if it was because she lacked enough rest, or if it was the drugs the military people had given her and Ami. She was just glad that she had not experienced it alone.

"They look like us, basically. Most of them seemed somewhat pale from living underground, but some of them have skin pigmentation from the plants and minerals they ingest. They also have a kind of glow about them."

In that moment, Ami thought of Mandy and started to reach out to her, wondering if she could communicate with Mandy through the messengers. She took a deep breath and concentrated on seeing her little ball of energy in front of her. It was not as clear to her as it had been in Lys, but she could feel the presence of her messenger, waiting to be imprinted with her thoughts.

She tried to focus her thoughts to form a clear message: *"Mandy! We're OK! We're back on the surface! Where are you?"* She repeated it several times in her mind and then thought, *"Go,"* commanding her messenger to deliver her communication.

"They told us about some kind of prophecy," shared Roya.

"Convergence, Integration, Emergence," Ami continued. "I remember."

"Yeah. They were debating the meaning of it, and somehow us coming down there was part of it." Roya was flashing back to the forum in Adinai, and she almost felt like she was there again. "They also got attacked by the military."

"Wow!" said Zack. "I can't believe all this stuff's happening underground! It sounds unbelievable. I don't think we would've believed you about Lys if we hadn't already stumbled onto a secret city ourselves."

"So, what else did they tell you about the prophecy?" queried Andrea.

"They said there were many different realities starting to collide, and if they could integrate, a whole new world could emerge," explained Roya.

"That's like finding Lex and Ram," said Aaron.

"Yeah," agreed Zack. "I wonder if us finding that city and Aaron going all the way in could be part of the same thing. We all certainly felt like worlds were colliding, and I'm sure Lex and Ram felt that way, too."

"So, you were in this place called Lys, and then you were captured by these military people, and then you got rescued," said Dominic. "Sounds like one hell of a trip."

"There's more," added Roya. "It's just coming back to me."

Ami was listening intently, ready to help recall whatever was coming up for Roya.

"It's on the edge of my awareness," said Roya. "Like I can almost taste it." She wanted to remember something the council had said, but then, her thoughts drifted to Claire and their families, wanting to know where they were.

Claire was frustrated with not being able to answer everyone's questions. The council had been adamant about returning the two families right way, but Soraya was having difficulty trusting the council's word that Roya and Ami were back on the surface. She knew she would not be able to communicate with Claire or the people of Lys once she returned herself. She was still afraid for the girls, even though Claire reassured her they were OK.

"Is there any way you can get word to us about what's happening if we don't hear from them?" pleaded Soraya frantically as they arrived at the pool where the boat was waiting for them.

"I can't promise you anything," apologized Claire. "We don't get to decide on our own whether or not to come to the surface. It was a very rare opportunity that brought us all together. I want you to trust that something greater is guiding all of us and protecting your girls." She looked intently at Frank, as well, to convey her reassurance.

"I can feel your daughter now," she said, looking at Soraya. "She's right where she needs to be, and she'll be waiting to hear from you. I wish I could be there to see this through, because I'm just as eager as you are to learn what happened. I need you to understand something, though." Claire focused in more directly on Soraya's heart, placing her hands on her shoulders.

"You saw what happened to Roya in the temple," she reminded her. "There's no telling what else she's been through since we last saw her. Ami may also have quite a lot to integrate. And coming down here has changed all of you. It's important that you all support each other to integrate with everything that's happened, because the world on the surface will no longer feel the same for you. I'm quite certain that your journey is just beginning, but I believe that all of you came into this world to make a powerful difference. You've all made a difference by being brave enough to trust in the forces that brought our lives together, and for that I am forever grateful."

Listening to Claire speak with such clarity and poise helped Frank feel a little better. She had a very grounded way of speaking truth that made it easy to trust her.

Just then, Mandy felt nudged very lightly on her brow by a thought bubble that burst into her mind with a communication from Ami. It came with a blue hue to it, and Mandy clearly heard Ami's message commanding her attention.

"Dad! I just heard from Ami!"

"What do you mean?" Frank lit up.

Claire knew exactly what was happening. The Formelle had timed the communication perfectly. This was just what the group needed to surrender to the journey ahead.

"I just heard her thoughts," said Mandy. "She said they're OK, and they're waiting for us on the surface." Mandy looked incredibly satisfied at her telepathic experience, and she had a big grin on her face. "Guys, they're OK. I can feel them both together."

Mandy's excitement broke the tension everyone was feeling about leaving Lys. Soraya's shoulders immediately relaxed, and she released a sigh of relief.

Claire could still see the blue light of Ami's thought resonance glowing on Mandy's forehead. For a second, she smiled inwardly, realizing that her new students would still be very receptive to their connection with her from the surface. They were all quick learners.

"If there's ever a way we can come here again, I hope it finds us," expressed Raymond.

Claire could sense his trust and gratitude, and she could already feel their souls embracing as if they were old friends. Gradually, she went around and hugged each of them.

"The boat will take you back to the surface," explained Amaron. "Just trust that the bubble of protection will last until you get there, and then you can just use the motor to get to shore."

"I don't think I ever thanked you," Raymond turned to Amaron. "We've been so caught up in everything that's happened. I just hope your people are all safe, as well."

"Thank you," he replied.

"And I'm so sorry to have burdened you both with my worries," said Soraya. "Thank you for being so supportive."

"We are all connected," Claire smiled, "and if we hold that we are all in this together, that awareness will continue to awaken in everyone."

There was something very profound in Claire's statement that they would ponder for a long time. She always spoke of the awareness that our thoughts matter and have an effect on the world. She lived as if every movement, word, and intention is a powerful creative act that has untold ripple effects, and that you can create the world to become more of what you focus on.

Her sense of personal power extended far beyond what most people considered possible, and it felt refreshing to be held in that kind of awareness. No one, not even Claire, could tell how much of this awareness they would retain after going back to the surface. But Claire knew that many seeds had been planted that would support them to continue growing.

Mandy was the first to board the boat, followed by Sarah. They each said their goodbyes and took a seat. It was strange to think of traveling through the water again without Claire being with them, but after two days of being in Lys, strange was starting to seem kind of normal.

Claire untied the boat and tossed the rope to Frank who secured it. Though the bubble of living energy that formed around them was mostly invisible, a sudden feeling of peace came over them as the boat began to turn around by itself and head into the tunnel. It was too dark to see by the time the boat fully submerged. They hardly felt any movement as it accelerated through the underwater tunnel and up through the bottom of the lake.

As soon as they exited the tunnel, they began to perceive the light of the morning sun above. The transition to the surface only took a minute. The energy bubble briefly refracted the light into a number of little rainbows as it broke the surface of the lake. The silence lasted only a little longer, and then, the bubble left completely, allowing in the sound of the water and a gentle breeze.

Raymond did not hesitate to start the motor, and then they were on their way. They all remained silent within their own thoughts. A residual peace and tranquility blessed them on their journey home.

Finding the dock was easy, given the landmarks they had passed before. There were several small islands to the right that had previously been on the left. Their vehicles were still there, and most importantly, their phones. They all moved with a little more urgency when they reached shore.

"You've got to be kidding me!" said Frank, fumbling with his phone.

"What?" asked Mandy.

"It's dead. I must have forgotten to turn it off when we left. How's yours?" he asked Soraya.

"Mine's still turning on," she said. It was the longest minute of her life, but as soon as the phone had booted up, she saw a voicemail message.

"Mom, it's me! We're OK! We're in Chicago, and some nice people are helping us. Call us back as soon as you get this. Ami's here with me and we're both fine."

Soraya burst into tears as she pressed the callback button, and everyone gathered around. Melanie was alert not to miss a call and had the ringer turned up all the way.

"Hello?" said Melanie.

"Yes, is my daughter Roya with you?"

"Sure, just a moment," she replied.

"Mom?"

"Baby, where are you? Are you OK?" and that was about all she could say before the tears overwhelmed her. She could only listen after that.

"We're fine, Mom. Are Dad and Sarah with you?"

Roya was feeling the intensity of everyone's emotions, and yet, somehow, she felt very calm.

"We're all right here," said Raymond. "Is Ami with you?"

"I'm right here," said Ami. "We're safe."

"Ami, thank God!" her dad sighed with relief. "They said you would be OK, but it's still hard to believe. Where exactly are you?"

"We're in Chicago at our new friend's apartment," explained Ami.

"How did you end up in Chicago?" asked Soraya. The mystery of it almost broke her out of her emotional state.

"We got taken by these military people," said Roya, "but these other guys helped us escape, and they got us to some friends of theirs on the surface. We're with six other people that are looking after us."

"It's a miracle!" exclaimed Raymond.

"Dad, I'm so sorry I left you guys, but I knew I had to go back for Roya."

"It's OK, Ami. You don't have to apologize for anything. We're just glad you're all right."

"I can't wait to see you guys," said Mandy. "You really freaked us out."

"How do you want to get them home?" Frank asked Raymond and Soraya.

"Let's see if we can just get them on a plane," suggested Raymond.

"Roya, can these people get you to an airport?"

Ami and Roya looked around the room, and heads were nodding.

"Yeah, Dad. What do you want us to do?"

"Just get to the airport, and we'll start working on the tickets," instructed Raymond. "Can we reach you at this number for a while?"

"Sure, I'll stay with you," offered Melanie. "You're welcome to use my phone."

The excitement of getting home to their families had suddenly overtaken the flow of the group's previous conversation. But remembering the picture of the doorway from *The Circle and the Stars*, Roya still felt there was something important about her connection with their new friends that needed to be explored further.

It was not long before the whole group jumped into Zack's van and was on their way to Chicago O'Hare Airport. Everyone wanted to be there to see the girls off, though Roya still felt incomplete about leaving so soon. She could not explain it, but she did not at all feel anxious about getting back to their families. Her thoughts kept turning toward her memories of Lys…something she had learned there was important to remember. She was certain that meeting this new group of people was destined to happen, but the context of this feeling eluded her.

"You know," said Zack. "We might want to think about this for a minute."

"What?" asked Echo, who was almost always riding in the front passenger seat.

"We have no idea how much those military people know about these two girls. If they're looking for them, they might consider at some point that they made it back to the surface."

"So…" said Echo.

Roya and the others were listening intently.

"Well, however improbable it might be, they might look for them at the airport. There's always a possibility that Lex and Ram might have been caught."

"Wait a minute," said Aaron. "That's right. And just in case, we should keep them well away from any security cameras that might be networked to the Eye."

"The Eye," questioned Roya. "What do you mean?"

"Jeez, I'm startin' to sound like my dad," admitted Aaron.

"Me, too," confessed Zack.

"Our dad's always talkin' about how most security cameras are feeding into the NSA's spy network," said Aaron. "He just calls it the Eye. He's always trying to find ways to go off the grid of electronic surveillance, and he's constantly worried about the government spying on his work. He even built a Faraday Cage in the basement that cancels out all electronic signals."

"What kind of work does your dad do?" asked Ami.

"He's a scientist and an engineer," answered Aaron.

"Wait a minute," inquired Roya, "he's a scientist?"

"Yeah," Aaron replied. "He used to work on patents for the aerospace industry, but he consults on all kinds of things technology related."

"Ami, I think I remember now," said Roya. "They said we would meet a scientist, and he needs our help."

"That's right!" she replied.

"He's the one! We have to go and see him!" stressed Roya.

"What makes you think my dad is the person you're supposed to meet?" questioned Aaron.

"Because they said this was important," Roya's mood had shifted to one of urgency. "The council we talked to in Lys…they talked about our connection to this man like it was something we dare not miss. They said he's in danger of missing the potential of his life's work."

"OK, well, I'm sure we can get in touch with him," said Aaron.

"No, we need to see him *now,*" insisted Roya.

"He doesn't live that far from here," mentioned Zack.

"I don't think Dad would like having all our friends show up on his doorstep," Aaron said skeptically, knowing how anti-social he could be sometimes.

"Don't you think he would know the best way to get these two home safely?" Zack pointed out.

"Yeah," admitted Aaron.

"Well, one thing's for sure," said Zack. "I'm not takin' them to the airport unless we know it's safe."

"He's right," agreed Aaron. "You should call your parents, so we can explore another way to get you home."

"Heck, I'd drive you home if your parents wouldn't mind paying for the gas," offered Zack.

"OK, I'll call my parents. But can we just call your dad, first?" urged Roya. "I wouldn't ask about this if I didn't feel it was important. We might not get another chance, since everyone wants us back home."

"What exactly did they say down there?" asked Andrea.

"They said there was a scientist that we would meet, and that he was very important to history. We're supposed to get in touch with him right away and tell him about what we witnessed. They talked about it like it was critical to the future," Roya said with greater urgency.

"OK, I'll give him a call and see if we can come over," accepted Aaron. He did not like calling his dad lately, because it seemed like he was on edge about something. Recently, he had noticed his dad's stress levels were higher than usual, which felt troubling because his dad had not opened up to him. Aaron felt concerned, but did not know what to do, other than give him more space. Up until now, this had felt disempowering, but somehow Roya's directive seemed to bring a supportive energy to the situation. "It's dialing, but I doubt I'll get him this early."

"Hello," Aaron heard his dad say on the other end.

"Dad…I didn't expect to get ahold of you. I have an unusual situation. I'm with some friends that witnessed something important, and we really need to talk with you in person."

Something about the way Aaron said the word 'unusual' had surprisingly piqued his interest.

"We can be there in fifteen minutes, if that works for you."

There was an uncomfortable silence. *Is he bothered or intrigued?* Aaron wondered. He was not expecting a warm welcome, but he could not help feeling that somehow, there was something right about making this connection for Roya. He felt motivated by his sense of recognition with her and wanted to be supportive.

"Sure, come on by. We'll talk when you get here," he said, and then hung up.

"Well, that was a green light," said Aaron, smiling at Roya.

"Seriously?" Zack was surprised.

"Yeah, he said come on by. I didn't tell him how many of us there were, or who was coming. He didn't even ask. He was like, come on by, and then, click."

Ami looked at Roya, and she nodded with approval.

"I hope you know what you're going to say," said Aaron. "Hard to know how opened-minded he is about this kind of stuff, but then again, he does know a lot about government conspiracies."

23

THE TECHNOLOGY OF LOVE

Dr. Daniel Tailor was about as nervous as he had ever been. For several weeks, he had contemplated a substantial offer made to him by some kind of government agent who had apparently been following his work. Despite all his efforts to keep the work in his lab concealed from outside attention, somehow, someone had found out that he was pursuing interests in energy technology. How much they knew was uncertain. They might know very little. They might, in fact, just be testing him to see if he would reveal that he *was* working on something. Then again, they might know everything.

It was upsetting to think that his work as an inventor was so vulnerable. To his knowledge, though, no one had entered his home lab or spied on any of the computers where he kept the data of his experiments offline. But he could not live with the uncertainty of how much the agent might know. The fact that anyone was asking the right questions was troublesome, and he was considering taking the deal just to get the attention off his back.

After all, his experiments had not yet been fruitful. He had not completely succeeded in producing an over-unity device as he had intended. At times, he wondered if he was just afraid to make a breakthrough. He was certain that other scientists had made similar discoveries, but they must have been suppressed. Some might have sold out to companies that wanted to keep such technologies off the market, or worse, some might have been killed. He had always known there was a risk to experimenting with any kind of energy technology that offered a viable replacement to fossil fuels.

Dr. Tailor had hoped to make a breakthrough without drawing any unwanted attention to himself. So, he pretended not to know what the man was talking about and insisted he had not made any breakthroughs, which was technically true. The man just said, "Whatever you're working on, we just want you to stop and hand it over, and we'll gladly pay you five million dollars." Whether or not the technology worked perfectly was irrelevant to the agent's offer.

Dr. Tailor was more concerned about avoiding government interference than with making money. If he refused to hand over a working technology, they would probably kill him to suppress the knowledge, but his device had never fully worked. At least the idea that inspired it in the first place never needed to be disclosed. *They probably already know,* he thought.

But why would his son call just when he was about to contact the man in the dark suit? He had been sitting by the phone all morning, contemplating what to do. He had all but decided to make the call, but something was holding him back. It was a strange and disturbing feeling, like staring at the doorway to the future, but not feeling safe enough to step through it; and yet *not* stepping through it was excruciatingly painful. It felt like he was selling out on his lifelong dreams.

His head was throbbing, and he had broken a sweat. This experience was making him emotional, and he almost never felt such a lack of emotional control. Something felt wrong about making the phone call, but he did not see any other way. He had started to convince himself that his work meant nothing, and that he was not capable of making the breakthrough of his dreams.

Why hang on to more disappointments? Why not at least have an extra five million dollars to play with?

He could easily justify having extra money to support his two boys, and yet some part of him was praying for a sign that would talk him out of making that call. The sound of his son's voice and his unusual request seemed like the answer to a prayer. Momentarily, it felt like a relief to have something else to focus on. The man in the dark suit would have to wait a little longer for an answer. It was time to go and splash some water on his face and get a bite to eat. Whatever this was about, he wanted to be present and feel more like himself.

Roya and Ami did not like changing plans with their families, who were anxious to see them, but they all remembered what the council had said about the scientist, and both their parents were supportive of them finding another way home besides the airport. The challenge now was how to share the information with Zack and Aaron's dad.

In order for Zack and Aaron to explain how they came to meet Roya and Ami, they would have to reveal what they had found. It was the best way to support the girls with their story, since Aaron had been all the way down into the underground city, and all of them had met Lex and Ram. This was going to be tricky, but Roya was adamant that they had to all commit to the idea of bringing Dr. Tailor into their circle of trust. Something deep inside her had been bubbling to the surface since the group had come together. It was a sense of mission and a feeling that her support system had finally arrived.

If she had not been given the opportunity to speak to the forum in Adinai, she might not have gained so much confidence in her own voice. This was all happening so fast, but she felt a perfection to the synchronicities that helped her trust what was unfolding. This was the new kind of experience that she had longed for, and everything that had happened was part of a plan that felt connected to her purpose. It reminded her of what Claire said about the educational process of Lys, where the goal is to gain a sense of knowing who you are until your purpose becomes clear.

Dr. Tailor had a nice two-story house in an upper middle class neighborhood with a big backyard and a well-maintained flower garden around the front lawn. The house had light blue siding and the front door had an oval-shaped window with flower designs etched into the glass. Even though Aaron still lived there, he knocked on the door before opening it to let his dad know they had arrived.

"Hang on a second," Aaron said to his friends, wanting to wait for his dad's invitation before welcoming everyone inside.

When Dr. Tailor came down the stairs, he was wearing a white, button-up shirt with khaki pants and a black belt. He was about 5 foot 8 and was slightly overweight. He had short, almost frizzy, light brown hair that was thinning on top. He also sported a mustache, and his arms were quite hairy. Ami started to imagine Mandy's wise-cracks, as if she was listening to a telepathic commentary track. It felt like she was right behind them saying, "Oh, you've met a Sasquatch. I thought they were extinct."

Ami smiled big at Dr. Tailor as he looked out onto the porch.

"Hello, welcome," he smiled right back, not knowing that Ami's smile was partly at Mandy.

"I'm Dr. Tailor, Zack and Aaron's dad. Why don't you all come in," he invited.

Roya sensed a warm welcome as they began the introductions, though she also sensed he was not expecting quite so many guests. Dr. Tailor guided them into the living room where they could talk.

"It's nice to meet you all," Dr. Tailor began. "So, what's this all about?"

They all took a seat on the couches in the living room with Ami and Roya sitting together directly across from Dr. Tailor.

"This is going to sound crazy at first," said Aaron, "but we just met these girls this morning, and they have something fantastic to share. The thing is, unless we share what we know…it might sound really hard to believe, but we've seen things, too, that will back them up, so just listen with an open mind."

"I'm intrigued," conceded Dr. Tailor, "but how old are you girls?"

"We're both sixteen," replied Ami.

"And how did you end up hanging out with my boys?"

"We weren't hanging out," clarified Roya. "They helped rescue us. They were just about to take us to the airport to go home to our families, but then they mentioned you, and I knew we had to come and see you. We were told we would meet a scientist and…"

"Wait a minute, where are your families?" he interrupted.

"They're in New York, but they know where we are," Roya quickly assured, trying to convey that nothing was out of place so as to stay on topic. She realized, though, that she was getting ahead of herself and needed to find the right starting place. Fortunately, Zack stepped in.

"None of this is going to make sense until we explain about the building," said Zack. "We were exploring this old abandoned factory when we found the entrance to a secret underground building."

"Sounds like you were doing something illegal."

"I know how it sounds," Zack replied a little defensively, "and I'm sure there are authorities that would totally object to us being down there, but what we found is also illegal. I didn't even think we would be sharing this with you, but these two girls brought it up for their own reasons."

"OK…go on," said Dr. Tailor, waiting patiently for more information.

"Dad, it wasn't just a hidden building. We stumbled onto a secret government *colony* underground." Aaron paused to let that statement sink in, trying to gauge his response.

"There's a whole city right beneath Chicago," Aaron continued, "and it's not the only one. What we saw was shocking! They have these super high speed trains that connect to other underground cities, and all these people living down there that have never even seen the surface."

"And *you* found a back door to one of these bases?" he questioned, slightly skeptical.

"Yes" said Zack emphatically. "We all found it. Plus, we have video. This is no joke!"

"OK, I believe you. I've known about this kind of stuff since before you two were born, so what you're saying is not outside the realm of possibility for me. What concerns me is that if you had been caught, you probably would have been killed. And how do you know that someone wasn't watching?"

"You're right," acknowledged Aaron. "It was dangerous to even discover something like this, but we didn't know what this was until we were all the way inside."

"Yeah, like twelve levels deep," blurted out Dominic.

"Something about this discovery didn't feel like an accident," Aaron further explained. "That's why we went back."

"You went back! That does *not* sound like a good idea. I hope you aren't planning on doing that again."

"Dad, it's OK. If we hadn't gone back, we wouldn't have been there to help Roya and Ami. We met these two guys that live down there who helped them escape. If they hadn't already known about us, they wouldn't have known where to bring the girls. It's probably the only reason they're still alive."

"I'm trying to suspend judgment for the moment, because I want to hear more, but this does not feel safe. If they've escaped from somewhere, someone might be looking for them."

"Dad, we have to help them," Aaron insisted. "They've seen even more than we have, and we need to protect the truth. This is bigger than all of us."

Aaron was having that feeling again where his heart expanded, and his sense of purpose strengthened. Zack, too, wanted to stay focused on getting his dad to trust that this was all happening for a reason.

"Now tell them about the other things you saw," Aaron prompted Roya and Ami.

"It wasn't just us," Ami began. "Both of our families were with us, but we got separated. We were in New York, and we got invited to an underground city by this woman named Claire."

"Another military base?"

"No, this one was a home for an ancient people that have been living underground for thousands of years. They are way more advanced than we are," Ami explained.

"A lost civilization?"

"Yes!" replied Roya. "They called themselves the people of Lys."

"So how did you end up in Chicago?" Dr. Tailor's mind was swimming with questions, but he wanted to fill in some of the basic gaps in the narrative, first.

"We were abducted," Ami disclosed. "The military raided the city we were in, and we were captured and taken to some other place. It was really scary," and that was all Ami cared to say about their experience with the aliens and the AI system. She knew Roya did not want to go there either.

"So why bring this to me?"

For a moment, Dr. Tailor could not imagine that such a complex web of unusual connections could have linked two teen girls from New York to a reclusive engineer in Chicago.

"They said that we would meet a scientist, and that he had an important role to play in history," explained Roya. She was finding her confidence to speak, despite sensing his skepticism.

That was not enough to convince Dr. Tailor. Lots of scientists had an important role to play in history. Why would he be special?

"Who are 'they'?"

"This council of leaders that we met with in Lys," answered Ami. "They said this was really important, like it might affect the outcome of history."

"Yeah, they told us that he was in danger of missing the potential of his work," added Roya.

Dr. Tailor swallowed hard. Roya's last sentence struck a chord, and that same feeling of stress and vulnerability came over him again, like he was on the verge of making a huge mistake.

He could feel it in his throat—a constriction that he had felt before, like he was completely alone in his truth. He had never trusted anyone with his discoveries, and this had contributed to a growing feeling of disconnection from society. His throat had been hurting all morning while he was contemplating calling the man in the dark suit, but he had not been able to understand what it meant.

Being in the presence of these young people was forcing him to confront the uneasy feeling he had about abandoning his work. He now realized he was facing the prospect of selling out on a potential future that did not just belong to him. It belonged to the younger generations, too, and all those that would inherit the legacy of these times. And then he began to ponder the moment of his epiphany. There was something about it that he was still having difficulty accepting. It was the moment that he heard the Voice.

I Am the Source of All Gravity, he recalled. The experience of hearing the Voice had terrified him. The vibration of those words seemed to declare that he was not only worthy of the secret, but that he was also responsible for stewarding the knowledge—a responsibility he felt challenged to accept in a world that he did not imagine would support him.

Now it was becoming evident that he needed to clear his conscience. He needed to be heard. Something about these two young women reflected into him. Each of them had witnessed something fantastic and unbelievable to most. They had been in grave danger with the same vast dark government that now threatened him. The parallels were breathtaking, and suddenly, he felt something shifting in his throat.

It was as if something had been stuck inside, trying to find its expression. He had not believed his work was supported, and it was dangerous to even have the knowledge he possessed. Why did it feel so scary to know things about the universe? After all, shouldn't that be our natural state of being? Why should we fear to have knowledge that connects us to a greater understanding of our place in the cosmos, or to the potential of greater freedom? He had often reflected on the fear he felt around making new discoveries, well aware that a secret institution was operating behind the scenes, forbidding and suppressing such knowledge, but he had little hope that this could change.

One thing he knew for certain was that he no longer wanted to keep his discovery a secret from his two sons. He had thought that doing so would protect them, but now it seemed they were potentially as exposed to the same threats that he was. For all he knew, the authorities could take them into custody at any moment citing national security reasons. It felt much better to reciprocate their trust in him by also sharing.

"It's hard for me to admit this, because I'm not used to trusting people with my work, but there may be something to what you're saying."

He swallowed hard again and took a drink of water, noticing that the moment he began to speak about his work, the constriction in his throat had eased. Perhaps through sharing, he could find the strength to make the right decision.

"You've caught me at an interesting time," Dr. Tailor began. "I've been struggling with that exact feeling…that I'm so close to my dream, but I feel compromised. I've been working on something that I believe is incredibly important. But my work has attracted the attention of the wrong people, and I'm not sure how much they know. They offered me a lot of money for it, but it would also mean abandoning all the progress I've made. If I give it up, I'm quite sure that the potential of this discovery would never see the light of day."

"What is it?" asked Zack.

"It might be a new way of generating clean energy. I had one of those Eureka moments that every scientist hopes for. I even felt guided by inspiration. But then I got discouraged."

Roya had been quietly searching for another clue about why she was there. And then, she remembered what the council wanted them to tell the scientist.

"That's why we're here!" Roya broke in. "We're supposed to tell you about the technology we witnessed. This thing that Ami and I found with my dad and her sister…it was a communication device that allowed us to talk to beings on the other side."

"You mean like dead people?" asked Dominic.

"Well, it can be used for that," responded Ami. "We used it to talk to my mom who crossed over several years ago. But we also talked with some spirit guides."

"They said that it was some kind of Resonator," explained Roya, "and it looked like a large egg. But what's amazing is that it created this connection with the other side without any kind of normal power source. Claire said that it was partly powered by the Earth and partly powered by the energy of the higher realms we were connecting with. When we were using it, there was light everywhere, and we could feel into these higher vibrations of reality. It was like a bridge between dimensions, and somehow, it was like part of our bodies at the same time."

"That's intriguing," considered Dr. Tailor, whose mood had lifted slightly. "I also work with something that I call a resonator. And what you're saying makes me think of the presence I felt around me when I first started working on my new discovery. I even wondered if the technology already existed in some form, like the consciousness of the unified field was teaching me how to create a technology that could tap into it. It just makes sense that we were meant to discover a way beyond our present barriers."

"Yeah," agreed Aaron. "I know what you mean. It's like you just know that reality can't really be as limited as what we've been told."

"I've always thought there was a way for us to travel faster than light, for example," Dr. Tailor continued. "It occurred to me that the universe might be set up for civilizations like ours to discover the secret once they've reached a certain point. What if this is how it always happens, like a puzzle that is solvable for any civilization in the universe that matures enough to see the greater whole?"

In the presence of people who listened with such open minds, the words were flowing out of him as if his ideas were being magnetized into the space for others to reflect on.

"I heard a mysterious voice say to me, *I Am the Source of All Gravity.* And after that, I realized that gravity is not what we've been led to believe. I began to glimpse a whole new world: one where all human beings understand the forces of physics in a different light. We've only understood one side of the equation, but there's another way of viewing gravity that's reversed."

Both Roya and Ami were recalling the messages about gravity from *The Circle and the Stars*. Perhaps Dr. Tailor *had* glimpsed the same world from which the book had come: a world where human beings experienced a living connection to the whole of gravity, the whole of light, and the whole of time.

"What do you mean, *reversed?*" asked Aaron.

"We've been looking at gravity through the lens of our current experience of it, but there's more to the human experience. Our current understanding creates us to believe that we're trapped. But in my glimpse of the future, it was a new understanding of gravity that made us free."

"It's just like the anti-mind," realized Roya. "Claire said that what our people call the mind is made up of the anti-mind. She said it was like a resistance to oneness, and if we release it, our bodies would be containers for a resonance of *universal* mind."

Ami was nodding, excited by the connections, while Dr. Tailor was shocked by the synchronicity. He was astonished at the fact that these teenagers were matching his intellect with something that expanded his own understanding. The insight paralleled his observations exactly.

"That's really interesting," he said, still dumbfounded. "It's the same with the truth of gravity. There's another form of it behind everything, and for that reason, it's possible to cancel the resonance of mass by aligning matter with the resonance of the source behind it."

Dr. Tailor's words triggered Roya to remember her dream about another solar system. She flashed back and was standing there in the library with planets and asteroids whizzing past her. She focused inwardly on the sensation of the memory to connect with what the book in her dream had said to her, and then it resonated into her mind as if she was hearing it again for the first time:

This is where the secret was first discovered.

The dream was somehow connected to this very moment, like she was witnessing a new chapter unfolding in the living records of the galaxy that the book was beginning to describe. The dream must have known that the question this statement provoked would be answered by something happening in physical reality, even though Roya was just catching up to the synchronicity more than a week later.

What secret? she had thought.

The secret must be connected to what Dr. Tailor was now discovering, and he was not the first. This *had* been discovered on other worlds before. Roya became very focused on discerning the next step of the recipe for change, believing in the potential of a joyful combination of forces. The lions. *Faith and Courage,* she thought. *That's what he needs,* but there was something more.

"I know I'm not the only one who has tapped into this kind of universal knowledge," Dr. Tailor went on. "Other inventors and scientists have made similar breakthroughs. The problem is that we have a secret government that is actively suppressing and controlling such discoveries. It's dangerous to have anything to do with it."

"But what if that's changing?" insisted Roya. She was having another one of her intense energy surges, but this time she knew that it was light coming through her to help create a shift in reality. "The Council of Lys seemed to think that your work was really important. Maybe you just need more support to finish what you started!"

"That would be great if it were true," he said. "I can't seem to make it work, though. Like a lot of scientists, I went looking for the Holy Grail of physics …but some missing ingredient keeps eluding me."

The Grail! thought Roya. *The secret ingredient…what's missing is Love!*

Roya could feel the Grail again, resonating in her heart, and she had the distinct feeling that the rim of the grail was reflecting up into her mind, like a halo of unity consciousness, energizing the feeling that they were all one. The more she focused on the circle in her mind, the more she felt as though she was energizing the presence of that same circle inside all of their minds.

A living technology of resonance, she thought.

"Dr. Tailor, you weren't meant to do this alone. Can you show us what you've been working on? I feel there's something we can do to help," suggested Roya compassionately.

Roya was speaking now for the energy of the circle resonating in the space between all of them. Ami could feel the energy of love and wholeness swelling inside both of them, like a cup that was overflowing. The feeling was contagious. The whole group had become engaged in breaking Dr. Tailor out of any doubts or fears. It was time to bring everything out into the open and share it with the circle. The will of the group presented a powerful invitation.

"My work is just down in the basement. I have a lab there."

Dr. Tailor hesitated for a moment, not sure if he wanted to go this far, but the words had already come out of his mouth, and he was trusting more and more in the flow of what was happening. After all, this was not a room full of corporate executives or government officials. It was his two sons and a group of young people that felt worthy of the truth.

"I need you all to *promise* that anything I show you must remain secret."

"We swear," pledged Dominic, and everyone else nodded.

"Yeah, we're good at keeping secrets," reassured Andrea.

Zack and Aaron had been down there before—though it had been a while. Dr. Tailor led the group down to the bottom of the stairs and unlocked the door. They all piled into a large workroom with tables full of tools and electronic equipment. On the main table, at the center of the room, was a large, black, cylinder-shaped device, lying on its side. The base of it appeared to be flat, and wires coming out of it connected with other electronic instruments. The device was mounted on the table and was about a foot wide and two feet long.

"When I started this project, I was considering the problems of space travel. I wasn't looking to discover more about the rules of physics. I was looking for the *exception* to the rules. I knew that I was pursuing the impossible according to the known laws of physics. But something told me we've been looking at physics through a limiting psychological filter that obscures our connection to a greater reality. It's like studying the peel of an orange and thinking that you understand the whole orange without actually peeling it and tasting it. Basically, we've been studying the universe objectively without fully connecting to it."

"So how do we taste the universe?" Dominic wanted to know.

You should try one of Roya's Sunshine Cookies, thought Ami, smiling to herself.

"Well, what Roya and Ami experienced with the Resonator they found seems like a taste of that greater reality. It's just possible that this greater invisible reality is trying to reach us as much as we are trying to reach it. That might explain my epiphany about overcoming inertia."

"The key insight came to me when I experienced an awareness about the nature of physical reality. You see, we are used to perceiving matter as solid, but the awareness showed me that everything is actually fluctuating in a continuous cycle. It's a little like frames from a movie projector that create the illusion of motion, even though there's an imperceptible gap between the frames. The insight I had is that *there's no inertia inside the frame gap.*"

"If everything in reality is fluctuating—switching on and off—there must be intervals in the universal cycle where the resonance of mass is weaker, even approaching zero. The idea is that gravity and inertia are not constant, as we have believed. They *also* fluctuate between strong and weak intervals within the universal cycle. The challenge is that these low inertia intervals happen so incredibly fast, it's difficult to synchronize our technology with them."

"What exactly is inertia?" asked Ami. She was sure she had known the definition at some point, but she did not want to miss anything.

"Inertia is the tendency of an object at rest to stay at rest, and the tendency of an object in motion to stay in motion. It's a resistance to change unless acted upon by some external force, which is part of the essential problem in propulsion. Currently, we use combustible fuel to overcome the inertia of our planes and space vehicles, which is expensive and polluting. What our civilization needs is a quantum leap beyond this level of thinking. We're used to thinking of available energy spatially rather than dimensionally. What I was attempting to create was an over-unity device: one that produces more energy than you put into it."

Roya was amazed at the synchronicity between Dr. Tailor's words and the experience she was having of the Grail. She was beginning to see the energy of the heart as an over-unity device. The potential of the group's synergy felt like a generator that was powering up to channel a flow of universal energy. Through the field of oneness, she sensed each person's excitement about being part of the group, like there was a joy in combining energies that took each person's expression to another level of vibration.

"So how is this thing supposed to work?" asked Echo, bending over to get a closer look at the machine.

"Well, I wanted to create a generator that resonates with the low inertia part of the universal pattern. I've been experimenting with sound and electromagnetic frequencies to disrupt the generator's resonance with mass. In this way, I can reduce resistance to acceleration and create the right conditions to open a kind of bridge into the other dimensions."

Dr. Tailor was starting to switch on some of his instruments and computer monitors.

"I knew I was onto something when I got the system to produce slightly more energy than I was putting into it, but I haven't been able to get the system to stay in sync with the low inertia intervals. All of the right magnetic properties are there, but the bridge just won't engage. I assumed that the fluctuations happen too fast for our technology."

"And that's where you got stuck?" asked Melanie.

"Yes and no," replied Dr. Tailor. "I got stuck because someone found out about what I was doing, and it scared me."

"Who?" asked Aaron.

"There was a man in a dark suit that came to me in the parking lot of one of the companies I consult for. He offered me five million dollars for the blueprints I was developing, and in return, I would have to sign over all legal rights to the technology. I wasn't sure if he really knew what I was working on, unless they had me under surveillance. I had a hunch that he was just testing me to see if I would reveal that I *was* working on something, but I didn't want to say anything to suggest that he was right. He called me again last week and reiterated the offer, which makes me think that he *does* know something."

"So, what if he does," retorted Zack. "Can't you just blow him off?"

"It's not that simple. The Shadow Government has maintained absolute authority over this kind of technology. All they have to do is cite national security, and they could raid my lab and treat me like a terrorist, or even force me to work for them."

"Wait a minute," interjected Aaron. "I can't believe that the whole potential of human history is controlled by darkness. Somehow, against all odds, I walked right into the heart of one of their most super-secret underground bases in the world and walked right back out undetected. If we hadn't met these two girls, I would've thought it was just dumb luck, but now I believe there's something happening. Something's protecting us that wants to support our ability to create our own reality." Aaron was thinking of the lion in his mural.

"Dr. Tailor," added Melanie. "If this is really universal knowledge that you're tapping into, then it doesn't belong to anybody. The idea that anyone can own it is false. You're letting this Shadow Government intimidate you with an illusion of power. Nobody can own humanity's future. That future belongs to all of us."

Roya could feel that the presence of the circle was strengthening the part of Dr. Tailor that was struggling to trust in his destiny. It was clear that he had been afraid to succeed, because then, he would become more vulnerable to those driven by greed. Somehow, Roya knew that if she kept focusing on the oneness between them, she could help close the gap that would bridge him into an energy of protection and safety. She held the vision with confidence until she could feel that he was beginning to flow with the potential of a new outcome for history. His resonance was changing, and they could all feel Dr. Tailor's presence tilting into alignment with them.

He had just turned on the generator, and they could hear the components inside accelerating to a gentle hum.

"This is just the power up cycle," he explained. "Right now, there's power feeding into it from electricity. Now, I'm going to turn on the resonator. You might want to cover your ears, because some of the peaks are quite intense."

Everyone had their ears covered but Aaron. He wanted to hear the sequence, but was ready to plug his ears, if needed. The resonator started out pulsing tones at a low vibration, but they quickly accelerated in frequency and pitch. Dr. Tailor was watching one of the monitors when the speed of the generator surged for a moment.

"Did you see that?" he said, pointing to a monitor. "If I keep adjusting the frequencies, I get these surges, but I've never been able to keep the machine calibrated long enough to sustain them."

Roya looked at Ami, and their eyes widened together as they both saw what they knew was a Formelle move through the space between them and right over to the generator. They could both see a large purple orb hovering over the device, and a number of other smaller orbs were zipping around the room.

"What was that?" asked Andrea who had just seen a flash of light out of the corner of her eye.

"I just saw something, too," added Aaron.

"It's the Formelle," Roya and Ami both said in unison.

"They're energy beings that want to help us," Roya added.

Dr. Tailor was still focused on the monitor and was not paying full attention to the conversation, but then he turned back toward the group and noticed that several of them were looking around the room in curiosity.

"You can feel the presence, can't you? I've felt this before. This is as far as I've come, though. You see this monitor? It shows the output of electrical energy. You can see that it jumps when the vibration interacts with the universal pattern and disrupts the resonance of mass. I can't seem to calibrate it correctly, though. No matter what frequency I use, I haven't been able to find the right match."

Just then, there was a spike in the output, and everyone felt a rush of energy move through the room.

"Did you feel that just now?" asked Dominic.

"I definitely felt something," responded Echo.

"It's just like the Egg!" exclaimed Roya.

Dr. Tailor turned his focus toward the machine as he also sensed something shifting. The feeling of the Grail was still vibrating in Roya's heart, and she felt guided to hold the field of the circle with the generator. She imagined all of their hearts connected with a ring of light that encompassed the machine, and the Formelle seemed to respond by joining with it. Roya knew that everyone was feeling the magic of the group's energy.

Suddenly, the generator surged for a few seconds, and the presence of living light in the room increased. Dr. Tailor did not need to look back to the monitor to know that the power was building. Another surge lit up the generator, followed by yet another that lasted longer.

"It's the sound!" announced Ami. "The beings of light are helping us through the sound."

Each surge elongated until the generator began to hold its acceleration. The vibrations grew more intense, and then a *pulse* of living energy flashed through the room. Everyone felt connected to it, and the generator was now sustaining a new peak vibration. It was as if the energy of both people and machine had broken through a barrier as one. The bridge to the invisible world was open.

Our story, Andrea thought. The Book had just opened in her heart, and she could feel a whole new shared human reality extending from what they were all creating with their love. It was not just a bridge to a new source of energy. It was a bridge to a future of human unity.

Dr. Tailor then reached across the table, flipped a couple of switches on the generator, and unplugged it from the original power source. The generator glowed and pulsated with energy and everyone clearly felt that a marriage had taken place between the device and the living consciousness of the unified field. A living energy now permeated the room, and it was not just coming from the machine. Everyone could feel a joyful presence that reflected the group's betweenergy.

"It works! I don't know how, but it works!" Dr. Tailor reached over and first hugged his son Zack and then Aaron. "But what was missing? I didn't even do anything different this time."

The Circle and the Stars, thought Roya. *The Circle...and the* Energy *of the Stars!*

"It the energy!" beamed Roya. "It's *living* energy, and it's helping us because we have the right intentions. I remember it from the book: *The most powerful calling to direct energy and resources into alignment with your vision is a shared purpose.*"

"That sounds like the missing piece of my epiphany," realized Dr. Tailor. "If that's true, then the frequency match I've been searching for was not just technological. It was a matter of matching the right kind of human energy with the consciousness of the unified field."

"Yes," agreed Roya. "The energy knows that we all want to help humanity. As soon as you decided to share your work with us, it aligned you with the support of the invisible world."

Roya reached out and took Ami's hand, and then Melanie's. They all began to join hands together, including Dr. Tailor.

"We just have to intend for this energy to be shared with everyone," emphasized Ami. "That's the key. That's why it wants to flow for us. You weren't meant to do this alone. We have to help you share this with the world."

"Totally," agreed Andrea. "We have to stick together and not give in to fear."

They were right, and Dr. Tailor knew it. If he believed in the world of competition and ownership, he would resonate with the reality where people steal from each other and control through fear. But there was another kind of reality emerging: one where love governed the fair distribution of resources—one where the goal was to empower everyone. Dr. Tailor had reached the deciding point between the two worlds, and he was beginning to realize that he *did* have a choice.

"I like the way you all think," he said. "I don't want to believe that I'm trapped and that I have no choice anymore. It just doesn't feel right. When I align with what you're all saying, it feels like the power of this knowledge is coming back into the sacred circle of trust where it belongs. I just don't know what to do about this man now."

"Dad, that man doesn't have any power over you," stated Aaron. The faith and courage of his journey to the secret city had brought him a powerful message that resonated clearly into his mind.

"That man," he continued, "was just a manifestation of your fears. He intimidated you, because you were willing to believe that you were trapped. But in reality, you were just afraid of your own potential. Some part of you wanted out, because your potential is so big it's scary. So, you created an out and nearly sold out on your dream. I almost did the same with my artwork."

"We're in this together," assured Roya. "You don't have to resonate with that man. If you just focus on *our* energy, those kinds of people won't be able to plug into you."

Once again, Roya realized how her experiences leading up to this had staged the exact insights that she needed. The timing of everything was perfect.

"You're a brilliant man," complimented Melanie. "You deserve all the support that life can give you."

"You've come this far," acknowledged Echo. "Don't give up on humanity, just because somebody tried to shake you down."

Dominic nodded and bumped fists with Echo.

"You're not selling this invention, Dad," affirmed Zack. "We have to see this through as a family."

"And our families will help you, too," encouraged Ami. "We were meant to."

Dr. Tailor's eyes began to tear up a little, though he remained mostly composed in front of the group. For a long time, he did not believe that something as innocent as love could thwart the dark webs of power that seemed like such a threat to progress. It had felt like a stain upon his soul to believe that humanity could be so lost and unreceptive to change. But something had just healed inside him. Before, he could not have imagined including all of these innocent faces in his dilemma, out of fear of sharing the danger. Now, he was beginning to feel that love actually *was* the more powerful force, and that those who had the courage to be the change would ultimately be victorious.

24

A GUIDING FORCE

After listening to the details of their capture and escape, Dr. Tailor was reasonably certain that the girls could not be identified. Nobody had even asked for their names, and given the unusual circumstance of the blackout, they could not have made a cleaner getaway. It was doubtful that anyone from the secret underground could imagine that they had returned to the surface. And no mention of the girls was made on Dr. Tailor's police scanner. It felt like a miracle had brought them all together, and this elevated their feeling of safety around moving forward.

Dr. Tailor had suggested taking the train, so they could all sit facing each other while they were getting to know one another on the way to New York. Roya had never ridden on a train before, and it was an extra treat to share it with her best friend. It was an overnight train, and the two girls would have their own room with bunk beds.

For security reasons, Dr. Tailor had insisted on sharing the discoveries with Ami and Roya's families in person and was happy to get out of the city for a while. Aaron accompanied them as well, so he could share his experiences of the underground and learn more about Lys.

Standing there at Union Station in Chicago, Roya became entranced with the scene around her. At first, she was staring at a statue high above them of a woman holding an owl. But then the hypnotic echoes of people talking and the rhythm of people coming and going sent her into a dreamlike state. The expansive feeling of the cavernous Great Hall allowed Roya's attention to expand into the scene with no specific focus, just taking it all in. Aaron had gone to get everyone some snacks while his dad was getting the tickets, and Ami was silently standing by, wondering what her friend was thinking. Had they been engaged in conversation, Roya might have missed what was dancing on the edge of her awareness.

Something was different. It was not just Roya's ability to move more easily in and out of a waking dream state. They were both experiencing a long space of silence when they normally would have been talking endlessly. They were connected to an awareness that was much greater than themselves, and they both knew that the other was feeling it.

This time, it was different though, because they were surrounded by people. Ami, too, was caught up in the scene. She intuitively felt to share that silence again with Roya to see what would happen this time. Roya continued to relax her focus, scanning the room as if she had extended an invisible web of awareness to see if anyone else was resonating to that same state of openness. And then she saw something.

Across the room, sitting at a table in front of a café, was a woman whose aura was clearly visible. She was talking with a man, and a subtle, but vibrant, bluish-white haze surrounded her. As she watched, she could feel that the woman was sending light to the man, and after a couple of minutes, Roya started to see his aura, as well, though it was not as bright. She was about to turn to Ami who had just noticed what Roya was observing when a man walked in front of them. He was walking at a brisk pace with an angry look on his face. Something about him felt menacing, and Roya's heart started pounding, like she felt physically threatened by his presence. His aura was much less visible than the woman's, but she felt it very clearly. It was dark and shocking to feel, like this man was thinking of behaving violently.

"Did you just feel that?" Roya asked Ami.

"Yeah, he felt really scary," Ami concurred as they both watched until the man disappeared around the corner.

Both Roya and Ami noticed that they were in tune with each other and did not need to explain much about what they were witnessing. They just knew what the other was feeling.

"So, what do you think of that woman's aura?" asked Roya.

"You mean the woman at the café," she affirmed as she looked in that direction.

"That's the first person since Lys that I've seen with an aura that bright," observed Roya.

"Do you think she's from Lys?"

"I don't know, but it makes me wonder if our auras stand out that much to other sensitive people. I don't see ours as much as I did before…hardly at all, really," admitted Roya, putting her hands out in front of her to look for her aura. "But I still feel people more intensely."

"Same here, but I haven't stopped trying to see," said Ami, holding up her hands, too.

Though it was easier to see when the light was dimmer, or with a darker background, they could both still perceive a subtle glow in the space just around their skin. More noticeable was the flow of energy moving through their bodies, like a gentle current, connecting them to an intuitive awareness of their paths.

"Look around, do you see anything else?" suggested Roya.

Both of them scanned the room for a moment, extending their feeling senses. Roya was starting to figure out a technique that helped her focus on the subtle energetic level of what was happening all around her. It involved looking not with her eyes but with her presence. She would look without looking and focus on being present to the energy that she knew was radiating out from each person to feel how it was affecting the space. In Lys, she had noticed how people intentionally opened to reflect each other. It was a way of being vulnerable to a deeper state of connection. Now she was beginning to see how allowing reflectivity helped her read people's auras, noticing the reflective nature of her own presence when she was empathically open.

As she continued scanning the room, several interesting things leaped out at her. Over by some benches, two young children, a brother and sister perhaps, were entertaining themselves while their parents were sitting nearby. Roya instantly recognized a vibration of wholeness in the children that reached out to touch everything around them. She aligned with their vibration and opened more to feel their presence reflecting into her, noticing they were self-aware of the joy they were sharing with others.

Then, she saw two men standing quietly with a noticeably different vibration. They were also observing the whole scene, but something about them felt alien. She could tell from their auras that they were concealing something about who they were and how much they knew. She wondered if they were conversing telepathically, and a feeling of caution arose to not cross wires with them psychically. Then, something happened that took her totally by surprise. She clearly heard a voice speak to her inwardly.

"We have given you both discernment that few people have. This is part of a master teaching that, in time, you will grow to embody and share."

The angel, Roya thought, instantly wanting to hear more. She was certain that this was the Voice she had heard in the tree as a child; the same angel depicted in the book. She felt the soft glow of the Angelic Presence all around her, and was about to share the message with Ami, when the feeling of connection was disrupted.

Across the room, a man seemed to have taken notice of them, and both Roya and Ami felt penetrated for a moment by a very cold and emotionless presence. The man was wearing a dark suit with a hat and sunglasses, even though it was not nearly bright enough to need them. Roya was certain that he was staring at them from behind his shades, and she wondered if someone from the underground had discovered them. The man had pale skin, and something about him did not feel like normal human energy.

Just then, Aaron walked up behind them.

"Are you two ready to go?"

"Don't look now," said Roya quietly as they turned to face Aaron. "There's a man staring at us, and something doesn't feel right about him."

"What does he look like?" Aaron asked.

"He was looking right at us, so don't give away that we're checking him out. He's just over my left shoulder wearing a hat and sunglasses, and he has pale skin like the people from the underground."

Both Ami and Roya had moved around and positioned themselves with their backs to the man so that Aaron could glance at him without being noticed. As Aaron lifted his gaze, he immediately found the man who *did* look noticeably pale.

"He's not looking at you anymore."

"How can you tell? He's wearing sunglasses," said Ami.

"His head is turned."

"Maybe he's just pretending like he's not interested," guessed Ami. "Can you feel anything about him?"

"Now that you mention it, something does feel strange about him. It's weird, but he seems really cold."

"I felt the same thing," agreed Roya, "and it felt like he wasn't just staring in this direction, but he was looking at us with his mind. We should keep an eye on him. What if he was sent here to find us?" she whispered, as she leaned a little toward Aaron playfully. She was playing into a dynamic that she and Ami had noticed, and she thought Ami would be highly entertained if she could engage it a bit more.

"OK, let me handle that," Aaron said confidently. "You two just pretend like everything is normal, and I'll hang back to see if he boards the same train as us."

Roya and Ami looked at each other with muted smiles and raised eyebrows, and they both knew they were thinking the same thing. Aaron really wanted to give himself the role of protector, which they both thought was cute. His attention was even flattering, but neither of them quite knew what he intended by it. For the moment, their mutual interest in avoiding detection by dark agents was displaced slightly by what seemed like a subtle game of flirtation.

A moment later, Dr. Tailor walked up with the tickets.

"OK, we're all set. Is everybody ready?"

"Ready when you are," replied Roya who was anxious to get underway. She could not help feeling exposed being in such a public place, and she was not used to cities. The moment they began walking toward the train, she felt more at ease.

Roya continued to survey the room to see if she noticed anything else out of the ordinary. After all, she now knew that people from Lys sometimes came to the surface on missions, and it was reasonable to think that some of the people from the breakaway civilization also came here on missions. What other kinds of interesting people could she sense that were pretending to blend in with the surface culture? It was not just a matter of curiosity for Roya, but rather one of sharpening her discernment so she could stay safe and alert to both danger and opportunity. Would she be able to recognize another person like Claire, just by sensing auras?

Ami had that same heightened sense of both caution and awareness. The caution gave her a reason to sharpen her newly activated range of inner senses. Were it not for having a shared experience of Lys with Roya, she might not have stayed so open. They had both awakened into a new and larger energetic world, and they could not wait to reconnect with Mandy. Even Aaron acknowledged feeling incredibly different after all that he had seen and experienced in the last week. He had not been contacted again by Lex, but something about his experiences with Lex had increased his awareness of his own telepathic nature. The train ride ahead would hold some interesting discussions.

Roya felt how easy it would be to get lost exploring the energy of the people around her, but the ominous presence of the man with the sunglasses made her feel a need to pull back and not draw unwanted psychic attention. Blending energies with other people held some fascination but focusing on Ami and Aaron made it easier to find her own frequency and to feel the support of her soul family. Her connection to them, and Dr. Tailor as well, felt like a womb of safety where she could stay open, but more contained.

Just before they entered the hallway to the main concourse, Roya noticed the woman at the café look over quite intently at the four of them as they passed by. She could not tell if the woman was just returning her glance, or if it was something more. She felt a subtle rush of the woman's energy and a feeling of connection that seemed to linger, even after they disappeared from her view.

When they boarded the train, they headed straight for their rooms to check them out. Aaron hung back to see if he noticed the man coming, but there was no sign of him. He waited until the train was moving before joining the others, feeling satisfied that they were not being followed.

When he finally met up with them, he was happy to report that they were free and clear. "I think that man might have actually been from the underground, but he wasn't here for us," Aaron explained. "They must have agents on the surface, but I don't think they have any idea who you are."

"I hope you're right," said Roya. "I just know that I feel safer with all of us together."

Ami and Roya had never been so excited to see their families, and Aaron had never felt closer to his father. Connecting these three families together felt like a reunion of some kind that was always destined to happen.

Aaron and his father stayed for almost a week as they all explored each other's experiences, and the feeling of a shared purpose was very noticeable. Raymond even took them to the trail where they had found the Egg and the cave where they had first experienced it. Lots of questions remained to be answered, but over the course of their time together, an exciting and unexpected plan emerged.

Dr. Tailor was the first to suggest it, but it would take some time for the seed that he planted to fully take root. To him, the group energy of the younger generation felt like a container for his work, and the other adults had already been told by the Council of Lys how important it was that they help the scientist they would meet. The connection that all of them had to the invisible realms felt enhanced when they were around each other, so the next logical step was for all of them to come together as a community. That would involve both Roya and Ami's families moving to Chicago.

This was not such a stretch for Frank, Ami, and Mandy who had moved around quite a bit. Chicago was just as well connected to many of the places that Frank would need to go to for his nature photography, and the girls were ready for anything. Roya's family, on the other hand, was faced with financial challenges that seemed like real obstacles. For that reason, Dr.

Tailor offered to support them in any way he could, including help with the moving costs, adamant that money should not impede them. He could not explain it, but his work felt inseparable now from the whole group, and he would do whatever it took to serve the project's needs. It was more than a technology project now; they were all working together to disclose the truths they were stewarding.

What made the difference was the realization that this was exactly the opportunity that Roya's family needed. Their financial challenges had brought them to the point of needing to try something new, and there were not a lot of options living in such a remote area. For months, Raymond had been wondering how to make things work in Adams, and the thought of moving to a big city had not even occurred to him.

Having someone offer to pay for their move was the miracle they did not even know they needed. Now everything had changed, and the inspiration for the move was flowing. The families were bound by a force of historical momentum that was guiding them together, as if some promising future was folding over to touch them in the past and seed them with new potentials.

It took several months for the two families to prepare for the move, and over this time, Roya spent almost every day with Ami and Mandy. Given that Roya was the only real friend both of them had, she sometimes noticed a bit of competition for her attention. Mandy could be a little jealous of Roya's connection to Ami, especially given the added adventure the two of them had experienced together. Mandy was determined to forge a unique bond with Roya apart from her sister, so she would not ever feel like a third wheel. So, one day, Mandy proposed that the sisters take turns sleeping over at Roya's, and they all realized that it was a perfect solution to the dynamic of their friendships; like a balancing process had begun that felt more inclusive. Sometimes, they each took turns staying with Roya, and sometimes Roya would sleep over with both of them.

The best surprise had come at the end of the summer when they all decided to do home school together. To Mandy, this felt like her wish had come true: to be in the same class with Roya and Ami. Even though she would not be in the same grade, they would all study together. Their awareness had changed so dramatically since their unusual adventures together that they wanted the freedom to explore new educational paths. The girls had spent several weeks researching home school programs for high schoolers and found one that allowed the greatest amount of flexibility to customize the program according to their interests. Roya could not help noticing that all of their lives were rearranging themselves to create the maximum cohesion of everyone's passions and interests, which felt nothing short of miraculous.

Frank would continue to travel for his photography work, but now Mandy and Ami would be welcome to stay with Roya when he was away, and they had even planned a trip where Roya could come. Frank would be able to teach them all photography as an elective. And after Raymond considered what he could offer to the home school program, he decided to develop a wellness class that he could also teach online. This was an entirely separate venture from home school, but the success of launching the first online course increased his confidence in supporting his family in Chicago.

Roya's mother was preparing to enter the corporate world again if necessary, but for most of the summer, she was preoccupied with Sarah's departure for college. Sarah was anxious to get away and begin a new life with greater independence. For Soraya, it was a prolonged process of letting go of her oldest daughter. She worried that she had not done enough to raise her in the right way, but Sarah had stopped letting her mother raise her a long time ago.

She had been accepted to Syracuse University. It had been part of the plan since well before the decision to move to Chicago, but the fact that her family would not be close by anymore did not bother Sarah. She was a fiercely independent young woman and saw her family's move as a bonus. She would much rather come to visit them in Chicago than come back to Adams, anyway.

What challenged Roya was that she did not feel as connected with Sarah as she had when they were in Lys. Initially, after returning to the surface, they enjoyed some deeper conversations, but they became fewer and farther between. Occasionally, Sarah would still be very present and acknowledging, making a connection just long enough for Roya to feel a bit of the unspoken dialogue between their souls. She was learning to read the messages of Sarah's soul behind her outer expression. Sometimes, these brief connections resonated with both sadness and joy about the big departure, but mostly, she felt gratitude and a soulful goodbye. Roya could only hope that the other levels of connection they had experienced together had been imprinted and might still be activated again.

It wasn't long before Sarah became absorbed with her own friends again. Sometimes, it even felt to Roya like Sarah was deliberately pulling away.

But when she really tuned in, she realized that Sarah was just in a letting go process as their lives were heading in different directions. All she wanted was for Sarah to know that it meant so much to have her as a sister, but time kept passing by without finding the right moment to really say goodbye in the way that would satisfy Roya's heart.

As luck would have it, one day, not long before Sarah left for college, she came into Roya's room and surprised her with a gift.

"I've been saving this for the right moment," she explained as she presented a small box. "I wanted you to have this before I left. Go ahead, open it."

Roya was touched even before she opened the box but was even more surprised when she saw what was inside. It was Sarah's crystal necklace, Roya's favorite. The necklace had a small Herkimer diamond, set in silver, just above a piece of blue apatite.

"I always knew you admired it. I was wearing it the whole time we were in Lys, so maybe it has a bit of Lys energy."

Roya beamed with emotion, not knowing what to say, but the tears in the corners of her eyes said everything.

"Thank you so much," Roya gushed as she pulled her sister into a hug, though her gratitude was about much more than the necklace. "Are you sure? I thought this was your favorite?"

"I'm sure," affirmed Sarah. "You know, you've really impressed me. I know I don't always say so, but I'm really glad that you're my sister."

Sarah took the words right out of Roya's mouth. It was as if Sarah had momentarily stepped back into the deeper reflectivity between them, where their thoughts and feelings resonated.

"I'm really glad that you're my sister, too," said Roya.

After that, Roya felt at peace with Sarah's departure. It didn't matter as much that Sarah seemed more focused on normal life. After all, Roya had her best friends Ami and Mandy to share her experiences of Lys with, whereas Sarah was going away to college where no one would even believe such a story.

Overall, it seemed like Sarah's connection to Lys had faded rather quickly, whereas Roya was intent on maintaining it as much as possible. She had, for example, taken to lying in the backyard in the afternoons to practice what Claire had told her about plugging into the Earth, as this was the best way to connect with the energy of Lys.

Ami and Mandy had tried it as well, but Roya was the only one who did it regularly. She would go out in the afternoon when the heat had died down and spread a thin sheet over the grass. Lying on her belly, she would relax as if taking a catnap, extending her energy into the Earth to activate a deeper state of connection. Claire had said that the Earth was a powerful ally and healer, and if she greeted the Earth like a true companion would, the Earth would respond, and so would the spirits of nature.

She was guided not to have any attachments to what would happen, and she found that it was different almost every time. Sometimes, she would feel a connection that would last for half an hour, and other times, it only lasted a few minutes. Each time she blended her energies with the Earth, she felt enveloped by an energetic cocoon of peace.

First, she would focus on listening to all the sounds that she could hear. Then, she would take a few deep breaths to relax and feel herself in her body. Finally, she would invite the healing energies of the Earth to connect with her and help her to expand her awareness. After relaxing for a while and continuing to breathe, a subtle shift in awareness would arrive. Her thoughts would suddenly become quieter, and she would lose her sense of time. It was a feeling of inner stillness that would balance her flow of attention no matter how much noise or activity was happening around her. This felt distinctly different from taking a catnap, because it felt like she was connecting with an awareness much larger than her own; an awareness that seemed to know her personally.

She had hoped this practice might lead to a reconnection with Claire, but in all this time, Roya had not heard from her. Only once, in a dream, did she feel like Claire had been with her momentarily. On another occasion, Roya even felt like she was flying into the Earth and connecting with the cities of Lys, but the experience only lasted a few minutes, and she was not able to hone in on Claire's vibration. She was determined to keep practicing the art of listening that Claire had spoken about, but was truly missing Lys. It even felt like she had left a part of herself behind there.

The nature of her and Ami's sudden departure had felt like being ejected from the womb of heaven into the pit of darkness. Such an abrupt shift had left a lingering feeling of shock, despite the miracle of support that had guided them back to safety. She never imagined when she was still in Lys that she would not have a proper goodbye, and she longed for the presence of her new mentor to help her process the meaning of these events. Surely, a being as sensitive as Claire could feel Roya's calling, but her silence was a mystery.

On her last day in Adams, it occurred to her that she would soon live in a big city; a city full of people that were not as sensitive to energy as she now was. Her whole life had felt so sheltered up to now. She would not have the same sense of safety that she had grown up with. It might be harder to feel so close to nature. For once, being surrounded by countryside did not feel so limiting. Her little town had been a blessing in more ways than one.

It was time to say goodbye. Time to let go of all the memories. Everything was about to change, once again. She was excited about what laid ahead. A feeling of mystery surrounded all that was unfolding; an uncertainty mixed with a sense of faith about a subtle force that she could feel was guiding all of their lives.

It was time for one last walk to her favorite field where she liked to go to look at the stars. She remembered how much harder it was to see the stars in Chicago, but unfortunately, she would not be stargazing tonight. She had promised to be home for dinner and to stay in for the night before the move.

It was not even late enough to see the sunset, but the field was as beautiful to her as it had ever been. A thousand sunsets were dancing in her memories as she walked through the tall grass to her favorite spot next to a tree. The field was surrounded by residential property but was large enough that you did not feel like you were in the middle of a town. Here, she could take one last look around, and say goodbye to the land.

Sitting cross-legged on the ground, Roya leaned against the tree and wondered about Feather. What would he think of the town where she grew up? Would she ever see him again?

She could not deny that she had felt an attraction to him, but she had held back from feeling it any stronger, because she knew that Ami had felt something, too. The last thing she wanted was to end up liking the same guy as her friend, but this was different. They might not ever see him again, and something about the attraction felt worthy of exploration, because it connected her to Lys. The thought occurred to her that meeting people his own age from the surface must have left quite an impression on him, and she decided to try an experiment.

Roya focused inwardly, calling upon her messenger to receive her communication and deliver it to him. She focused on all her feelings about the land and the town she grew up in, imagining a beautiful ball of energy at the center of her chest. She focused on some of her happiest memories, the kind that she would have loved to share with him. Then, she focused on how grateful she was for meeting him, and how much she loved Lys.

As she was creating this ball of telepathic energy, she could feel the presence of her messenger strengthening, and she had the distinct feeling that it was helping her to form the communication. She felt guided to concentrate all her feelings and memories into the ball of energy, rolling them together and spinning the ball faster and faster. She imagined it growing brighter and began to add colors, like orange and pink. Then, she sealed it with a single enthusiastic message that said: *"I think you're amazing!"*

With that, she released the energy and opened her awareness back into the field, assuming that her messenger had whizzed away, guiding her communication to where it needed to go.

Roya smiled big, as if she could already feel Feather smiling back at her. She wondered if that meant he had received her message with all the added details. She did not expect to receive a response right away, and she was not sure if she would receive one at all. She had practiced messaging Ami and Mandy before, but never with the fullness of what she had just felt inspired to create. Using the phone or texting was still so automatic to their culture that the idea of practicing telepathy was not as present as it had been in Lys. Sadly, there was no more time to linger in the field. There were still a few things to pack, and Roya knew she would be expected home soon. Something told her the feeling of this field would come with her wherever she would go. She could always find this feeling of home if she needed it.

As she took one last look around, a window of reflectivity seemed to open in her inner field of awareness. And then, with very little warning, she was struck by a beam of communication. The energy carried a force of excitement and interest that she recognized as Feather's, and in the instant that she felt it, the image of a white feather appeared in front of her.

The image was made of light, very subtle, but still completely real, and it must have had a tiny amount of mass, because it began to fall immediately after it appeared. Roya's reached out to catch it, and the feather landed softly in her hands. She actually felt its form for a few seconds just before she held it to her heart. It was like a telepathic emoticon that was made of living energy, and it showed that Feather had a level of mastery to the art of communication that she had not expected. The feather absorbed right into her heart as she held her hands there for a moment, breathing deeply and feeling the dance of his energy in her being.

Perhaps there was more to their connection than she had imagined. Her response to feeling his energy swirling around her was surprisingly exciting, and it made her feel, well, light as a feather. It definitely put a spring in her step as she began to walk home.

As she reached the edge of the field, she closed her eyes, feeling their connection for a moment, and thought she could see him in the gardens.

And then, she heard the distinct words of his inner voice reflecting back to her: *"Thank you! I think you're amazing, too!"*

It was more than she had hoped for, and there was something else…a surprising hidden wish that she could sense in Feather's aura. He longed to see the surface just as much as she longed to return to Lys. And now, it felt undeniably real, that a field of possibilities existed between them.

How interesting, that in this very moment, Feather had felt called to go to the platform overlooking the gardens, where he had stood with his new friends only months before. Such a powerful memory; and such a sweet acknowledgment. The synchronistic timing revealed the presence of a guiding force between them, as if to confirm his dream.

Somehow, Feather thought, *we will all see each other again.*

EPILOGUE

Deep beneath the surface levels of the Pentagon, two officers exited a highly secure, secret elevator and walked toward an office, following their orders. Both men were alert with anticipation, believing they were being summoned for something akin to a special promotion. They were in their late twenties, muscular, and had military style haircuts. The shorter of the two wore glasses.

"Mr. Secretary," said the taller one, as they both entered the office and stood at attention.

"At ease, gentlemen," responded the older man wearing a highly decorated uniform. He was carefully reading a document in a file folder for several minutes while they waited. On the wall behind him, an antique clock was ticking, giving both of the officers the feeling that they were on someone else's time. Finally, he looked up from his desk.

"You're both highly trained remote viewers and skilled at psychic interrogation," he began. "And you've both recently completed the process of severing ties with the surface."

"Yes, sir!" said the shorter one emphatically, and the other officer nodded with agreement.

"You both realize there's no going back. When you're in this deep, your life belongs to the program. But don't worry, we always take care of our own down here."

"Understood," remarked the tall one, and they both nodded again.

"Good. I'm reassigning you both to a new experimental psy-ops division. You start training immediately, and you'll be working entirely below the surface from now on. Here are your orders," he said as he handed them both a file. "We recently had an incident. Two subjects escaped that had been retrieved during an important away mission. Circumstances were highly unusual. You've both been briefed on Project Shortcut," he affirmed, and the two nodded silently.

"The team you'll be joining works very closely with that project, but the tech has a different aim. We're not going to be sending you anywhere physically at first, just psychically. We need your help to locate the subjects and bring them in."

"The subjects are two teenage girls, sir?" remarked the tall one, as they both read the project files, a little perplexed.

"Apparently. They were scheduled for termination, but since they escaped, the team hasn't been able to re-establish a link to where they were originally found. The connection just won't form. We think that somehow, these two girls were part of the bridge that the team crossed to get in there. We need them now to make the bridge work, and we're counting on both of you to make it happen. We don't have any pictures of them for you to work with, so you'll have to rely entirely on your abilities with this new tech. That's why we need the best."

"You can count on us, sir," said the one with the glasses.

"Good. This assignment is now the top priority of this new division. Do whatever it takes men but *find those two girls.*"

ACKNOWLEDGMENTS

First and foremost, I would like to thank my partner, Dixie Pond, also a co-editor, and my personal cheerleader who stood by me through every step of finishing this first novel—I am forever grateful. My sincere thanks: to Angela Valentine for her impeccable editing skills, and for making the editing process fun; to my publisher, Patricia Cagganello, for coaxing even more good ideas out of me; and to Brad Walrod, Julie Dillon and Alexandra Brandt, who each played a role in helping me hold the vision. I am honored to work with such professional people that inspire me.

It takes many eyes on a book to help it reach its potential, and for that I want to thank all of my proofreaders. Most notably, I want to thank Nina Quinn for her excellent suggestions, Cristiana Elena Ciupitu for her proofreading superpowers, as well as Angela Ota, Linda Radford, and Chet Nichols. Special thanks also to my teen focus group: Kateli Pond, Xander Henry and Zoe Henry—three honor students who each made meaningful contributions. And thanks to our adult focus group readers Karol and Lynn Stephens, Jayson Pond, and especially Jennifer Pond for her attention to detail.

I am also grateful for the financial contributions that helped move this project along, with special thanks to Heather Dancer, Victoria Triana, Theresa Haislip, Dawn Benner, and everyone who participated in my Launch Team. And my sincere gratitude to all those that have helped sponsor my work over the years.

Thanks to Colin and Analita for hosting Dixie and I while we worked out-of-state on the editing with Angela. Thanks to Gary Acevedo for empowering me to overcome some of my inner obstacles at the final stage of the creative process. Thanks to Lori Spagna for being a true friend and helping me get discovered. I am eternally grateful to my mom, who has always supported me in numerous ways. Thanks also to John Burgos for the generosity of his support, and others like him who have helped my work get noticed.

Thank you to all of my muses, on Earth and in Spirit. I especially want to acknowledge: J. K. Rowling for inspiring me to become a fiction author; Barbara Marciniak, whose channeled books from the Pleiadians introduced me to the concept of the Earth as a Living Library; and James Redfield, whose Celestine Prophecy series helped awaken me in my teens. I'd also like to acknowledge the work of Marshall Vian Summers, whose revelations about the challenges of ET contact have paralleled my own.

Last but not least, I am eternally grateful for the love, wisdom, guidance and support of my teacher, Louix Dor Dempriey, whose devotion to helping me realize my potential has never wavered and never failed to take me higher.

ABOUT THE AUTHOR

Saryon Michael White is an author, world traveler, and transformational leader whose work has touched the lives of people throughout the world. Inspired by visions of humanity's peace potential, part of his global mission is to link people with the emerging potential of human unity through his visionary writings and speeches.

Saryon is also the founder and teacher of the School of Manifestation, an online resource of teachings to educate humanity about new potentials of conscious evolution. As an intuitive reader, Saryon offers private sessions to help his clients clear obstacles to their personal growth and to develop their connection to divine guidance.

Roya Sands and the Bridge Between Worlds is Saryon's first fiction novel—Book One of a new series, and a precursor to a forthcoming nonfiction series of transformational teachings.

For more info and free bonus content, visit:
www.Saryon.com
www.RoyaSands.com